"WHO ARE YOU?" he whispered.

Her chin lifted at that, her lips parting in surprise. She studied him with wide, shining eyes, and appeared to be as confused by him as he was by her. Kamran took comfort in this, in the realization that they'd confounded each other equally.

"Will you not tell me your name?" he asked.

She shook her head, the movement slow, uncertain. Kamran felt paralyzed. He could not explain it; his body seemed anchored to hers. He drew closer by micrometers, propelled to do so by a force he could not hope to understand. What mere minutes ago might've struck him as lunacy now seemed to him essential: to know what it might be like to hold her, to breathe in the scent of her skin, to press his lips to her neck. He was scarcely aware of himself when he touched her—light as air, faint as fading memory—a stroke of his fingers against her lips.

She vanished.

THIS
WOVEN
KINGDOM

TAHEREH MAFI

HARPER

An Imprint of HarperCollinsPublishers

Library of Congress Control Number: 2021946101

ISBN 978-0-06-297245-3

Typography by Jenna Stempel-Lobell

23 24 25 26 27 LBC 7 6 5 4 3

❖

First paperback edition, 2022

For Ransom

I turn to right and left, in all the earth
I see no signs of justice, sense or worth:
A man does evil deeds, and all his days
are filled with luck and universal praise;
Another's good in all he does— He dies
a wretched, broken man whom all despise.

But all this world is like a tale we hear—
Men's evil, and their glory, disappear.

—Abolghasem Ferdowsi, *Shahnameh*

THIS
WOVEN
KINGDOM

ONE

یک

ALIZEH STITCHED IN THE KITCHEN by the light of star and fire, sitting, as she often did, curled up inside the hearth. Soot stained her skin and skirts in haphazard streaks: smudges along the crest of a cheek, a dusting of yet more darkness above one eye. She didn't seem to notice.

Alizeh was cold. No, she was *freezing*.

She often wished she were a body with hinges, that she might throw open a door in her chest and fill its cavity with coal, then kerosene. Strike a match.

Alas.

She tugged up her skirts and shifted nearer the fire, careful lest she destroy the garment she still owed the illegitimate daughter of the Lojjan ambassador. The intricate, glittering piece was her only order this month, but Alizeh nursed a secret hope that the gown would conjure clients on its own, for such fashionable commissions were, after all, the direct result of an envy born only in a ballroom, around a dinner table. So long as the kingdom remained at peace, the royal elite—legitimate and illegitimate alike—would continue to host parties and incur debt, which meant Alizeh might yet find ways to extract coin from their embroidered pockets.

She shivered violently then, nearly missing a stitch, nearly toppling into the fire. As a toddling child Alizeh had once been so desperately cold she'd crawled onto the searing hearth on purpose. Of course it had never occurred to her that she might be consumed by the blaze; she'd been but a babe following an instinct to seek warmth. Alizeh couldn't have known then the singularity of her affliction, for so rare was the frost that grew inside her body that she stood in stark relief even among her own people, who were thought to be strange indeed.

A miracle, then, that the fire had only disintegrated her clothes and clogged the small house with a smoke that singed her eyes. A subsequent scream, however, signaled to the snug tot that her scheme was at an end. Frustrated by a body that would not warm, she'd wept frigid tears as she was collected from the flames, her mother sustaining terrible burns in the process, the scars of which Alizeh would study for years to come.

"*Her eyes*," the trembling woman had cried to her husband, who'd come running at the sounds of distress. "See what's happened to her eyes— They will kill her for this—"

Alizeh rubbed her eyes now and coughed.

Surely she'd been too young to remember the precise words her parents had spoken; no doubt Alizeh's was a memory merely of a story oft-repeated, one so thoroughly worn into her mind she only imagined she could recall her mother's voice.

She swallowed.

Soot had stuck in her throat. Her fingers had gone numb. Exhausted, she exhaled her worries into the hearth, the action disturbing to life another flurry of soot.

Alizeh coughed for the second time then, this time so hard she stabbed the stitching needle into her small finger. She absorbed the shock of pain with preternatural calm, carefully dislodging the bit before inspecting the injury.

The puncture was deep.

Slowly, almost one at a time, her fingers closed around the gown still clutched in her hand, the finest silk stanching the trickle of her blood. After a few moments—during which she stared blankly up, into the chimney, for the sixteenth time that night—she released the gown, cut the thread with her teeth, and tossed the gem-encrusted novelty onto a nearby chair.

Never fear; Alizeh knew her blood would not stain. Still, it was a good excuse to cede defeat, to set aside the gown. She appraised it now, sprawled as it was across the seat. The bodice had collapsed, bowing over the skirt much like a child might slump in a chair. Silk pooled around the wooden legs, beadwork catching the light. A weak breeze rattled a poorly latched window and a single candle blew out, taking with it the remaining composure of the commission. The gown slid farther down the chair, one heavy sleeve releasing itself with a hush, its glittering cuff grazing the sooty floor.

Alizeh sighed.

This gown, like all the others, was far from beautiful. She thought the design trite, the construction only passably good. She dreamed of unleashing her mind, of freeing her hands to create without hesitation—but the roar of Alizeh's imagination was quieted, always, by an unfortunate need for self-preservation.

It was only during her grandmother's lifetime that the Fire Accords had been established, unprecedented peace agreements that allowed Jinn and humans to mix freely for the first time in nearly a millennia. Though superficially identical, Jinn bodies had been forged from the essence of fire, imbuing in them certain physical advantages; while humans, whose beginnings were established in dirt and water, had long been labeled *Clay*. Jinn had conceded to the establishment of the Accords with a variegated relief, for the two races had been locked in bloodshed for eons, and though the enmity between them remained unresolved, all had tired of death.

The streets had been gilded with liquid sun to usher in the era of this tenuous peacetime, the empire's flag and coin reimagined in triumph. Every royal article was stamped with the maxim of a new age:

MERAS
May Equality Reign Always Supreme

Equality, as it turned out, had meant Jinn were to lower themselves to the weakness of humans, denying at all times the inherent powers of their race, the speed and strength and elective evanescence born unto their bodies. They were to cease at once what the king had declared "such supernatural operations" or face certain death, and Clay, who had exposed themselves as an insecure sort of creature, were only too willing to cry cheat no matter the context. Alizeh could still hear the screams, the riots in the streets—

She stared now at the mediocre gown.

Always she struggled not to design an article too exquisite, for extraordinary work came under harsher scrutiny, and was only too quickly denounced as the result of a preternatural trick.

Only once, having grown increasingly desperate to earn a decent living, had Alizeh thought to impress a customer not with style, but with craftsmanship. Not only was the quality of her work many orders of magnitude higher than that of the local modiste, but Alizeh could fashion an elegant morning gown in a quarter of the time, and had been willing to charge half as much.

The oversight had sent her to the gallows.

It had not been the happy customer, but the rival dressmaker who'd reported Alizeh to the magistrates. Miracle of miracles, she'd managed to evade their attempt to drag her away in the night, and fled the familiar countryside of her childhood for the anonymity of the city, hoping to be lost among the masses.

Would that she might slough off the burdens she carried with her always, but Alizeh knew an abundance of reasons to keep to the shadows, chief among them the reminder that her parents had forfeited their lives in the interest of her quiet survival, and to comport herself carelessly now would be to dishonor their efforts.

No, Alizeh had learned the hard way to relinquish her commissions long before she grew to love them.

She stood and a cloud of soot stood with her, billowing

around her skirts. She'd need to clean the kitchen hearth before Mrs. Amina came down in the morning or she'd likely be out on the street again. Despite her best efforts, Alizeh had been turned out onto the street more times than she could count. She'd always supposed it took little encouragement to dispose of that which was already seen as disposable, but these thoughts had done little to calm her.

Alizeh collected a broom, flinching a little as the fire died. It was late; very late. The steady *tick tick* of the clock wound something in her heart, made her anxious. Alizeh had a natural aversion to the dark, a rooted fear she could not fully articulate. She'd have rather worked a needle and thread by the light of the sun, but she spent her days doing the work that really mattered: scrubbing the rooms and latrines of Baz House, the grand estate of Her Grace, the Duchess Jamilah of Fetrous.

Alizeh had never met the duchess, only seen the glittering older woman from afar. Alizeh's meetings were with Mrs. Amina, the housekeeper, who'd hired Alizeh on a trial basis only, as she'd arrived with no references. As a result, Alizeh was not yet permitted to interact with the other servants, nor was she allotted a proper room in the servants' wing. Instead, she'd been given a rotting closet in the attic, wherein she'd discovered a cot, its moth-eaten mattress, and half a candle.

Alizeh had lain awake in her narrow bed that first night, so overcome she could hardly breathe. She minded neither the rotting attic nor its moth-eaten mattress, for Alizeh knew herself to be in possession of great fortune. That any grand house was willing to employ a Jinn was shocking enough, but that she'd been given a room—a respite from the winter streets—

True, Alizeh had found stretches of work since her parents' deaths, and often she'd been granted leave to sleep indoors, or in the hayloft; but never had she been given a space of her own. This was the first time in years she had privacy, a door she might close; and Alizeh had felt so thoroughly saturated with happiness she feared she might sink through the floor. Her body shook as she stared up at the wooden beams that night, at the thicket of cobwebs that crowded her head. A large spider had unspooled a length of thread, lowering itself to look her in the eye, and Alizeh had only smiled, clutching a skin of water to her chest.

The water had been her single request.

"A skin of water?" Mrs. Amina had frowned at her, frowned as if she'd asked to eat the woman's child. "You can fetch your own water, girl."

"Forgive me, I would," Alizeh had said, eyes on her shoes, on the torn leather around the toe she'd not yet mended. "But I'm still new to the city, and I've found it difficult to access fresh water so far from home. There's no reliable cistern nearby, and I cannot yet afford the glass water in the market—"

Mrs. Amina roared with laughter.

Alizeh went silent, heat rising up her neck. She did not know why the woman laughed at her.

"Can you read, child?"

Alizeh looked up without meaning to, registering the

familiar, fearful gasp before she'd even locked eyes with the woman. Mrs. Amina stepped back, lost her smile.

"Yes," said Alizeh. "I can read."

"Then you must try to forget."

Alizeh started. "I beg your pardon?"

"Don't be daft." Mrs. Amina's eyes narrowed. "No one wants a servant who can read. You ruin your own prospects with that tongue. Where did you say you were from?"

Alizeh had frozen solid.

She couldn't tell whether this woman was being cruel or kind. It was the first time anyone had suggested her intelligence might present a problem to the position, and Alizeh wondered then whether it wasn't true: perhaps it *had* been her head, too full as it was, that kept landing her in the street. Perhaps, if she was careful, she might finally manage to keep a position for longer than a few weeks. No doubt she could feign stupidity in exchange for safety.

"I'm from the north, ma'am," she'd said quietly.

"Your accent isn't northern."

Alizeh nearly admitted aloud that she'd been raised in relative isolation, that she'd learned to speak as her tutors had taught her; but then she remembered herself, remembered her station, and said nothing.

"As I suspected," Mrs. Amina had said into the silence. "Rid yourself of that ridiculous accent. You sound like an idiot, pretending to be some kind of toff. Better yet, say nothing at all. If you can manage that, you may prove useful to me. I've heard your kind don't tire out so easily, and I expect your work to satisfy such rumors, else I'll not scruple to toss you back into the street. Have I made myself clear?"

"Yes, ma'am."

"You may have your skin of water."

"Thank you, ma'am." Alizeh curtsied, turned to go.

"Oh—and one more thing—"

Alizeh turned back. "Yes, ma'am?"

"Get yourself a snoda as soon as possible. I never want to see your face again."

TWO

دو

ALIZEH HAD ONLY JUST PULLED open the door to her closet when she felt it, felt *him* as if she'd pushed her arms through the sleeves of a winter coat. She hesitated, heart pounding, and stood framed in the doorway.

Foolish.

Alizeh shook her head to clear it. She was imagining things, and no surprise: she was in desperate need of sleep. After sweeping the hearth, she'd had to scrub clean her sooty hands and face, too, and it had all taken much longer than she'd hoped; her weary mind could hardly be held responsible for its delirious thoughts at this hour.

With a sigh, Alizeh dipped a single foot into the inky depths of her room, feeling blindly for the match and candle she kept always near the door. Mrs. Amina had not allowed Alizeh a second taper to carry upstairs in the evenings, for she could neither fathom the indulgence nor the possibility that the girl might still be working long after the gas lamps had been extinguished. Even so, the housekeeper's lack of imagination did nothing to alter the facts as they were: this high up in so large an estate it was near impossible for distant light to penetrate. Save the occasional slant of the moon through a mingy corridor window, the attic presented opaque in the night; black as tar.

Were it not for the glimmer of the night sky to help her navigate the many flights to her closet, Alizeh might not have found her way, for she experienced a fear so paralyzing in the company of perfect darkness that, when faced with such a fate, she held an illogical preference for death.

Her single candle quickly found, the sought after match was promptly struck, a tear of air and the wick lit. A warm glow illuminated a sphere in the center of her room, and for the first time that day, Alizeh relaxed.

Quietly she pulled closed the closet door behind her, stepping fully into a room hardly big enough to hold her cot.

Just so, she loved it.

She'd scrubbed the filthy closet until her knuckles had bled, until her knees had throbbed. In these ancient, beautiful estates, most everything was once built to perfection, and buried under layers of mold, cobwebs, and caked-on grime, Alizeh had discovered elegant herringbone floors, solid wood beams in the ceiling. When she'd finished with it, the room positively gleamed.

Mrs. Amina had not, naturally, been to visit the old storage closet since it'd been handed over to the help, but Alizeh often wondered what the housekeeper might say if she saw the space now, for the room was unrecognizable. But then, Alizeh had long ago learned to be resourceful.

She removed her snoda, unwinding the delicate sheet of tulle from around her eyes. The silk was required of all those who worked in service, the mask marking its wearer as a member of the lower classes. The textile was designed for hard work, woven loosely enough to blur her features without obscuring necessary vision. Alizeh had chosen this profession with great forethought, and clung every day to the anonymity her position provided, rarely removing her snoda even outside of her room; for though most people did not understand the strangeness they saw in her eyes, she feared that one day the wrong person might.

She breathed deeply now, pressing the tips of her fingers against her cheeks and temples, gently massaging the face she'd not seen in what felt like years. Alizeh did not own a looking glass, and her occasional glances at the mirrors in Baz House revealed only the bottom third of her face: lips, chin, the column of her neck. She was otherwise a faceless servant, one of dozens, and had only vague memories of what she looked like—or what she'd once been told she looked like. It was the whisper of her mother's voice in her ear, the feel of her father's calloused hand against her cheek.

You are the finest of us all, he'd once said.

Alizeh closed her mind to the memory as she took off her shoes, set the boots in their corner. Over the years, Alizeh had collected enough scraps from old commissions to stitch herself the quilt and matching pillow currently laid atop her mattress. Her clothes she hung from old nails wrapped meticulously in colorful thread; all other personal affects she'd arranged inside an apple crate she'd found discarded in one of the chicken coops.

She rolled off her stockings now and hung them—to air them out—from a taut bit of twine. Her dress went to one of the colorful hooks, her corset to another, her snoda to the last. Everything Alizeh owned, everything she touched, was clean and orderly, for she had learned long ago that when a home was not found, it was forged; indeed it could be fashioned even from nothing.

Clad only in her shift, she yawned, yawned as she sat on her cot, as the mattress sank, as she pulled the pins from her hair. The day—and her long, heavy curls—crashed down around her shoulders.

Her thoughts had begun to slur.

With great reluctance she blew out the candle, pulled her legs against her chest, and fell over like a poorly weighted insect. The illogic of her phobia was consistent only in perplexing her, for when she was abed and her eyes closed, Alizeh imagined she could more easily conquer the dark, and even as she trembled with a familiar chill, she succumbed quickly to sleep. She reached for her soft quilt and drew it up over her shoulders, trying not to think about how cold she was, trying not to think at all. In fact she shivered so violently she hardly noticed when he sat down, his weight depressing the mattress at the foot of her bed.

Alizeh bit back a scream.

Her eyes flew open, tired pupils fighting to widen their aperture. Frantically, Alizeh patted down her quilt, her pillow, her threadbare mattress. There was no body on her bed. No one in her room.

Had she been hallucinating? She fumbled for her candle and dropped it, her hands shaking.

Surely, she'd been dreaming.

The mattress groaned—the weight shifting—and Alizeh experienced a fear so violent she saw sparks. She pushed backward, knocking her head against the wall, and somehow the pain focused her panic.

A sharp snap and a flame caught between his barely there fingers, illuminated the contours of his face.

Alizeh dared not breathe.

Even in silhouette she couldn't see him, not properly, but then—it was not his face, but his voice, that had made the devil notorious.

Alizeh knew this better than most.

Seldom did the devil present himself in some approximation of flesh; rare were his clear and memorable communications. Indeed, the creature was not as powerful as his legacy insisted, for he'd been denied the right to speak as another might, doomed forever to hold forth in riddles, and allowed permission only to persuade a person to ruin, never to command.

It was not usual, then, for one to claim an acquaintance with the devil, nor was it with any conviction that a person might speak of his methods, for the presence of such evil was experienced most often only through a provoking of sensation.

Alizeh did not like to be the exception.

Indeed it was with some pain that she acknowledged the circumstances of her birth: that it had been the devil to first offer congratulations at her cradle, his unwelcome ciphers as inescapable as the wet of rain. Alizeh's parents had tried, desperately, to banish such a beast from their home, but he had returned again and again, forever embroidering the tapestry of her life with ominous forebodings, in what seemed a promise of destruction she could not outmaneuver.

Even now she felt the devil's voice, felt it like a breath loosed inside her body, an exhale against her bones.

There once was a man, he whispered.

"No," she nearly shouted, panicking. "Not another riddle—please—"

There once was a man, he whispered, *who bore a snake on each shoulder.*

Alizeh clapped both hands over her ears and shook her head; she'd never wanted so badly to cry.

"Please," she said, "please don't—"

Again:

There once was a man
who bore a snake on each shoulder.
If the snakes were well fed
their master ceased growing older.

Alizeh squeezed her eyes shut, pulled her knees to her chest. He wouldn't stop. She couldn't shut him out.

What they ate no one knew, even as the children—

"Please," she said, begging now. "Please, I don't want to know—"

What they ate no one knew,
even as the children were found
with brains shucked from their skulls,
bodies splayed on the ground.

She inhaled sharply and he was gone, gone, the devil's voice torn free from her bones. The room suddenly shuddered around her, shadows lifting and stretching—and in the warped light a strange, hazy face peered back at her. Alizeh bit her lip so hard she tasted blood.

It was a young man staring at her now, one she did not recognize.

That he was human, Alizeh had no doubt—but something about him seemed different from the others. In the dim light the young man seemed carved not from clay, but marble, his face trapped in hard lines, centered by a soft mouth. The longer she stared at him the harder her heart raced. Was this the man with the snakes? Why did it even matter? Why would she ever believe a single word spoken by the devil?

Ah, but she already knew the answer to the latter.

Alizeh was losing her calm. Her mind screamed at her to look away from the conjured face, screamed that this was all madness—and yet.

Heat crept up her neck.

Alizeh was unaccustomed to staring too long at any face,

and this one was violently handsome. He had noble features, all straight lines and hollows, easy arrogance at rest. He tilted his head as he took her in, unflinching as he studied her eyes. All his unwavering attention stoked a forgotten flame inside her, startling her tired mind.

And then, a hand.

His hand, conjured from a curl of darkness. He was looking straight into her eyes when he dragged a vanishing finger across her lips.

She screamed.

IN THE BEGINNING

در آغاز

THE STORY OF THE DEVIL had worn thin in the retelling, but Iblees, Iblees, his true name like a heartbeat on the tongue, was lost to the catacombs of history. His own people knew best that the beast was wrought not from light, but fire. Not angel, but *Jinn*, an ancient race who'd once owned the earth, who'd once celebrated this young man's extraordinary elevation to the heavens. They knew best whence he came, because they were there when he was returned, when his body cracked against the earth and their world was left to rot in the wake of his arrogance.

Birds froze when his body fell out of the sky, their sharp beaks parted, broad wings pinned open in midair. He glistened in his descent, flesh slick with fresh melt, heavy drops of liquid fire rolling off his skin. His drippings, still steaming, would hit the earth before his heft would, disintegrating frogs and trees and the shared dignity of an entire civilization who would be forced forever to scream his name at the stars.

For when Iblees fell, so too did his people.

It was not God, but the occupants of the expanding universe that would soon forsake the Jinn; every celestial body had borne witness to the genesis of the devil, to a creature of darkness heretofore unknown, unnamed—and none wished to be seen as sympathetic to an enemy of the All-Powerful.

The sun was the first to turn its back on them. A single wink and it was done; their planet, Earth, was plunged into perpetual night, armored in ice, flung out of orbit. The moon faded next, knocking the world off its axis, warping its oceans. All was soon flooded, then frozen; the population neatly halved in three days. Thousands of years of history, of art and literature and invention: obliterated.

Still, the surviving Jinn dared to hope.

It was when the stars finally devoured themselves, one by one; when land sank and fissured underfoot; when maps of centuries past were suddenly rendered obsolete. It was when they could no longer find their way in the perpetual dark that the Jinn felt truly, irrevocably, lost.

They soon scattered.

Iblees had been charged for his crime with a single task: to haunt forever the dirt forms that would soon crawl out of the earth. Clay—that crude, rudimentary form before which Iblees would not kneel—would inherit the world the Jinn had once owned. Of this, the Jinn were certain. It had been foretold.

When? They did not know.

The heavens observed the devil, the half-life he was forced to live. All watched silently as frozen seas overwhelmed the shores, tides rising parallel to his wrath. With every passing moment the darkness grew thicker, denser with the stench of death.

Without the skies to guide them, the remaining Jinn could not determine how long their people spent compressed under cold and darkness. It felt like centuries but might've been days. What was time when there were no moons to mind the hour, no suns to define a year? Time was told only through birth, through the children who lived. That their souls were forged from fire was the first of two reasons any Jinn had survived the infinite winters, the second: that they required only water for nourishment.

Clay shaped itself slowly in such waters, shuddering into a finished form while another civilization died, en masse, of heartbreak, of horror. The Jinn who endured against all odds were plagued always by a rage trapped in their chests, a rage held at bay only by the weight of an unyielding shame.

Jinn were once the sole intelligent beings on Earth; they were creatures built stronger, faster, simpler, and more cunning than Clay would ever be. Still, most had gone blind in the perpetual blackness. Their skin grew ashen, their irises white, stripped of pigment in the dark. In the torturous absence of the sun, even these fiery beings had grown weak, and when Clay, freshly formed, finally stood tall on steady legs, the sun flared back to life—swinging their planet back into focus, and bringing with it a searing pain.

Heat.

It desiccated the Jinns' unaccustomed eyes, melted the remaining flesh from their bones. For the Jinn who'd sought shelter from this heat, there was hope: with the return of the sun came the moon, and with the moon, the stars. By starlight they navigated their way to safety, taking refuge at the apex of the earth, in a blistering cold that had begun to feel like home. Quietly, they built a modest new kingdom, all the while pressing their supernatural bodies so hard against the planes of space and time as to practically disappear.

It did not matter that Jinn were stronger than the Clay bodies—human beings, they called themselves—that now owned the earth and its skies. It did not matter that Jinn possessed more power and strength and speed. It did not matter how hot their souls burned. Dirt, they had learned, would smother a flame. Dirt would eventually bury them all.

And Iblees—

Iblees was never far.

The devil's everlasting, shameful existence was a powerful reminder of all they'd lost, of all they'd endured to survive. With profound regret, Jinn surrendered the earth to its new kings—and prayed never to be found.

It was yet another prayer that went unanswered.

THREE

ALIZEH SHOVED INTO THE EARLY morning light.

She'd shoved out of bed, shoved on her clothes, shoved pins in her hair, shoved shoes on her feet. She usually took greater care with her toilette, but she'd slept later than she'd intended and had no time to do more than run a damp cloth over her eyes. The finished commission was due for delivery today, and she'd wrapped the glittering gown in layers of tulle, securing the package with twine. Alizeh handled the large parcel carefully as she tiptoed downstairs and, after building the fire in the kitchen hearth, pushed open the heavy wooden door—only to be met with fresh snowfall up to her knees.

Alizeh's body nearly sagged with disappointment. She squeezed her eyes shut, took a steadying breath.

No.

She would not return to bed. It was true she did not yet own a proper winter coat. Or hat. Or even gloves. It was also true that if she raced back up the stairs this very instant she might manage to sleep a full hour before she was needed.

But no.

She forced her spine straight, clutched the precious bundle to her chest. Today, she would be getting paid.

Alizeh stepped into the snow.

The moon was so large this morning it blotted out most of the sky, its reflected light suffusing all in a dreamy glow. The sun was but a pinprick in the distance, its outline shining through a soufflé of clouds. Trees stood tall and white, branches heavy with powder. It was early yet—snow still untouched along the paths—and the world shimmered, so white it looked almost blue. Blue snow, blue sky, blue moon. The air seemed even to smell blue, it was so cold.

Alizeh huddled deeper into her thin jacket, listening as the wind tore through the streets. Plowmen appeared as suddenly as if they'd been conjured by her thoughts, and she watched their choreographed movements, red trapper hats bobbing to and fro as shovels scraped to reveal stripes of gold cobblestone. Alizeh hurried herself onto a quickly clearing path and shook the snow from her clothes, stamped her feet against the glimmering stone. She was wet up to her thighs and did not want to think on it.

Instead, she looked up.

The day was not yet born, its sounds not yet formed. Street vendors had yet to set up their kiosks, shops had yet to unlatch their shuttered windows. Today, a trio of bright-green ducks waddled down the powdered median as wary shopkeepers peered out of doorways, poking broomsticks into the snow. A colossal white bear lounged on an icy corner, a street child sleeping soundly against its fur. Alizeh gave the bear a wide berth as she rounded the corner, her eyes following a spiral of smoke into the sky. Outdoor food carts were lighting their fires, preparing their wares. Alizeh inhaled the unfamiliar scents, testing them against her mind.

She'd studied cookery—could identify eatables by sight—but she'd not had enough experience with food to be able to name things by smell.

Jinn enjoyed food, but they did not need it, not the way most creatures did; as a result, Alizeh had forgone the decadence for several years. She used her income to pay instead for sewing supplies and regular baths at the local hamams. Her need for cleanliness grew parallel to her need for water. Fire was her soul, but water was her life; it was all she needed to survive. She drank it, bathed in it, required often to be near it. Cleanliness had, as a result, become a foundational principle of her life, one that had been hammered into her from childhood. Every few months she trekked deep into the forest to find a miswak tree—a toothbrush tree—from which she harvested the brush she used to keep her mouth fresh and her teeth white. Her line of work often left her filthy, and any truly idle time she had, she spent polishing herself to a shine. It was in fact her preoccupation with cleanliness that had led her to consider the benefits of such a profession.

Alizeh stopped.

She'd happened upon a shaft of sunlight and stood in it now, warming in the rays as a memory bloomed in her mind.

A soapy bucket.

The coarse bristles of a floor brush.

Her parents, laughing.

The memory felt not unlike a handprint of heat against her sternum. Alizeh's mother and father had thought it critical to teach their child not only to care and clean for her own home, but to have basic knowledge of most all technical

and mechanical labor; they'd wanted her to know the weight
of a day's work. But then, they'd only meant to teach her a
valuable lesson—they'd never meant for her to earn her living this way.

While Alizeh had spent her younger years being honed by
masters and tutors, so, too, had her parents humbled her in
preparation for her imagined future, insisting always upon
the greater good, the essential quality of compassion.

Feel, her parents had once said to her.

*The shackles worn by your people are often unseen by the
eye. Feel,* they'd said, *for even blind, you will know how to
break them.*

Would her mother and father laugh if they saw her now?
Would they cry?

Alizeh didn't mind working in service—she'd never
minded hard work—but she knew she was likely a disappointment to her parents, even if only to their memories.

Her smile faltered.

The boy was fast—and Alizeh had been distracted—so
it took her a second longer than usual to notice him. Which
meant she hadn't noticed him at all until the knife was at her
throat.

"Le man et parcel," he said, his breath hot and sour
against her face. He spoke Feshtoon, which meant he was
far from home, and probably hungry. He towered over her
from behind, his free hand roughly gripping her waist. By
all appearances she was being assaulted by a barbarian—and
yet, somehow, she knew he was just a boy, one overgrown
for his age.

Gently, she said: "Unhand me. Do it now and I give you my word I will leave you unharmed."

He laughed. "Nez beshoff." *Stupid woman.*

Alizeh tucked the parcel under her left arm and snapped his wrist with her right hand, feeling the blade graze her throat as he screamed, stumbling back. She caught him before he fell, caught his arm and twisted it, dislocating his shoulder before pushing him into the snow. She stood over him as he sobbed, half-buried in the drift. Passersby were averting their eyes, uninvested as she knew they would be in the lower rungs of the world. A servant and a street urchin could be counted upon to do away with each other, save the magistrates the extra work.

It was a grim thought.

Carefully, Alizeh retrieved the boy's blade from the snow, examined its crude workmanship. She appraised the boy, too. His face was nearly as young as she'd suspected. Twelve? Thirteen?

She knelt beside him and he stiffened, his sobs briefly ceasing in his chest. "Nek, nek, lotfi, lotfi—" *No, no, please, please—*

She took his unbroken hand in her own, uncurled the dirty fingers, pressed the hilt back into his palm. She knew the poor boy would need it.

Still.

"There are other ways to stay alive," she whispered in Feshtoon. "Come to the kitchens at Baz House if you are in need of bread."

The boy stared at her then, turned the full force of his

terrified gaze upon her. She could see him searching for her eyes through her snoda. "Shora?" he said. *Why?*

Alizeh almost smiled.

"Bek mefem," she said quietly. *Because I understand.* "Bek bidem." *Because I've been you.*

Alizeh did not wait for him to respond before she pushed herself to her feet, shook out her skirts. She felt a bit of moisture at her throat and retrieved a handkerchief from her pocket, which she pressed to the wound. She was still standing, unmoving, when the bell tolled, signaling the hour and startling into flight a constellation of starlings, their iridescent plumage glittering in the light.

Alizeh breathed deep, pulling the cold air into her lungs. She hated the cold, but the chill was bracing, at least, and the perpetual discomfort kept her awake better than any cup of tea had done. Alizeh had slept maybe two hours the night prior, but she could not allow herself to dwell on the deficit. She was expected to start work for Mrs. Amina in precisely one hour, which meant she'd have to accomplish a great deal in the next sixty minutes.

Even so, she hesitated.

The knife at her throat had discomposed her. It was not the aggression she found unnerving—in her time on the streets she'd dispatched far worse than a hungry boy wielding a knife—it was the timing. She'd not forgotten the events of last night, the devil's voice, the young man's face.

She'd not forgotten; she'd simply set it aside. Worrying was its own occupation—for Alizeh, a third occupation. It was a job that required of her the free time she seldom

possessed, so she often shelved her distress, leaving it to collect dust until she found a moment to spare.

Still, Alizeh was no fool.

Iblees had been haunting her all her life, had driven her
near to madness with his indecipherable riddles. She'd never
been able to fathom his abiding interest in her, for though she
knew the frost in her veins made her unusual even among
her own people, it seemed an insufficient reason to recommend the girl for all this torture. Alizeh hated how her life
had been plaited with the whispers of such a beast.

The devil was universally reviled by Jinn and Clay, but it
had taken humans millennia to discern this truth: that Jinn
hated the devil perhaps more than anyone else. Iblees was
responsible, after all, for the downfall of their civilization,
for the lightless, unforgiving existence to which Alizeh's
ancestors had long been sentenced. Jinn suffered dearly as
a result of Iblees's actions—his arrogance—at the hands of
humans who for thousands of years considered it their divine
duty to expunge the earth of such beings, beings seen only as
descendants of the devil.

The stain of this hatred was not so easily lifted.

One certainty, at least, had been proven to Alizeh over
and over: the devil's presence in her life was an omen, a por-
tending of imminent misery. She'd heard his voice before
every death, every sorrow, before every inflamed joint upon
which her rheumatic life turned. Only when she was feeling
particularly soft of heart did she acknowledge a nagging suspicion: that the devil's missives were in fact a perverse sort of

kindness, as if he thought he might blunt an inevitable pain with a warning.

Instead, the dread often made it worse.

Alizeh spent her days wondering what torture might befall her, what agony lay in wait. There was no telling how long it—

Her hand froze, forgot itself; her bloody handkerchief fluttered to the ground, unnoticed. Alizeh's heart suddenly pounded with the force of hooves, beating against her chest. She could scarcely draw breath. That face, that inhuman face. *Here*, he was *here*—

He was already watching her.

She noticed his cloak at almost the same time she noticed his face. The superfine black wool was heavy, exquisitely crafted; she recognized its subtle grandeur even from here, even in this moment. It was without question the work of Madame Nezrin, the master seamstress of the empire's most eminent atelier; Alizeh would recognize the woman's work anywhere. In point of fact, Alizeh would recognize the work of most any atelier in the empire, which meant she often needed only a single look at a stranger to know how many people might pretend to mourn them at a funeral.

This man, she decided, would be mourned by a great many sycophants, his pockets deeper, no doubt, than Dariush himself. The stranger was tall, forbidding. He'd drawn the hood over his head, casting most of his face in shadow, but he was far from the anonymous creature he hoped to be. In the wind, Alizeh glimpsed the lining of his cloak:

the purest ink silk, aged in wine, cured with frost. *Years*, it took, to create such a textile. Thousands of hours of labor. The young man likely had no idea what he wore, just as he seemed to have no idea that she could tell, even from here, that the clasp at his throat was pure gold, that the cost of his simple, unadorned boots would feed hundreds of families in the city. He was a fool to think he might disappear here, that he might have the advantage of her, that he might—

Alizeh went deathly still.

Understanding awoke slowly in her mind, and with it a thick, disorienting unease.

How long had he been standing there?

*There once was a man
who bore a snake on each shoulder*

In truth, Alizeh might not have noticed him at all were he not looking directly at her, pinning her in the air with his eyes. It hit her then—she gasped—hit her with the force of a thunderclap: she saw him now only because he allowed it.

Who was the fool, then?

She.

Panic set fire to her chest. Alizeh tore herself from the ground and fairly disappeared, tearing off through the streets with the preternatural swiftness she usually saved for her worst altercations.

Alizeh did not know what darkness this strange, Clay face would bring. She only knew she'd never be able to outrun it.

Still, she had to try.

FOUR

چهار

THE MOON SAT SO LARGE in the sky Kamran thought he might lift a finger to its skin, draw circles around its wounds. He stared at its veins and starbursts, white pockmarks like spider sacs. He studied it all as his mind worked, his eyes narrowing in the aftermath of an impossible illusion.

She'd fairly disappeared.

He'd not meant to stare, but how, also, was he meant to look away? He'd seen danger in the assailant's movements even before the man drew his knife; worse, no one paid the altercation any attention. The girl could've been maimed or abducted or murdered in the worst ways—and even though Kamran had been sworn to anonymity in daylight, his every instinct compelled him to issue a warning, to step in before it was too late—

He needn't have worried.

Still, there was much that troubled him, not the least of which was that there'd seemed something amiss about the girl. She'd worn a snoda—a sheath of semi-transparent silk—around her eyes and nose, which did not obscure, exactly, but blur her features. The snoda itself was innocuous enough; it was required of all who worked in service. She was ostensibly a maid.

But servants were not required to wear the snoda outside

of work, and it was unusual that the girl had worn hers at this early hour, when the royals were still abed.

It seemed far more likely that she was not a maid at all.

Spies had been infiltrating the empire of Ardunia for years, but these numbers had been bloating dangerously in more recent months, feeding an unnerving concern that lately crowned Kamran's thoughts, and which he could not now shake.

He exhaled his frustration, shaping a cloud in the cold.

More in every moment, Kamran grew convinced the girl had stolen the servants' uniform, for her covert attempt had not only been poorly executed, but easily betrayed by an ignorance of the many rules and mannerisms that defined the lives of the lower classes. Her gait alone would've been warning enough; she'd walked too well for a servant, carrying herself with a kind of regal bearing established only in infancy.

No, Kamran felt certain now that the girl had been hiding something. It would not be the first time someone had used the snoda to mask themselves in public.

Kamran glanced at the clock in the square; he'd come into town this morning to speak with the Diviners, who'd sent a mysterious note requesting an audience with the young man despite his never having announced his return home. Today's meeting, it seemed, would have to wait; for much to his dismay, Kamran's always-reliable instincts would not quiet.

How, with only one free hand, had a maid so coolly disarmed a man holding a knife to her throat? When would a maid have had the time or coin to spare learning self-defense?

And what on earth had she said to the man to leave him weeping in the snow?

The suspect in question was only now stumbling to his feet. His shock of red curls screamed he was from Fesht, a region at least one month south of Setar, the capital city; not only was the assailant far from home, but he appeared to be in severe pain, one arm hanging lower than the other. Kamran watched as the redhead held his bad limb—dislocated, it seemed—with the good, carefully steadying himself. Tears had tracked clean paths down his otherwise dirty cheeks, and for the first time, Kamran got a good look at the criminal. Had he more practice with outward displays of emotion, Kamran's features might've registered surprise.

The assailant was quite young.

Kamran moved swiftly toward him, sliding a mask of intricate chain mail over his face as he went. He walked into the wind, his cloak snapping against his boots, and only when he'd all but collided with the child did he stop. It was enough that the Fesht boy jumped back at his approach, wincing as the movement jostled his injury. The boy cradled his wounded arm and curled inward, head to his chest like a humbled millipede, and with an unintelligible murmur, tried to pass.

"Lotfi, hejj, bekhshti—" *Please, sir, excuse me—*

The gall of this child, Kamran could scarce believe it. Still, it was a comfort to know that he'd been correct: the boy spoke Feshtoon and was far from home.

Kamran had every intention of handing the child over

to the magistrates; it had been his sole purpose in seeking out the boy. But now, unable to pry loose his suspicions, he found himself hesitating.

Again, the child tried to pass, and again, Kamran blocked his path. "Kya tan goft et cheknez?" *What did the young woman say to you?*

The boy startled. Stepped back. His skin was a shade or two lighter than his brown eyes, with a smattering of darker freckles across his nose. Heat blossomed across his face in unflattering splotches. "Bekhshti, hejj, nek mefem—" *I'm sorry, sir, I don't understand—*

Kamran stepped closer; the boy nearly whimpered.

"Jev man," he said. "Pres." *Answer me. Now.*

The boy's tongue came loose then, almost too quickly to be comprehensible. Kamran translated in his head as the child spoke:

"Nothing, sir—please, sir, I didn't hurt her, it was only a misunderstanding—"

Kamran clamped a gloved hand around the boy's dislocated shoulder and the Fesht boy cried out, gasping as his knees buckled.

"*You dare lie to my face—*"

"Sir—please—" The child was crying now. "She only gave me back my knife, sir, I swear it, and—and then she offered me bread, she said—"

Kamran rocked backward, dropping his hand. "You continue to lie."

"On m-my mother's grave, I swear. On all that is holy—"

"She returned your weapon and offered to feed you," Kamran said sharply, "after you nearly killed her. After you tried to steal from her."

The boy shook his head, tears welling again in his eyes. "She showed me mercy, sir— Please—"

"*Enough.*"

The boy's mouth snapped shut. Kamran's frustration was mounting; he wanted desperately to throttle someone. He searched the square once more, as if the girl might appear as easily as she'd evaporated. His gaze landed again on the boy.

It was like thunder, his voice.

"You pressed a blade to a woman's throat like the worst coward, the most detestable of men. That young woman might've shown you mercy but I see no reason to do the same. You expect to walk away from this without judgment? Without justice?"

The boy panicked. "Please, sir—I will go and die, sir—I will slit my own throat if you ask me to, only don't hand me over to the magistrates, I beg you."

Kamran blinked. The situation grew more complicated by the second. "Why do you say such a thing?"

The boy shook his head then, growing only more hysterical. His eyes were wild, his fear too palpable for theater. Soon he began to wail, the sound ringing through the streets.

Kamran did not know how to calm the urchin; his own dying soldiers had never allowed themselves such weakness in his presence. Too late, Kamran considered letting the boy go, but he'd hardly begun to formulate the thought when, without warning, the child drove the length of the crude blade into his own throat.

Kamran inhaled sharply.

The boy—whose name he did not know—choked on his own blood, on the knife still buried in his neck. Kamran caught him when he fell, could feel the outline of the boy's ribs under his fingers. He was light as a bird, bones hollowed out, no doubt, by hunger.

Old impulses prevailed.

Kamran issued commands to passersby with the voice he used to lead a legion, and strangers appeared as if out of thin air, abandoning their own children to carry out his orders. His head was so dense with disbelief he hardly noticed when the boy was lifted from his arms and carried out of the square. The way he stared at the blood, the spotted snow, the red rivulets circling a manhole cover—it was as if Kamran had never seen death; hadn't seen it a thousand times over. He had, he had, he thought he'd seen all manner of darkness. But Kamran had never before witnessed a child commit suicide.

It was then that he saw the handkerchief.

He'd watched the young woman press it to her throat, to the wound inflicted by a boy who was now presumably dead. He'd watched this strange girl manage her own near-death with the forbearance of a soldier, meting out justice with the compassion of a saint. He held no doubt now that she was indeed a spy, one in possession of an astuteness of mind that surprised him.

She'd known in but a moment how to handle the child, had she not? She'd done far better than he, had judged better; and now, as he processed her earlier escape, his fears only ratcheted higher. It was rare that Kamran experienced shame, but the sensation roared inside him now, refusing to be quieted. With a single finger, he lifted the embroidered square out of the snow. He'd expected the white textile to be stained with blood.

It was pristine.

FIVE

پنج

KAMRAN'S HEELS KNOCKED AGAINST THE marble floors with unusual force, the sounds echoing through the cavernous halls of his home. Upon his father's death Kamran had discovered that he could be propelled through life by a single emotion; carefully cultivated, it grew hot and vital inside his chest, like an experimental organ.

Anger.

It kept him alive better than his heart ever had.

He felt anger always, but he felt it especially now, and Lord save the man who crossed him when he was at his worst.

After tucking the girl's handkerchief into his breast pocket, he'd pivoted sharply, single-minded as he strode toward his horse, the animal patiently awaiting his return. Kamran liked horses. They did not ask questions before doing as they were told; at least not with their tongues. The jet stallion had not minded his master's bloodied cloak nor his distracted temper.

Not the way Hazan did.

The minister trailed him now with impressive speed; his the second set of boots pounding the stone floors. Had they not grown up together, Kamran might've reacted to this insolence with an inelegant method of problem-solving: brute force. But then, it was his incapacity for awe that made

Hazan perfect for his role as minister. Kamran could not countenance sycophants.

"You are worse than an idiot, did you know?" Hazan said with great serenity. "You should be nailed to the oldest Benzess tree. I should let the scarabs strip the flesh from your bones."

Kamran said nothing.

"It could take weeks." Hazan had caught up, and now he kept pace easily. "I would watch, happily, as they devoured your eyes."

"Surely, you exaggerate."

"I assure you, I do not."

Without warning, Kamran stopped walking; Hazan, to his credit, did not falter. The two young men turned sharply to face each other. Hazan had once been the kind of boy whose knees resembled arthritic knuckles; as a child, he could hardly stand up straight to save his life. Kamran could not help but marvel at the difference in him now, at the boy who'd grown into the kind of man who felt comfortable threatening to murder the crown prince with a smile.

It was with a begrudging respect that Kamran met his minister's eyes. They were nearly the same height, he and Hazan. Similar builds.

Wildly different features.

"No," Kamran said, sounding tired even to himself. The sharp edge of his anger had begun to fade. "As to your enthusiasm for my brutal death, I have no doubt. I refer only to your assessment of the damage you claim I've done."

Hazan's hazel eyes flashed at that, the only outward sign

of his frustration. Still, he spoke calmly when he said, "That there lingers any uncertainty in your mind that you've not committed a grievous error says only to me, sire, that you should have your neck checked by the palace butcher."

Kamran almost smiled.

"You think this is funny?" Hazan took a measured step closer. "You've only alerted the kingdom to your presence, only shouted into a crowd every proof of your identity, only *marked yourself as a target while entirely unguarded—*"

Kamran unlatched the clasp at his throat, stretched his neck, let the cloak drop. The article was caught by unseen hands, a specter-like servant scraping in, then out of sight with the bloodied garment. In the fraction of a second he saw the blur of the servant's snoda he was reminded, again, of the girl.

Kamran dragged a hand down his face, with grim results. He'd forgotten about the boy's dried blood on his hands and hoped he might forget again. In the interim, he only half listened to the minister's reprimands, with which he did not at all agree.

The prince neither saw his actions as foolish, nor did he think it beyond him to be interested in the affairs of the lower classes. Privately, Kamran might allow an argument defending the futility of such an interest—for he knew if he were to concern himself with every violent attack on the city streets he'd scarcely find time to breathe—but apart from the fact that an interest in the lives of the Ardunian people was entirely within the prince's purview, the morning's bloodletting had seemed to him more than a random act of violence. Indeed the more he'd studied the situation the more nefarious it had presented, its actors more complex than first appeared. It had seemed wise, at the time, to insert himself in the situation—

"A situation that concerned two worthless bodies better off extinguished by their own kind," Hazan said with little emotion. "The girl had seen fit to let the boy go, as you claim—and yet, you found her judgment wanting? You felt it necessary to play God? No, don't answer that. I don't think I want to know."

Kamran only glanced at his minister.

Hazan's lips pressed into a thin line. "I might've been motivated to consider the wisdom of your intervention had the boy actually killed the girl. Barring that," he said flatly, "I can see no excuse for your reckless behavior, sire, no explanation for your thoughtlessness save a grotesque need to be a hero—"

Kamran looked up at the ceiling. He'd loved little in his life, but he'd always appreciated the comfort of symmetry, of sequences that made sense. He stared now at the soaring, domed ceilings, the artistry of the alcoves carved into alcoves. Every expanse and cavity was adorned with starbursts of rare metals, glazed tiles expertly arranged into geometric patterns that repeated ad infinitum.

He lifted a bloody hand, and Hazan fell silent.

"Enough," Kamran said quietly. "I've indulged your censure long enough."

"Yes, Your Highness." Hazan took a step back but stared curiously at the prince. "More than usual, I'd say."

Kamran forced a sardonic smile. "I beg you to spare me your analysis."

"I would dare to remind you, sire, that it is my imperial duty to provide you the very analysis you detest."

"A regrettable fact."

"And a loathsome occupation, is it not, when one's counsel is thusly received?"

"A bit of advice, minister: when offering counsel to a barbarian, you might consider first lowering your expectations."

Hazan smiled. "You are not at all yourself today, sire."

"Chipper than usual, am I?"

"Your mood is a great deal darker this morning than you would care to admit. Just now I might inquire as to why the death of a street child has you so overwrought."

"You would be wasting your breath in the effort."

"Ah." Hazan still held his smile. "I see the day is not yet ripe enough for honesty."

"If I am indeed overwrought," said the prince, losing a modicum of composure, "it is no doubt a symptom of my enthusiasm to remind you that my father would've had you hung for your insolence."

"Just so," Hazan said softly. "Though it occurs to me now that you are not your father."

Kamran's head snapped up. He drew his sword from its scabbard without thinking, and not until he saw the barely contained mirth in his minister's eyes did he stall, his hand frozen on the hilt.

Kamran was rattled.

He'd been gone from home for over a year; he'd forgotten

how to have normal conversations. Long months he'd spent in the service of the empire, securing borders, leading skir-mishes, dreaming of death.

Ardunia's rivalry with the south was as old as time.

Ardunia was a formidable empire—the largest in the known world—and their greatest weakness was both a well-kept secret and a source of immense shame: they were running out of water.

Kamran was proud of Ardunia's existing qanat systems, intuitive networks that transported water from aquifers to aboveground reservoirs, and upon which people relied for their drinking water and irrigation. The problem was that qanats relied entirely upon the availability of groundwater, which meant large swaths of the Ardunian empire were for centuries rendered uninhabitable—a problem mitigated only by barging freshwater via marine vessel from the Mashti River.

The fastest path to this titanic waterway was located at the nadir of Tulan, a small, neighboring empire affixed to Ardunia's southernmost border. Tulan was much like a flea they could not shake free, a parasite that could neither be eliminated nor exhumed. Ardunia's greatest wish was to build an aqueduct straight through the heart of the south-ern nation, but decade after decade its kings would not bow. Tulan's only peaceful offering in exchange for such access was a punishing, ruinous tax, one too great even for Ardunia. Several times they'd tried simply to decimate Tulan, but the Ardunian military had suffered astonishing losses as a result—Kamran's own father had died in the effort—and none in the north could understand why.

Hatred had grown between the two nations not unlike an impassable mountain range.

For nearly a century the Ardunian navy had been forced instead to take a far more dangerous route to water, traveling many months for access to the tempestuous river. It was lucky, then, that Ardunia had been blessed not only with a reliable rainy season, but with engineers who'd built impressive catchment areas to capture and store rainwater for years at a time. Even so, the clouds never seemed quite as full these days, and the empire's cisterns were running low.

Every day, Kamran prayed for rain.

The empire of Ardunia was not officially at war—not yet—but peace, too, Kamran had learned, was maintained at a bloody price.

"Your Highness." Hazan's tentative voice startled the prince, returning him to the present moment. "Forgive me. I spoke thoughtlessly."

Kamran looked up.

The details of the hall in which he stood came suddenly into sharp focus: glossy marble floors, towering jade columns, soaring opalescent ceilings. He felt the worn, leather hilt of his sword against his palm, growing all the while incrementally aware of the musculature of his body, the dense weight he carried always and seldom considered: the heaviness in his arms, the heft of his legs. He forced himself to return the sword to its scabbard, briefly closing his eyes. He smelled rosewater and fresh rice; a servant bustled past carrying a copper tray laden with tea things.

How long had he been lost in his own thoughts?

Kamran had grown anxious and distracted of late. The recent swell of Tulanian spies discovered on Ardunian land had done little for his sleep; alone it would've been a disturbing enough discovery, but this intelligence was compounded by his own myriad worries, for not only did the prince fear for their reservoirs, but he'd seen things on his recent tour of duty that continued to unnerve him.

The future seemed dim, and his role in it, bleak.

As was expected, the prince sent his grandfather frequent updates while away. His most recent letter had been rife with news of Tulan, whose small empire became only bolder as the days went on. Rumors of discord and political maneuvering grew louder each day, and despite the tenuous peace between the two empires, Kamran suspected war might soon be inevitable.

His return to the capital the week prior was for two reasons only: first, after completing a perilous water journey, he'd had to replenish the central cisterns that fed the others throughout the empire, and then deliver his troops safely home. Second, and more simply: his grandfather had asked it of him.

In response to Kamran's many concerns, the prince had been instructed to return to Setar. For a respite, his grandfather had said. An innocuous enough request, one Kamran knew to be quite irregular.

The prince had been restored to the palace for a week now, and every day he grew only more unsettled. Even after seven days home the king had yet to respond directly to his note, and Kamran had grown restless without a mission, without his soldiers. He was just then listening to Hazan articulate these same thoughts, allowing that this very restlessness was—

"—perhaps the only plausible explanation for your actions this morning."

Yes. Kamran could at least agree that he was eager to return to work. He would need to leave again, he realized.

Soon.

"I grow tired of this conversation," the prince said curtly. "Do assist me in welcoming its swift conclusion and tell me what it is you require. I must be on my way."

Hazan hesitated. "Yes, sire, of course, but— Do you not wish to know what has become of the child?"

"What child?"

"The boy, of course. The one whose blood stains your hands even now."

Kamran stiffened, his anger sparking suddenly back to life. It took little, he realized, to rekindle a fire that only dulled, but never died. "I would not."

"But it might comfort you to know that he is not yet dead."

"*Comfort* me?"

"You seem distressed, Your Highness, and I—"

Kamran took a step forward, his eyes flashing. He studied Hazan closely: the broken slope of his nose, his cropped ash-blond hair. Hazan's skin was so densely freckled one could scarcely see his eyebrows; he'd been bullied mercilessly as a child for what seemed a myriad of reasons, tragic in all ways save one: it was Hazan's suffering that had conjured their

first introduction. The day Kamran defended the illegitimate child of a courtier was the same day that nobby-kneed
child pledged fealty to the young prince.

Even then, Kamran had tried to look away. He'd tried
valiantly to ignore the affairs deemed beneath him, but he
could not manage it.

He could not manage it still.

"You forget yourself, minister," Kamran said softly. "I
would encourage you now to get to your point."

Hazan bowed his head. "Your grandfather is waiting to
see you. You are expected in his rooms at once."

Kamran briefly froze, his eyes closing. "I see. You were
not exaggerating your frustration, then."

"No, sire."

Kamran opened his eyes. In the distance, a kaleidoscope
of colors bedimmed, then brightened. Soft murmurs of conversation carried over to him, the gentle footfalls of scurrying
servants, a blur of snodas. He'd never paid much attention to
it; the centuries-old uniform. Now every time he saw one
he would think of that accursed servant girl. *Spy.* He nearly
snapped his neck just to clear the thought. "What, pray, does
the king want from me?"

Hazan prevaricated. "Now that your people know you are
home, I expect he will ask you to do your duty."

"Which is?"

"To host a ball."

"Indeed." Kamran's jaw clenched. "I'm certain I would
rather set myself on fire. If that is all?"

"He's quite serious, Your Highness. I've heard rumors that

the announcement for a ball has already been—"

"Good. You will take this"—Kamran retrieved the hand-kerchief from his jacket, pinching it between thumb and forefinger—"and have it examined."

Hazan quickly pocketed the white handkerchief. "Shall I have it examined for anything in particular, Your Highness?"

"Blood."

At Hazan's blank look, the prince went on: "It belonged to the servant girl whose neck was nearly slit by the Fesht boy. I think she might be Jinn."

Now Hazan frowned. "I see."

"I fear you do not."

"Forgive me, Your Highness, but in what way does her blood concern us? As you know, the Fire Accords give Jinn the right to w—"

"I am well acquainted with our laws, Hazan. My concern is not merely with her blood, but with her character."

Hazan raised his eyebrows.

"I don't trust her," Kamran said sharply.

"Need you trust her, sire?"

"There's something false about the girl. She was too refined in her manners."

"Ah." Hazan's eyebrows lifted higher, comprehension dawning. "And in light of all our recent friendliness from Tulan—"

"I want to know who she is."

"You think her a spy."

It was the way he said it, as if he thought Kamran delu-sional, that soured the prince's expression. "You did not see her the way I did, Hazan. She disarmed the boy in a single motion. Dislocated his shoulder. You know as well as I do how the Tulanians covet the Jinn for their strength and fleet-footedness."

"Indeed," Hazan said carefully. "Though I should remind you, sire, that the child she disarmed was weak from hunger to the point of death. His bones might've been unhinged by a strong gust of wind. An ailing rat might've bested him."

"Just the same. You will have her found out."

"The servant girl."

"Yes, the servant girl," Kamran said irritably. "She fled the scene when she saw me. She looked at me as if she knew me."

"Forgive me, sire—but I thought you could not see her face?"

Kamran took a sharp breath. "Perhaps you will thank me, minister, for employing you with such a task? Unless, of course, you would rather I seek your replacement."

Hazan's lips twitched; he bowed. "It is a pleasure, as always, to be at your service."

"You will tell the king I must bathe before our meeting."

"But, sire—"

Kamran strode away, his retreating footfalls ringing out once more through the cavernous hall. His anger had again begun to percolate, bringing with it a humidity that seemed to fog his vision, dim the sounds around him.

It was a shame, then, that Kamran did not dissect himself. He did not stare out of windows wondering what other emotions might be lurking beneath the veneer of his ever-present anger. It did not occur to him that he might be experiencing a muddied sort of grief, so it did not strike him as unusual that he was fantasizing, just then, about driving a sword through a man's heart. In fact, he was so consumed by his imaginings that he did not hear his mother calling his name, her bejeweled robes dragging, sapphires scoring the marble floors as she went.

No, Kamran seldom heard his mother's voice until it was too late.

SIX

شش

ALIZEH'S MORNING HAD BEEN, AMONG other things, disappointing. She'd sacrificed an hour of sleep, braved the winter dawn, narrowly escaped an attempt on her life, and eventually returned to Baz House with only regret to report, wishing her pockets weighed as heavy as her mind.

She'd carried the unwieldy parcel through several snowdrifts before arriving at the servants' entrance of the Lojjan ambassador's estate, and, after forcing her frozen lips to stammer out an explanation for her appearance at the threshold, the bespectacled housekeeper had handed Alizeh a purse with her pay. Alizeh, shivering and fatigued, had made the mistake of counting the coin only after relinquishing her commission, and then, forgetting herself entirely, dared to say aloud that she thought there'd been some kind of mistake.

"Forgive me, ma'am—but this is only h-half of what we agreed upon."

"Mm." The housekeeper sniffed. "You'll get the rest once my mistress decides she likes the dress."

Alizeh's eyes went round.

Perhaps if her skirts hadn't been stiff with frost, or if her chest had not felt as if it might fissure from cold—perhaps if her lips had not been so very numb, or if her feet had not lost all sensation—perhaps then she might've remembered to bite her tongue. Instead, Alizeh managed only to contain the worst of her outrage. A miracle, really, that she spoke with some measure of equanimity when she said, "But Miss Huda might decide she doesn't like the dress simply to avoid payment."

The housekeeper recoiled, as if she'd been struck. "Careful what you say, girl. I won't hear anyone call my mistress dishonest."

"But surely you can see that this is indeed dishon—" Alizeh said, slipping on a spot of ice. She caught herself against the doorframe, and the housekeeper shrank back farther, this time with an undisguised revulsion.

"*Off,*" the woman snapped. "Get your filthy hands off my door—"

Startled, Alizeh jumped back, miraculously avoiding another patch of ice just two inches to her left. "Miss Huda won't even allow me in the h-house," she stammered, her body now trembling violently with cold. "She wouldn't allow me to do a single fitting—she could decide for any number of reasons that she doesn't like my w-work—"

The door slammed shut in her face.

Alizeh had experienced a sharp pinch in her chest then, a pain that made it hard to breathe. The feeling had remained with her all day.

She felt for the little purse now, its weight in her apron pocket, resting against her thigh. She'd been delayed getting back to Baz House, which meant she'd had no time to deposit her earnings somewhere safer. The world had begun to come alive on her journey back, fresh snowfall dotting every effort to awaken the city of Setar. Preparations for the Wintrose Festival had overtaken the streets, and though Alizeh appreciated the heady scent of rosewater in the air, she would've preferred a moment of quiet before the bell tolled for work. She could not have known then that the quiet she sought might not come at all.

Alizeh was in the kitchen when the clock struck six, broomstick in hand, standing silently in the shadows and as near to the fire as she could manage. The other servants had gathered an hour earlier around the kitchen's long wooden table for their morning meal, and Alizeh watched, rapt, as they finished the last of their breakfast: bowls of haleem, a kind of sweet porridge blended with shredded beef.

As a trial employee Alizeh was not yet allowed to join them—nor did she have any interest in their meal, the mere description of which made her stomach turn—but she enjoyed listening to their easy banter, witnessing the familiarity with which they spoke to one another. They engaged like friends. Or family.

It was a kind of ordinariness with which Alizeh was little acquainted. Her parents' love for her had filled her whole life; Alizeh had wanted for little, and was denied in her childhood nothing but the company of other children, for her mother and father were adamant that, until the moment Alizeh was ready, her existence remain otherwise undiscovered. Alizeh could recollect only one little boy—whose mother was a dear friend of her parents—with whom she was allowed on occasion to play. His name she could not now recall; she remembered only that his pockets were always full of hazelnuts, with which he taught her to play a game of jacks.

Only a select few other trustworthy souls—mostly the masters and tutors with whom she spent a great deal of her time—had been allowed in her life. She had been as a result sheltered to an uncommon degree, and, having spent little time in Clay company, was now spellbound by a great many of their customs. Alizeh had been punished in her previous positions for lingering too long in a breakfast room, for example, hoping for a glimpse of a gentleman eating an egg or buttering a slice of toast. She was endlessly fascinated by their forks and spoons, and this morning was no different.

"What do you think you're doing here?" Mrs. Amina barked at her, startling Alizeh nearly to death. The housekeeper grabbed Alizeh by the scruff of her neck and shoved her into the adjoining hall. "You forget yourself, girl. You don't eat with the other servants."

"I was— I was only waiting," Alizeh said, wincing as her fingers fluttered around her neck, gently pulling her collar back into place. The cut at her throat was still tender, and Alizeh had not wanted to draw attention to herself by wrapping it. She felt the telltale moisture of what could only be fresh blood, and clenched her fists to keep from touching the wound. "Forgive me, ma'am. I never meant to be impertinent. I was only awaiting your instruction."

It happened so fast Alizeh didn't even realize Mrs. Amina had slapped her until she felt the pain in her teeth, saw the flash of light behind her eyes. Too late Alizeh flinched and shrank back, her ears ringing, hands grasping for purchase against the stone wall. She'd made too many mistakes today.

"What did I tell you about that mouth of yours?" Mrs. Amina was saying. "You want this position, you will learn your place." She made a sound of disgust. "I told you to rid yourself of that absurd accent. *Impertinent*," she scoffed. "Where you even learned to talk like that—"

Alizeh felt the change when Mrs. Amina cut herself off, watched her eyes darken with suspicion.

Alizeh swallowed.

"Where *did* you learn to talk like that?" Mrs. Amina asked quietly. "Knowing your letters is one thing, but you begin to strike me as a bit too high in the instep for a scullery girl."

"Not at all, ma'am," Alizeh said, lowering her eyes. She tasted blood in her mouth. Already her face was tender; she resisted the impulse to touch what was no doubt a purpling bruise. "I beg your pardon."

"Who taught you to read, then?" Mrs. Amina rounded on her. "Who taught you to put on airs?"

"Forgive me, ma'am." Alizeh flinched, forced herself to talk slowly. "I don't mean to put on airs, ma'am, it's only that I don't know how else to spe—"

Mrs. Amina looked up then, distracted by the sight of the clock, and the fight went out of her eyes. They'd lost precious minutes of the workday already, and Alizeh knew they could not afford to lose more to this conversation.

Still, Mrs. Amina stepped closer.

"Speak to me like you're some fancy toff one more time

and not only will you see the back of my hand, girl, you'll be back on the street."

Alizeh felt suddenly ill.

If she closed her eyes, she could still feel the rough stone of the cold, vermin-infested alley pressed against her cheek; she could still hear the sounds of the sewer lulling her into unconsciousness for minutes at a time—the longest she'd ever dared to keep her eyes closed on the street. Alizeh sometimes thought she'd rather run in front of a carriage than return to such darkness.

"Yes, ma'am," she said softly, her pulse racing. "Forgive me, ma'am. It won't happen again."

"Enough of your pompous apologies," Mrs. Amina snapped. "Her ladyship is in a frightful state today, and wants every room scrubbed and polished as if the king himself were coming to visit."

Alizeh dared to look up.

Baz House had seven floors, and 116 individual rooms. Alizeh wanted more than anything to ask: *Why? Why every room?* Instead, she held her tongue, grieving quietly. Scrubbing all 116 in one day, she knew, would leave her body in ribbons.

"Yes, ma'am," she whispered.

Mrs. Amina hesitated.

Alizeh could see then that Mrs. Amina was not such a monster that she wouldn't acknowledge the near impossibility of this demand. The housekeeper's tone softened a bit when she said: "The others will help, of course—but they

have their regular duties to attend to as well, you understand? The bulk of the work will be yours."

"Yes, ma'am."

"Do this well, girl, and I will see about hiring you on per-
manently. But I make no promises"—Mrs. Amina lifted a
finger, then pointed it at Alizeh—"if you don't learn to keep
that mouth shut."

Alizeh took a sharp breath. And nodded.

SEVEN

هفت

KAMRAN HAD ONLY JUST ENTERED the antechamber leading to his grandfather's rooms when he felt it: a breath of movement. There was a glimmer of unnaturally refracted light along the walls, a hint of perfume in the air. Kamran purposely slowed his stride, for he knew his predator would not resist such an easy mark.

There.

A flutter of skirts.

Not a moment too soon, Kamran had clamped a hand over his assailant's fist, her fingers clenched around the hilt of a ruby dagger, which she held happily at his throat.

"I tire of this game, Mother."

She twisted out of reach and laughed, her dark eyes gleaming. "Oh, darling, I never do."

Kamran watched his mother with an impassive expression; she was so covered in jewels she glittered even standing still. "You find it diverting," he said, "to play at murdering your own child?"

She laughed again and spun around him, velvet skirts shimmering. Her Royal Highness Firuzeh, the princess of Ardunia, was empyreal in her beauty—but then, this was not such an extraordinary accomplishment for a princess. Loveliness was to be expected of any royal who aspired to the throne, and it was no secret that Firuzeh resented the untimely death of her husband, who seven years ago had lost his head in a senseless battle and had left her forever a princess, never a queen.

"I am tragically *bored*," she said. "And as my child pays so little attention to me, I am forced to be creative."

Kamran was freshly bathed, his clothes pressed and scented, but he wanted desperately to be back in his military uniform. He'd always disliked his formal clothes for their impracticality, their frivolousness. He resisted the urge now to scratch his neck, where the stiff collar of his tunic scraped against his throat. "No doubt there are innumerable other ways," he said to his mother, "to inspire my attention."

"Tedious other ways," she said tersely. "Besides, I should not have to inspire your interest. I did enough work growing you inside my own body. I am owed, at the very least, a modicum of devotion."

Kamran bowed. "Indeed."

"You patronize me."

"I do not."

Firuzeh slapped Kamran's hand away from his neck. "Do cease scratching yourself like a dog, my love."

Kamran stiffened.

It did not matter how many men he'd killed, his mother would forever treat him like a child. "You would blame me for my discomfort when the collar of this ridiculous costume clearly seeks the decapitation of its wearer? Pray can we not, in all the empire, find someone to stitch together two pieces of reasonable clothing?"

Firuzeh ignored this.

She said, "It is a dangerous thing to keep an intelligent woman from performing a single practical task," and slipped her arm through her son's, forcing them to walk together toward the king's main chamber. "I am not to blame for my fits of creativity."

Kamran stopped, surprised, and turned to his mother. "Do you mean to say you have a desire to work?"

Firuzeh made a face. "Don't be intentionally stupid. You know what I mean."

Kamran had once thought there could never in all the world exist his mother's equal, not in beauty or elegance, not in grace or intelligence. He'd not known then how critical it was to also possess a heart. "No," he said. "I'm afraid I haven't the slightest idea."

Firuzeh sighed theatrically, waving him away as they entered the king's reception chamber. Kamran had not known his mother would be joining them for this meeting. He suspected that, more than anything else, she'd come along merely for another look at the king's rooms, as his were her favorite in the palace, and seldom was anyone invited inside.

His grandfather's rooms were designed entirely with mirrors; with what seemed an incalculable number of these small, reflective tiles. Every inch of the interior space, high and low, glittered with arrangements of star-like patterns, all interwoven into a series of larger geometric shapes. The soaring domed ceilings glimmered from high above, a mirage of infinity that seemed to reach the heavens. Two large windows were thrown open to grant entrée to the sun: sharp shafts of light penetrated the room, further illuminating constellation after constellation of shattered glow. Even the floors were covered in mirrored tiles, though the delicate work was protected by a series of rich, intricately woven rugs.

The overall effect was ethereal; Kamran imagined it was not unlike standing in the belly of a star. The room itself was sublime, but the effect it had on its occupants was perhaps the greater accomplishment. A visitor stepped into this room and felt at once exalted, transported to the heavens. Even Kamran was not immune to its effects.

His mother, however, grew mournful.

"Oh, my dear," she said, spinning around the room, a hand clasped to her chest. "This should've all been mine one day."

Kamran watched as his mother peered into the nearest wall, admiring herself; she fluttered her fingers, making her jewels sparkle and dance. Kamran always found it a bit disorienting, entering this space. It inspired a feeling of magnificence, yes, but he found the feeling chased always by a feeling of inadequacy. He felt his small footprint in the world never more acutely than when surrounded by true strength, and he never felt this feeling with more precision than when he drew nearer his grandfather.

The prince looked around then for a sign of the man.

Kamran peered through a crack in one of the adjoining doors, the one he knew led to the king's bedchamber, and was weighing the impertinence of searching the bedroom when Firuzeh tugged on his arm.

Kamran looked back.

"Life is so unfair, is it not?" she said, her eyes shining with feeling. "Our dreams so easily shattered?"

A muscle jumped in Kamran's jaw. "Indeed, Mother. Father's death was a great tragedy."

She made a noncommittal noise.

Often, Kamran thought he could not leave this palace quickly enough. He did not resent his inheritance to the throne, but neither did he relish it. No, Kamran knew too well the gore that accompanied glory.

He'd never once hoped to be king.

As a child, people spoke to Kamran of his position as if he were blessed, fortunate to be in line for a title that first demanded the deaths of the two people he cared for most in the world. It had always seemed to him a disturbing business, and never more so than the day his father's head had been returned home without its body.

Kamran was eleven years old.

He was expected to show strength even then; only days later he was forced to attend a ceremony declaring him the direct heir to the throne. He was but a child, commanded to stand beside the mutilated remains of his father and show no pain, no fear—only fury. It was the day his grandfather gave him his first sword, the day his life changed forever. It was the day a boy was forced to leap, unformed, into the body of a man.

Kamran closed his eyes, felt the press of a cold blade against his cheek.

"Lost in your head, darling?"

He looked at his mother, irritated not merely with her,

but with himself. Kamran did not know the precise shape of the discomfort that addled him; he could not fathom an explanation for his disordered thoughts. He only knew he felt every day a creeping dread, and worse: he feared such uncertainty of mind would only exacerbate matters, for these lost moments, Kamran knew, could cost him his life. His mother had proven that just now.

She seemed to read his mind.

"Don't worry. It's decorative, mostly." Firuzeh stepped back, tapping the glimmering ruby blade with the tip of a perfectly rounded fingernail. She tucked the weapon into her robes. "But I *am* quite angry with you today, and we must speak about it quickly."

"Why is that?"

"Because your grandfather has things he wishes to say to you, but I mean to say my things first."

"No, Mother, I meant: why are you angry?"

"Well, certainly we must discuss this servant girl you have s—"

"There you are," boomed a voice just behind them, and Kamran spun around to see the king approach, transcendent in vibrant shades of green.

Firuzeh fell into a deep curtsy; Kamran bowed.

"Come, come." The king motioned with one hand. "Let me look at you."

Kamran stood and stepped forward.

The king took Kamran's hands and held them, his warm eyes appraising the prince with an undisguised curiosity. Kamran understood that he would be reprimanded for his actions today, but he also knew he would bear the repercussions with dignity. There was no one alive he respected more than his grandfather, and Kamran would honor the king's wishes, whatever they were.

King Zaal was a living legend.

His grandfather—his father's father—had overcome all manner of tribulations. When Zaal was born, his mother had thought she'd given birth to an old man, for the baby's hair was already white, his eyelashes white, his skin so pale it was nearly translucent. Despite the protests of the Diviners, the child had been declared cursed, and his horrified father refused to own him. The wretched king ripped the newborn child from his mother's arms and carried him to the peak of the highest mountain, where the infant was left to die.

Zaal's salvation came in the form of a majestic bird that discovered the crying infant and carried it away, raising it as one of its own. Zaal's eventual return to claim his rightful place as heir and king was one of the greatest stories of their time, and his long reign over Ardunia had been just and merciful. Of his many achievements, Zaal was the only Ardunian king who'd seen fit to put an end to the violence between Jinn and Clay; it was by his order that the controversial Fire Accords had been established. Ardunia was, as a result, one of the only empires living in peace with Jinn, and for that alone Kamran knew his grandfather would not be forgotten.

Finally, the king drew away from his grandson.

"Your choices today were exceedingly curious," Zaal said as he seated himself on his mirrored throne, the sole piece of furniture in the room. Kamran and his mother did what was expected and folded themselves onto the floor cushions before him. "Do you not agree?"

Kamran did not immediately respond.

"I think we can all agree that the prince's behavior was both hasty and unbecoming," his mother interjected. "He must make amends."

"Indeed?" Zaal turned his clear brown eyes on his daughter-in-law. "What kind of amends do you recommend, my dear?"

Firuzeh faltered. "I cannot think of any at present, Your Majesty, but I am certain we shall think of something."

Zaal steepled his hands under his chin, against the carefully trimmed cloud of his beard. To Kamran, he said, "You neither deny nor justify your actions today?"

"I do not."

"And yet, I see that you are not remorseful."

"I am not."

Zaal turned the full force of his gaze upon his grandson. "You will, of course, tell me why."

"With all due respect, Your Majesty, I do not think it unbecoming of a prince to care for the welfare of his people."

The king laughed. "No, I daresay it is not. What is unbecoming is a fickleness of character and an unwillingness to speak the truth to those who know you best."

Kamran stiffened, heat prickling along the nape of his neck. He knew a rebuke when he heard one, and he was not yet immune to the effects of an admonishment from his grandfather. "Your Highness—"

"You have walked among your people for some time now, Kamran. You've seen all manner of suffering. I might accept an explanation of idealism more readily were your actions symptomatic of a larger philosophical position, which we both know they are not, as you've never before taken an active interest in the lives of street children—or servants, for that matter. Certainly there is more to this story than the sudden expansion of your heart." A pause. "Do you deny that you acted out of character? That you put yourself in danger?"

"I will not attempt to deny the first. As to the second—"

"You were alone. Unarmed. You are heir to an empire that spans a third of the known world. You solicited the help of passersby, put yourself at the mercy of strangers—"

"I had my swords."

Zaal smiled. "You persist in insulting me with these ill-considered protests."

"I mean no disrespect—"

"And yet you are aware, are you not, that a man in possession of a sword is not invincible? That he might be attacked from above? That he might be slain by arrow, that he might be mobbed or overrun, that he might be knocked on the head and dragged away for ransom?"

Kamran bowed his head. "Yes, Your Majesty."

"Then you accept that you acted out of character. That you put yourself in danger."

"Yes, Your Majesty."

"Very good. I am asking now only for your explanation."

Kamran took a deep breath and exhaled, slowly, through

his nose. He considered telling the king what he'd told Hazan: that he'd involved himself in the situation because the girl had appeared to him conspicuous, untrustworthy. And yet, Hazan had all but laughed at his explanation, at his instinct that something was amiss. How might Kamran forge into words the influence of an intuition invisible to the eye?

Indeed the more he deliberated, the more the prince's justifications, which had earlier struck him as cogent, seemed now, under the searing gaze of his grandfather, as scattered as sand.

Quietly, Kamran said, "I have no explanation, Your Majesty."

The king hesitated at that, the smile evaporating from his eyes. "You cannot mean it."

"I beg you will forgive me."

"What of the girl? I would not judge you too harshly if you admitted to some weakness of the mind there. Perhaps you will tell me she was a disorienting beauty—that you interfered for some lesser, sordid reason. That you fancy yourself in love with her."

"I did not." Kamra's jaw tensed. "I do not. I most certainly would not."

"Kamran."

"Grandfather, I could not even see her face. You could not expect me to own such a lie."

For the first time, the king grew visibly concerned. "My child, do you not understand how precarious your position is? How many would celebrate any excuse to have your faculties examined? Those who covet your position would invite any reason to deem you unworthy of the throne. It disturbs me more to know that your actions were born not of recklessness, but thoughtlessness. Stupidity is possibly your worst offense."

Kamran flinched.

True, he deeply respected his grandfather, but so, too, did the prince respect himself, and his pride would no longer allow him to endure an onslaught of insults without protest.

He lifted his head, looking the king directly in the eye when he said, with some sharpness, "I believed the girl might be a spy."

King Zaal visibly straightened, his countenance revealing nothing of the tension visible in his hands, clenched now around the arms of his throne. He was silent for so long that Kamran feared, in the interlude, he'd made a terrible mistake.

The king said only: "You thought the girl a spy."

"Yes."

"It is the single true thing you have spoken."

Instantly, Kamran was disarmed. He stared at the king then, bewildered.

"I may now understand your motivations," said his grandfather, "but I am yet to comprehend your lack of discretion. You thought it wise to pursue such a suspicion in the middle of the street? You thought the girl a spy, so you say—and what of the boy? Did you think him a saint? That you carried him through the square, allowing him to bleed all over your body?"

For the second time, Kamran experienced an unnerving heat inflame his skin. Again, he lowered his eyes. "No, Your Majesty. There, I had not been thinking clearly."

"Kamran, you are to be king," said his grandfather, who sounded suddenly close to anger. "You have no choice but to think clearly. The people may discuss all manner of gossip pertaining to their sovereign, but the soundness of his mind should never be a topic of discussion."

Kamran kept his head bowed, his eyes trained on the intricate, repeating patterns of the rug underfoot. "Do we need worry what anyone thinks of my mind? Surely there's no need to concern ourselves with such matters at this juncture. You are strong and healthy, Grandfather. You will rule Ardunia for many years yet—"

Zaal laughed out loud, and Kamran looked up. "Oh, your sincerity does move me. Truly. But my sojourn here is coming to an end," he said, his eyes searching for the window. "I have felt it for some time now."

"Grandfather—"

King Zaal held up a hand. "I will not be distracted from our present discussion. Neither will I insult your intelligence by reminding you how profoundly your every action affects the empire. A simple announcement of your return home would've been enough to stir up all manner of theater and excitement, but your actions today—"

"Indeed," said his mother, interjecting herself, reminding everyone she was still there. "Kamran, you should be ashamed of yourself. Acting the part of a commoner."

"Ashamed?" Zaal looked at his daughter-in-law in surprise. To Kamran, he said, "Is that why you think I've summoned you?"

Kamran hesitated.

"I expected you might be angry with me, yes, Your Majesty. I was also told you might expect me to host a ball now that I've inadvertently announced my return."

Zaal sighed, his white brows knitting together. "Hazan told you that, I imagine?" The king's frown grew deeper. "A ball. Yes, a ball. Though that is the least of it."

Kamran tensed. "Your Highness?"

"Oh, my child." Zaal shook his head. "I see only now that you do not realize what you've done."

Firuzeh looked from her son to the king and back again. "What has he done?"

"It was not your mere interference that caused such talk today," Zaal said softly. He was staring out the window again. "Had you left the boy to die in his own blood, it would've been little remarked upon. These things occasionally happen. You could've quietly summoned the magistrates, and the boy would've been carted away. Instead, you held him in your arms. You let the blood of a street orphan touch your skin, sully your clothes. You showed care and compassion for one of their own."

"And am I to be punished, Your Majesty? Am I to be cut down for a display of mercy?" Kamran said, even as he felt the ascent of an unsettling apprehension. "I thought it expected of a prince to be in service of his people."

His grandfather almost smiled. "Do you mean to

purposely misunderstand me? Your life is too valuable, Kamran. You, heir to the largest empire on earth, recklessly exposed yourself to danger. Your performance today might go unquestioned by the people, but it will be severely scrutinized by the nobles, who will wonder whether you've gone mad."

"*Gone mad?*" the prince said, struggling now to control his anger. "Is that not a gross overreaction? When there were no repercussions— When I did nothing but assist a dying boy—"

"You did nothing but cause a riot. They are only chanting your name in the streets."

Firuzeh gasped and ran to the window, as if she might see or hear anything from within the palace walls, which were notoriously impenetrable. The prince, who knew better than to hope for a glimpse of a mob, sank back down.

He was stunned.

Zaal sat forward in his seat. "I know in your heart you would fight to the death for your empire, child, but this is not at all the same kind of sacrifice. A crown prince does not risk his life in the town square for a thieving street urchin. It is not done."

"No," said the prince, subdued. He felt suddenly leaden. "I expect it is not."

"We must now temper your recklessness with displays of solemnity," said his grandfather. "Such performances will be for the benefit, in particular, of the noble families of the Seven Houses, upon whose political influence we heavily rely. You will host a ball. You will be seen at court. You will pay your respects to the Seven Houses, House of Piir, in particular. You will relieve them of any fears they might have as concerns your character. I will have them question neither the soundness of your mind nor your ability to rule. Is that clear?"

"Yes, Your Majesty," said the prince, discomposed. Only now was he beginning to understand the weight of his error. "I will do as you bid me, and I will remain in Setar for as long as you think it necessary to repair this damage. Then, if you will allow it, I'd like to return to my troops."

Briefly, Zaal smiled. "I'm afraid it is no longer a good idea for you to be far from home."

Kamran did not pretend to misunderstand.

"You are healthy," he said with more heat than he intended. "Fit and strong. Of sound mind. You could not be certain of such a thing—"

"When you get to be my age," Zaal said gently, "you can indeed be certain of such things. I've grown weary of this world, Kamran. My soul is eager to depart. But I cannot leave without first ensuring that our line is protected—that our empire will be protected."

Slowly, the prince looked up into his grandfather's eyes.

"You must know." Zaal smiled. "I did not ask you to come home merely to rest."

At first, Kamran did not understand. When he did, a beat later, he felt the force of the realization like a blow to the head. He could scarcely form the words when he said:

"You need me to marry."

"Ardunia requires an heir."

"*I* am your heir, Your Majesty. I am your servant—"

"Kamran, we are on the brink of war."

The prince held steady even as his heart pounded. He stared at his grandfather in something akin to disbelief. This was the conversation he'd been waiting to have, the news he'd been waiting to discuss. Yet even now, King Zaal seemed disinclined to say much.

This, Kamran could not countenance.

His grandfather was threatening to die—threatening to leave him here alone to wage a war, to defend their empire— and instead of equipping him for such a fate, was tasking him with marriage? No, he could not believe it.

Through sheer force of will was Kamran able to keep his voice steady when he said, "If we are to go to war, Your Highness, surely you might assign me a more practical task? There's no doubt a great deal more I could do to protect our empire at such a time than court some nobleman's daughter."

The king only stared at Kamran, his expression serene. "In my absence, the greatest gift you could give your empire is assurance. *Certainty.* War will come, and with it, your duty"—he held up a hand to prevent Kamran from speaking—"which I know you do not fear.

"But if something should happen to you on the battlefield, we will be in chaos. Worthless relations will claim the throne, and then lay waste to it. There are five hundred thousand soldiers under our command. Tens of millions who rely on us to manage their well-being, to ensure their safety, to procure the necessary water for their crops, to guarantee food for their children." Zaal leaned forward. "You must secure the line, my child. Not just for me, but for your father. For your legacy. *This*, Kamran, is what you must do for your empire."

The prince understood then that there was no choice to be made. King Zaal was not asking a question.

He was issuing a command.

Kamran rose on one knee, bowed his head before his king. "Upon my honor," he said quietly. "You have my word."

EIGHT

هشت

THIS DAY HAD BEEN MORE difficult than most.

Alizeh had boiled water until the steam seared her skin. She'd plunged her hands into soapy, scalding-hot liquid so many times that the grooves in her knuckles had split. Her fingers were blistered, warm to the touch. The sharp edges of her floor brush had dug into her palms, rubbing the skin raw until it bled. She'd bunched her apron in her fists as often as she dared, but every desperate search for her handkerchief turned up only disappointment.

Alizeh had little time to dwell on the many thoughts haunting her mind that day, though neither did she desire to think upon such disheartening matters. Between the devil's visit, the terrifying appearance of the hooded stranger, the cruelty of Miss Huda, and the boy she'd left broken in the snow, Alizeh did not lack for fuel to feed her fears.

She considered, as she scrubbed clean yet another latrine, that it was probably for the best that she ignore the lot. Better not to think on any of it, better to simply push every day through the pain and the fear until she, too, was finally consumed by eternal darkness. It was a bleak thought for a young woman of eighteen, but she thought it nonetheless: that perhaps only in death might she find the freedom she so desperately sought, for she had long ago given up hope of finding solace in this world.

Indeed most hours of the day Alizeh could hardly believe who she'd become, how far she'd strayed from the plans once held for her future. Long ago there'd been a blueprint for her life, a quiet infrastructure designed to support who she might one day be. She'd been left little choice but to abandon that imagined future, not unlike a child shedding an imagined friend. All that remained of her old existence was the familiar whisper of the devil, his voice growing under her skin at intervals, snuffing her life of light.

Would that he, too, might vanish.

The clock had just struck two when, for the twelfth time that day, Alizeh placed her empty buckets on the kitchen floor.

She looked around for any sign of Cook or Mrs. Amina before stealing to the back of the room, and only when she was certain of her solitude did she do what she'd already done eleven times before, and wrench open the heavy wooden door.

Alizeh was struck straightaway by the intoxicating smell of rosewater.

The Wintrose Festival was one of the few things familiar to her in this foreign, royal city, for the Wintrose season was celebrated all throughout the empire of Ardunia. Alizeh had fond memories of harvesting the delicate pink blooms with her parents, straw baskets colliding as they walked, heads dense with perfume.

She smiled.

Nostalgia nudged her feet across the threshold, sense

memory encouraging her legs, articulating her limbs. A zephyr moved through the alley, tumbling rose petals toward her, and she drew the heady, floral fragrance deep into her lungs, experiencing a rare moment of unqualified joy as the breeze ruffled her hair, the hems of her skirts. The sun was but a nebulous glow through an exhalation of clouds, painting the moment in diffuse, golden light that made Alizeh feel as if she'd stepped into a dream. She could hardly help her need to draw nearer to such beauty.

One at a time, she began picking the wind-scattered roses out of the snow, gently tucking the wilting blossoms into the pockets of her apron. These Gol Mohammadi roses were so heavily scented, their perfume would last for months. Her mother had always used theirs to make a rose-petal jam, saving a few corollas to press between the pages of a book, which Alizeh liked t—

Without warning, her heart began to race.

It was that familiar pinch in her chest, her pulse pounding in her bleeding palms. Her hands shook without warning, petals falling loose from her fists. Alizeh was struck with a frightening need to run from this place, to strip the apron from her body and tear across the city, lungs blazing. She wanted desperately to return home, to fall at her parents' feet and grow roots there, at the base of their bodies. She felt all this in the span of a second, the feeling flooding her with a riotous force and leaving her, in its wake, strangely numb. It was a humbling experience, for Alizeh was again reminded that she had no home, no parents to whom she might return.

It had been years since their deaths, and still it seemed to Alizeh an outrageous injustice that she could not see their faces.

She swallowed.

Once, Alizeh's life had meant to be a source of strength for the people she loved; instead, she often felt her birth had exposed her parents to bloodshed, to the brutal murders that would take them both—first her father, then her mother— in the same year.

Jinn had been viciously slaughtered for ages, it was true; their numbers had been decimated, their footprint reduced near to nothing—and with it, much of their legacy. The deaths of her parents, too, had seemed to the unsuspecting eye much like the deaths of countless other Jinn: random acts of hatred, or even unfortunate accidents.

And yet—

Alizeh was plagued always by an unsettling suspicion that her parents' deaths had not been random. Despite their diligent efforts to keep Alizeh's existence concealed, she worried; for it was not only her parents, but all those whose lives had once touched hers who'd vanished in a series of similar tragedies. Alizeh could not help but wonder whether the true target of all this violence had been someone else entirely—

Her.

With no proof to corroborate such a theory, Alizeh's mind was unable to rest, devoured every day a bit more by the voracious appetite of her fears.

Heart still thudding in her chest, she retreated inside.

Alizeh had searched the back alley beyond the kitchen each of the twelve times she'd come downstairs, but the Fesht boy had never turned up, and she couldn't understand why. She'd scavenged from the remains of breakfast a few chunks of pumpkin bread, which she'd carefully wrapped in wax paper, and hid the rations under a loose floorboard in the pantry. The boy had seemed so hungry this morning that Alizeh could not imagine an explanation for his absence, not unless—

She added firewood to the stove, and hesitated. It was possible she'd hurt the boy too badly during their scuffle.

Sometimes Alizeh did not know her own strength.

She checked the kettles she'd set to boil, then glanced at the kitchen clock. There were still many hours left in the day, and she worried her hands wouldn't survive the onslaught. Sacrifices would have to be made.

Alizeh sighed.

Quickly, she tore two strips of fabric from the hem of her apron. Alizeh, who made all her own clothes, quietly mourned the ruin of the piece, and then bandaged her wounds as best she could with blistered fingers. She would need to find time to visit the apothecary tomorrow. She had some coin now; she could afford to purchase salve, and maybe even a poultice.

Her hands, she hoped, would recover.

Having wrapped her wounds, the sharp edge of her torment began slowly to abate, the modicum of relief unbolting the vise from around her chest. In the aftermath she took a deep, bracing breath, experiencing a prickle of embarrassment at her own thoughts, at the dark turns they took with so little encouragement. Alizeh did not want to lose faith in this world; it was only that every pain she owned seemed to extract hope from her as payment.

Still, she considered, as she refilled her buckets with freshly boiled water, her parents would've wanted more for her. They would've wanted her to keep fighting.

One day, her father had said, *this world will bow to you.*

Just then came a sharp knock at the back door.

Alizeh straightened so quickly she nearly dropped the kettle. She tossed another glance around the unusually empty kitchen—there was so much work to be done today that the servants were granted no breaks—and snatched the hidden parcel from the pantry.

Carefully, she opened the door.

Alizeh blinked, then stepped back. It was Mrs. Sana staring at her, the bespectacled housekeeper from the Lojjan ambassador's estate.

Stunned as she was, Alizeh nearly forgot to curtsy.

Housekeepers, who ruled their own little kingdoms, were not considered servants and did not wear snodas; as a result, they were due a level of respect that Alizeh was still learning. She bobbed a curtsy, then straightened.

"Good afternoon, ma'am. How may I help you?"

Mrs. Sana said nothing, only held out a small purse, which Alizeh accepted in her injured hand. She felt the weight of the coin at once.

"*Oh*," she breathed.

"Miss Huda was very pleased with the dress and would like to engage your services again."

Alizeh went suddenly solid.

She dared not speak, dared not move for fear of ruining the moment. She tried to remember if she'd fallen asleep, if perhaps she was dreaming.

Mrs. Sana rapped her knuckles on the doorframe. "You've gone deaf, girl?"

Alizeh took a sharp breath. "No, ma'am," she said quickly. "That is—yes, ma'am. I would— It would be my honor."

Mrs. Sana sniffed at her, in a way that was becoming familiar. "Yes. I daresay it would be. And you'll remember it the next time you speak ill of my mistress. She meant to send her maid, but I insisted on delivering the message myself. You understand my meaning."

Alizeh lowered her eyes. "Yes, ma'am."

"Miss Huda will need at least four gowns for the upcoming festivities, and one showpiece for the ball."

Alizeh's head snapped up. She did not know to which upcoming festivities Mrs. Sana was referring, and she did not care. "Miss Huda wants *five* gowns?"

"Will that be a problem?"

Alizeh heard a roar in her ears, experienced a terrifying disorientation. She worried she might cry, and she did not think she'd forgive herself if she did. "No, ma'am," she managed to say. "No problem at all."

"Good. You may come to the house tomorrow at nine in the evening." A heavy pause. "After you finish your shift here."

"Thank you, ma'am. Thank you. Thank you for und—"

"Nine o'clock sharp, you understand?" And Mrs. Sana was gone, the door slamming shut behind her.

Alizeh could hold it in no longer. She slid to the floor and sobbed.

NINE

IN THE MILKY EYE OF the moon the silhouettes of passersby merged into one gelatinous mass rumbling with sound; raucous cries rang out, laughter tearing through trees, lamplight flickering as people stumbled through the streets. The night was pure madness.

Alizeh suppressed a shudder.

It disturbed her always to be enveloped by the dark, for it brought to life a fear of blindness she could not fully rationalize. Her ancestors had once been sentenced to an existence without light or heat—she knew this, yes—but that she should carry the fear *still* struck her as most peculiar. Worse, it seemed her strange fate to be tethered always to the dark, for these days she moved most freely through the world only in the absence of daylight, when the yoke of duty had been removed.

Alizeh had emerged from Baz House long after the sun had been extinguished, and though the good news of more work for Miss Huda had done a great deal to buoy her spirits, Alizeh was burdened anew by the state of her hands. The day's tasks had torn fresh wounds into her already split palms, and the strips of fabric she'd carefully wrapped around her injuries had grown damp and heavy with blood. Alizeh, who now needed to create five gowns in addition to performing her regular duties, suddenly required her hands more than ever—which meant her journey to the apothecary could not wait until tomorrow.

It was on aching feet that Alizeh dredged through the evening's snowfall, arms tight against her chest, chin tucked into her collar. Frost grew steadily along the wet tendrils of her hair, unruly strands whipping in the wind as she went.

Already Alizeh had paid a visit to the local hamam, where she'd washed the day's filth from her body. She always felt better when she was clean, and though the task had cost her physically, she felt it ultimately worthwhile. More: the night air was bracing, and the cold shock to her uncovered head kept her thoughts focused. Alizeh required a sharpness of mind never more than when she walked the streets at night, for she knew well the dangers posed by desperate strangers in the dark. She was careful to remain quiet as she moved, keeping to the light, and to herself.

Still, it was impossible to ignore the uproar.

People were chanting in the streets, some singing, some yelling, all too drunk to be understood. There were large crowds dancing, all of them working together to hold aloft what appeared to be a scarecrow; the straw figure wearing a crude iron crown. Masses of people were sitting in the middle of the road smoking shisha and drinking tea, refusing to clear the streets even as horses whinnied, carriages teetered, and noblemen emerged from the plush interiors of their conveyances shouting and brandishing whips.

Alizeh walked through a cloud of apricot-flavored smoke, shook off an evening peddler, and pushed through a narrow gap in a group laughing uproariously at the story of a child who'd caught a snake in its hands and, delighted, had dipped the serpent's head over and over again into a bowl of yogurt.

Privately, Alizeh smiled.

Some people, she noticed, were carrying signs—some held high, others dragging behind like a dog on a leash. She tried to make out the printed words, but none could be deciphered in the dim, flickering light. One thing was for certain: this was an unusual level of merriment and madness, even for the royal city, and for a moment Alizeh's curiosity threatened to overcome her better senses.

She tamped it down.

Strangers jostled her, a few swiping at her snoda, laughing in her face, stepping on her skirts. She'd learned long ago that servants of her station were the most universally despised, considered fair game for all manner of cruelty. Others in her position were eager to remove their snodas in public spaces for fear of drawing unwanted attention, but Alizeh could not remove her snoda without great risk to herself; though she felt certain she was being hunted, she did not know by whom, which meant she could never let down her guard.

Alizeh's face was—unfortunately—too easily remembered.

Hers was the rare exception; it was otherwise difficult to spot the difference between Jinn and Clay, as Jinn had thousands of years ago regained not only their vision but the varying levels of melanin in their hair and skin. Alizeh, like many in Ardunia, had yards of glossy, coal-black curls and an olive complexion. But her eyes—

She did not know the color of her eyes.

Occasionally they took on the familiar brown of burnt umber, which she believed to be the natural color of her irises, but more often her eyes were a piercing shade of ice blue, so light they were hardly a color at all. It was no wonder then that Alizeh lived always with a perpetual chill, one she felt even in the sockets of her eyes. Ice sluiced through her clear veins even in the pit of summer, immobilizing her in the way she imagined only her ancestors could understand, for it was from them that she'd inherited this irregularity. The resulting effect was so disorienting few could bear to look at the girl—and yet, Alizeh's face might've been more readily ignored had her irises only ceased to change shades, which they had not. Instead, they flickered, alternating color constantly; it was a problem over which she had no control, and whose provocation she did not understand.

Alizeh felt a touch of moisture on her lips then and looked up. Fresh snow had begun to fall.

She pulled her arms tighter across her chest and darted down a familiar road, her head bowed against the wind. She'd been growing slowly aware of a pair of footsteps behind her—unusual only in their consistency—and felt a frisson of fear, which she forcefully dismissed. Alizeh felt she was growing too easily paranoid of late, and besides, the glow of the apothecary's shop was just up ahead. She sprinted toward it now.

A bell chimed as she pushed open the wooden door, and she was nearly shoved right back out by the crowd jammed within. The apothecary was unusually busy for the hour, and

Alizeh could not help but notice that its standard aroma of sage and saffron had been exchanged for the mephitic vapors of unwashed latrines and aged vomit. Alizeh held her breath as she took her place in line, resisting the urge to stamp the snow from her boots on the rug underfoot.

Present clientele were shouting obscenities at each other, jostling for space while cradling fractured arms and broken noses. Some were dripping red blood from the crowns of their heads, their mouths. One man was presenting a child with the bloody tooth he'd plucked from his head, a souvenir from another who'd thought to bite his skull.

Alizeh could scarcely believe it.

These people needed baths and surgeons, not an apothecarist. She could only imagine they were either too stupid or too drunk to know better than to seek aid here.

"All right, enough," boomed an angry voice over the crowd. "The lot of you: *get out*. Out of my shop before you—"

There was the abrupt sound of glass shattering, vials knocking to the ground. The same booming voice shouted renewed epithets as the crowd grew only more agitated, and there was a veritable stampede for the door when he brandished a cane and threatened not only to horsewhip the group of them, but to turn them over to the magistrates on charges of public indecency.

Alizeh flattened herself as best she could against the wall, so successful in her aim that when the horde had finally cleared, the shopkeeper almost missed her.

Almost.

"Get out," he barked, advancing on her. "Get out of my

store, *out*, you heathen—"

"Sir— Please—" Alizeh shrank back. "I'm here only for some salve and bandages. I'd be terribly grateful for your help."

The shopkeeper froze, the angry expression still etched onto his face. He was a narrow man, tall and wiry, with dark brown skin and coarse black hair, and he very nearly sniffed her. His assessing eyes took in her patched—but clean—jacket, the tidiness of her hair. Finally he took a deep, steadying breath, and stepped away.

"All right, then, what'll it be?" He moved back around the main counter, staring down at her with large, ink-dark eyes. "Where's the damage?"

Alizeh clenched her fists, stuffed them in her pockets, and tried to smile. Her mouth was the only part of her face unobscured, and it was as a result a point of focus for most people. The apothecarist, however, seemed determined to stare at her eyes—or, where he thought her eyes might be.

For a moment, Alizeh was unsure what to do.

It was true that, from the outside, Jinn were mostly unde-tectable. It was in fact their stunning physical resemblance to Clay that had made them the biggest threat, the more dif-ficult to suspect. The Fire Accords had attempted to bring organization to these sorts of problems, but under the veneer of peace there remained always an uneasiness among the people—an ingrained hatred of their kind, of their imagined association with the devil—that was not easily forgotten. Presenting strangers with clear proof of her identity had always inspired in Alizeh a halting fear, for she never knew how they might react. More often than not, people could not hide their contempt; and more often than not, she did not have the energy to face it.

Quietly, she said, "I've only a few scrapes on my hands that need tending—and a few blisters. If you've fresh bandages and a salve you'd recommend, sir, I'd be most obliged."

The apothecarist made a sound in his mouth, something like a *tsk*, drummed his fingers on the counter, and turned to study his walls; the long wooden shelves housed stoppered bottles of untold remedies. "And what of your neck, miss? The cut there seems severe."

Unconsciously, Alizeh touched her fingers to the wound. "I beg—I beg your pardon, sir?"

"You have a laceration at your throat, of which I doubt you're unaware. You must be feeling the pain at the incision, miss. The wound is likely warm to the touch, and"—he peered closer—"yes, it looks like there's a bit of swelling. We must get ahead of any major infection."

Alizeh went suddenly rigid with fear.

The Fesht boy had cut her with a crude, dirty blade. She'd seen it herself, had examined the tool in her own hand; why had she not realized there'd be consequences? Certainly, she'd been unwell and in pain all day, but she'd compartmentalized the sensations, experiencing it all as one large unpleasantness. She'd never had a chance to pinpoint the many discrete origins of her discomfort.

Alizeh squeezed her eyes shut and grabbed at the counter, steadying herself. She could ill afford much of anything these days, but she could least afford to be sick. If she caught a fever—if she could not work—she would be turned out onto the street, where she'd doubtless die in the gutter. It was this cold reality that propelled her actions every day, this larger instinct that demanded she survive.

"Miss?"

Oh, the devil always did know when to pay a visit.

TEN

KAMRAN STOOD IN THE SHADOW of a shuttered store-front, the hood of his cloak whipping in the wind, snapping against his face like the leathery wings of a bat. The snow had softened to rain, and he listened to the drops pop along the awning overhead, watched as they pelted the white drift frosting the streets. Long minutes passed, piles of snow perforating, then dissolving at his feet.

He should not have come.

After their meeting, the king had taken Kamran aside to ask further questions about the suspected servant girl, questions Kamran only too gladly answered, having felt validated by his grandfather's concern. It was in fact at the king's behest that Kamran was to continue his inquiries into the girl's whereabouts, for Zaal, too, had seemed perturbed upon hearing a more detailed accounting of the morning's events. He'd dispatched the prince into town to fulfill various obligations—among them a visit to the Fesht boy—and to then surveil the city.

Naturally, Kamran had obliged.

A focused task was precisely what he needed, as it would allow him a reprieve from his own mind, from the weight of all that his grandfather had recently imparted. The prince had thought to see the mobs for himself, in any case; he wanted to hear the commotion he had caused, to bear witness to the consequences of his actions.

In the end, it had led to this: darkness.

No, he should not have come at all.

First was his visit to the street child, who'd been installed at the Diviners Quarters in the Royal Square. The king had made it clear to Kamran that to ignore the boy now would make his earlier actions appear rash and hotheaded. Subsequent actions of care and compassion toward the boy would not only be expected, Zaal had said, but anticipated, and as Kamran already owed the Diviners a visit, it had not seemed too great a waste of his time.

Instead, it had been infuriating.

As it turned out, magic alone had saved the boy from the brink of death. This revelation, which should have been a relief, was to the prince grim news indeed, for it had been upon his perceived orders that the Diviners had acted—and rarely, if ever, was magical assistance offered to any outside the imperial family.

Vast though Ardunia was, magic as a substance was exceptionally rare. The unstable mineral was mined from the mountains at great risk, and as a result existed only in small, precious quantities, meted out only by royal decree. Kamran's call for help had been interpreted as just that; marking yet another reason why his actions toward a thieving street urchin had been so significant, and would not be easily forgotten.

He sighed at the reminder.

Though the boy was healing still, he'd managed to flinch

when Kamran arrived in his room. The child had inched backward in his bed as best he could, scrambling out of reach of his unlikely savior. They both knew it; knew that the scene within which they'd been trapped was a farce; that Kamran was no hero; that there existed no amity between them.

Indeed, Kamran felt nothing but anger toward the boy.

Through the careful dissemination of new rumors, the crown had actively sought to distort the story of the street urchin; King Zaal decided it would be more difficult to convince an audience that the prince had done good by saving a murderous child, and so had modified the tale to exclude any mention of harm done to the servant girl. This bothered Kamran far more than it ought, for privately he felt the rascal deserved neither the efforts made to spare him, nor the care he received now.

Carefully, Kamran had approached the boy's bed, claiming a small victory as fear flared to life in the child's eyes. From this he gained impetus enough to hone his frustration, which gave his visit focus. If the prince was to be forced into the company of this disgraceful child, he would use the opportunity to demand answers to his innumerable questions.

By the angels, he had questions.

"Avo, kemem dinar shora," he'd said darkly. *First, I want to know why.* "Why did you beg me not to hand you over to the magistrates?"

The boy shook his head.

"Jev man," Kamran had said. *Answer me.*

Again, the boy shook his head.

Kamran stood sharply, clasping his hands behind his back. "You and I both know the real reason you are here, and I will not soon forget it. I have no interest in forgiving you for your actions today merely because you nearly died in the effort. You would've murdered a young woman just to steal her wares—"

"Nek, nek hejjan—" *No, no, sire—*

"And were willing to kill yourself so you would not have to stand trial—so you would not be turned over to the magistrates and pay the price for your debased actions." Kamran's eyes flashed with barely suppressed anger. "Tell me why."

For the third time, the child shook his head.

"Perhaps I will turn you over to the magistrates now. Perhaps they might be more effective at yielding results."

"No, sire," the boy had said in his native tongue, his brown eyes large in his sunken face. "You would not do that."

Kamran's eyes widened a fraction. "How dare y—"

"Everyone thinks you saved my life because you are compassionate and kind. If you threw me in the dungeon now, it would not look good for you, would it?"

Kamran's fists clenched, unclenched. "I *did* save your life, you ungrateful wretch."

"Han." *Yes.* The child almost smiled, but his eyes were strangely distant. "Pet, shora?" *But, why?* "After this, I will be returned to the street. To the same life as before."

Kamran felt an unwelcome pang in the region of his chest; a flicker of conscience. He was quite unaware that the edge to his voice had gone when he said, "I do not understand why you would rather kill yourself than go to prison."

"No, you do not understand, sire." The redheaded boy would not meet his eyes. "But I have seen what they do to kids like me. Being turned over to the magistrates is worse than death."

Kamran straightened, then frowned. "What can you mean? How can it be worse than death? Our prisons are not so foul as that. You would be offered a daily meal, at the very least—"

The boy was now shaking his head hard, looking so agitated Kamran feared he might bolt from the room.

"All right—enough," the prince said reluctantly, and sighed. "You may instead tell me what you know of the girl."

The boy froze at that, the inquiry unexpected enough to have disarmed him. "Know of her? I do not know her, sire."

"How, then, were you able to communicate with her? Do you speak much Ardanz?"

"Very little, sire."

"And yet, you spoke with her."

"Yes, sire." The boy blinked. "She spoke Feshtoon."

Kamran was so surprised by this revelation he failed to mask his expression fast enough. "But there are no servants in the royal city who speak Feshtoon."

"Begging your pardon, sire, but I didn't know you were acquainted with all the servants in the royal city."

At that, Kamran experienced a swell of anger so large he thought it might break open his chest. It took all he had to bite out the words: "Your insolence is astonishing."

The boy grinned; Kamran resisted the urge to smother him.

This redheaded Fesht boy had the uncommon ability to move Kamran to a swift, discomposing anger—an anger of the most dangerous variety. Kamran knew this, for he knew well his own weaknesses, and implored himself to defuse what he knew to be an irrational reaction. There was no reason to scare away the child, after all, not now that the boy might provide him with information he needed to hunt down the duplicitous servant girl.

"I beg you will help me understand," Kamran had said flatly. "You claim that a servant girl with little education—a servant girl who is likely illiterate—somehow spoke to you in Feshtoon. You claim she gave you bread, which you di—"

"No, sire. I said that she *offered* me bread."

Kamran's jaw tensed. This was the second time the child had interrupted him. "I see little difference," he'd said. "*Gave* and *offered* are interchangeable words."

"No, sire. She told me to come to the kitchens at Baz House if I was in need of bread."

Here, Kamran experienced a moment of triumph.

"Then she lied to you," said the prince. "I know Baz House, and that girl is no servant there. In fact, if it has not yet been made obvious to you, you should know: that girl was no servant at all."

The child shook his head. "You're wrong, sire."

Impertinent, disrespectful, shameless boy. Kamran found he no longer cared that the child had nearly died; he seemed well enough now, with the audacity of an impudent street rat, speaking to a member of the royal household with so little deference. And yet—Kamran was now shackled to him in this strange way, compelled to be kind to the precocious imp.

Omid. His name was Omid.

He was the son of saffron farmers in the south. His parents had been imprisoned for failing to pay taxes on a meager harvest, and their official complaint—Kamran had since pulled the report—was that the taxes were a fixed amount, instead of a percentage. Paying the fixed amount, they had insisted, would've meant starvation for their family, as the season's crop had been so small. They had appealed to the courts for leniency, but had contracted lung fever in prison and died days later, leaving the boy to fend for himself.

Twelve, he'd said he was. Twelve years old.

"You are either very brave or very stupid," Kamran had said to him. "To disagree with me so readily."

"But, sire, you didn't see her hands," Omid insisted. "And I did."

Kamran had only scowled.

In his haste to take his leave of the insufferable child, Kamran had forgotten, yet again, to pay his respects to the honorable priests and priestesses. He was instead intercepted by a halo of Diviners on his way out—who'd said little, as they were wont to do—and accepted as payment but a moment of his time before they pressed a small parcel into his hands. The prince offered his many thanks, but his mind, full and disordered as it was, bade him tuck away the untitled gift, to be opened at a later date.

The parcel would remain forgotten, for some days, in the interior pocket of Kamran's cloak.

Unnerved by his conversation with Omid, the prince had gone straight from the Diviners Quarters to Baz House, the home of his distant aunt. He knew exactly where the kitchens were; he'd spent a great deal of his youth at Baz House, sneaking belowstairs for snacks after midnight. He considered going through the front doors and simply asking his aunt whether she'd employed such a servant, but he thought of his grandfather's warning that his actions were now under intense scrutiny.

Kamran had many reasons for seeking out the girl—not the least of which was King Zaal's confirmation that Ardunia was destined for war—but he did not think it wise to over-hastily spread word of this to the happy public.

In any case, Kamran was good at waiting.

He could stand in one position for hours without tiring, had been trained to practically disappear at will. It was no trouble at all to him to waste an hour standing in an alley to capture a criminal, not when his aim was to protect his empire, to spare his people the machinations of this faceless girl—

Lie.

True, that he found her actions suspect; true, too, that she might be a Tulanian spy. But there was also a possibility that he was wrong about the girl, and his unwillingness to accept this fact should've concerned him. No, the unadulterated truth, which he was only now willing to admit, was that there was a grain more to his motivations: something about this girl had burrowed under his skin.

He couldn't shake it.

She—a supposed poor, lowly servant—had acted this morning with a mercy he could not understand, with a compassion that enraged him all the more for its inconstancy. The young woman had entered his empire, ostensibly, to do harm. Why should she have been the more benevolent actor this morning? Why should she have inspired in him a feeling of unworthiness?

No, no, it made no sense.

Years of training had taught the prince to recognize even the slightest inconsistencies in his opponents; weaknesses that could be mined and promptly manipulated. Kamran knew his own strengths, and his instincts in this instance could not be denied. He'd seen her contradictions from the moment he laid eyes on her.

She was without question hiding something.

He'd wanted to out her as the liar he knew her to be; to uncover what seemed to him one of only two possibilities: a treasonous spy, or a frivolous society girl playing pretend.

He had, instead, ended up here.

Here, standing in the dark so long the mobs had begun to disperse, the streets littered now with the drunk, sleeping bodies that dared not drag themselves home. Kamran had let the cold brace him until his bones shook, until he felt nothing but a large emptiness yawn open inside him.

He did not want to be king.

He did not want his grandfather to die, did not want to marry a stranger, did not want to father a child, did not want to lead an empire. This was the secret he seldom shared even with himself—that he did not want this life. It was hard enough when his father had died, but Kamran couldn't even begin to imagine a world without his grandfather. He did not think he was good enough to lead an empire alone, and he did not know who he might rely upon instead. Sometimes he wasn't even sure he could trust Hazan.

Instead, Kamran had distracted himself with his anger, had allowed his mind to focus on the irritations of the Fesht boy, the false face of a servant girl. The truth was that he'd been forced to return home against his will and was now running from himself, from the counterintuitive burden of privilege, from the responsibilities laid upon his shoulders. In moments like these he'd always consoled himself with the reassurance that he was at least a capable soldier, a competent leader—but today had disproven even that. For what good was a leader who could not even trust his own instincts?

Kamran had been bested by this servant girl.

Not only had she proven him wrong on all counts, she'd proven him worse. When she'd finally appeared in the alley behind Baz House, he'd recognized her at once—but had the privilege now of inspecting her more closely. Right away he noticed the angry cut at her throat, and from there he followed the elegant lines of her neck, the delicate slope of her shoulders. For the second time that day he noticed the way she carried herself; how different she seemed from other servants. There was a gracefulness even in the way she held her head, the way she drew her shoulders back, the way she'd tilted her face up at the sun.

Kamran did not understand.

If not a spy or society girl, she might perhaps be the fallen daughter of a gentleman, or even the bastard child of one; such circumstances might explain her elegant carriage and knowledge of Feshtoon. But for a well-educated child of a noble to have fallen this low? He thought it unlikely. The scandals in high society were most everyone's business, and such a person in his aunt's employ would doubtless have been known to him.

Then again, it was hard to be certain of anything.

In vain he'd fought for a better look at her face and was given instead only a mouth to study. He'd stared at her lips for longer than he cared to admit, for reasons that were not lost on him. Kamran had arrived at the frightening realization that this girl might be beautiful—a thought so unexpected it nearly distracted him from his purpose. When she suddenly bit her lip, he drew a breath, startling himself.

She seemed worried.

He watched as she searched the alley, all the while clutching a small parcel to her chest. Kamran remembered what Omid had said about her hands, peered closer, and was dealt at once a powerful blow to his pride, to his fragile conscience. The girl's hands were so damaged he could see the injuries even from his distant vantage point. Her skin was painful to look at. Red. Blistered. Raw.

Without a doubt the hands of a servant.

Kamran rocked back on his heels as this truth washed over him. He'd been so determined the girl was a liar, had so eagerly anticipated the moment her ugliness would be uncovered. Instead, he'd made a discovery about himself.

He was the villain in this story, not she.

Not only had the girl kept her promise to Omid, but she'd made preparations; it grew increasingly obvious that what she sought in that alley had been the street child himself.

Twice in one day this faceless girl had inspired in Kamran a shame so vast he could hardly breathe around it. She'd reached into his chest and broken something essential inside of him, managed it all without even acknowledging his existence. Was Kamran so weak as to be dismantled thus by a stranger? Was he so unworthy?

Worse: how would he explain this embarrassment to his grandfather? So enthusiastically had Kamran added to the king's worries with his poorly supported suspicions, and now the prince's arrogance would prove only his own idiocy; an instability of mind that would further substantiate the king's fears for his grandson. In a single day Kamran had made himself into a joke, and he wanted to sink into the earth.

It was his single thought, repeating like a drumbeat in his head, when Hazan finally found him.

ELEVEN

یازده

"MISS?"

The apothecarist cleared his throat again, and Alizeh startled. When she looked up, she saw the shopkeeper staring at her hands, which she snatched out of sight.

"I can see that you're in pain, miss. A good deal, too, it seems."

Slowly, Alizeh met his eyes.

"You need not fear me," he said quietly. "If I'm to do my job, I must see the damage."

Alizeh thought again of her work, how her safety and security depended on her waking up tomorrow and scrubbing yet more floors, stitching more gowns. But if this man saw her clear blood and realized she was Jinn, he might refuse to serve her; and if he turned her out of his store she'd have to walk to the apothecary on the other side of the city—which, though not impossible to manage, would be both difficult and exhausting, and would take another day to arrange.

Alizeh sighed. She was left with little choice.

With painful effort, she unwrapped the damp, makeshift bandages and rested her bare hands atop the counter, palms up, for the apothecarist to examine.

He sucked in his breath at the sight.

Alizeh tried to see her injuries through his eyes: the raw,

shredded skin, the blistered fingers, the blood most people mistook for water. The normally pale skin of her palms was now a garish red, throbbing with pain. She wanted desperately to wrap them anew, to clench her fists against the searing burn.

"I see," said the man, which Alizeh took as her cue to withdraw. She waited, body tensed for a hostile attack, but the apothecarist did not insult her, nor did he ask her to leave his store.

By degrees, Alizeh relaxed.

In fact, he said nothing more as he collected items from around his shop, measuring into burlap pouches various herbs, snipping strips of linen for her wounds. She felt immeasurable gratitude as she stood there defrosting in her boots, snowmelt puddling in shallow pools around her feet. She could not see the eyes watching her from the window, but she soon felt them, felt the disturbing, specific fear of one who knows she's being watched but cannot prove it.

Alizeh swallowed.

When the apothecarist finally returned to his post, he was carrying a small basket of remedies, which he proceeded to crush into a thick paste with mortar and pestle. He then procured from under the counter what looked like a paintbrush.

"Please have a seat"—he gestured to one of the tall stools at the counter—"and pay attention to what I do, miss. You'll need to repeat these next steps at home."

Alizeh nodded, grateful as her tired body sank into the upholstered seat. She feared she might never stand up again.

"Please hold out your hands."

Alizeh complied. She watched closely as he painted a bright blue salve onto her palms in a single stroke, the calming effect so immediate she nearly cried out from relief.

"You must keep everything clean," he was saying, "and change the bandages every other day. I'll show you how to wrap them properly."

"Yes, sir," she breathed. She squeezed her eyes shut as he wound fresh strips of linen around her hands, between her split fingers. It was a bliss unlike any she'd experienced in recent memory.

Quietly, he said: "It isn't right."

"The bandages?" Alizeh looked up. "Oh, no, sir, I think—"

"*This,*" he said, lifting her hands closer to the lamplight. Even half-wrapped and covered in salve, the picture was tragic. "They work you too hard, miss. It isn't right."

"Oh." Alizeh returned her eyes to the counter. "It's no trouble."

She heard the ire in his voice when he said, "They work you like this because of what you are. Because of what you can bear. A human body could not withstand so much, and they take advantage of you because they can. You must realize that."

"Indeed, I do," Alizeh said with some dignity. "Though you must also realize that I'm grateful to have the work, sir."

"You may call me Deen." He retrieved another brush, which he used to paint a different salve onto the cut at her neck. Alizeh sighed as the medicine spread, closing her eyes when the pain dulled, then faded altogether.

It was a moment before Deen cleared his throat and said,

"You know, I don't think I've ever seen a servant wear a snoda at night."

Alizeh froze, and the apothecarist felt it. When she made no reply, he said quietly, "You are perhaps, as a result, unaware of the large bruise spanning your cheek."

"*Oh.*" Alizeh lifted one newly bandaged hand to her face. "I . . ."

She'd not realized her bruise had bled beyond the lines of her snoda. It was illegal for housekeepers to beat their servants, but Alizeh had never met a housekeeper who'd observed this law, and she knew bringing attention to it now would only cost her her job.

She said nothing.

Deen sighed. "If you would only remove your snoda, miss, I might inspect the damage for you."

"No," Alizeh said too quickly. "That is— I thank you for your concern, but I'm quite all right."

It was a long while before Deen said quietly, "Very well. But when I am done, I ask that you come back in one week so that I might check for signs of improvement or infection."

"Yes, sir." She hesitated. "I mean, Deen, sir."

He smiled. "If, however, you develop a fever in the interim, you must send for a surgeon at once."

To this, Alizeh merely nodded. Even with five dresses worth of income she knew she'd not be able to afford a surgeon, but did not see the point in expressing so.

Deen was winding a narrow bandage around her neck—precisely the sort of spectacle she'd been trying to avoid—when he made one last attempt at conversation. "This is an interesting wound, miss," he said. "More interesting for all the conflicting stories we've been hearing in town today."

Alizeh stiffened.

She knew, objectively, that she'd done nothing wrong, but Alizeh lived in this city only because she'd had to escape her own attempted execution. It was seldom, if ever, that she stopped worrying. "Which conflicting stories, sir?"

"Stories of the prince, of course."

Almost at once, Alizeh relaxed. "Oh," she said. "I don't believe I've heard any."

Deen was pinning her bandage in place when he laughed. "With all due respect, miss, you'd have to be deaf not to have heard. The whole of the empire is discussing the prince's return to Setar."

"He's come back?" Beneath her snoda, Alizeh's eyes widened. She, who was new to the city, had heard only rumors about the empire's elusive heir. Those who lived in Setar lived in the royal heart of Ardunia; its lifelong residents had seen the prince in his infancy, had watched him grow. Alizeh would be lying if she said she wasn't curious about the royals, but she was far from obsessed, the way some were.

Just then—in a flash of understanding—the day's events made sense.

The festivities Mrs. Sana had mentioned—the impending ball. It was no wonder Miss Huda needed five new gowns. Of course Duchess Jamilah had demanded every one of her rooms be cleaned. She was a distant cousin of the king, and it was rumored she had a close relationship with the prince.

Perhaps she was expecting a visit.

"Indeed, he is come home," Deen was saying. "And no small thing either, is it? Already they're planning a ball, and no fewer than a dozen festivities. Of course"—he grinned—"not that the likes of us should care. I don't expect we'll be seeing the inside of a palace ballroom anytime soon."

Alizeh matched Deen's smile with one of her own. She'd often longed for moments like these—opportunities to speak with people in her own city, as if she were one of them. She'd never felt free to do so, not even as a child.

"No, I expect not," she said softly, still smiling as she sat back in her seat, absently touching the fresh bandage at her neck. She felt so much better already, and the flood of relief and gratitude was loosening her tongue to an unfamiliar degree. "Though I'm not sure I understand all the excitement, if I'm being honest."

"Oh?" Deen's smile grew broader. "And why's that?"

Alizeh hesitated.

There was always so much she wanted to say, but she'd been forbidden—over and over—from speaking her mind, and she struggled now to overcome that impulse.

"I suppose— I suppose I would ask why the prince should be so lavishly celebrated merely for arriving home. Why is it that we never ask who pays for these festivities?"

"Begging your pardon, miss." Deen laughed. "I'm not sure I understand your meaning."

Alizeh thawed a bit at the sound of his laughter, and her own smile grew wider. "Well. Do not the taxes paid by common folk fund the royal parties they're not even allowed to attend?"

Deen, who was rewinding a roll of linen, went suddenly still. He looked up at Alizeh, his expression inscrutable.

"The prince never even shows his face," she went on. "What kind of prince does not mix with his own society? He is praised—and well liked, yes—but only on account of his noble birth, his inheritance, his circumstances, his inevitable ascent to king."

Deen frowned a bit. "I suppose—perhaps."

"On what merit, then, is he celebrated? Why should he be entitled to the love and devotion of a public that does not even know him? Does not his distaste of the common people reek of arrogance? Does not this arrogance offend?"

"I do not know, miss." Deen faltered. "Though I daresay our prince is not arrogant."

"Pretentious, then? Misanthropic?"

Alizeh couldn't seem to stop talking now that she'd started. It should've worried her that she was having so much fun; it should've reminded her to bite her tongue. But it had been so long since she'd had a single conversation with someone, and Alizeh, who was demanded always to deny her own intelligence, had grown tired of keeping her mouth shut. The thing was, she was *good* at talking, and she dearly missed that exchange of wits that exercised the mind.

"And does not misanthropy indicate a miserliness of spirit, of the human heart?" she was saying. "Loyalty and duty and a general sense of—of awe, perhaps—might induce his royal subjects to overlook such shortcomings, but this generosity serves only to recommend the proletarian, not the prince. It remains rather cowardly then, does it not, to preside over us all as only a mythical figure, never a man?"

The dregs of Deen's smile evaporated entirely at that, his eyes going cold. It was with a horrible, sinking feeling that Alizeh realized the depth of her mistake—but too late.

"Goodness." Deen cleared his throat. He no longer seemed able to look at her. "I've never heard such talk, least of all from one in a snoda." He cleared his throat again. "I say. You speak mighty well."

Alizeh felt herself stiffen.

She'd known better. She'd learned enough times by now not to speak so much, or with such candor. She'd known better, and yet— Deen had shown her compassion, which she mistook for friendship. She swore to herself right then that she would never again make such a mistake, but for now— for now, there was nothing to be done. She could not take back her words.

Fear clenched a fist around her heart.

Would he report her to the magistrates? Accuse her of treason?

Deen inched away from the counter and quietly packaged up her things, but Alizeh could feel his suspicion; could feel it coming off him in waves.

"He's a decent young man, our prince," said the shopkeeper curtly. "What's more: he's away from home on duty, miss, protecting our lands, not cavorting in the streets. He's neither a drunk nor a womanizer, which is more than we can say for some.

"Besides, it is not for us to decide whether he's deserving. We owe our gratitude to anyone who defends our lives with his own. And yes, he keeps to himself, I suppose, but I don't think a person should be crucified for their silence. It's a rare thing, is it not? Lord only knows how many there are who would benefit"—Deen looked up at her—"from biting their tongues."

A shock of heat struck her through the heart then; a shame so potent it nearly cured her of that ever-present chill. Alizeh cast down her gaze, no longer able to meet the man's eyes.

"Of course," she said quietly. "I spoke out of turn, sir."

Deen did not acknowledge this. He was tallying up the total cost of her items with pencil and paper. "Just today," he said, "just today our prince saved a young beggar's life— carried the boy off in his arms—"

"You must forgive me, sir. It was my mistake. I do not doubt his heroism—"

"That'll be six coppers, two tonce, please."

Alizeh took a deep breath and reached for her coin purse, carefully shaking out the amount owed. *Six* coppers. Miss Huda had paid her only eight for the gown.

Deen was still talking.

"Some Fesht boy, too—quite merciful to spare him, considering how much trouble we get from the southerners— shock of red hair so bright you could see it from the moon. Who knows why the child did it, but he tried to kill himself in the middle of the street, and our prince saved his life."

Alizeh startled so badly she dropped half her pay on the floor. Her pulse raced as she scrambled to collect the coins, the thudding of her heart seeming to pound in her head.

When she finally placed her payment on the counter, she could scarcely breathe.

"The Fesht boy tried to kill himself?"

Deen nodded, counting out her coin.

"But why? What did the prince do to him?"

Deen looked up sharply. "*Do* to him?"

"That is, I mean— What did he do to help the boy?"

"Yes, quite right," Deen said, his expression relaxing. "Well, he picked the boy up in his own arms, didn't he? And called for help. The good people came running. If it weren't for the prince, the boy would surely be dead."

Alizeh felt suddenly ill.

She stared at a glass jar in the corner of the shop, at the large chrysanthemum trapped within. Her hearing seemed to fade in and out.

"—not entirely clear, but some people are saying he'd attacked a servant girl," Deen was saying. "Put a knife to her neck and cut her throat, not unlike y—"

"Where is he now?" she asked.

"Now?" Deen startled. "I wouldn't know, miss. I imagine he's at the palace."

She frowned. "They took the Fesht boy to the palace?"

"Oh, no, the boy is at the Diviners' in the Royal Square. No doubt he'll be there a while."

"Thank you, sir," she said quickly. "I'm very grateful for your help." She drew herself up, forced her mind firmly back into her body, and attempted to be calm. "I'm afraid I must now be on my way."

Deen said nothing. His eyes went to her throat, to the

bandage he'd only just wrapped around her neck.

"Miss," he said finally, "why is it you do not remove your snoda so late at night?"

Alizeh pretended to misunderstand. She forced out another goodbye and rushed for the exit so quickly she almost forgot her packages, and then ran out the door with such haste she hardly had time to register the change in weather.

She gasped.

She'd run straight into a winter storm, rain lashing the streets, her face, her uncovered head. It was but a moment before Alizeh was soaked through. She was trying, while balancing an armful of parcels, to pull the sopping wet snoda away from her eyes, when she suddenly collided with a stranger. She cried out, her heart racing wildly in her chest, and through miracle alone caught her packages before they hit the ground. Alizeh gave up on her snoda then, darting deeper into the night, moving almost as fast as her feet could carry her.

She was thinking of the devil.

There once was a man
who bore a snake on each shoulder.
If the snakes were well fed
their master ceased growing older.

What they ate no one knew,
even as the children were found
with brains shucked from their skulls,
bodies splayed on the ground.

The vision she'd seen, the nightmare delivered by Iblees in the night—

The signs seemed clear enough now: the hooded man in the square; the boy who'd never turned up at her kitchen door; the devil whispering riddles in her heart.

That face had belonged to the prince.

Who else could it be? It had to be the prince, the elusive prince—and he was murdering children. Or perhaps he was trying to murder children. Had he tried to murder the child and failed? When Alizeh had left the Fesht boy earlier today he'd not seemed in danger of killing himself.

What had the prince done to him?

Alizeh's feet pounded the slick cobblestone as she ran, desperately, back to Baz House. Alizeh had hardly enough time to breathe lately; she'd even less time to solve a riddle sent down from the devil. Her head was spinning, her boots slipping. The rain was falling so hard she hardly saw where she was going, much less the hand that darted out of the darkness, clamping down on her wrist.

She screamed.

TWELVE

دوازده

KAMRAN DID NOT LOOK AT Hazan as the latter approached through what was fast becoming a violent storm, choosing to stare instead at a stripe of wet cobblestone shimmering under orange gaslight. The rain had grown only more brutal, thrashing all and sundry while a vengeful wind rattled around their bodies, unseating ribbons of frost from a stand of trees.

It was unlike Hazan to overlook Kamran's cold reception, for though the minister knew his place—and knew that he was owed little of Kamran's attentions—he relished any opportunity to provoke his old friend, as the prince was easily provoked.

Theirs was an unusual friendship, to be sure.

The solidarity between the two was real—if varnished over with a thin layer of acerbity—but the foundations of their comradeship were so steeped in the separation of their classes that it seldom occurred to Kamran to ask Hazan a single question about his life. The prince assumed, because they'd been acquainted since childhood, that he knew all there was to know about his minister, and it had never once occurred to him that he might be wrong, that a subordinate might possess in his mind as many dimensions as his superior.

Still, the general effect of proximity over time meant that Kamran was at least well versed in the language of his minister's silence.

That Hazan said nothing as he stepped under the battered awning was Kamran's first indication that something was wrong. When Hazan shifted his weight, a moment later, Kamran had his second.

"Out with it," he said, straining a bit to be heard over the rain. "What have you discovered?"

"Only that you were right," said Hazan, his expression dour.

Kamran turned his gaze up at the gaslight, watched the flame batter the glass cage with its tongues. He felt suddenly uneasy. "I am often right, Minister. Why should this fact distress you tonight?"

Hazan did not respond, reaching instead into his coat pocket for the handkerchief, which he held out to the prince. This, Kamran accepted wordlessly.

Kamran studied the handkerchief with his fingers, running the pad of his thumb over its delicate lace edges. The textile was of a higher quality than he'd originally considered, with an embroidered detail in one corner that the prince only now noticed. He struggled to distinguish the details in the dim light, but it appeared to be a small, winged insect—just above which hovered an ornamental crown.

The prince frowned.

The heavy fabric was neither damp nor dirty. Kamran turned it over in his hands, finding it hard to believe that such a thing was in fact stained with the girl's blood. More curious, perhaps, was that as the day wore on, Kamran grew only more interested in its mysterious owner.

"Your Highness."

Kamran was again studying the embroidered fly, trying to name the uncommon insect, when he said: "Go on, then. I take it you've discovered something dreadful?"

"Indeed."

Kamran finally looked up at Hazan, his heart constricting in his chest. The prince had only just reconciled himself to the idea of the girl's innocence; all this uncertainty was reeking havoc on his mind.

"What, then?" Kamran forced a laugh. "She is a Tulanian spy? A mercenary?"

Hazan grimaced. "The news is bleak indeed, sire."

Kamran took a deep, bracing breath, felt the chill fill his lungs. He experienced, for an extraordinary moment, a pang of what could only be described as disappointment—a feeling that left him both stunned and confused.

"You worry yourself overmuch," the prince said, affecting indifference. "Certainly the situation is far from ideal, but we have the better of her now. We know who she is, how to track her. We may yet get ahead of any sinister plotting."

"She is not a spy, sire. Nor is she a mercenary." Hazan did not appear to rejoice in the statement.

"An assassin, then? A turncoat?"

"Your Highness—"

"Enough of your filibustering. If she is neither spy nor assassin why are you so aggrieved? What could possibly—"

A sudden *oof* from his minister and Kamran took an elbow

to the gut, knocking, for a moment, the air from his lungs. He straightened in time to hear the sharp splash of a puddle, the retreating sound of footsteps on slick stone.

"What the devil—?"

"Forgive me, Your Highness," Hazan said breathlessly. "Some ruffian barreled into me, I didn't mean t—"

Kamran was already stepping away from the protection of the awning. It was possible they'd been knocked into by a drunkard, but Kamran's senses felt unusually heightened, and intuition implored him now to explore.

Just an hour ago the prince had been convinced of his own ineptitude, and though he took some comfort in his recent vindication as pertained to the servant girl, he worried now that he'd been so willing to doubt his better judgment.

He had been right to mistrust her all along, had he not?

Why, then, was he disappointed to discover that she was somehow duplicitous, after all?

Kamran's mind had been thoroughly exhausted from the upheaval of the day's emotional journey, and he thought he'd rather drive his head into a wall than lose another moment to the dissection of his feelings. He decided right then that he'd never again deny his instincts—instincts that were now insisting that something was amiss.

Carefully, he moved deeper into the night, fresh rain pelting his face as he scanned for the culprit.

A blur. *There.*

A silhouette struck gold in a flicker of gaslight, the figure illuminated in a flash.

A girl.

She was there and gone again, but it was all he needed to
be certain. He saw her snoda, the length of linen wrapped
around her neck—

Kamran froze.

No, he could not believe it. Had he conjured the girl to
life with his own thoughts? He felt a moment of triumph,
quickly chased by trepidation.

Something was wrong.

Her movements were frantic, unrehearsed. She ran
through the rain as if she were afraid, as if she were being
chased. Kamran followed swiftly, homing in on her before
panning out again, surveying the area for her aggressor. He
saw a fresh blur of movement, a form heavily obscured by
the torrential downpour. The figure sharpened into focus by
degrees; Kamran could only make out the true shape of him
when he reached out, grabbing the girl by the arm.

She screamed.

Kamran did not think before he reacted. It was instinct
that propelled him forward, instinct that bade him grab the
man and throw him bodily against the pavement. Kamran
drew his sword as he approached the fallen figure, but just
as he lifted his blade, the cretin disappeared.

Jinn.

The unnatural act was enough to sentence the lout to
death—and yet, how could you kill a man you could not
catch?

Kamran muttered an oath as he sheathed his sword.

When he spun around, he spotted the girl only paces
away, her clothes sagging with rainwater. The skies had not

ceased their torment, and Kamran watched as she struggled to run; she appeared to be balancing packages in one arm, stopping at intervals to pull the wet snoda away from her face. Kamran could hardly see three feet in front of him; he could not imagine how she saw anything at all with a sheet of wet fabric obscuring her eyes.

"Miss, I mean you no harm," he called out to her. "But you must remove your snoda. For your safety."

She froze at that, at the sound of his voice.

Kamran was heartened by this and dared to approach her, overcome not only by concern for the girl, but by an impassioned curiosity that grew only stronger by the moment. It occurred to him, as he dared to close the gap between their bodies, that the wrong move might spook her—might send her running blindly through the streets—so he moved with painstaking carefulness.

It was no good.

He'd taken but two steps toward her and she went flying into the night; in her haste she slipped, landing hard on cobblestone, scattering her packages in the process.

Kamran ran to her.

Her snoda had slipped an inch, the wet netting sealing around her nose, suffocating her. In a single motion she tore the mask from her face, gasping for air. Kamran hooked his arms under hers and dragged her to her feet.

"My—my packages," she gasped, raindrops pelting her closed eyes, her nose, her mouth. She licked the rainwater from her lips and caught her breath, keeping her eyes shut, refusing to meet his gaze. Her cheeks were flush with color—with cold—her sooty lashes the same shade as her sable curls, wet tendrils spiraling away from her face, some plastered to her neck.

Kamran could hardly believe his fate.

Her reluctance to open her eyes provided him the rare opportunity to study her at length, without fear of self-consciousness. All this time he'd been wondering about the girl and now here she was, in his arms, her face mere inches from his own and—devils above, he could not look away from her.

Her features were both precise and soft, balanced in every quadrant as if by a master. She was finely designed, loveliness rendered in its truest sense. This discovery was surreal to him to the point of distraction, all the more so because Kamran's calculations had been wrong. He'd suspected she might be beautiful, yes—but this girl was not merely beautiful.

She was stunning.

"Hang the packages," he said softly. "Are you hurt?"

"No, no—" She pushed against him like she might be blind, still refusing to open her eyes. "Please, I need my packages—"

Try as he might, Kamran could not understand.

He *knew* she was not blind, and yet she pretended at it now, for reasons he could not fathom. At every turn this girl had baffled him, and just as he was beginning to digest this, she threw herself to the ground, sparing Kamran only seconds to catch the girl before her knees connected with stone. She pulled away from him, paying him no mind even as her skirts sank into the old slush of the filthy street, her hands fumbling in the wet for sign of her wares. She moved suddenly into a stroke of gaslight, the flame bracing her in its glow.

It was then that Kamran noticed the bandages.

Her hands were wrapped almost to the point of immobility; she could hardly bend a finger. It was no wonder she struggled to hold on to her things.

He quickly scooped up the scattered items, depositing them into his satchel. He didn't want to scare her by shouting over the rain, so he bent low and said close to her ear: "I've got your packages, miss. You may be easy now."

It was the surprise that did it. It was the sound of his voice so near her face, his warm breath against her skin.

Alizeh gasped.

Her eyes flew open, and Kamran froze.

It was only seconds that they studied each other, but it seemed to Kamran a century. Her eyes were the silver-blue of a winter moon, framed by wet lashes the color of pitch. He'd never seen anyone like her before, and he had the presence of mind to realize he might never again. Sudden movement caught his attention: a raindrop, landing on her cheek, traveling fast toward her mouth. Only then, with a shock, did he notice the bruise blooming along her jaw.

Kamran stared perhaps too long at the discolored mark, the faint impression of a hand it formed. He wondered then that he hadn't recognized it right away, that he'd so easily dismissed it as an indiscriminate shadow. The longer he stared at it now the harder his heart moved in his chest, the faster heat flooded his veins. He experienced a sudden, alarming desire to commit murder.

To the girl he said only: "You are hurt."

She made no response.

She was trembling. Drenched through. Kamran was suffering, too, but he had the benefit of a heavy wool cloak, a protective hood. The girl wore only a thin jacket, no hat, no scarf. Kamran knew he needed to convey her home, to make certain she did not catch her death in this weather, but just then he could not seem to move. He didn't even know this girl's name and somehow he'd been stricken by her, reduced to this, to stupidity. For the second time that night, she licked the rainwater from her lips, drawing his gaze to her mouth. Had any other young woman done such a thing in his presence, Kamran might've thought it a coquettish affectation. But this—

He'd read once that Jinn had a particular love of water. Perhaps she could not help licking the rain from her lips any more than he could help staring at her mouth.

"Who are you?" he whispered.

Her chin lifted at that, her lips parting in surprise. She studied him with wide, shining eyes, and appeared to be as confused by him as he was by her. Kamran took comfort in this, in the realization that they'd confounded each other equally.

"Will you not tell me your name?" he asked.

She shook her head, the movement slow, uncertain. Kamran felt paralyzed. He could not explain it; his body seemed anchored to hers. He drew closer by micrometers, propelled to do so by a force he could not hope to understand. What mere minutes ago might've struck him as lunacy now seemed to him essential: to know what it might be like to hold her, to breathe in the scent of her skin, to press his lips to her neck. He was scarcely aware of himself when he touched her—light as air, faint as fading memory—a stroke of his fingers against her lips.

She vanished.

Kamran fell backward, landing hard in a puddle. His heart was racing. He tried and could not collect his thoughts—he scarcely knew where to begin—and he'd been rooted to the spot for at least a minute when Hazan came running forward, out of breath.

"I couldn't see where you'd gone," he cried. "Were you set upon by thieves? Good God, are you hurt?"

Kamran sank fully into the street then, letting himself be absorbed by the wet, the cold, the night. His skin had cooled too quickly, and he felt suddenly feverish.

"Sire, I do not think it advisable to sit here, in th—"

"Hazan."

"Yes, sire?"

"What were you going to tell me about the girl?" Kamran turned his gaze up to the sky, studying the stars through a web of branches. "You say she is not a spy. Not a mercenary. Not assassin nor turncoat. What, then?"

"Your Highness." Hazan was squinting against the rain, clearly convinced the prince had lost his mind. "Perhaps we should head back to the palace, have this conversation over a warm cup of—"

"*Speak*," Kamran said, his patience snapping. "Or I shall have you horsewhipped."

"She— Well, the Diviners—they say—"

"Never mind, I shall horsewhip you myself."

"Sire, they say her blood has ice in it."

Kamran went deathly still. His chest constricted painfully and he stood up too fast, stared into the darkness. "Ice," he said.

"Yes, Your Highness."

"You are certain."

"Quite."

"Who else knows about this?"

"Only the king, sire."

Kamran took a sharp breath. "The king."

"He, too—as you know—had been convinced there was something unusual about the girl and bade me report to him my findings straightaway. I would have come to you sooner with the news, sire, but there were a great many arrangements to be made, as you can well imagine." A pause. "I confess I've never seen the king quite so overwrought."

"No," Kamran heard himself say. "This is terrible news, indeed."

"Her collection has been set for tomorrow evening, sire." A pause. "Late night."

"Tomorrow." Kamran's eyes were on a single point of light in the distance; he hardly felt a part of his own body. "So soon?"

"The king's orders, Your Highness. We must move with all possible haste and pray no one else gets to her before we do."

Kamran nodded.

"It feels almost divine, does it not, that you were so swiftly able to identify her?" Hazan managed a stiff smile. "A servant girl in a snoda? Lord knows we might never have found her out otherwise. You've most assuredly spared the empire the loss of countless lives, sire. King Zaal was deeply impressed with your instincts. I'm sure he will tell you as much when you see him."

Kamran said nothing.

There was a tense stretch of silence, during which the prince closed his eyes, let the rain lash his face.

"Sire," Hazan said tentatively. "Did you come upon cutthroats earlier? You look as if you came to blows."

Kamran placed two fingers in his mouth and whistled. Within moments his horse came galloping toward him, the stunning beast rushing to a reckless halt at his master's feet. Kamran placed a foot in the stirrup and swung himself onto the slick seat.

"Sire?" Hazan shouted to be heard over the wind. "Did you meet with anyone out here?"

"No." Kamran grabbed the reins, gave the horse a gentle nudge with his heels. "I saw no one."

THIRTEEN

سیذدہ

ALIZEH HAD BROKEN NO FEWER than seven different laws since fleeing the scene with the prince. She was breaking one right then, daring to remain invisible as she entered Baz House. The consequences for such offenses were severe; if she were caught materializing she'd be hung at dawn.

Still, she felt she was left with little recourse.

Alizeh hurried to the hearth, stripping her coat, unlacing her boots. Public undressing of any kind was considered an act of stateliness, one deemed beneath those of her station. She might be forgiven for removing her snoda late at night, but a servant was forbidden from removing any essential article of clothing in common gathering areas.

Not a coat, not a scarf. Certainly not her shoes.

Alizeh took a deep breath, reminding herself that she was invisible to Clay eyes. She suspected there were a handful of Jinn employed at Baz House, but as she'd not been allowed to speak with any of the others—and none had dared compromise their positions by reaching out—she'd no way of knowing for certain. She hoped that any who might come upon her now might be willing to look the other way.

Alizeh drew nearer the fire, trying as best she could to roast her sopping jacket and boots. Alizeh had a spare dress, but only one jacket and one pair of boots, and there was little chance the articles would dry out overnight in the musty closet that was her bedroom. Though perhaps if she remained indoors all day tomorrow she'd not have need of her jacket—at least not until her appointment with Miss Huda. The idea gave her some comfort.

When the jacket lost the worst of its wet, Alizeh slipped her arms back into the still-damp piece, her body tensing at the sensation. She wished she could lay the article out by the fire overnight, but she'd not risk leaving it here, where it might be noticed by anyone. She picked up her boots then, holding them as close to the flames as she dared.

Alizeh shivered without warning, nearly dropping the shoes in the fire. She calmed her shaking hands and chattering teeth by taking steady, even breaths, clenching her jaw against the chill. When she felt she could bear it, she put her mostly wet boots back on.

Only then did Alizeh finally sink down onto the stone hearth, her trembling legs giving out beneath her.

She removed her illusion of invisibility—fully dressed, she'd not be reprimanded for taking a moment by the fire— and sighed. She closed her eyes, leaned her head against the outer brick. Would she allow herself to think about what transpired tonight? She wasn't sure she could bear it, and yet—

So much had gone wrong.

Alizeh still worried over her treasonous comments to the apothecarist, and a bit about the man who'd tried to attack her—no doubt to steal her parcels—but most of all she worried about the prince, whose attentions toward her were so baffling as to be absurd. Where had he come from? Why had he cared to help her? He'd touched her just as the devil had foretold, as she'd seen in her nightmares the very night before—

But why?

What had possessed him to touch her so? Worse: Was he not a murderer of children? Why, then, had he acted with such compassion toward a servant girl?

Alizeh dropped her head in her hands.

Her throbbing, bandaged hands. The medicine had been all but washed out of her wounds, and the ache had returned in full force. If she allowed herself to consider for even a moment the devastating loss of her packages, she thought she might faint from heartache.

Six coppers.

The medicine had cost her nearly all the coin she had, which meant she'd not be able to afford replacements without further work. And yet, without her medicine, Alizeh didn't know whether her hands would recover quickly enough; Miss Huda would no doubt require the five dresses in short order, as the royal festivities would be arranged without delay.

Hers was a simple tragedy: without work Alizeh would not be able to afford medicine; without medicine she might not be able to work. It tore her heart to pieces to think of it. No longer was she able to conquer her despair. She felt the familiar prick of tears, swallowed against the burn in her throat.

The cruelty of her life seemed suddenly unbearable.

She knew her thoughts to be infantile even as they arrived, but she lacked the strength to stop herself from wondering then, as she'd done on so many other nights, why it was that others had parents, a family, a safe home, and she did not. Why had she been born with this curse in her eyes? Why was she tortured and hated merely for the way her body had been forged? Why had her people been so tragically condemned alongside the devil?

For centuries before the bloodshed between Jinn and Clay had begun, Jinn had built their kingdoms in the most uninhabitable lands, in the most brutal climates—if only to be far from the reach of Clay civilization. They'd wanted to exist quietly, peacefully, in a state of near invisibility. But Clay, who had long considered it their divine right—no, duty— to slaughter the beings they saw only as scions of the devil, had mercilessly hunted Jinn for millennia, determined to expunge the earth of their existence.

Her people had paid a high price for this delusion.

In her weaker moments Alizeh longed to lash out, to allow her anger to shatter the cage of her self-control. She was stronger than any housekeeper who struck her; she was capable of greater force, greater strength and speed and resilience than any Clay body that oppressed her.

And yet.

Violence alone, she knew, would accomplish nothing. Anger without direction was only hot air, there and gone. She'd seen this happen over and over to her own people. Jinn had tried to flout the rules, to exercise their natural abilities despite the restrictions of Clay law, and they'd all suffered. Daily, dozens of Jinn bodies had been strung up in the square like bunting, more charred at the stake, still others beheaded, disemboweled.

Their divided efforts were no good.

Only the unification of Jinn might hope to affect real change, but such a feat was hard to hope for in an age where Jinn had fled their ancestral homes, scattering across the globe in search of work and shelter and anonymity. Their numbers had always been small, and their physical advantages had offered them much protection, but they'd lost hundreds of thousands of people over the last centuries. What was left of them could hardly be cobbled together overnight.

The fire snapped in its brick cove, flames flickering urgently. Alizeh wiped her eyes.

It was rare that she allowed herself to think on these cruelties. It did not comfort her to speak aloud her agonies the way it did for some; she did not enjoy reanimating the string of corpses she dragged with her everywhere. No, Alizeh was the kind of person who could not dwell on her own sorrows for fear of drowning in their bottomless depths; it was her physical pain and exhaustion tonight that'd weakened her defenses against these darker meditations—which, once torn free from their graves, were not easily returned to the earth.

Her tears fell now with abandon.

Alizeh knew she could survive long hours of hard labor, knew she could persevere through any physical hardship. It was not the burden of her work or the pain in her hands that broke her—it was the loneliness. It was the friendlessness of her existence; the days on end she spent without the comfort that might be derived from a single sympathetic heart.

It was grief.

The price she still paid with her soul for the loss of her parents' lives. It was the fear she was forced to live with every day, the torment that was born from an inability to trust even a friendly merchant to spare her the noose.

Alizeh had never felt more alone.

She scrubbed at her eyes again and then, for the umpteenth time that day, searched her pockets for her handkerchief. Its disappearance had not bothered her so much the first few times she searched for it, but the loss was beginning to worry her now that she considered it might not be misplaced—but well and truly lost.

The handkerchief had been her mother's.

It was the only personal possession Alizeh had salvaged intact from the ashes of her family home. Her memories of the dreadful night she lost her mother were strange and horrible. Strange that she remembered feeling warm—truly warm—for the first time in her life. Horrible that the roaring flames that engulfed her mother had only made Alizeh want to sleep. She still remembered her mother's screams that night, the wet handkerchief she'd used to cover her daughter's face.

There'd been so little time to flee.

They'd come in the night, when Alizeh and her sole surviving parent had been abed. The two tried, of course, to escape, but a wooden rafter had fallen from the ceiling, pinning them both to the ground. Had it not been for the blow she'd taken to the head, her mother might've been strong enough to lift the beam from their bodies that night.

For hours, Alizeh screamed.

For what felt like an eternity, she screamed. And yet, their home had been so expertly hidden away that there was no one to hear the sound. Alizeh clung to her mother's body as it burned, taking the embroidered handkerchief from her parent's limp hand and gathering it up in her own fist.

Alizeh had remained with her dead mother until daylight. If not for the eventual disintegration of the beam that trapped her body, Alizeh would've stayed there forever, would've died of dehydration alongside her mother's charred flesh. Instead, she emerged from the inferno without a scratch, her skin pristine, her clothes in tatters, the handkerchief all she'd possessed intact.

It was the second time in her life she'd survived a fire unscathed, and Alizeh had wondered then, as she often did, whether the ice that ran through her veins would ever truly matter.

She startled, suddenly, at the rattle of the back door.

Alizeh dared not breathe as she got to her feet. She pressed herself against the wall, tried to calm her racing heart. Her mind knew she had little reason to be afraid here, within the protection of this grand home, but her frayed nerves could not comprehend such logic. Upon entering Baz House she'd been single-minded in her haste to reach the fire; in the process she'd forgotten to lock the kitchen door.

She wondered whether to risk doing so now.

In a split second, Alizeh made the decision. She flew to the door and threw the bolt just as the handle began to turn, and when the mechanical movement came to a sudden halt, she sagged with relief. She fell back against the door, clasping both hands to her chest.

She could hardly catch her breath.

The knock that came next was so unexpected she jumped a foot in the air. She looked around for signs of servants lurking, but none appeared. One glance at the clock and she was reminded: anyone with sense was now abed. She alone was left to manage the destitute stragglers no doubt seeking shelter from the rain. It broke Alizeh's heart to deny them relief from the desperation she understood only too well, but she also knew she had no choice—not unless she wanted to be tossed into the street alongside them.

The knock came again, and this time she felt it, felt the door shake with it. She pressed her back harder against the wood, keeping it from moving in its frame. There was a brief reprieve.

Then: "I beg your pardon, but is someone there? I have a rather urgent delivery."

Alizeh went deathly still.

She recognized his voice right away; indeed, she doubted she'd ever forget it. He'd discomposed her with a few gentle words, had stripped her of all composure with mere syllables. Even then she'd recognized the strangeness of her reaction— she did not think it common to be so moved by the sound of a voice—but his was rich and melodic, and when he spoke she seemed to feel it inside her.

Another knock. "Hello?"

She steadied herself and said, "Sir, you may leave any deliveries at the door."

There was a beat of silence.

The prince's voice seemed changed when he next spoke. Softer. "I pray you will forgive me that I cannot, miss. These packages are very important, and I fear they'll be destroyed in the rain."

For a moment, Alizeh wondered whether this wasn't a cruel trick; no doubt he'd come to arrest her for vanishing illegally into the night. There seemed no other plausible explanation.

Certainly the prince of Ardunia had not braved a torrential downpour to personally deliver a stock of trivial goods to the lowly servant residing at Baz House? And at this late hour?

No, she could not believe it.

"Please, miss." His voice again. "I should only like to return the parcels to their owner."

Alizeh felt suddenly awake with fear. She supposed a different person might be flattered by such attentions, but Alizeh could not help but be wary, for not only did she doubt his motives, but she couldn't imagine how he'd known to find her when she'd said but a few words in his presence.

She swallowed, squeezing her eyes shut.

Then again, what did any of it matter if there was a chance she might be returned her parcels? To Alizeh, those packages were everything; without them, her immediate future appeared nothing short of disastrous. If the prince had come all this way only to torture her, she couldn't see what he might gain by it, for she was perfectly capable of defending herself.

No, what confounded her above all else was why the devil had shown her this young man's face.

Perhaps tonight she would finally know.

Alizeh took a deep breath and turned the lock.

The door groaned as it opened, bringing with it a shower of windswept rain. She quickly stepped aside, allowing the prince entrée, for he was, as she suspected, soaked to the bone. His arms were crossed tightly against his chest, his face obscured almost entirely by the hood of his cloak.

He closed the kitchen door behind him.

Alizeh took several steps back. She felt horribly exposed meeting him like this, without her snoda. She knew there was little to hide, not now that he'd already seen her face in full, had borne witness to her strange eyes.

Still. Habit was hard to overcome.

Wordlessly, the prince unhooked the satchel from his body and held it out to her. "The packages are within. I trust they're all accounted for."

Alizeh's hands were shaking.

Had he really come all this way only to deliver her a kindness?

She tried to affect calm as she opened the bag and was uncertain of her success. One at a time, she withdrew the packages, balancing them carefully in the crook of her arm. They were all there, only slightly worse for wear.

Alizeh couldn't quell the sigh of relief that escaped her

then. Fresh tears pricked her eyes and she blinked them away, composing herself as she returned the bag to its owner.

The prince froze as he accepted the satchel.

He appeared to be staring at her, but with much of his face so hidden from view, Alizeh couldn't be sure.

"Your eyes," he said quietly. "They just"—he shook his head an inch, as if to clear it—"I could've sworn they just changed color."

Alizeh retreated farther, putting several pieces of furniture between them. Her thudding heart would not slow. "Please accept my sincerest gratitude," she said. "You've rendered me an unaccountable service by returning my packages. Truly, I do not know how to thank you. I am in your debt, sir."

She winced.

She should have said *sire*, should she not?

Thankfully, the prince in question did not seem to take offense. Instead, he pulled back his hood, revealing his face in full for the first time. Alizeh took a sharp breath and a step back, catching herself against a chair.

It was mortifying, truly, that she could not bear to look at him.

She'd seen his face in her nightmare, but rendered in real life the effect was entirely different; he was startling to behold in the flesh, the sharp planes of his face illuminated by firelight. He had piercing eyes the color of coal, his olive skin so golden it seemed to glow. Indeed there was something almost unnaturally illuminated about him—as if he was limned with light around the edges—and she could not pinpoint its origin.

He took a step toward her.

"First they were blue," he said softly. "Then brown. Silver. Ah. Now they're brown again."

She stiffened.

"Blue."

"Stop, I beg you."

He smiled. "I see now why you never remove your snoda."

Alizeh lowered her eyes and said, "You cannot know that I never remove my snoda."

"No," he said, and she heard the humor in his voice. "I daresay you're right."

"I must bid you good night," she said, and turned to go.

"Wait. Please."

Alizeh froze, her body turned toward the exit. She wanted desperately to take her parcels up to her room, where she might reapply the miraculous salves to her injuries. Pain was lancing across her palms, her throat.

She held the back of her hand to her forehead.

That she was warm at all meant she was warmer than usual, though she consoled herself with the knowledge that there might, at the moment, be several reasons for her elevated temperature.

Slowly she turned around, locking eyes with the prince.

"You must forgive my inability to grant you an audience at this hour," she said quietly. "I've no doubt you are generous enough to comprehend the difficulty of my position. I've precious few hours to sleep before the work bell tolls, and I must return to my quarters with all possible haste."

The prince seemed taken aback by this, and indeed took a

step back. "Of course," he said softly. "Forgive me."

"There is nothing to forgive." She bobbed a neat curtsy.

"Yes." He blinked. "Good night."

Alizeh turned the corner and waited in the dark, her heart racing, for the sound of the back door opening, then closing. When she was certain the prince was gone, she returned quietly to the kitchen to lock up and bank the fire.

Only then did she realize she was not alone.

FOURTEEN

چھارده

SLEEP, THAT ELUSIVE FIEND, CAME so unwillingly to the prince that it refused to remain long. Kamran awoke before dawn with a sharpness that surprised him, for he was both abed and then out of it before the sun had even met the horizon. His body was fatigued, yes, but his mind was clear. It had been running all night; his dreams fevered, his imaginings frenzied.

He'd begun to wonder whether the girl had cursed him.

She clearly knew not what she'd done to him, nor could she be blamed for her success in so thoroughly disordering his faculties, but Kamran could not conceive a more elegant explanation for what had overcome him. He was moved neither by a base need to physically possess the girl, nor was he deluded enough to think he might be in love with her. Still, he could not understand himself. Never before had he been so consumed by thoughts of anyone.

The girl was going to be murdered.

She was going to be murdered by his own grandfather, and it seemed to Kamran the worst kind of tragedy.

The prince was one of the few people who knew, of course. He and Hazan both knew of the prophecy, the foretelling of a creature with ice in its veins. Every king in the history of the Ardunian empire had received a prophecy, and King

Zaal had felt it his duty to manage the prince's expectations of such an event. Long ago his grandfather had explained to him that, on the day of his coronation, Kamran would receive two visits.

The first, from a Diviner.

The other, from the devil.

The devil would offer him a bargain, the terms of which Kamran should under no circumstances accept. The Diviner, his grandfather had said, would make a prediction.

When Kamran asked what prediction the Diviners had made for him, King Zaal had grown unnaturally reticent, saying only that he'd been warned of the rise of a fearsome adversary, a demon-like creature with ice in its veins. It was said to be an enemy with allies so formidable its mere existence would lead to the king's eventual demise.

Enraged, the young prince had promised his grandfather right then that he would search all of Ardunia for this monster, that he would slay the beast and deliver its head to the king on a pike.

You need not worry, his grandfather had said, smiling. *I will slay the beast myself.*

Kamran closed his eyes and sighed.

He splashed water on his face, performing his morning ablutions with care. It seemed impossible that the terrifying monster of his childhood imaginings was in fact the stunning young woman he'd encountered last night.

Kamran towel dried his face and applied orange blossom oil to his neck, to the pulse points at his wrists. He took a deep breath and drew the intoxicating scent into his body, relaxing as it warmed his chest, lowered his heart rate.

Slowly, he exhaled.

He was so unfamiliar with the feelings that possessed him now that he wondered for a moment whether he might well and truly be ill. How he'd even delivered himself to his chambers the evening prior he knew not, for he rode home through the blustery night as if in a trance. The girl's beauty had first rendered him speechless under the most unflattering conditions—in the half-light of a vicious storm—but seeing her face by firelight had dealt him a physical blow from which he had no hope of recovering.

Worse, far worse: he thought her fascinating.

He found himself captivated by her contradictions, the choices she made, even the way she moved.

Who was she, precisely? Where had she come from?

His ambitions upon arriving at her door last night had been scattered by a battering of his senses. He'd hoped to accomplish a great deal by going to her; he'd wanted to return her packages, yes, but there was something more that had compelled his senseless visit, a motivation of which he was entirely ashamed. Had his visit been successful Kamran might've betrayed his king, his empire. He would've been reduced to the most repellant variety of idiot, instead of the next king of Ardunia.

He'd gone to warn her.

He'd gone to tell her to run, to pack her bags and flee, to find a safe place to hide and remain there, possibly forever. And yet, when he saw her face, he realized that he could not simply ask her to run; no, she was an intelligent girl, she would have questions. If he told her to flee, she would want to know why. And what reason would she have to trust him?

He'd hardly begun to process this when she'd all but dismissed him.

It was possible she'd not known who he was—she'd called him *sir*, at one point—but he suspected that even if she'd known she were speaking to a prince she'd have treated him the same.

In any case, it did not seem to matter.

Kamran had known his grandfather's position on the girl; going against the king would've been an act of treason. Had Kamran been found out, his head would've been removed from his body in short order. It was some small miracle, then, that he'd lost his nerve.

Or perhaps regained his good sense.

He did not know this girl. He did not understand why the thought of killing her left him feeling ill. He only knew that he had to at least *try* to find another way—for surely she, a humble servant, was not the demon-like creature with an abundance of formidable allies prophesied all those years ago.

No, most assuredly not.

Kamran finished dressing himself without the assistance of his still-sleeping valet, and then—to the shock and horror of the palace servants—stole belowstairs to filch a cup of tea from the kitchens on his way out.

He needed to speak with his grandfather.

Kamran had lived at the royal palace his whole life and yet he never tired of its resplendent views, its acres of manicured gardens, its endless pomegranate groves. The grounds were of course always magnificent, but the prince never loved them more than he did at sunrise, when the world was still quiet. He stopped where he stood then, lifting the still-steaming cup to his lips.

He was standing in the illusion of a glittering infinity; the single mile of ground beneath his feet was in fact a shallow pool three inches deep. A sudden wind nudged water against his boots, the soothing sounds of gentle waves a welcome balm for his tired mind.

Kamran took another drink of his tea.

He was staring up at the soaring, open-air archways, their tens of dozens of exquisite columns planted into the shallow depths around him. The smooth white stonework of the structures was inlaid with vibrant jewels and vivid tiles, all of which benefited now from the blossom of a waking sun. Fiery light refracted against the bezel-set gems, fracturing endless prismatic colors along the sleeping grounds. More golden rays shattered through the open arches, gilding the water beneath his feet so that it looked almost like liquid bullion.

The beauty of Kamran's life was often lost on him, but not always. There was some mercy in that.

He finished the last of his tea and hooked a finger through its glass handle, letting the cup swing as he strode onward. With the rise of the sun came the stir of servants; snodas were popping up all around him, bustling past with vessels and trays.

Baskets of pomegranates were balanced precariously on

heads, under arms. There were silver trays heaving with baklava and delicate honey grapes, others stacked high with fresh barbari bread, each oblong sheet the length of a setar. And flowers—manifold bouquets of flowers—tens of servants rushing by carrying armloads of the fragrant stems. There were copper bowls filled with glossy green tea leaves; basil and mint and tarragon piled high on gold platters. Another endless procession of snodas carried rice—innumerable, incalculable sacks of rice.

Sudden foreboding caught Kamran by the throat; he went unearthly still.

Then he spun around.

There was more; there were more. More servants, more trays, more baskets and tureens and bushels and platters. Wheels of feta cheese were shuttled past; trolleys overstuffed with fresh chestnuts. There were stockpiles of vivid-green pistachios and salvers laden with saffron and tangerines. There were towers of peaches; an abundance of plums. Three servants shuffled past with a tremendous dripping honeycomb, the mass of sticky beeswax spanning the width of an oversized door.

Every second seemed to bring more.

More crates, more hampers, more sacks and wheelbarrows. Dozens and dozens of servants rushing to and fro.

It was madness.

While it was true that there was often a great deal happening at the palace, this level of activity was unusual. To see the servants getting started so early—and with so much to occupy their arms—

Kamran drew a sharp breath.

The teacup slipped from his finger, shattering as it hit the ground.

These were preparations for a ball.

Kamran couldn't believe it. His grandfather had said he might wait at least a week before confirming the date, but this—this meant the king had made the decision without him.

For him.

Kamran's heart seemed to beat in his throat. He knew what this meant. He knew it to be an intentional unkindness. It was subterfuge glossed over with the shellac of benevolence. His grandfather wasn't willing to wait a moment longer, instead forcing him, now, to choose a bride.

Why?

The question pounded over and over in his head, steady as a heartbeat, as he all but ran to the king's chambers.

Kamran wasted no time upon arrival.

He pounded on his grandfather's door in as polite a manner as he could manage, stepping back when it swung open, ignoring the servant who addressed him. He pushed forward into the room, his earlier arguments in favor of the girl's life all but forgotten in the wake of this—*this*—

He turned the corner and discovered the king in his dressing room.

Kamran came to a sudden halt, his chest heaving with barely suppressed frustration. He bowed before the king, who bade him rise with a gesture of his hand.

Kamran stood, then stepped back.

It would not do to speak on the subject until the king was fully dressed, and besides, his grandfather's valet—a man named Risq—was still in the room, assisting the king with his long velvet robes. Today King Zaal wore a scarlet set with fringed epaulets; Risq buttoned the golden center strip that was the placket, then draped a pleated blue sash across the king's chest. This, he anchored with a heavy, intricately designed pearl belt, which he secured at the center with a single medallion: an eight-pointed star.

Dressing the king took an agonizingly long time.

There were endless layers, an infinite number of details. Kamran himself was expected to undergo a great deal of fanfare in his dress, but as he was seldom seen or required in public, he was more often spared the pomp and ceremony. Watching the king now, Kamran realized with a creeping dread that he would one day be expected to perform every tedious practice his grandfather undertook.

He clenched, unclenched his fists.

Only once every military badge and royal insignia was secured—the miniature of King Zaal's late wife, Elaheh, was pinned in a position of prominence over his heart—and his pearl harnesses were crisscrossed over his chest, did the king ask his man to leave them. His grandfather's ornate crown—so heavy it could be used to bludgeon a man—he held in his arms.

Kamran stepped forward, hardly parting his lips to speak, when his grandfather lifted a hand.

"Yes," he said. "I know you've come to change my mind."

Kamran stiffened.

For a moment, he wasn't sure to which problem the king was referring. "Yes, Your Majesty," he said carefully. "Indeed, I've come to try."

"Then I will be sorry to disappoint you. My position on the matter is resolute. The girl is a threat; such a threat must be removed immediately."

The impending ball was at once forgotten.

Kamran only stared, for a moment, at the face of his grandfather: his clear brown eyes, his rosy skin, his shock of white hair, white beard, white eyelashes. This was a man he loved; one he dearly respected. Kamran had admired King Zaal his entire life, had seen him always as a paragon of justice and greatness. He wanted, with his entire soul, to agree with the king—to stand always beside this extraordinary man—but for the first time, Kamran struggled.

For the first time, he doubted.

"Your Majesty," Kamran said quietly. "The girl has committed no crime. She's done nothing to threaten the empire."

King Zaal laughed, his eyes widening in amusement. "Done nothing to threaten the empire? She is the sole surviving heir to an ancient kingdom—on our own land—and not a threat to our empire? She is the very *definition*."

Kamran froze. "She—what?"

"I see you've not figured it out, then." Zaal lost his smile by inches. "She is not a mere servant girl."

Kamran felt a bit like he'd been impaled on a dull blade. He'd known there was something unusual about the girl, but this—

"How can you know for certain who she is?"

"You forget, child, that I have been searching for precisely such a creature since the day I became king. In fact I'd thought for certain I'd found her once; I assumed her dead some years ago. That she was alive was a surprise to me, but if there is ice in her veins, there can be no doubt."

The prince frowned. This was too much to process. "You say she is the sole surviving heir to an ancient kingdom. But wouldn't that make her—"

"Yes," said his grandfather. "Yes. She is, among her people, considered a queen."

Kamran took a sharp breath. "Why have you never told me about this? That there are other kingdoms in Ardunia?"

Zaal touched two fingers to his temple; he looked suddenly tired. "They died out thousands of years ago. They are not like us, Kamran; they do not pass down their line through their children. They claim their sovereigns are chosen by the earth, marked by the infinite cold they were once forced to endure. It is said that the ice chooses only the strongest among them, for there are very few who can survive the brutality of the frost inside the body." A pause. "Surely you must see that she is not some ordinary girl."

"And yet— Forgive me, but she seems wholly unaware of who she is. She lives a life of the lowest status, spends her days doing backbreaking labor. Do you not think—"

"That she might be ignorant of her own self? Of what she might be capable?"

"I do think it's possible, yes, that she doesn't know. She appears to have no family—perhaps no one has told her—"

King Zaal laughed again, though sadly this time. "Ice runs

through the girl's veins," he said, shaking his head. "Ice so rare it is revered, even as it damages the body. That kind of power leaves its marks, child. The girl no doubt carries the proof of her identity on her own flesh—"

"Your Majesty—"

"But yes, yes, let us pretend. For your sake let us pretend and say you are right, that she does not know who she is. What then?" The king steepled his hands under his chin. "If you do not think there are others searching for her right now, you are not paying close enough attention. Pockets of unrest in the Jinn communities continue to disturb our empire. There are many among them deluded enough to think the resurrection of an old world is the only way to move forward."

Kamran's jaw tensed. He did not appreciate the condescension in his grandfather's tone. "Indeed I am well aware," he said flatly. "I would humbly remind my grandfather that I was away from home for over a year, overseeing our armies, witnessing such accounts firsthand. It is not the threat I misunderstand, Your Highness, but the tactic. To take a preemptive strike against an innocent young woman— Would it not be worse? What if our actions against her were discovered? Would that not result in greater chaos?"

For a moment, King Zaal was silent.

"It is indeed a risk," he said finally. "But one that has been thoroughly considered. If the girl were to claim her place as the queen of her people, it is possible, even with the brace of the Fire Accords, that an entire race would pledge their allegiance to her on the basis of an ancient loyalty alone. The

Accords would be forgotten in the time it took to light a torch. The Jinn of Ardunia would form an army; the remaining civilians would riot. An uprising would wreak havoc across the land. Peace and security would be demolished for months—years, even—in the pursuit of an impossible dream."

Kamran felt himself growing irritated and forced himself to remain calm. "With all due respect, Your Majesty, if we can imagine our Accords so easily broken, should we not be compelled to wonder what makes them brittle? If the Jinn among us would move so easily to revolt—to pledge allegiance to another—should we not first consider addressing the dissatisfaction that might move them to revolution? Perhaps if they felt more reason to be loyal to us, they would not—"

"Your idealism," King Zaal said sharply, "is romantic. Diplomatic. And unrealistic. Can you not see my motivation for the establishment of the Accords? The entire reason I so desperately sought the unification of the races was to get ahead of the prophecy, to suture together the two groups so the Jinn could not be so easily claimed by a new sovereign—"

"My apologies," Kamran bit out angrily. "I thought you established the Accords to bring peace to our empire, to finally end the unnecessary bloodshed—"

"And that is precisely what I did," King Zaal thundered, more than matching his grandson's tone. "Your own eyes cannot deny it. You have seen since the day you were born that my every effort has been in the service of our people. With my very life I've tried always to prevent war. To circumvent tragedy. To protect our legacy.

"One day, Kamran, I've no doubt you will be a great king. Until then there is much you do not see, and a great deal more you must try to anticipate. Tell me: can you imagine such a revolt finding success?"

"Does it matter?" the prince nearly shouted.

King Zaal raised his chin, drew a sharp breath.

"Forgive me." Kamran lowered his eyes and collected himself. "But does it matter whether they are capable of success? Is there not a greater danger, Your Highness, in demanding obedience from unwilling subjects? And should any sovereign be satisfied with the tenuous allegiance of a people merely biding their time, waiting for the right moment to unleash their anger—to revolt? Would it not be wiser to allow such a people a voice now—to cool their anger now—in the interest of preventing an eruption later?"

"You are quite good," his grandfather said coldly, "at taking clear and logical arguments and elevating them to a level so esoteric they are rendered ineffectual.

"Your reasoning, while admirably impassioned, will not weather the storms of the real world. This is not about *rights*, child, but reason. It is about preventing the kind of bloodshed so horrific it would keep a man from ever again closing his eyes. What astounds me most is that you, the impending heir to this throne, would even consider allowing the birth of another monarchy on your own land." His grandfather hesitated a moment, studied Kamran's face. "You've met this girl, I take it? Spoken with her?"

Kamran tensed; a muscle jumped in his jaw.

"Yes," said the king. "As I thought."

"I do not know her, Your Majesty. Only of her, and from afar. My arguments are not influenced b—"

"You are young," said his grandfather. "As such, you are well within your rights to be foolish. Indeed it is natural at your age to make mistakes, to fall for a pretty face and pay dearly for your folly. But this— Kamran, this would not be foolish. This would not be folly. This would be a *travesty*. No good can come of such an alliance. I gave you a direct command, bade you find a wife—"

A moment of madness prompted Kamran to say, "This girl has royal blood, does she not?"

King Zaal rose to his feet, abandoning his throne with an agility that belied his age. He carried a golden mace, which he slammed against the glittering floor. Kamran had never seen his grandfather angry like this—had never seen him unleash the weight of his temper—and the transformation was chilling. Kamran did not see a man in that moment, but a king; a king who'd ruled the world's largest empire for nigh on a century.

"You would dare make a tasteless joke," he said, chest heaving as he stared down at his grandson, "about a creature predestined to orchestrate my demise."

Kamran swallowed. The words felt like ash in his throat when he said, "I beg you will forgive me."

King Zaal took a deep breath, his body trembling with the effort to remain calm. It felt like centuries before he finally resumed his throne.

"You will now answer me honestly," said his grandfather

quietly. "Knowing the might of Ardunia—tell me sincerely whether you can imagine the eventual victory of such a revolt."

Kamran lowered his eyes. "I cannot."

"No," said the king. "Nor I. How would they ever hope to win against us? Our empire is too old, our armies too strong, our bases scattered generously across the land. It would be a long and bloody war, and all for naught. How many lives would be lost in the pursuit of an impossible revolution?"

Kamran closed his eyes.

"You would consider risking the peace of millions," his grandfather went on, "the unnecessary deaths of tens of thousands—to spare the life of one girl? Why? Why spare her when we already know who she will become? What she will go on to do? My dear child, these are the kinds of decisions you will be forced to make, over and over, until death strips your soul from this world. I hope I never led you to believe your task here would be easy."

A length of silence stretched between them.

"Your Majesty," the prince said finally. "I do not dare deny your wisdom, and I do not mean to take lightly such a prophecy from our Diviners. I only argue that perhaps we wait to cut her down until she becomes the enemy once foretold."

"Would you wait for poison to ravage your body, Kamran, before taking the antidote you hold all the while in your hand?"

Kamran studied the floor and said nothing.

There was so much the prince longed to say, but this conversation felt impossible. How might he hope to argue in favor of leniency toward a person believed to be the provocation of his grandfather's demise?

Were the girl to make even the slightest move against King Zaal, Kamran's choice would be clear, his emotions undiluted. He would not scruple to defend his grandfather with his life.

The problem was that Kamran could not believe that the girl—as she existed now—had any interest in overthrowing the throne. Murdering her as an innocent seemed to him an action dark enough to dissolve the soul.

Still, he could not say any of this for fear of offending the king, in addition to losing what little respect his grandfather had left for him. They'd never fought like this, never been so far apart on such an important issue.

Even so, Kamran felt he had to try. Just once more.

"Could we not consider," he said, "perhaps—keeping her somewhere? In hiding?"

King Zaal canted his head. "You mean to put her in prison?"

"Not— No, not prison, but— Perhaps we could encourage her to leave, live elsewhere—"

His grandfather's face shuttered closed. "How can you not see? The girl cannot be free. While she is free, she can be found, she can be rallied, she can become a symbol of revolution. So long as I am king, I cannot allow it."

Kamran returned his gaze to the floor.

He felt a savage pain lance through him then, the blade of failure. Grief. The girl would be sentenced to death because of *him*, because he'd had the audacity to notice her, and the self-importance to announce what he'd seen.

"Tonight," said the king gravely, "the girl will be dealt with. Tomorrow night, you will choose a wife."

Kamran looked up in an instant, his eyes wild. "Your Majesty—"

"And we will never discuss this again."

FIFTEEN

پانزده

IN THE SILKY GLIMMER OF a sunlit window, she saw motion, then heard it: a flutter of wings, the sound like blades of grass in the wind, pushing together, then apart. Alizeh was washing the windows of Baz House on this beautiful morning, and when compared to her tasks the day before, the work seemed almost luxurious.

The sound of wings grew suddenly louder then, and a tiny body careened into the window with a soft *bop*.

Alizeh shooed it away.

The fluttering insect repeated this action twice more. Alizeh checked to make sure she was alone before she held up a single finger to her lips. "You must be quiet," she whispered. "And remain close to me."

The firefly did as it was bade, and landed gently on the nape of her neck, where it folded its wings, crawled downward, and ducked its head underneath her collar.

Alizeh dipped her sponge in its bucket, wrung the excess water, and continued scrubbing the smudged glass. She'd reapplied the salve to her hands and throat last night, which had made her pain quite manageable this morning. In fact, in the presence of the sun, all the terrors induced by the events of the evening prior had faded. It was easier for Alizeh to declare her fears dramatic when the skies were so clear, when her hands no longer throbbed in agony.

Today, she swore, would be easier.

She would not fear the condemnations of the apothecarist; nor would she concern herself with the prince, who had only done her a kindness. She would not worry over her missing handkerchief, which would doubtless be found; she would not fear for her health, not now that she had her salves. And the devil, she reasoned, could go to hell.

Things were going to get better.

Tonight, she had an appointment *inside* the Lojjan ambassador's estate. She was engaged to design and execute the creation of five gowns, for which she might hope to collect a total of forty coppers, which was nearly half a stone.

Goodness, Alizeh had never even held a stone.

Her mind had already run wild with the possibilities such a sum of coin might provide. Her wildest hope was to secure enough customers to make a regular living, for only then might she be able to leave Baz House. If she was careful and kept to a tight budget, she prayed she'd be able to afford a small room of her own—maybe somewhere sparsely populated on the outskirts of town—somewhere she might never be bothered.

Her heart swelled at the thought.

Somehow, she would manage it. She'd keep her head down and work hard, and one day she'd be free of this place, these people.

She hesitated, her sponge pressed against the glass.

Alizeh could not help but think how strange it was that she worked in service. All her life she'd known she wanted to spend her life in the service of others, though not at all like this.

Life, it seemed, possessed a sense of irony.

Alizeh had been brought up to lead, to unify, to free her people from the half-lives they'd been forced to live.

Once, she'd been meant to revive an entire civilization.

The painful frost growing inside her veins was a primitive phenomenon, one thought lost to her people a millennia ago. Alizeh knew only a little of the abilities she was rumored to possess, for though there was an inherent power in the ice that pulsed through her, it was a power that could not be tapped until she came of age, and even then would not mature without the assistance of an ancient magic buried deep in the Arya mountains, where her ancestors had built their first kingdom.

And then, of course, she would require a kingdom.

The idea struck her as so preposterous it nearly made her laugh, even as it broke her heart.

Still, it had been at least a thousand years since there'd been news of a Jinn born with ice in their blood, which made Alizeh's mere existence nothing short of miraculous. Nearly two decades ago whispers of Alizeh's strange, cold eyes had spread among the Jinn the way only a rumor might, expectations building every day upon the slopes of her young shoulders. Her parents, who knew she would not be safe until she came of age at eighteen, had removed their daughter from the noisy, needy world, secreting her away for so long that the whispers, without fuel, were soon reduced to ash.

Alizeh, too, was forgotten shortly thereafter.

All those who knew of her had been killed, and Alizeh, who had no ally, no kingdom, no magic, and no resources, knew her life was best spent simply trying to survive.

She no longer had any ambition beyond a desire to live a quiet, undetected existence. In her more hopeful moments Alizeh dreamed of living somewhere lost in the countryside, tending to a flock of sheep. She'd sheer them every spring, using their wool to weave a rug as long as the world was round. It was a dream at once simple and implausible, but it was an imagining that gave her comfort when her mind required an escape.

She promised herself things wouldn't always be this hard. She promised herself that the days would get better, bit by bit.

In fact, things were already better.

For the first time in years, Alizeh had company. And as if to remind her, the firefly nudged her neck.

Alizeh shook her head.

The firefly nudged her again.

"Yes, I know, you've made it very clear that you'd like me to come outside with you," she said, scarcely breathing the words. "But as you can plainly see, I'm not allowed to leave this house at will."

She could almost feel the firefly grieve. It wilted against her neck, rubbing one little arm over its eyes.

The creature had snuck into Baz House last night, during the brief window of time it took for the prince to open and close the back door. It had flown hard and fast in her direction, pelting her in the cheek with its little body.

It'd been so long since Alizeh had seen a firefly that, at first, she hadn't recognized the creature. When she did, she smiled so wide she hardly knew herself.

Alizeh had been sent a firefly.

A communiqué.

From whom? She did not know. Though not for a lack of effort on the part of the insect. The poor thing had been trying to drag her outside since the moment it found her.

There was a special relationship between Jinn and fireflies, for though they could not communicate directly, they understood each other in ways unique only to the two species. Fireflies were to Jinn what some animals were to Clay. Beloved companions. Loyal friends. Comrades in arms.

Alizeh knew, for example, that this firefly was a friendly one, that it already knew who she was, and that it wanted now to guide her to a meeting with its owner. Though it appeared neither the firefly nor its owner understood the limits surrounding Alizeh's freedom.

She sighed.

She took as much time as she dared scrubbing each delicate windowpane, enjoying the expansive view to the outside. It was rare that she was afforded so much time to take in the beauty of Setar, and she relished it now: the shattering, snowcapped Istanez mountain range in the distance; the frosted green hills in between. Dozens of narrow rivers fractured the landscape, the valleys blue with turquoise and rainwater, bookended on either side by miles of saffron and rose fields.

Alizeh was from the very north of Ardunia—from Temzeel province—an icy, elevated region so close to the stars she'd often thought she could touch them. She missed her home desperately, but she could not deny the splendors of Setar.

Without warning, the bell tolled.

It was noon, the morning now officially at an end. The sun had slid discreetly into position at the apex of the horizon, and Alizeh marveled at it through the glass, at the jolly warmth it emanated across the land.

She really was in a fine mood.

She recognized that it had been good for her to cry last night, to release a bit of the pressure in her chest. She felt lighter this morning, better than she had in a long ti—

The sponge dropped from her fingers without warning, landing with a dull thud in its soapy bucket, spraying her fresh snoda with dirty water. Anxiously, she dried her wet hands on her apron and pressed closer to the window.

Alizeh could not believe her eyes.

She clapped a hand over her mouth, overcome by an irrational happiness to which she was almost certainly not entitled. That wretched Fesht boy had nearly slit her throat; what reason did she have to be delighted to see him now? Oh, she didn't know, and she didn't care.

She couldn't believe he'd come.

Alizeh watched him as he came up the walk, marveling anew at his shock of red hair and prematurely long frame. The boy was an entire head taller than her, and at least five years younger; it was a wonder to her how he grew at all for a child who ate so little.

The boy arrived at the fork in the footpath then, making a sharp right where he should've gone left, his unsettling choice directing him straight to the main entrance. When Alizeh was certain his vivid figure had disappeared for good, her joy evaporated.

Why had he gone to the front door?

She'd instructed the boy to come to the kitchens, not the main house. If she hurried right this second she might, under the pretense of collecting more water, be able to rush down to meet him. But if he was discovered at the front door not only would he be whipped for the impudence—she'd be cast out for having promised him bread.

Alizeh sat back, her heart racing at the thought.

Was this her fault? Should she have explained things more thoroughly to the boy? But what street child was deluded enough to think he might be admitted through the front door of a grand estate?

She dropped her face in her hands.

The firefly fluttered its wings against her neck, asking the obvious question.

Alizeh shook her head. "Oh, nothing," she said softly. "Just that I'm fairly certain I'll be thrown out onto the street . . . any minute now."

At that, the firefly grew animated, taking flight and tossing its body once more at the window.

Bop. Bop.

Alizeh couldn't help her smile then, however reluctant. "Not in a good way, you silly creature."

"Girl!" A familiar voice barked at her.

Alizeh froze.

"*Girl!*"

In a flash, the firefly flew up the cuff of Alizeh's sleeve, where it shuddered against her skin.

Alizeh turned slowly from her seat in the window bay to face Mrs. Amina, where the housekeeper somehow managed to tower over her even from below.

"Yes, ma'am?"

"Who were you talking to?"

"No one, ma'am."

"I saw your lips moving."

"I was humming a song, ma'am." Alizeh bit her lip. She wanted to say more—to offer up a more robust lie—but she was warier than ever of saying too much.

"Your job is to disappear," Mrs. Amina said sharply. "You're not allowed to hum, you're not allowed to speak, you're not allowed to look at anyone. You don't exist when you work here, especially when you're abovestairs. Do I make myself clear?"

Alizeh's heart was racing. "Yes, ma'am."

"Get down here. *Now.*"

Alizeh's body felt suddenly heavy. She climbed down the rickety wooden ladder as if in a dream, her heartbeats growing louder as she went. She kept her eyes on the ground as she approached the housekeeper.

"Forgive me," she said quietly, keeping her head down. "It won't happen again."

"I daresay it will not."

Alizeh braced herself, waiting for what seemed the inevitable strike, when Mrs. Amina suddenly cleared her throat.

"You have a guest," she said.

Very slowly, Alizeh looked up. "I beg your pardon, ma'am?"

"You may meet him in the kitchen. You will have fifteen minutes."

"But— Who—"

"And not a minute more, do you understand?"

"Y-yes. Yes, ma'am."

Mrs. Amina marched off, leaving Alizeh sagging in place. She couldn't believe it. *A visitor?* It had to be the boy, did it not? The Fesht boy.

And yet— How could a street child have been admitted into the home of a duchess? How might he then be granted an audience with the lowest servant in the order?

Oh, her curiosity would not quiet.

Alizeh did not walk, but flew to the kitchens, lifting her sleeve to her mouth as she went. "It looks as if I won't be tossed into the street after all," she breathed, hardly daring to move her lips. "That's good news, isn't it? And now I've got a . . ." She trailed off, slowing down when she realized she could no longer feel the firefly's legs on her arm, nor its wings against her skin. She peered inside her sleeve.

"Where are you?" she whispered.

The firefly was nowhere to be found.

SIXTEEN

شانزده

THE AFTERNOON ROSE BRIGHT AND clear, the sun proud in the sky. The prior evening's storm had washed clean the city of Setar, leaving in its wake a freshness and clarity its crown prince did not share.

Kamran sighed in the direction of the sun, cursing its shine, its beauty. He'd been swallowed whole by many a dark mood in his eighteen years, but his disposition at this hour was singularly volatile.

Still, the boy was not cruel.

He knew better than to grant such darkness an audience, and had abandoned the palace for Surati Forest, whose towering pink trees were like something out of a dream. It was one of the prince's favorite places, not only for its beauty but for its seclusion, for it was accessible only by mountain cliff—from which one was required to jump, and often to their death.

Kamran never much minded this risk.

He'd brought with him only a small, patterned red rug, which he'd unfurled upon the snowy forest floor, and upon which he now reclined. He stared impassively at the impressive grove, the fluorescent pink trunks and their fluorescent pink leaves. Fresh snowfall had obscured the miles of green moss blanketing the ground, but the endless white drift lent its own cold beauty to the scene.

Kamran closed his eyes as a breeze skated along his face, mussing the glossy black waves of his hair. He heard the sweet chirp of a pair of songbirds, the buzz of a rare dragon-fly. The hawk circling high above might've witnessed only a young man in repose, but the humble ant would've known better, would've felt the violent tremble emanating from his limbs, fracturing across the forest floor.

No, Kamran's anger could not be contained.

It was no wonder, then, that he remained undisturbed as he lay exposed in the middle of uncharted land. Snake and spider, scarab and snow leopard, insects large and small, bears both white and brown. They all knew to give the young prince a wide berth, for there was no greater repellant than anger, and the woods shook with this warning now.

Today, Kamran had begun to doubt everything.

He had felt only sadness upon leaving his grandfather's rooms that morning, but as the day wore on and his mind continued to work, his anger had grown over him like ivy. He was experiencing the grief of disillusionment, going over and over again in his mind his every memory of his grandfather; every moment he'd thought the man just and benevolent. All that King Zaal had done for the common good—had it been only in the interest of his own protection?

Even now he heard his grandfather's voice in his head—

In fact I'd thought for certain I'd once found her
I assumed her dead some years ago

Kamran had not questioned the statement when first spoken by the king, but now, at his leisure, he combed over every word of their earlier conversation, turned it inside out for analysis.

What had his grandfather meant when he'd said he was surprised the girl was alive? Did that mean he'd tried to kill her before?

Some years ago, he'd said.

The girl couldn't have been a day older than Kamran—of that, he felt certain—so what conclusion was he left to draw? That his grandfather had tried to murder a child?

The prince sat up, dragged his hands down his face.

He knew, intellectually, that these were not ordinary circumstances.

That the girl's animus had been foretold by the Diviners meant a great deal, for the mouths of the priests and priestesses were touched with binding, brutal magic before they were even allowed to take their vows. They were as a result beings physically incapable of telling lies, and whose prophecies were the fodder of legend.

Never once had they been wrong.

But try as he might shape his heart to the painful context of the situation, the prince could not condone the killing of an innocent. He could not fathom the murder of the girl, not now, not for the crime of merely existing.

So it had become, in the aftermath of their meeting, critically important to Kamran to reconcile his heart and mind. He'd wanted, desperately, to side with his grandfather, who in eighteen years had always treated Kamran with an abundance of love and loyalty. The prince could learn to accept his grandfather as imperfect; all else might be forgiven if he could only prove today the merit of the king's argument—that the girl was indeed a threat. It was with this in mind that the prince had consoled himself with a single plan of action:

He would find evidence.

He would prove to himself that the girl was plotting against the crown; that she had ambitions of bloodshed; that she hoped to incite a revolt.

It certainly seemed possible.

For the more he'd thought on it, the more impossible it seemed to Kamran that the girl did not know who she was.

On that score, his grandfather had to be right. Why else the refinement, the elegance and education, the knowledge of multiple languages? She'd been bred for royalty, had she not? Was it not a disguise, the lowering of herself into obscurity? Was not the snoda merely an excuse to hide her unusual eyes, which were likely proof of her identity?

Devils above, Kamran had not been able to decide.

For it was not entirely a performance, was it? She worked every day for her living, scrubbed the floors of her lessers, cleaned the toilets of a gentlewoman.

Deeply agitated, Kamran had drawn his hood low over his head, pulled the chain mail over his face, and gone straight from his grandfather's chambers into the center of town.

He'd been determined to find reason in what seemed like madness, and the parcels seemed his straightest path to clarity.

Kamran had recognized their seal the night prior; they were from the apothecary in town. Only this morning had it occurred to him that the girl might've overreacted to their loss. It had suddenly seemed strange to him that anyone would grow hysterical at the thought of losing a few medicinal herbs—items that were easily found, easily replaced.

It was possible, then, that there was more to their contents.

The parcels might help prove her hand in some nefarious scheme, tie her to some underhanded plotting; uncovering their truth might establish her as a real threat to the empire. It was perhaps not too late, he'd consoled himself, to find a way to support the king's decision against her.

So he'd gone.

It was a simple matter for him to locate the apothecary, disguise himself as a magistrate, ask questions of the proprietor. He'd pretended to be going shop to shop, asking questions about possible criminal acts committed during the previous evening's revelry, and had hounded the poor man for every detail concerning his late-night customers.

One, in particular.

"Sir, I confess I don't understand," the proprietor had said nervously. He was a wiry man, with black hair and brown skin; a man named Deen. "She purchased only what I recommended for her injuries, nothing more."

"And what had you recommended?"

"Oh," he said, faltering a bit as he remembered. "Oh, just— well, there were two different kinds of salve. She had very different injuries, sir, though both treatments were meant to help with the pain and guard against infection, albeit in slightly different ways. Nothing unusual. That was all, really. Yes, it was just some salve and—and some linen bandages."

Salve and linen bandages.

She'd fallen to her knees in the gutter to save a few coppers' worth of salve and linen bandages?

"You're quite certain?" Kamran had asked. "There was nothing else—nothing of considerable value? Nothing particularly precious or expensive?"

At this, the tension in Deen's body seemed to vanish. The apothecarist blinked curiously at the man wearing a face of chain mail—the man he considered a magistrate—and said, with surprising calm, "When a person is in tremendous pain, sir, is not its remedy worth everything? Valued above all else?"

Kamran managed an indifferent tone when he said, "You mean to say the girl was in tremendous pain?"

"Most certainly. She did not complain of it aloud, but her wounds were severe and had been festering all day. I've witnessed many a man in my shop weep over lesser injuries."

Kamran had felt the words like a blow.

"Forgive me," Deen said carefully. "But as magistrate you must surely know that the wages of a snoda are paid out predominantly in the form of shelter? I rarely see a snoda in my shop, for most receive only three tonce a week in addition to their housing. Lord only knows how the girl scraped together the coppers to pay me." Deen hesitated. "I explain all this only because you have asked, sir, if the girl left my store with anything of considerable value, and—"

"Yes, I see," Kamran had said sharply.

He'd felt sick with self-loathing, with shame. He'd hardly heard Deen as the man prattled on, providing details Kamran no longer cared to hear. He did not want to know that the girl was friendly or evidently hardworking. He did not want to hear Deen describe the bruise on her face or discuss at length his suspicions that she was being abused by her employer.

"She was a nice girl," Deen had gone on. "Oddly well-spoken for a snoda, but a little jumpy, too, easily frightened. Though—that may have been my fault. I feel I may have come down too hard on the poor girl. She'd said some things . . . and I . . ." Deen trailed off. Looked out the window.

Kamran had stiffened at that. "Said what things?"

Deen shook his head. "Oh, she was only making conversation, really. I fear I might've scared her. She left the store so quickly I never had a chance to give her the brushes she'll need, though I suppose she could use her hands just so long as she keeps them clean . . ."

Kamran heard a roaring in his ears then, the sound so loud it drowned out all else, blurring his vision.

The magenta trees of Surati Forest came back into focus with agonizing slowness, the present world materializing one sensation at a time. The coarse fibers of the red rug under his head and hands, the weight of his swords against his torso, the whistling of the wind in the thicket, the bracing scent of winter pine filling his nose.

Kamran swiped a finger along the snow as one might an iced cake; he studied for a moment the shimmering dollop sat atop his finger and then popped it in his mouth, shivering a bit as the frost melted on his tongue.

A red fox darted up through the snow just then and wrinkled its nose, shaking flakes from its eyes before diving back into the earth, not long after which a quintet of reindeer appeared in the distance. The herd came to an abrupt halt still yards away, their large eyes wondering, no doubt, why Kamran had come.

He would answer, had they asked.

He would tell them he'd come for escape. To flee his mind, his strange life. He would tell them that the information he'd sought as an antidote had proven instead to be a poison.

She was going to be killed.

He understood it, but he did not know how to accept that she would be killed, she who treated with mercy a boy who'd tried to murder her, who was born a queen but made her living by scrubbing floors and was, in return, thanked for her hard work with only abuse and tyranny. He'd thought her mad for falling to pieces over a few coppers' worth of medicine, never considering that those few coppers might be all she had in the world.

Kamran exhaled, closed his eyes.

She did not seem to him in any way a criminal. He supposed he could find new ways to investigate her life, but his always-reliable instincts insisted there was no point. He'd known it even before he'd set off on his earlier task, but had been too deep in denial to face it: no matter the prophecy, the version of the girl who lived today did not deserve to die, and there was nothing he could do about it.

In point of fact, it would be his fault.

He had done this to her, had shone a spotlight on her when she'd seemed to want nothing more than to disappear. Kamran would live with this regret for the rest of his life.

Indeed, the prince felt so much in that very moment he found he could not move—dared not move. If he allowed himself to shift even an iota he thought he might crack, and if he cracked he thought he might set fire to the world.

He opened his eyes.

A single pink leaf fell slowly, spinning as it drifted from a nearby tree, landing on Kamran's nose. He plucked the leaf from his face, spun it around by the stem.

Madness prompted him to laugh.

SEVENTEEN

هفده

THEY WERE NOT ALONE.

Cook had frozen in place, her cleaver aloft, staring agog at the two unlikely allies sitting nervously at the kitchen table. A cluster of servants peered around the corner, three heads stacked like tomatoes on a skewer. More peered out of doorways, others slowing down as they walked past. Everyone was waiting for a single word to be spoken.

Alizeh could not blame them for their interest.

She, too, was stunned by this turn of events. Neither she nor the Fesht boy had said much yet, for as soon as they'd made their initial, exuberant greetings, they'd realized half the staff had crowded around to gawk. Even so, Alizeh felt an uncommon happiness as he and she stared at each other from across the table, smiling awkwardly.

"Et mist ajeeb, nek? Hef nemek vot tan sora." *It is very strange, no? That I can't see your eyes.*

Alizeh smiled. "Han. Bek nemekketosh et snoda minseg cravito." *Yes. But I can't take off the snoda when I'm working.*

At that indecipherable exchange, most of the servants made audible sighs of frustration and returned to work. Alizeh glanced at the few who remained, then at the fifteen-minute sand timer sitting atop the table. The grains slid steadily from one glass bulb to the other, each loss filling her with dread. She doubted there were many—if any—servants in Setar who spoke Feshtoon, but Alizeh could not rely upon such an uncertainty.

They would simply have to be careful.

She returned her gaze to the Fesht boy, who'd benefited greatly from the attentions of the Diviners. Regular baths and meals had left him remarkably transformed; he was, underneath all that dirt, a rosy-cheeked stalk of a child, and when he smiled at her now, she knew he meant it.

Her heart warmed at the thought.

In Feshtoon, she said, "There's so much I'd like to ask you, but I fear we have very little time. Are you well, my young friend? You look quite well."

"I am, miss, thank you. I wish I could say the same for you, but I can't see your face."

Alizeh fought back a laugh.

"I'm glad you got some bandages for your hands, though." He made as if to look closer, then jerked back, paling. "And I did damage to your neck, miss, I see that now. I'm ever so sorry."

"Oh," she said quietly. "It's just a scratch."

"'Tis more than a scratch, miss." The boy sat up straighter. "And I've come to you today to make amends for what I done."

She smiled then, feeling a complicated fondness for the boy. "Forgive me," she said. "But my curiosity has overcome my manners, and I must know: how on earth did you convince them to admit you through the front door?"

The boy beamed at that, displaying a set of teeth still a

touch too big for his face. "You mean why was a slippery, no good, thieving street urchin allowed through the front door?"

Alizeh matched his smile. "Yes. Precisely that."

For some reason, the boy seemed pleased by her response, or perhaps he was relieved that she would not pretend the ugliness between them had never happened.

"Well," he said, "because I'm an important person now, aren't I? The prince saved my life, didn't he? And the king himself said he was very glad I didn't die. *Very* glad. And I've got the papers to prove it."

"Is that so?" Alizeh blinked at him. She believed little of what the boy was saying but found his enthusiasm charming. "How wonderful that must be for you."

He nodded. "They've been feeding me eggs most mornings, miss, and honestly, I can't complain. But today," he said, "today I've come to see you, miss, to make amends for what I done."

Alizeh nodded. "As you said."

"That's right," he said, just a little too loudly. "I've come to invite you to a party!"

"I see," said Alizeh, glancing nervously around the near-empty kitchen. Mercifully, most onlookers had dispersed, having given up hope of hearing the two of them speak Ardanz. Alizeh and the boy were now alone but for the occasional servant passing through the kitchens; Mrs. Amina was doubtless far too busy with her own tasks to waste time hovering over a pair of nobodies.

"Goodness, a party. That's very kind of you . . ." Alizeh

hesitated, then frowned. "Do you know, I don't believe I know your name."

The boy leaned forward at that, arms folded on the table. "I'm Omid, miss. Omid Shekarzadeh. I come from Yent, of Fesht province, and I'm not ashamed to say it."

"Nor should you be," Alizeh said, surprised. "I've heard so much about Yent. Is it really as beautiful as they say?"

Omid blinked, regarding her for a moment as if she might be mad. "Begging your pardon, miss, but these days all I ever hear about any place in Fesht is probably not fit to be repeated in present company."

Alizeh grinned. "Oh, but that's only because a great many people are stupid, aren't they? And what's left of them have never actually been to Fesht."

Omid's eyes widened at that, and he sputtered a laugh.

"I was quite young the last time I went south," Alizeh was saying, "so my memories of the region are dim. But my mother told me the air in Yent always smells of saffron—and that its trees grow so tall they fall over and stay that way, with their branches growing along the ground. She said the rose fields are so near the rivers that when heavy summer winds tear the flowers from their stems, the petals fall in the streams and steep, perfuming the water. She said there was never a more heavenly drink than river rosewater in the heat of summer."

Very slowly, Omid nodded.

"*Han*," he said. "Your mother is right." He sank back in his seat, drawing his hands into his lap. It was a moment before he looked up again, and when he did his eyes were bright with an emotion he'd not been able to fight.

Softly, Alizeh said, "I'm so very sorry you had to leave."

"Yes, miss." Omid took a deep breath. "But it's real nice to hear you talk about it. Everyone hates us, so they think Fesht is all donkeys and idiots. Sometimes I start to think my life there was all a dream." A pause. "You're not from Setar, either, are you?"

Alizeh's smile was strained. "I am not."

"And is your mother still with you, miss? Or did you have to leave her behind?"

"Ah." Alizeh turned her gaze to the unfinished wood of the weathered table. "Yes," she said softly. "My mother is still with me. Though only in my soul."

"*Mizon,*" Omid said, slapping the table with feeling.

Alizeh looked up.

Mizon was a Fesht word that did not translate easily, but was used to describe the inexpressible emotion of an unexpected moment when two people understood each other.

"Mizon," Omid said again, this time gravely. "As my mother is in mine."

"And my father," Alizeh said, smiling softly as she touched two fingers to her forehead, then to the air.

"And mine." The boy echoed the gesture—two fingers to his forehead, then to the air—even as his eyes glistened. "Inta sana zorgana le pav wi saam." *May their souls be elevated to the highest peace.*

"Inta ghama spekana le luc nipaam," she returned. *May their sorrows be sent to an unknown place.*

This was a call-and-response familiar to most Ardunians,

a prayer offered up always when remembering the dead.

Alizeh looked away then, focused her eyes on the timer. She would not cry here. They had only several minutes left, and she did not want to spend them feeling sad.

She sniffed, then said brightly: "So. You've come to invite me to a party. When shall we celebrate? I wish I could join you for an afternoon outing, but sadly I'm not allowed to leave Baz House during the day. Perhaps we might find a clear patch of forest in the evening? Enjoy a moonlit picnic?"

To her great surprise, Omid laughed.

"No," he said, shaking his head vigorously. "Miss, I mean to ask you to a *real* party." He laughed again. "I've been invited to the ball tomorrow night as a special guest of the king." He retrieved a heavy, gilded scroll from his inside pocket, unfurling it on the table before her.

"See? It says just there"—he pointed several times—"just there it says I can bring one guest to the royal ball." Omid unearthed two other scrolls, flattening them both before her. They were numbered, hand-lettered invitations rendered in heavy calligraphy, and stamped with the royal seal. Each admitted one guest.

Omid pushed the spare invitation across the table.

Carefully, Alizeh gathered up the heavy sheaf. She studied it for a long time, and then looked up at the boy.

She was dumbfounded.

"Is that not what it says, miss?" Omid asked after a moment. He peered again at the scroll. "I know little Ardanz, but I think they're correct. Aren't they?"

Alizeh could hardly speak for the shock she felt.

"I'm sorry," she said finally. "I don't— I'm afraid I still don't— *Oh.*" She gasped, covering her mouth with one bandaged hand. "Is this the reason you were admitted through the front door? Is this why you were allowed an audience with me? You— Oh my goodness. So these are real, then?"

"Are you very pleased, miss?" Omid beamed at her, puffing out his chest a bit. "At first I weren't allowed to bring a guest, see, but I've been thinking hard for a while now how to make amends, and then"—he snapped his fingers—"it just struck me, miss, just like that!

"So the next time they came to see me I said to them that I'm ever so grateful for the invitation, but I'm only twelve, understand, still but a child, and a child can't attend a ball without a chaperone, so may I please have another, else I won't be able to go at all! And can you believe it, miss, they didn't question me, not one bit. I fear the king's ministers might be stupid."

Alizeh picked up the scroll, examined the wax seal. "So this . . . but it must be real. I never dreamed . . ."

There were all manner of astonishments to contend with in that moment, but perhaps the most shocking was Alizeh's realization that—even with all her duties at Baz House—she might actually be able to go. Royal balls didn't even begin until at least nine or ten o'clock in the evening, which meant Alizeh could leave Baz House at her leisure. It would not be the first time she'd forfeited an entire night of sleep—and it was a price she would happily pay.

Even better: she'd need not tell anyone where she was going, for it was not as if she had any friends who might notice her prolonged absence. In fact, had she a proper room in the servants' wing, she might've had more trouble getting away, for most servants shared rooms and were able to keep few secrets as a result.

Not that it needed, strictly, to be kept a secret.

Alizeh's attendance at such a ball would not technically be unlawful—though she doubted there was much precedence for a snoda attending any royal function—but it seemed unlikely that others would take kindly to the idea of the lowest, most disposable servant of Baz House being invited to a royal event. She would be surprised, indeed, if they did not hate her for it merely out of spite, but then—

Alizeh frowned.

If Omid had been admitted entry to Baz House on the basis of these papers, did not Mrs. Amina already know about the invitations? Had she not already been informed on the matter, and made her decision? The housekeeper could've easily barred the boy from entering, could've denied Alizeh even a moment to speak with him. Could it be, then, that her fifteen minutes with the child were tacit approval of precisely such an outing? Had Mrs. Amina done her a kindness?

Alizeh bit her lip; it was hard to know.

Still, this uncertainty did not keep her from dreaming. Such an evening would be a rare treat for anyone, though perhaps especially so for the likes of Alizeh, who'd not been invited anywhere in years.

In fact, she'd not done anything purely recreational in what felt like a painfully long time. This would be a singular experience, then, for not only was it an evening of excitement by any metric, but it would be embarked upon with a friend, a friend with whom she might conspire and share stories. Alizeh thought she'd be content merely to stand at the back of the ballroom and stare, to admire the gowns and glittering details of a living, breathing world so different from the drudgery of her own waking hours. It sounded decadent.

It sounded *fun*.

"And we can eat fancy food the whole night long!" Omid was saying. "There should be all kinds of fruits and cakes and nuts and oh, I bet there will be sweet rice and beef skewers, and all sorts of stews and pickled vegetables. The palace chef is said to be a legend, miss. It's bound to be a real feast, with music and dancing and—"

The boy hesitated then, the words dying in his mouth.

"I do hope," he said, faltering a bit, "I do hope you see, miss, that this is my way of apologizing for my wrongdoing. My ma wouldn't have been proud of me that morning, and I been thinking about it every day since. You can't know how ashamed I am for trying to steal from you."

Alizeh conjured a faint smile. "And for trying to murder me?"

At that Omid turned bright red; even the tips of his ears went scarlet. "Oh, miss, I weren't going to murder you, I swear, I never would've done it. I was only"—he swallowed—"I only— I was so hungry, see, and I couldn't think straight— It was like a demon had possessed me—"

Alizeh covered his freckled hand with her own bandaged one and squeezed gently. "It's quite all right," she said. "The demon is gone now. And I accept your apology."

Omid looked up. "You do?"

"I do."

"Just like that? No groveling or nothing?"

"No, no groveling necessary." She laughed. "Though—may I ask you a rather impertinent question?"

"Anything, miss."

"Well. Forgive me for how this sounds, for I mean no disrespect—but it strikes me as odd that the king's men agreed to your request so readily. All of high society must be devouring itself for a chance at one of these invitations. I can't imagine it was a small thing to offer you two."

"Oh that's true, miss, no doubt about it, but as I said, I'm pretty important now. They need me."

"Oh?"

He nodded. "Pretty sure I'm meant to be there as a trophy," he said. "Living proof, miss."

Alizeh was surprised to discover that Omid's tone did not project arrogance, but a quiet wisdom rare for his age.

"A trophy?" she said, realization dawning. "A trophy for the prince, you mean?"

"Yes, miss, exactly that."

"But why would the prince require such a trophy? Is he not enough on his own?"

"I can't say, miss. I only think I'm supposed to remind the people, you understand, of the merciful empire. To tell the tale of the heroic prince and the southern street rat."

"I see." Alizeh's enthusiasm dimmed. "And was he?" she asked after a moment. "Heroic?"

"I can't honestly say, miss." Omid shrugged. "I was

near-dead for the part where he saved my life."

Alizeh went quiet then, laid low by the reminder that this vibrant, eager child had tried to take his own life. She was trying to think of what to say next, and faltered.

"Miss?"

She looked up. "Yes?"

"It's only—I just realized you never told me your name."

"Oh." She startled. "Yes. Of course."

Alizeh had managed to live a long time without needing to supply her name to anyone. Even Mrs. Amina had never demanded to know—preferring instead to call her *you* and *girl*. But oh, what harm would it do if she told Omid her name now? Who was listening, anyway?

Quietly, she said, "I am Alizeh."

"Alizeh," said the boy, testing the shape of it in his mouth. "I th—"

"*Enough.*" Mrs. Amina snatched the sand timer from the table. "That is quite enough. Your fifteen minutes are up. Back to work, girl."

Alizeh swiped the scroll with lightning speed, slipping it up her sleeve with the artistry of an experienced thief. She jumped to her feet and curtsied.

"Yes, ma'am," she said.

She chanced a glance in Omid's direction, offered him a barely perceptible nod, and was already darting into the hall when he shouted—

"Minda! Setunt tesh." *Tomorrow! Nine o'clock.* "Manotan ani!" *I'll meet you there!*

Mrs. Amina straightened, her arms pinned angrily to her

sides. "Someone please escort this child outside. *Now.*"

Two footmen appeared in an instant, arms outstretched as if to manhandle the boy, but Omid was undaunted. He was smiling, clutching his scrolls to his chest and slipping out of reach when he said—

"Bep shayn aneti, eh? Wi nek snoda." *Wear something nice, okay? And no snoda.*

EIGHTEEN

هجده

KAMRAN TILTED HIS HEAD UP at the blue mosaic work of the war room, not merely to admire the geometric ingenuity executed upon the domed ceiling, but to exercise his tortured neck away from the stiff collar of his tunic.

The prince had been willing to don this shirt only because he'd been assured by his valet that it was made of pure silk—and silk, he'd assumed, would prove more comfortable than that of his other formal wear. Silk was purported to be a smooth and quiet textile, was it not?

How, then, to explain the atrocity he wore now?

Kamran could not understand why the blasted article was so crisp, or why it made so much noise when he moved.

His valet was clearly an idiot.

It had taken hours, but Kamran's earlier anger had abated just long enough to carry him home. His frustrations still simmered at a low, constant heat, but when the haze of fury had lifted, Kamran looked about himself and decided the only way through this day was to focus on things he could control. He feared he might otherwise spend every minute staring angrily at the clock until he could be certain the girl was dead.

It wouldn't do.

Much better, the prince thought, would be to exorcise

his demons in the pursuit of a known enemy—and he bade
Hazan assemble a gathering of a dozen high-ranking military officials. There was a great deal to discuss with respect
to the brewing tensions with Tulan, and Kamran hoped to
spend the remainder of the day working through strategy in
the palace war room. Work, he thought, would calm him.

He had miscalculated.

As if this day hadn't been from its birth an abomination,
Kamran seemed doomed now to spend the rest of it accosted
by halfwits; imbeciles whose jobs it was to dress him and
guide him and advise him poorly in all matters both foreign
and domestic.

Idiots, all of them idiots.

He was listening to one of those idiots now. The empire of
Ardunia had a redundant, useless defense minister, and not
only was the greasy creature present in the war room today,
he wouldn't cease speaking long enough to allow a more reasonable person to contradict him.

"Certainly, there are some concerns about relations with
Tulan," the minister was saying, dispensing words at a slug-
gardly pace so tedious Kamran wanted to throttle the man.
"But we have the situation well in hand, and I would humbly
remind His Highness—for our esteemed prince had yet to
set foot on a battlefield when these provisions were made—
that it was covert Ardunian intelligence that brought to bear
the promotions of several of Tulan's highest ranking officials,
who might now be counted upon to report any information
of note to their Ardunian allies . . ."

Kamran briefly closed his eyes, clenching his fists to keep

from boxing his own ears or tearing the shirt from his body. He'd been forced to change into formal wear for the purposes of this meeting, which was one of the more ludicrous customs of peacetime. The near decade they'd spent away from the battlefield had made the once legendary leaders of Ardunia now thick and lethargic, stripping these military summits of their urgency, degrading them all in the process.

Kamran was not only prince of Ardunia, but one of only five lieutenant generals responsible for the five respective field armies—each a hundred thousand soldiers strong—and he took his position quite seriously.

When the time came for Kamran to inherit the throne, so, too, would he inherit his grandfather's role as commanding general of the entire Ardunian military, and there were few who did not resent the prince's impending elevation to the distinguished rank at such a young age. The title should have gone to his father, yes, but such was Kamran's fate. He could not run from it any more than he could reanimate the dead. His only recourse was to work harder—and smarter—to show what he was worth.

This, among other reasons, might explain why his comrades had not taken kindly to Kamran's overly aggressive counsel, and had all but called him an unschooled child for daring to suggest a preemptive attack on Tulanian soil.

Kamran did not care.

It was true that these men had the benefit of age and decades of experience to support their ideas, but so too had they been idle in the last several years of peace, preferring to laze about on their large estates, abandoning their wives and children to toss coin instead at courtesans; to dull their minds with opium.

Kamran, meanwhile, had actually been reading the weekly reports sent in from the divisions.

There were fifty divisions spanning the empire, each comprising ten thousand soldiers, and each commanded by a major general whose job, among others, was to compile weekly briefings based on essential findings from lower battalions and regiments.

These fifty disparate briefings were then issued *not* to direct superiors, but to the defense minister, who read the materials and disseminated pertinent information to the king and his five lieutenant generals. Fifty briefings from across the empire, each five pages long.

That made for two hundred and fifty pages a week.

Which meant every month, a thousand pages of essential material was bequeathed to a single unctuous man upon whom the king himself relied for critical intelligence and instruction.

This, *this* was where Kamran lost his patience.

The dissemination of key information through a defense minister was an ancient practice, one that had been established during wartime to spare the highest-ranking officials the critical hours that might otherwise be spent poring over hundreds of pages of material. Once upon a time, it had made sense. But Ardunia had been at peace now for seven years, and still his fellow lieutenants did not read the reports for themselves, relying instead upon a minister who grew only more unqualified by the hour.

Kamran had long ago circumvented this impotent practice, preferring to read the briefings in full through the lens of his own mind and not the minister's.

Had anyone else in the room bothered to read the sitrep from these different reaches of the empire they might see as Kamran did: that the observations were at once fascinating and worrying, and together drew a bleak picture of Ardunia's relations with the southern kingdom of Tulan. Sadly, they did not.

Kamran's jaw clenched.

"Indeed," the minister was droning on, "it is often to our benefit to maintain a sense of rivalry with another powerful nation, for a common enemy helps keep the citizens of our empire united, reminding the people to be grateful for the safety promised not only by the crown, but by the military—to which their children will devote four years of their lives, and whose movements have been so well calculated in this last century, under the guidance of our merciful king.

"Our prince was divinely blessed to inherit the fruits of a kingdom built tirelessly over many millennia. Indeed the empire he is one day to inherit is now so magnificent it stands as the largest of the known world, having so successfully conquered its many enemies that its millions of citizens may now enjoy a stretch of well-deserved peace."

By the angels, the man refused to shut his mouth.

"Surely there is proof in this, is there not?" the minister was saying. "Proof not only of Ardunia's skillful leadership, but in the collective wisdom of its leaders. It is our hope that His Highness, the prince, will see in time that his experienced elders—who are also his most humble servants—have worked diligently to make thoughtful, considered decisions at every turn, for certainly we can see how—"

"*Enough.*" Kamran stood up with such force he nearly knocked over his chair.

This was madness.

He could neither continue sitting here in this damned hair shirt, nor could he listen any longer to these insipid excuses.

The minster blinked slowly, his vacant eyes shining like glass beads. "I beg your pardon, Your Highness, bu—"

"Enough," Kamran said again, angrily. "Enough of your blathering. Enough of your insufferable stupidity. I can no longer listen to another ridiculous word that comes out of your mouth—"

"Your Highness," Hazan cried, jumping to his feet. He shot Kamran a look of death and dire warning, and Kamran, who was usually in far better control of his faculties, could not summon the presence of mind to care.

"Yes, I see," Kamran said, looking his minister in the eye. "You've made it plain: you think me young and foolish. Yet I am not so young and foolish as to be blind to your ill-concealed passive aggressions, your weak attempts to pacify my genuine concerns. Indeed I know not how many times I will need to remind you, gentlemen"—he looked around the room now—"that I have only a week ago returned from an eighteen-month tour of the empire, in addition to recently accompanying our admiral on a treacherous water journey, during which half our men nearly drowned after we collided with an invisible barrier near the border of Tulan.

Upon arrival in Ardunia, traces of magic were found on the hull of our ship—"

Gasps. Whispers.

"—a discovery which should concern everyone in this room. We have been at odds with Tulan for centuries, and sadly, I suspect our incumbent officials have grown comfortable with that which has become commonplace. You seem to grow blind when you turn your gaze south," the prince said sharply. "No doubt our exchanges with Tulan have become as familiar to you as your own bowel movements—"

There were several protests at that, exclamations of outrage that Kamran ignored, instead raising his voice to be heard above the din.

"—so familiar, in fact, that you no longer see an obvious threat for what it is. Let me refresh your memories, gentlemen!" Kamran pounded the table with his fist, calling to order the moment of chaos. "In the last two years," he said, "we have captured sixty-five Tulanian spies, who even under extensive duress would not reveal more than limited information about their interests in our empire. With great effort we were able to conclude only that they seek something of value here; something they hope to mine from our land, and recent reports indicate that they are nearing their goal—"

More protests broke out at this, and Hazan, who'd gone scarlet to his hairline, looked as if he might soon strangle the prince for his effrontery.

"I say, gentlemen," Kamran said, shouting now to be heard. "I say I do much prefer this method of discourse, and I would encourage you to direct your anger at me more regularly, so that I might respond to you in kind. We are discussing *war* are we not? Should we not shed the delicacy with which we approach these hardened subjects? I confess that when you speak to me in circles I find it both detestable"—he raised his voice further—"both detestable and tiresome, and I do wonder whether you hide behind wordplay merely to disguise your own ignorance—"

"*Your Highness*," Hazan cried.

Kamran met his minister's eyes, finally acknowledging the barely restrained wrath of the only man in the room he marginally respected. The prince took a steadying breath, his chest lifting with the effort.

"Yes, Minister?"

Hazan's voice all but shook with fury as he spoke. "It has only just occurred to me, sire, that I require your immediate guidance on a matter of great importance. Might I convince you to meet me outside so that we might discuss this crucial business at once?"

At that, the fight left Kamran's body.

It was no fun to fight a horde of idiots when Hazan suffered an apoplectic fit as a result. He tilted his head at his old friend. "As you wish, Minister."

The remaining officials exploded with outrage in their wake.

Hazan said nothing until he'd all but bullied the prince up to his chambers, where, only once the rooms had been cleared of servants, did he close the door.

Were Kamran in a different frame of mind, he might've

laughed at the demented look in Hazan's eyes.

The young man had gone nearly purple.

"What the devil is the matter with you?" Hazan said with dangerous calm. "You ordered these men to leave their posts—for some, dozens of miles away—on a *whim* for what you deemed an essential meeting—and then you all but rip their throats out? Are you mad? You will lose their respect before you've even claimed the throne, which y—"

"You don't mind if I ring for tea, do you? I'm quite parched." Kamran pulled the bell without waiting for a response, and his minister sputtered at the impertinence.

"You ring for tea? Now?" Hazan had gone rigid with anger. "I'm of a mind to snap your neck, sire."

"You lack the heart to snap my neck, Hazan. Do not pretend otherwise."

"You underestimate me, then."

"No, Minister. I only know that, deep down, you thoroughly enjoy your position, and I daresay you can't imagine your life without me."

"You are deluded, Your Highness. I imagine my life without you all the time."

Kamran raised his eyebrows. "But you do not deny that you enjoy your position."

There was a brief, taut silence before Hazan sighed, reluctantly. The sound severed the tension between them, but was chased quickly by an epithet.

"Come now, Hazan," the prince was saying. "Surely you can see the logic in my arguments. Those men are idiots. Tulan will come for all our throats soon enough, and then they will see, too late, how blind they've been."

Hazan shook his head. "These *idiots*, as you call them, make up the necessary framework of your empire. They've been loyal to Ardunia since before you were born. They know more about your own history than you do, and they deserve your basic respect—"

There was a sharp knock at the door, and Hazan halted his speech to answer it, intercepting the tea tray before the servant could enter the room. He kicked the door shut, placed the tray down on a nearby table, poured them both a cup, and said—

"Go on, then. I believe I was in the middle of making an excellent point, and you were just about to interrupt me."

Kamran laughed, took a quick sip of tea, and promptly swore out loud. "Why is this tea so hot?"

"Apologies, sire. I'd always hoped that one day your tongue might be irreparably damaged. I see now that my prayers were answered."

"Good God, Hazan, you should be shot." The prince shook his head as he placed the teacup on a low table. "Pray tell me," he said, turning to face his minister. "Tell me why— *why* am I considered the fool when I am in fact the sole voice of reason?"

"You are a fool, sire, because you act like a fool," Hazan said impassively. "You know better than to insult your peers and subordinates in the pursuit of progress. Even if you make a good point, this is not how it's done. Nor is this the time to court enemies in your own house."

"Yes, but is there ever a time for that? Later, perhaps?

Tomorrow? Would you make the appointment?"

Hazan threw back the last of his tea. "You are acting the part of a ridiculous, spoiled prince. I cannot countenance your recklessness."

"Oh, leave me be."

"How can I? I expect more from you, sire."

"No doubt that was your first mistake."

"You think I don't know why you pick fights today? I do. You sulk because the king intends to host a ball in your honor, because he has bade you choose a wife from a bevy of beautiful, accomplished, intelligent women—and you would much rather take up with the one destined to kill him." Hazan shook his head. "Oh, how you suffer."

Kamran had reached for the teapot and froze now mid-movement. "Minister, do you mock me?"

"I'm only making the evident observation."

Kamran straightened, the tea forgotten. "And yet the observation that is so evident to you renders me, in the same breath, an insensate human being. Tell me: do you think me incapable of suffering? Am I so unworthy of the experience?"

"With all due respect, sire, I don't believe you know what it is to suffer."

"Indeed?" Kamran sat back. "What sage wisdom from my minister. You've been inside my mind, have you? You've taken a tour of my soul?"

"Enough of this," Hazan said quietly. He would no longer look at the prince. "You are being absurd."

"Absurd?" Kamran said, picking up his glass. "You think me absurd? A girl is going to die tonight, Hazan, and her death was provoked by my own arrogance."

"Spoken like a vainglorious fool."

Kamran smiled, but it was a tortured expression. "And yet? Is it not true? That I was so determined to doubt a poor servant girl? That I thought her so incapable of such basic decency as to show mercy to a hungry child that I had her hunted, her blood dissected?"

"Don't be stupid," Hazan said, but Kamran could tell his heart wasn't in it. "You know it is more than that. You know it is about far more than you."

Kamran shook his head.

"I have sentenced her to death, Hazan, and you know that is true. It's why you were loath to tell me who she was that night. You knew even then what I had wrought."

"Yes. That." Hazan dragged a hand down his face. He looked tired suddenly. "And then I saw you with her, in the street that night. You miserable liar."

Kamran lifted his head slowly. He felt his pulse pick up.

"Oh yes," Hazan said quietly. "Or did you think me so incapable of finding you in a rainstorm? I am not blind, am I? Neither am I deaf, unfortunately."

"How very accomplished you are," Kamran said softly. "I admit I had no idea my minister aspired to the stage. I suspect you'll be changing careers imminently."

"I'm quite satisfied where I am, thank you." Hazan shot a sharp look at the prince. "Though I think it is I who should be congratulating you, sire, on your fine performance that evening."

"All right. Enough," said Kamran, exhausted. "I've let you

berate me at your leisure. No doubt we've both had our fill of this unpleasantness."

"Nevertheless," Hazan said. "You cannot convince me that your concern for the girl is all about the goodness of her heart—or yours, for that matter. You are perhaps in part moved by her innocence; yes, I might be persuaded to believe that; but you are also at war within yourself, reduced to this state by an illusion. You know nothing of this girl, meanwhile it has been foretold by our esteemed Diviners that she is to usher in the fall of your grandfather. With all due respect, sire, your feelings on the subject should be uncomplicated."

At that, Kamran fell silent, and a quiet minute stretched out between them.

Finally, Hazan sighed. "I admit I could not see her face that night. Not the way you did. But I gather the girl is beautiful?"

"No," said the prince.

Hazan made a strange sound, something like a laugh. "No? Are you quite certain?"

"There's little point in discussing it. Though if you saw her, I think you would understand."

"I think I understand enough. I must remind you, sire, that as your home minister, my job is to keep you safe. My chief occupation is ensuring the security of the throne. Everything I do is to keep you alive, to protect your interests—"

Kamran laughed out loud. Even to himself he sounded a bit mad. "Don't fool yourself, Hazan. You have not protected my interests."

"Removing a threat to the throne is a protection of your

interests. It does not matter how beautiful the girl is, or how kind. I will remind you once more that you do not know her. You've never spoken more than a few words to the girl—you could not know her history, her intentions, or of what she might be capable. You must put her out of your mind."

Kamran nodded, his eyes searching the tea leaves at the bottom of his cup. "You do realize, Minister, that by having the girl murdered my grandfather is ensuring that she remains embedded in my mind forever?"

Hazan released a breath, exhaling an obvious frustration. "Do you not see what power she already holds over you? This young woman is your direct enemy. Her very existence is a threat to your life, to your livelihood. And yet—look at yourself. Reduced to these infantile behaviors. I fear, sire, you will be disappointed to discover that your mind at the moment is as common and predictable as the infinite others who came before you. You are neither the first nor the last man on earth to lose his sensibilities over a pretty face.

"Does it not frighten you, sire? Are you not terrified to imagine what you might do for her—what you might do to yourself—if she became suddenly real? If she were to become flesh and blood under your hands? Does this not strike you as a terrible weakness?"

Kamran felt his heart move at the thought, at the mere imagining of her in his arms. She was everything he'd never realized he wanted in his future queen: not just beauty, but grace; not just grace, but strength; not just strength, but compassion. He'd heard her speak enough to know she was not only educated but intelligent, proud but not arrogant.

Why should he not admire her?

And yet, Kamran did not hope to save her for himself. Hazan might not believe it, but the prince didn't care: saving the girl's life was about so much more than himself.

For to kill her—

To kill her now, innocent as she was, seemed to him as senseless as shooting arrows at the moon. That kind of light was not so easily extinguished, and what was there to celebrate in a success that would only leave the earth dimmer as a result?

But did it frighten him, the power she wielded over his emotions in so brief a time? Did it frighten him what he might be driven to do for such a girl if she became real? What he might be inspired to give up?

He drew a sudden breath.

No, it was not merely frightening. It felt more like terror; a feverish intoxication. Of all the young women to want, it was madness to want her. It shook him to admit this truth even in the privacy of his mind, but his feelings could no longer be denied.

Did it frighten him?

Quietly, he said, "Yes."

"Then it is my job," Hazan said softly, "to make certain she disappears. With all possible haste."

NINETEEN

نوزده

MRS. AMINA WAS A STRANGE woman.

It was a thought Alizeh could not shake as she pushed through the dark, ducking her head against the blustery wind of yet another brutally cold night. She was on her way to Fol-lad Place—the grand home of the Lojjan ambassador—for what was doubtless one of the most important appointments of her short career. As she walked she could not help but reflect not only on the day's many strange events, but on the mercurial housekeeper without whose permission they might not have occurred.

Alizeh had timed her exit from Baz House that evening so she'd not be noticed by Mrs. Amina; for though Alizeh was not breaking any rules by leaving the house after the day's work was done, she remained wary of having to explain to anyone what she was doing in her spare time, least of all Mrs. Amina. The woman had so often threatened Alizeh for putting on airs that Alizeh worried she'd be seen as reaching above her station by pursuing extra work as a seamstress.

Which indeed she was.

Alizeh had been struck dumb, then, when Mrs. Amina had come upon her just as Alizeh made to leave, one hand reaching for the door, the other clutching the handle of her modest carpet bag, which she'd fashioned herself. Alizeh had been but a sturdy three-year-old the day she climbed up onto the bench of a loom, settling her small bottom between the warm bodies of her parents. She'd watched their deft hands work magic even without a pattern, and had demanded right then to be taught.

When her mother died, and Alizeh sank into a resolute stoicism, she'd forced her trembling fingers to work. It was during this dark time that she'd fashioned the carpet bag she carried with her always—that which housed her sewing supplies and few precious belongings—and which she dis-assembled whenever she found a place to rest. Most days it remained on the ground next to her cot, transformed into a small rug she used for much appreciated warmth in the room.

She'd been carrying it the day she arrived at Baz House.

Tonight the housekeeper had appraised Alizeh upon her exit, examining the girl from crown to boot, her keen eyes settling just a bit too long on the bag.

"Not running away, are we?" Mrs. Amina had said.

"No, ma'am," Alizeh said quickly.

The housekeeper almost smiled. "Not before the ball tomorrow night, anyway."

Alizeh dared not breathe at that; dared not speak. She held still for so long her body began to shake, and Mrs. Amina laughed. Shook her head.

"What a strange girl you are," she said quietly. "To behold a rose and perceive only its thorns, never the bloom."

Alizeh's heart thudded painfully in her chest.

The housekeeper studied Alizeh a moment longer before

her expression changed; moods shifting as reliably as the phases of the moon. Sharply, she said, "And don't you dare forget to bank the fire before you go to bed."

"No, ma'am," said Alizeh. "I would never."

Mrs. Amina had turned on her heel and stalked out of the kitchen after that, leaving Alizeh to step into the cold night, her mind spinning.

She walked along the road now with caution, taking care to remain as near as possible to the glow of the hanging gaslights as she went, for the bulk of her carpet bag was not only a bit difficult to handle, but would certainly attract unwanted attention.

Alizeh was seldom spared when she was out alone, though nighttime was always worse. A young woman of her station was reduced to such circumstances more often than not because she had no one upon whom to rely for her safety or well-being. As a result, she was more frequently accosted than others; considered an easy target by thieves and scoundrels alike.

Alizeh had learned to cope with this over time—had found ways to protect herself with small measures—but she was well aware that it was her many physical strengths that'd saved her from worse fates over the years. It was easy, then, for her to imagine how many young women in her position had suffered greater blows than she ever would, though the understanding offered her cold comfort.

The sharp trill of a nightjar suddenly pierced the silence, the sound promptly followed by the hoot of an eagle owl. Alizeh shivered.

What had she been thinking about?

Ah, yes, Mrs. Amina.

Alizeh had been working at Baz House for nearly five months now, and in that time the housekeeper had shown her both unexpected kindness and stunning cruelty. She'd strike the girl across the face for minor infractions, but never once fail to remember Alizeh's promised allotment of water. She'd threaten the girl constantly, finding fault in faultless work, and demand Alizeh do it again, and again. And then, for no apparent reason at all, she'd permit the lowest ranked servant in the house a fifteen-minute audience with a questionable guest.

Alizeh did not know what to make of the woman.

She realized her musings were strange—strange to be pondering the strangeness of a housekeeper who was doubtless strange even to herself—but this evening was quieter than she liked, causing her hands to twitch from more than mere cold. Alizeh's reliable, creeping fear of the dark had evolved from uncomfortable to unsettling in the last several minutes, and with so much less to distract the senses tonight than the evening prior, she needed to keep her thoughts loud, and her wits about her.

This last bit was harder to achieve than she'd have hoped. Alizeh felt sluggish as she moved, her eyes begging to close even with the incessant snap of winter against her cheeks. Mrs. Amina had worked the girl to within an inch of her life in the wake of Omid's visit, tempering a single act of generosity with swift punishment. It was almost as if the housekeeper had sensed Alizeh's happiness and had made it her business to disabuse the girl of such fanciful notions.

It was unfortunate, then, that Mrs. Amina had very nearly accomplished her goal.

By the end of the workday Alizeh had been so ragged with exhaustion she'd startled when she walked past a window and discovered it dark. She'd been abovestairs most of the day and hardly noticed when the sun was siphoned off into the horizon, and even now, as she stepped from one pool of gaslit cobblestone to another, she could not fathom where the day had gone, or what joys it once held.

The glow of Omid's visit had faded in the aftermath of many hours of physical toil, and her melancholy was made worse by what seemed the permanent loss of her firefly. Alizeh realized only in its absence that she'd conjured an unreasonable amount of hope at the insect's initial appearance; the sudden and complete loss of the creature made her think the firefly had found her only by mistake, and that upon realizing its error, had left to begin a fresh search.

A shame, for Alizeh had been looking forward to meeting its owner.

The walk from Baz House to Follad Place came to an abrupt and startling finish; Alizeh had been so lost in her own thoughts, she'd not realized how quickly she'd covered the distance. Her spirits lifting at the prospect of imminent warmth and lamplight, she headed eagerly to the servants' entrance.

Alizeh stamped her feet against the cold before knocking twice at the imposing wooden door. She wondered, distantly, whether she'd be able to use some of her new earnings to buy a bolt of wool for a proper winter coat.

Maybe even a hat.

Alizeh wedged her carpet bag between her legs, crossed her arms tightly against her chest. It was far more painful to remain unmoving in this weather. True, Alizeh was unnaturally cold at all times—but it really was an uncommonly frigid night. She peered up at the staggering reach of Follad Place, its sharp silhouette pressed in relief against the night sky.

Alizeh knew it to be rare for an illegitimate child to be raised in such a noble home, but it was said that the Lojjan ambassador was an unusual man and had cared for Miss Huda alongside his other children in relative equality. Though Alizeh doubted the veracity of this rumor, she did not dwell upon it. She'd never met Miss Huda, and did not think her own uninformed opinions on the matter would make a jot of difference in the facts as they stood now:

Alizeh was lucky to be here.

Miss Huda was as close to high society as her commissions had ever come, and she'd only even been granted the commission via Miss Huda's lady's maid, a woman named Bahar, who'd once stopped Alizeh in the square to offer a compliment on the draping of her skirts. Alizeh had seen an opportunity there and had not squandered it; she quickly informed the young woman that she was a seamstress in her spare hours and offered such services at excellent prices. It was not long thereafter that she'd been engaged to fashion the woman a wedding gown, which her mistress, Miss Huda, had then admired at the ceremony.

Alizeh took a deep, steadying breath. It had been a long and circuitous path to this moment, and she would not fritter it away.

She knocked on the door once more, a bit harder this time—and this time, it opened immediately.

"Yes, girl, I heard you the first time," Mrs. Sana said irritably. "Get inside, then."

"Good evening, ma'am, I was j— *Oh*," Alizeh said, and startled. Something like a pebble had struck her against the cheek. She looked up, searching the clear sky for hail.

"Well? Come on, then," Mrs. Sana was saying, waving her forward. "It's cold as death out there and you're letting all the heat out."

"Yes, of course. I beg your pardon, ma'am." Alizeh quickly crossed the threshold, but instinct bade her look back at the last moment, her eyes searching the dark.

She was rewarded.

Before her eyes burned a single, disembodied prick of light. In a flash it moved, striking her again on the cheek.

Oh.

Not hail, then, but a firefly! Was it the same as before? What were the odds that she should be found by two different fireflies in such a short window of time? Very low, she considered.

And *there*—

Her eyes widened. Just there, in the tall hedge. Was that a flutter of movement?

Alizeh turned to ask the firefly a question and promptly froze, lips parted around the shape of the interrogative.

She could scarcely believe it.

The fickle creature had disappeared for the second time. Frustrated, Alizeh returned her gaze to the shadows, trying again to see through veils of darkness.

This time, she saw nothing.

"If I have to tell you to get inside one more time, girl, I'll simply push you out the door and be done with it."

Alizeh started, then scrambled without delay across the threshold, stifling a shudder as a rush of warmth gathered around her frozen body.

"Forgive me, ma'am— I just thought I saw—"

A glowering Mrs. Sana pushed past her and slammed the door shut, nearly snapping off Alizeh's fingers in the process.

"Yes?" the housekeeper demanded. "What did you see?"

"Nothing," Alizeh said quickly, pulling the carpet bag up into her arms. "Forgive me. Do let us begin."

TWENTY

بیست

NIGHT HAD COME TOO QUICKLY.

Kamran lay sprawled across his bed in nothing but a scowl, crimson sheets tangling around his limbs. His eyes were open, staring into the middle distance, his body slack as if submerged in a bath of blood.

He cut a dramatic figure.

The sea of dark red silk that enveloped him served to compliment the bronze tones of his skin. The golden glow of the artfully arranged lamps further sculpted the contours of his body, depicting him more as statue than sentient being. But then Kamran would not have noticed such things even had he cared to try.

He had not chosen these sheets. Nor the lamps.

He'd not chosen the clothes in his wardrobe, or the furnishings in his room. All he owned that were truly his were his swords, which he'd forged himself, and which he carried with him always.

All else in his life was an inheritance.

Every cup, every jewel, every buckle and boot came with a price, an expectation. A legacy. Kamran hadn't been asked to choose; instead, he'd been ordered to obey, which had never before struck him as particularly cruel, for his was not such a difficult life. He had struggles, certainly, but Kamran owned no proclivity for fairy tales. He wasn't so deluded as to imagine he might be happier as a peasant, nor did he dream of living a humble life with a woman of common stock and weak intelligence.

His was a life he'd never before questioned, for it had never before constrained him. He'd wanted for nothing, and as a result deigned not to lower himself to the experience of desire, for desire was the pastime of poorer men, men whose only weapons against the world's cruelty were their imaginations.

Kamran desired nothing.

He cared little for food, for it had always been abundant. He looked upon material objects with contempt, for nothing was rare or uncommon. Gold, jewels, the most singular objects on earth—had he cared even a little he'd need only tell Hazan, and all that he wanted would be procured. But what were such trifles worth? Who did he hope to impress with baubles and trinkets?

No one.

He detested conversation, for there was always an abundance of callers, endless invitations, doubtless hundreds of thousands—if not millions—across the empire who wished to speak with him.

Women—

Women, he desired least of all. For what appeal was there in an arrangement with no uncertainty? Every eligible woman he'd ever met would happily have him even had they found him eminently unworthy.

Women were perhaps his greatest plague.

They hounded him, haranguing him en masse whenever he was forced, by order of the king, to give them cause. He shuddered even at the memories of his rare appearances at court, social events at which his presence was required. He was suffocated by imitations of beauty, of poorly disguised ambition. Kamran did not possess the necessary stupidity to desire anyone who sought only to claim his money, his power, his title.

The very idea filled him with revulsion.

There was once a time when he'd thought to look beyond his own society for companionship, but it was quickly revealed to him that he'd never get on with an uneducated woman, and as a result, could never look beyond his peers. Kamran could not countenance dullards of any vintage; not even the most extraordinary beauty could recompense, in his mind, for brainlessness. He'd learned this lesson thoroughly in the first flush of youth, when he'd been foolish enough to be taken in by a pretty face alone.

Since then, Kamran had been disappointed over and over by the young women foisted upon him by their sycophantic guardians. As he did not, and would never, possess the infinite time required to comb through hordes of women on his own, he'd promptly extinguished any expectations he might've once had with regard to marriage. Dismissing the possibility of his own happiness had made it easy to accept his fate: that the king—and his mother—would choose him the most suitable bride. Even in a partner, he had learned to want and hope for nothing, resigning himself instead to what seemed inevitable.

Duty.

It was too bad, then, that the sole object of the young man's first and only desire was now—he glanced up at the clock—yes, almost certainly dead.

Kamran dragged himself out of bed, tied on a dressing robe, and walked over to the tea tray set down earlier by his minister. The simple service had been abandoned there hours ago: silver teapot, two short tea glasses, a copper bowl filled with jagged, freshly cut sugar cubes. There was even a small painted plate laden with thick dates.

Kamran lifted his cup from the tray, weighed it in his hand. The glassware was no bigger than his palm and shaped a bit like an hourglass; it was without a handle, meant to be held by the rim alone. He cradled the cup now in a loose fist, curling his fingers around its small body. He wondered whether he should exert a bit more pressure, whether he should crush the delicate drinkware in his hand, whether the glass might then shatter and lacerate his skin. The pain, he thought, might do him good.

He sighed.

Carefully, he replaced the glass on the tray.

The prince poured himself a cold cup of tea, tucked a sugar cube between his teeth, and threw the drink back in a single shot, the bracing, bitter liquid cut only by the grit of the sugar cube dissolving slowly on his tongue. He licked a drop of tea from his lips, refilled the short cup, and began a slow walk around his room.

Kamran paused at the window, staring for a long while at the moon. He shot back the second cold cup of tea.

It was nearly two o'clock in the morning, but Kamran did not hope for sleep. He dared not close his eyes. He feared what he might see if he slept; what nightmares might plague him in the night.

It was his own fault, really.

He hadn't asked to know the details. He hadn't wanted to know how they'd come for her; he hadn't wanted to be alerted when the deed was done.

What Kamran hadn't realized, of course, was how much worse it would be to leave such details to his imagination.

He drew in a deep breath.

And startled, suddenly, at the sound of furious pounding at his door.

TWENTY-ONE

بیست و یک

THE ROARING FIRE CRACKLED MERRILY in its cove, so merrily, in fact, that Alizeh was struck by the oddest notion to envy the burning logs. Even after three hours—she glanced at the clock, it was just after midnight—of standing in a toasty room, she'd not been able to draw the frost from her body. She watched hungrily now as the flames licked the charred wood and, exhausted, closed her eyes.

The sound of burning kindling was comforting—and strange, too, for its pops and crackles were so similar to that of moving water. If she hadn't known it was fire beside her, Alizeh thought she might be convinced she was listening instead to the pitter-patter of a gentle rain; a staccato beat against the roof of her attic room.

How bizarre, she found herself thinking, that elements so essentially different could ever sound the same.

Alizeh had been waiting several minutes while Miss Huda tried on yet another dress, but she did not entirely mind the wait, for the fire was good company, and the evening had been pleasant enough.

Miss Huda had certainly been a surprise.

Alizeh heard the groan of a door and her eyes flew open; she quickly straightened. The young woman in question now entered the room, wearing what Alizeh could only hope was the last gown of the evening. Miss Huda had insisted on trying on every article in her wardrobe, all in the pursuit of proving a point that had already been made hours ago.

Goodness, but *this* gown really was hideous.

"There," Miss Huda said, pointing at Alizeh. "You see? I can tell merely from the set of your jaw that you hate it, and how right you are to disdain such a monstrosity. Do you see what they do to me? How I am forced to suffer?"

Alizeh walked over to Miss Huda and did a slow revolution around her, carefully examining the gown from every possible angle.

It had not taken long for Alizeh to comprehend why Miss Huda had granted an unproven nobody such an opportunity with her attire. Within minutes of meeting the young woman, in fact, Alizeh had understood nearly all there was to understand.

Indeed, it had been a relief to understand.

"Am I not the very picture of a trussed walrus?" Miss Huda was saying. "I look a fool in every gown, you see? I'm either bulging out or pinched in; a powdered pig in silk slippers. I could run away to the circus and I daresay they'd have me." She laughed. "I swear sometimes I think Mother does it on purpose, merely to vex me—"

"Forgive me," Alizeh said sharply.

Miss Huda ceased speaking, though her mouth remained open in astonishment. Alizeh could not blame her. A snoda was a mere tier above the lowest scum of society; Alizeh could scarce believe her own audacity.

She felt her cheeks flush.

"Forgive me, truly," Alizeh said again, this time quietly. "It is not my intention to be discourteous. It's only that I've listened silently all evening while you've disparaged yourself and your looks, and I begin to worry that you will mistake my silence as an endorsement of your claims. Please allow me to make myself unambiguously plain: your criticisms strike me not only as unfair, but fabricated entirely from fantasy. I would implore you never again to make unflattering comparisons of yourself to circus animals."

Miss Huda stared at her, unblinking, her astonishment building to its zenith. To Alizeh's great consternation, the young woman said nothing.

Alizeh felt a flutter of nerves.

"I fear I have shocked you," she said softly. "But as far as I can tell, your figure is divine. That you've been so thoroughly convinced otherwise says only to me that you've been injured by the work of indifferent dressmakers who've not taken the time to study your form before recommending its fit. And I daresay the solution to your troubles is quite simple."

At that, the young woman finally released an exaggerated sigh, collapsed onto a chaise longue, and closed her eyes against the glittering chandelier overhead. She threw an arm over her face as a single sob escaped her.

"If it is indeed as simple as you say then you must save me," she cried. "Mother orders identical gowns for me and all my sisters—merely in different colors—even though she *knows* my figure is markedly different from the others. She puts me in these horrid colors and all these horrendous ruffles, and I can't afford a traditional seamstress on my own, not with only my pin money to spend, and I'm afraid to breathe a word of it to Father, for if Mother finds out it'll only make things worse for me at home." She heaved another sob. "And now I've got nothing at all to wear to the ball tomorrow and I'll be the laughingstock of Setar, as usual. Oh, you cannot imagine how they torment me."

"Come now," Alizeh said gently. "There's no need to be overwrought when I am here to help. Come and I will show you how easily the situation can be mended."

With dramatic reluctance, Miss Huda dragged herself over to the circular dais built into the dressing room, nearly tripping over her abundant skirts in the process.

Alizeh attempted a smile at Miss Huda—she suspected they were nearly the same age—as the young woman stepped onto the low platform. Miss Huda returned the smile with an anemic one of her own.

"I really don't see how the situation can be salvaged," she said. "I thought I'd have time to get a new gown made in time for the ball, for I assumed the event would be weeks away—but now that it's nearly upon us Mother is insisting I wear *this*"—she faux-gagged, glancing down at the dress—"tomorrow night. She says she's already paid for it, and that if I don't wear it it's only because I'm an ungrateful wretch, and she's begun threatening to cut my pin money if I don't stop whining."

Alizeh studied her client a moment.

She'd been studying the young woman all night, really, but Alizeh had said very little in the three hours she'd been here.

As the night wore on it had become abundantly clear, however, through a series of offhand comments and anecdotes, that Miss Huda suffered a great deal of cruelty and unkindness throughout her life; not only due to her improper birth, but for all else about her that was judged uncommon or irregular. Her pain she unsuccessfully cloaked in a veneer of sarcasm and poorly feigned indifference.

Alizeh snapped open her carpet bag.

She carefully buttoned her pincushion around her wrist, buckled her embroidered toolbelt around her waist, and unspooled the measuring tape in her bandaged hands.

Miss Huda, Alizeh knew, was not only uncomfortable in her gowns, but in her own body—and Alizeh understood that she would accomplish nothing at all if she did not first manage to activate the girl's confidence.

"Let us, for the moment, forget about your mother and your sisters, shall we?" Alizeh smiled wider at the young woman. "First, I'd like to point out that you have beautiful skin, whi—"

"I most certainly do not," said Miss Huda automatically. "Mother tells me I've grown too brown and that I should wash my face more often. She also tells me my nose is too big for my face, and my eyes too small."

It was some kind of miracle that Alizeh's smile did not waver, not even as her body tensed with anger. "Goodness," she said, struggling to keep the disdain from her voice. "What strange things your mother has said to you. I must say I think your features fine, and your complexion quite beautif—"

"Are you blind, then?" Miss Huda snapped, her scowl

deepening. "I would ask you not to insult me by lying to my face. You need not feed me falsehoods to earn your coppers."

Alizeh flinched at that.

The insinuation that she might be willing to swindle the girl for her coin cut a shade too close to Alizeh's pride, but she knew better than to allow such blows to land. No, Alizeh understood well what it was like to feel scared—so scared you feared even to hope, feared the pitfall of disappointment. Pain made people prickly sometimes. It was par for the course; a symptom of the condition.

Alizeh knew this, and she would try again.

"I mentioned your glowing complexion," she said carefully, "only because I wanted, first, to assure you that we are in possession of a bit of good luck tonight. The rich, jewel tones of this dress do you a great service."

Miss Huda frowned; she studied the green gown.

The dress was a shot silk taffeta, which gave the fabric an iridescent sheen, and which in certain light made it look more emerald than forest green. It was not at all the textile Alizeh would've chosen for the girl—next time, she would choose something more fluid, maybe a heavy velvet—but for the moment, she'd have to make do with the taffeta, which she believed could be repurposed beautifully. Miss Huda, on the other hand, remained visibly unconvinced, though not aggressively so.

It was a step forward.

"Now, then." Gently, Alizeh turned the girl to face the mirror. "I would ask you, secondly, to stand up straight."

Miss Huda stared at her. "I am standing up straight."

Alizeh forced a smile.

She stepped onto the dais, praying she'd come far enough into the girl's confidence tonight to be able to take certain liberties. Then, with a bit of force, she pressed the flat of her hand against Miss Huda's lower back.

The girl gasped.

Her shoulders drew back, her chest lifted, her spine straightened. Miss Huda raised her chin reflexively, staring at herself in the mirror with some surprise.

"Already," Alizeh said to her, "you are transformed. But this dress, as you see, is overwrought. You are statuesque, miss. You have prominent shoulders, a full bust, a strong waist. Your natural beauty is suffocated by all the fuss and restriction of the modern fashion. All these embellishments and flounces"—Alizeh made a sweeping gesture at the gown—"are meant to enhance the assets of a woman with a more modest figure. As your figure is in no need of enhancement, the exaggerated shoulders and bustle only overwhelm you. I would recommend, going forward, that we not mind what's currently en vogue; let us focus instead on what best complements your natural form."

Without waiting to be countermanded, Alizeh tore open the high neck, sending buttons flying across the room, one pelting the mirror with a dull *plink*.

Alizeh had learned by now that words had done too much damage to Miss Huda to be of any use. Three hours she'd listened quietly as the girl vented her frustrations, and now it was time to offer a prescription.

Alizeh procured a pair of scissors from her toolbelt, and,

after asking the startled girl to stand very, very still, she sliced open the inseams of the massive, puffed sleeves. She cut loose the remaining collar of the gown, splitting it open from shoulder to shoulder. She used a seam ripper to carefully strip the ruffles laid overtop the bodice, and opened the central darts compressing the girl's chest. Another few snips and she wrenched apart the pleated bustle, allowing the skirt to relax around the young woman's hips. As carefully as she could with her bandaged fingers, Alizeh then proceeded to drape and fold and pin an entirely new silhouette for the girl.

Alizeh transformed the high, ruffled neckline into an unembellished boatneck. She refashioned the bodice, carefully refining the darts so they emphasized the narrowest point of the girl's waist instead of restraining her bust, and reduced the monstrously puffed arms to simple, fitted bracelet sleeves. The skirt Alizeh draped more simply, adjusting the silk to flow around the young woman's hips in a single clean wave instead of many tight flounces.

When she was finally done, she stood back.

Miss Huda clasped a hand over her mouth. "Oh," she breathed. "Are you a witch?"

Alizeh smiled. "You need very little embellishment, miss. You can see here that I did nothing just now but remove the distractions from the gown."

Miss Huda went a bit slack when the fight finally left her body. She studied herself now with a cautious optimism, first drawing her fingers down the lines of the gown, then carefully touching those same fingers to her face, to the slant of her cheekbone.

"I look so elegant," Miss Huda said softly. "Nothing at all like a trussed walrus. What incomprehensible magic this is."

"It's not magic, I assure you," Alizeh said to her. "You have always been elegant, miss. I'm only sorry you've been tortured into thinking otherwise for so long."

Alizeh did not know what time it was when she finally left Follad Place, only that she was so exhausted she'd begun to feel dizzy. It had been at least an hour since the last time she'd checked the time, which meant that, if her calculations were correct, it was well past one o'clock in the morning. She would be spared only a handful of hours to sleep before the work bell tolled.

Her heart sank in her chest.

Alizeh forced her eyes open as she plodded along, even stopping to gently pinch her own cheeks when, in her fogginess, she thought she'd seen two moons in the sky.

She was carrying her carpet bag as carefully as possible in the bitter cold, for it now held Miss Huda's green gown, which she'd promised to finish mending before tomorrow's ball. Bahar, Miss Huda's lady's maid, would be arriving to retrieve the gown at eight o'clock, precisely one hour after Alizeh finished her shift.

She exhaled a sigh at that, staring for a moment at the icy plume her breath painted against the dark.

Alizeh had taken all of Miss Huda's measurements; the five additional gowns were to be designed however Alizeh saw fit, as per the young woman's instructions. This was both a boon and a burden, for while it gave Alizeh full artistic license, it also placed the whole of the sartorial responsibility on her shoulders.

Alizeh was at least grateful that the other gowns would not be due for another week. Already she couldn't imagine how she'd manage all of tomorrow's work in addition to finding something suitable for herself to wear to the ball, but she consoled herself with the reminder that what she wore would not matter, for no one would be looking at her anyway—and all the better.

It was just then that Alizeh heard an unusual sound.

It was unusual in that it was not a sound endemic to the night; it was more like the rasp of a kicked pebble, a skittering there and gone in a flash.

It was enough.

Sleep fled her brain as adrenaline moved through her body, heightening her senses. Alizeh dared not break her stride; dared not speed up or slow down. She acknowledged, quietly, that the sound could've been provoked by an animal. Or a large insect. She might've even blamed the wind except that there was no breeze.

There was in fact no evidence to support Alizeh's sudden, chilling fear that she was being followed, none but a basic instinct that cost her nothing to take seriously. If she should appear foolish for overreacting, so be it.

Alizeh would take no chances at this hour.

As casually as she could manage, she hefted the carpet bag up, into her arms, and snapped it open. As she walked, she strapped her pincushion to her left wrist, pulling free handfuls of the sharp objects and tucking several needles between each of her knuckles. She retrieved her sewing scissors next, which she kept clenched in her right fist.

The footsteps—soft, nearly undetectable—she heard soon thereafter.

Alizeh dropped her carpet bag to the ground, felt her heartbeat rocket in her chest. She stood planted to the pavement, chest heaving as she bade herself be calm.

She then closed her eyes and listened.

There was more than one pair of footsteps. How many, then? Four. Five.

Six.

Who would send six men to chase down a defenseless servant girl? Her pulse raced, her thoughts spinning. Only someone who knew who she was, who knew what she might be worth. Six men sent to intercept her in the dead of night, and they'd found her here, halfway to Baz House, far from the safety of her own room.

How had they known where she was? How long had they been tracking her? And what else had they learned?

Alizeh's eyes flew open.

She felt her body tense with awareness, go suddenly solid with calm. Six heavily shadowed figures—each clad in black—approached her slowly from all sides.

Alizeh sent up a silent prayer then, for she knew she would require forgiveness before the night was done.

The assailants had her completely surrounded when she finally broke the silence with a single word:

"Wait."

The six forms came to a surprised halt.

"You do not know me," she said quietly. "You are no doubt indifferent to me and do not personally harbor me ill will. You are performing your duty tonight. I realize that."

"What's yer point?" one of them said gruffly. "Let's get on wiff it then if yer so understandin'. Business to do an' all 'at."

"I am offering you amnesty," Alizeh said. "I give you my word: walk away now and I will spare you. Leave in peace now and I will do you no harm."

Her words were met with a roar of laughter, guffaws that filled the night.

"My, wot cheek," a different man cried. "I think I will be sorry, miss, to kill ye tonight. I do promise to make it quick, though."

Alizeh briefly closed her eyes, disappointment flooding her body. "Then you are formally declining my offer?"

"Yes, Yer Highness." Another mocked her, feigning a bow with flourish. "We 'ave no need of yer mercy this night."

"Very well, then," she said softly.

Alizeh took a sharp breath, split the scissors open in her right hand, and lunged. She sent the blades flying, listening for contact—there, a cry—as a second assailant barreled toward her. She jumped, lifting her skirts as she spun and kicked him straight across the jaw, the force of her blow sending his head so far back she heard his neck snap just in time to face down her third opponent, at whom she threw an embroidery needle, aiming for his jugular.

She missed.

He roared, tearing the needle from his flesh as he

unsheathed a dagger, charging toward her with an unrestrained fury. Alizeh wasted no time launching herself forward, landing an elbow in his spleen before punching him repeatedly in the throat, the carefully placed pins and needles in her fist puncturing his skin over and over in the process. When she was done with the man, she'd buried all her needles in his neck.

He collapsed to the ground with a thud.

The fourth and fifth came running at her together, each carrying a glinting scimitar. Alizeh didn't flee; instead she bolted toward them and—within inches of contact—promptly disappeared, grabbing their sword arms, breaking their wrists, and flipping them onto their backs. She rematerialized then, confiscated their curved swords, and dropped to one knee, burying a blade in each of their chests simultaneously.

The sixth man was right behind her. She spun around in the time it took him to blink, catching him, without warning, by the throat.

She lifted the man in the air with a single hand, slowly squeezing the life from his body.

"Now," she whispered, "you might consider telling me who sent you."

The man choked, his face purpling. With great effort, he shook his head.

"You were the last of the six to approach me," she said quietly. "Which means you are either the smartest—or the weakest. Either way, you will serve a purpose. If the former, you will know better than to cross me. If the latter, your cowardice will render you pliable."

"I don'"—he choked, with sputtering difficulty—"I don' understand ye."

"Return to your master," she said. "Tell them I wish to be left alone. Tell them to consider this a warning."

She then dropped the man to the ground, where he fell badly and twisted an ankle. He cried out, wheezing as he struggled upright.

"Get out of my sight," said Alizeh softly. "Before I change my mind."

"Yes, miss, r-right away, miss." The brute hobbled away then, as quickly as his bad leg would allow.

Only when he'd disappeared from view did Alizeh finally exhale. She looked around her, at the bodies littering the street. She sighed.

Alizeh did not enjoy killing people.

She did not take lightly the death of any living being, for not only was it a difficult and exhausting business, but it left her tremendously sad. Alizeh had tried, over the years, only to injure, never to kill. She'd tried over and over to negotiate. She tried always to be merciful.

They laughed in her face every time.

Alizeh had learned the hard way that an unprotected woman of small stature and low station would never be treated with respect by her enemies. They thought her stupid and incapable; they saw only weakness in her for being kind.

It never occurred to most people that Alizeh's compassionate spirit was wrought not from a frail naïveté, but from a ferocious pain. She did not seek to steep in her nightmares. She sought instead, every day, to outgrow them. And yet never once had her offers of mercy been accepted. Never once had others set aside their darkness long enough to allow Alizeh a reprieve from her own.

What choice was she left, then?

With a heavy heart, she pulled free her sewing scissors from the ruin of a man's chest, wiping the blades clean on his coat before tucking them into her bag. She searched the cobblestone for her embroidery needle, then pulled each of her pins free from yet another dead man's throat, taking care to clean each needle before putting it away.

Would she have to move again? she wondered. Would she have to rebuild again?

So soon?

She sighed once more, taking a moment to adjust her skirts before picking up her carpet bag, snapping it closed.

Alizeh was so tired she couldn't imagine walking the short rest of the way home, and yet—

There lay the road, and below her, two feet.

She did not possess wings, nor did she own a carriage or a horse. She'd not enough money for a hackney, and no one would be along to carry her.

As always, the girl would have to carry herself.

One foot in front of the other, one step at a time. She would remain focused until she got back to Baz House. She

still had to bank the kitchen fire, but she would manage it.
She would manage it all, somehow. Perhaps only then would
she finally be able t—

She gasped.

A single prick of light flashed before her eyes, there and
gone again.

Alizeh blinked, slowly. Her eyes were dry, in desperate
need of rest. Heavens, but she was too tired for this.

"I demand you show yourself," she said, frustrated. "I've
had quite enough of this game. Show yourself or let me get
on. I beg you."

At that, a figure suddenly materialized. It was a young
man in silhouette—Alizeh could not discern his face—and
he fell suddenly on one knee before her.

"Your Majesty," he said softly.

TWENTY-TWO

بیست و دو

WAS HE GOING MAD? KAMRAN wondered.

Who on earth would be pounding at his door—at this hour? He'd have known, surely, if the palace were under siege, would he not? Surely there'd have been more madness, more commotion? He'd seen nothing amiss from his window, through which he'd been staring just moments ago.

Still, Kamran hastily dressed himself, and was tugging on his boots when the pounding grew suddenly louder. He knew it an indulgence, but he drew his sword belt around his waist anyway, for it was a habit so fully embedded it could not be spared even then.

The prince finally went to the door, having hardly opened it before he went suddenly blind. Someone had thrown a sack over his head while another grabbed his arms, twisting them painfully behind his back.

Kamran cried out, shock and confusion rendering him briefly paralyzed before he remembered himself and knocked his head back hard enough to break the nose of the monstrous figure restraining him. The man roared with anger but did not loosen his hold quite enough, and worse: the second assailant swiftly tightened the hood around Kamran's neck, choking him.

The prince gasped for breath and promptly tasted leather;

someone had shoved a stone into his mouth from the outside of the hood, lashing it in place with a strip of material
now being tied around his skull. Kamran tried to shout, to
spit it out, but managed only muffled sounds of protest. He
threw his body around instead, thrashing as best he could,
but both men held him securely, one torturing his arms into
an unnatural position while the other bound the prince's
hands together.

It soon became obvious that these men had been ordered
only to kidnap, not to murder, for if they'd been ordered to
kill the prince they'd certainly have done so by now.

Here, Kamran had the advantage.

They needed to keep him alive—but to Kamran, his life
was worth little, and he was more than willing to lose it in
any struggle for his freedom.

What's more, he'd been spoiling for a fight.

All day the prince had been containing his rage, trying to
fight back the storm in his chest. This was a relief, then.

He would unleash it now.

Kamran struck out with his foot, kicking backward
between the assailant's legs as hard as he could manage. The
man cried out, finally loosening his grip just enough to give
Kamran an inch of leverage, which the prince then used to
full advantage, decking the second man with the weight of
his shoulder, then his knee. With mere seconds to spare he
succeeded in getting his wrists free from their unfinished
bindings, but Kamran was still blind as he moved; striking
out with unseeing blows, not caring where his fists landed,
or how many ribs he broke.

When he'd finally knocked back both men enough to spare himself the moments necessary to tear off his hood, Kamran promptly drew his sword, blinking against the sudden light, drawing in lungfuls of air.

He moved toward his two attackers with all possible calm, appraising them as he went. One large, one average. Both crouched, breathing hard, and bleeding heavily from their mouths and noses.

The larger of the two lunged at the prince without warning and Kamran pivoted gracefully, leveraging the man's own weight to flip the sod over his shoulder and onto the floor. The assailant landed with a resounding *crack* on his back, knocking not merely the air from his lungs but possibly the vertebrae from his spine.

Kamran then tensed his fingers around the hilt of his sword and advanced upon the second brute, who glanced nervously at the supine figure of his much-larger comrade before meeting the prince's eyes.

"Please, sire," the man said, holding up both hands, "we wish ye no harm; we was only doing as we was told—"

Kamran grabbed the man by the scruff of his neck, pressing the point of his blade against the other's throat until he drew blood. The man whimpered.

"Who sent you here?" Kamran said angrily. "What do you want from me?"

The lout shook his head; Kamran dug the blade a bit deeper.

The man squeezed his eyes shut. "Please, sire, we—"

"*Who sent you?*" Kamran cried.

"I did."

Kamran dropped the man at once, drawing away as suddenly as if he'd been set aflame. The assailant slumped to the floor and the prince turned slowly around, astonishment reducing his motor functions near to nothing. A drop of blood dripped from his sword, landed on his boot.

Kamran met his grandfather's eyes.

"You will join me directly," the king said, "as we have a great deal to discuss."

TWENTY-THREE

بیست و سه

ALIZEH STARED, STUNNED, AT THE figure bowing before her.

"Forgive me," the stranger said quietly. "I only meant to keep close to you tonight should you need assistance—which, clearly, you did not." Even in shadow, she saw a flash of his smile. "My firefly, however, is quite taken with you and insists on seeking your attention whenever the opportunity arises."

"It is your firefly, then?"

The stranger nodded. "Normally she's more obedient, but when she sees you she seems to forget me entirely, and has been accosting you against my wishes these last two days. She first disobeyed me the night you met her at Baz House—she'd darted through the kitchen door even as I expressly forbid it. I apologize for any frustration her impulsiveness has caused."

Alizeh blinked at him, bewildered. "Who are you? How do you know me? How did you know I might need help tonight?"

The stranger smiled broadly at that, a gleam of white in the dark. He then held out a gloved hand, within which was a small glass orb the size of a marble. "First," he said. "This is for you."

Alizeh went suddenly still.

She'd recognized the object at once; it was called a *nosta*, an old Tulanian word for *trust*. To say that they were rare was a gross understatement of the truth. Alizeh had not seen one since she was a child; she thought they'd been all but lost to time.

Carefully, Alizeh took the small object into her hand.

In all of history, only several nostas had ever been made, for their creation required an ancient magic of which only the Diviners were capable. Alizeh's parents had often told her that the magic in Tulan was different—stronger—than it was in Ardunia, for the southern empire, while small, had a more potent concentration of the mineral in its mountains, and a far greater population of Diviners, as a result. Many Jinn had fled to Tulan in the early Clay wars for precisely this reason; there was something about the mountains there that called to them, imbued them with power.

Or so Alizeh had heard.

The few nostas that ever existed in Ardunia were widely believed to have been stolen from Tulan; a few small mementos of many failed wars.

How this stranger had gotten his hands on something so precious, Alizeh could not even begin to imagine.

She looked down at him in astonishment. "This is for me?"

"Please consider it a token of my loyalty, Your Highness. Keep it with you always, so that you never need wonder who your enemies might be."

Alizeh felt her eyes prick with unexpected emotion.

"Thank you," she whispered. "I hardly know what to say."

"Then I would be so bold as to ask for your forgiveness. You have suffered all these years alone, never knowing how many of us quietly searched for you. We are so grateful to have found you now."

"We?"

"Yes. We." Another flash of a smile, though this one was somber. "Your presence was only recently made known to me, Your Majesty, and I have been waiting every day for the right moment to approach you. In the interim, I've been tracking your movements so that I might offer protection if you should need it."

As he spoke, the nosta glowed warm in her hand. She knew that if he lied even a little, the orb would turn to ice. Alizeh's mind spun so fast she could scarcely draw breath.

"You may rise," she whispered.

He did, unfolding slowly to reveal a body much broader than she first suspected.

"Step into the light," she said.

He moved into the glow of a nearby gaslight, the flames setting fire to his pale hair and eyes. He was well dressed and groomed; his clothes were cut from fine cloth, his camel hair overcoat tailored to perfection. Were it not for the nosta, she did not think she'd believe this young man was fighting for her cause. He looked too well fed.

She struggled now to know what to make of him.

Still, the longer she stared, the more she saw. He was handsome in an unexpected way, his face composed of many small imperfections that added up to something interesting.

Strong.

Strange, but his features reminded her slightly of Omid—the dusky color of his skin, the generous smattering of freckles across his face. It was only his pale hair that kept him from looking like a native of the south.

Alizeh took a deep, steadying breath.

"You likely do not remember my mother," the young man said quietly, "but she was a courtier. This was after the establishment of the Fire Accords, when Jinn were finally allowed to join the court freely; but she had been by that time so used to hiding who she was that she continued to keep her identity a secret."

Alizeh's mind began to turn. As the nosta warmed in her hand, she realized there was something about this story that sounded familiar.

"On one of her many evenings at court," he went on, "my mother overheard the late queen speaking about the prophecy, and she knew then th—"

"A prophecy?" Alizeh frowned, cutting him off. "A prophecy about me, you mean?"

The young man went suddenly still. For a long moment he said nothing.

"Sir?" Alizeh prompted.

"You must accept my many apologies, Your Highness." He sounded a bit worried now. "I did not realize you were unaware."

Now Alizeh's heart was pounding. "Unaware of what?"

"I fear I must again beg your forgiveness, for this story is a rather long one, and there is not enough time tonight to tell it. Once the matters of your safety are settled, I promise to explain everything in greater detail. But tonight I cannot be away for too long, or I will be missed."

Again, the nosta burned hot.

"I see," Alizeh breathed.

A prophecy. Had her parents known? Was this the real reason why she'd been hidden away? Why all who knew her had been murdered?

The young man went on: "Allow me to say now only that my mother was once, long ago, acquainted with your parents. She acted as their eyes from inside the palace walls, and would visit your home often, always with the updates she was able to glean from the court. Occasionally, she took me along. I cannot imagine you remember me, Your Majesty—"

"No," she whispered, disbelief coloring her voice. "Can it be true? Is it possible you once taught me to play jacks?"

In response, the smiling young man reached into his pocket, and presented her with a single hazelnut.

A sudden, painful emotion seized her body then; a relief so large she could hardly fathom its dimensions.

She thought she might cry.

"I have been waiting close to the crown, as my mother once did, for any news of your discovery. When I learned of your existence I began at once to make arrangements for your safe transfer. I take it you've received your invitation to the ball tomorrow night?"

Alizeh was still stunned, for a moment, into silence. "The ball?" she said finally. "Did you— Was that—?"

The stranger shook his head. "The original thought

belonged to the child. I saw an opportunity and assisted. The context will help us."

"I fear I've been rendered speechless," she said softly. "I can only thank you, sir. I struggle now to think of anything else to say."

And in a gesture of goodwill, she removed her snoda.

The young man started, stepped back. He stared at her with wide eyes, with something like apprehension. She watched him struggle to look at her without appearing to look at all, and the realization almost made her laugh.

She realized, too late, that she'd put him in an awkward position. Doubtless he thought she expected a review.

"I know my eyes make me hard to look at," said Alizeh gently. "It's the ice that does it, though I don't entirely understand why. I believe my eyes are in fact brown, but I experience with some frequency a sharp pain in my head, a feeling like a sudden frost. It's the onslaught of cold, I think, that kills their natural color. It's the only explanation I have for their flickering state. I hope you will be able to overlook my strangeness."

He studied her then as if he were trying to sear her image into his memory—and then looked sharply away, at the ground. "You do not look strange, Your Majesty."

The nosta glowed warm.

Alizeh smiled, restored her snoda. "You say you are making arrangements for my safe transfer—what does that mean? Where do you mean to take me?"

"I'm afraid I cannot say. It is better, for now, that you know as little as possible, in the case that our plans go awry and you are apprehended."

Again, the nosta glowed warm.

"Then how will I know to find you?"

"You will not. It is imperative that you arrive at the ball tomorrow night. Will you require assistance in accomplishing this?"

"No. I think not."

"Very good. My firefly will seek you out when the moment is right. You may count on her to lead the way. Forgive me, Your Majesty." He bowed. "It grows later by the minute, and I must now be gone. Already I have said too much."

He turned to leave.

"Wait," she said softly, grabbing his arm. "Will you not at least tell me your name?"

He stared at her bandaged hand on his arm for a beat too long, and when he looked up, he said, "I am Hazan, Your Majesty. You may depend on me with your life."

TWENTY-FOUR

بیست و چهار

KAMRAN SAID NOTHING AT ALL during the long walk with his grandfather, his mind spinning with all manner of confusion and betrayal. He swore to himself he wouldn't jump to any absolute conclusions until he heard the whole explanation from the king, but it grew harder by the minute to ignore the rage simmering in his blood, for they did not appear to be heading to the king's chambers, as Kamran had first assumed, and he could not envisage now where his grandfather was leading him.

Never in his life could he have imagined the king sending mercenaries to his room in the dead of night.

Why?

What had happened to their relationship in so brief a time as to inspire such cruelty? Such lunacy?

Luckily, the king did not keep him wondering for long.

The path they followed grew darker and colder as they went, the circuitous path growing both familiar and alarming. Kamran had wandered this way precious few times in his life, for he'd seldom had cause to visit the palace dungeons.

A bolt of panic branched up his spine.

His grandfather was still several paces ahead, and the prince heard the groan of a metal cage opening before he saw its primeval design. That a trio of torches had been lit in anticipation of his arrival was shocking enough, but that the illumination forced the coarse, clawed-out corners of this sinister space into sharp relief rendered this horror only too real. Kamran's fear and confusion further electrified as the steady drip of some unnamed liquid beat the ground between them, the smell of rot and wet filling his nose.

He had stepped into a nightmare.

Finally, King Zaal turned to face his grandson, and the prince, who even now should have bowed before his sovereign, remained standing.

Neither did he sheath his sword.

King Zaal stared at that sword now, studied the insolence of the young man with whom he shared these shadows. Kamran saw the barely restrained anger in his grandfather's eyes, the outrage he did little to hide.

No doubt similar feelings were mirrored upon Kamran's own face.

"As your king," the older man said coldly, "I charge you presently with the crime of treason—"

"*Treason?*" Kamran exploded. "On what basis?"

"—and sentence you to an indefinite period of imprisonment in the royal dungeons, whence you will be released only to perform your duties, during which you will remain under strict surveillance, and after which you will be retur—"

"You would sentence me to this fate without trial, Your Majesty? Without proof? Have you gone mad?"

King Zaal took a sharp breath, his chin lifting at the insult. It was a moment before he spoke.

"As your king, I decree that your guilt is such that you

forfeit a right to trial. But as your grandfather," he added, with uncommon calm, "I offer you this single meeting during which you may attempt to exonerate yourself.

"If you fail to argue your own innocence in a timely manner, I will order the guards to shackle you without delay. If you then insist on fighting this modified sentence for so heinous a crime, you will force upon yourself the full punishment for treason and await your execution at sunrise, at which time you will die an honorable death by sword, in a location yet to be determined, your head severed from your body and impaled on a pike for seven days and seven nights for all the empire to bear witness."

Kamran felt the blow of this declaration with his entire body, felt it shudder through him with breathtaking pain.

It left him hollow.

His grandfather—the man who'd raised him, who taught him most everything he knew, who'd been his role model all his life—was threatening him with execution? That King Zaal was even capable of such cruelty to his own kin was stunning enough, but more shattering was that Kamran could not begin to fathom what had brought them both to this moment.

Treason?

Briefly, Kamran wondered whether the minister of defense had accused him so, but Kamran struggled to believe the oily man had influence enough to move his grandfather to this level of anger. Had the minister complained to the king, Kamran would've more likely heard about it in the light of day; would've been chastised and sent on his way with a warning to behave himself.

But this—

This was different. The king had enlisted armed men to fetch him from his private rooms in the dead of night. This was bigger than a moment of childishness in a boardroom.

Was it not?

A tense stretch of silence spun out between them, a long minute during which Kamran was forced to make peace with the worst. Kamran was a prince, yes, but he was a soldier first, and this was not the first time he'd been faced with such brutality.

With forced calm, he said, "I confess I know not, Your Majesty, how to defend myself against so baseless an accusation. Even all these moments of silence have not inspired my imagination to conjure a suitable explanation for these charges. I cannot now attempt to justify that which I have no hope of understanding."

King Zaal released an angry rasp of a laugh, an exclamation of disbelief. "You deny, then—in full—any and all allegations leveled against you? You make no effort to plead your case?"

"I have no case to plead," Kamran said sharply, "for I know not why I stand here before you, nor why you would send men to my rooms to restrain me in such an inhumane manner. In what way have I committed treason, pray tell? At what point in time might I have managed such a feat?"

"You insist on feigning ignorance?" King Zaal said angrily, his right hand clenched tight around his golden mace. "You would insult me even now, to my face?"

A muscle jumped in Kamran's jaw. "I see now that your

mind is already decided against me. That you refuse even to tell me what crime I have committed is evidence enough. If you wish me imprisoned, so be it. If you desire my head, you may have it. Worry not that I will struggle, Your Majesty. I would not defy the orders of my king."

The prince finally sheathed his sword and bowed. He kept his gaze on the filthy, pockmarked stone floor of the dungeons for what seemed a century but was more likely minutes. Or seconds.

When King Zaal finally spoke, his voice was subdued. "The girl is not dead," he said.

Kamran looked up. It was a moment before he could speak, a brief head rush leaving him, for an instant, unsteady. "You've not killed her?"

King Zaal stared, unblinking, at the prince. "You are surprised."

"Indeed I am, quite." Kamran hesitated. "Though I admit I don't understand the nature of the non sequitur. Of course, I'm deeply curious to know the reason for your changed mind toward the girl, but I am also anxious, Your Highness, to know whether I must soon make these grotesque quarters my home, and at the moment the latter point has claimed my full and undivided attention."

The king sighed.

He closed his eyes, pressed the tips of his fingers to his temple. "I sent six men after her tonight. And the girl is not dead."

Slowly, the frozen gears in Kamran's brain began to turn. His rusty mind had its excuses: the hour was late; the prince was exhausted; his consciousness had been preoccupied with a recent effort to defend himself against a surprise attack ordered by his own grandfather. Even so, he wondered that it had taken him so long to understand.

When he did, the breath seemed to leave his body.

Kamran closed his eyes as renewed anger—outrage— built in his bones. His voice, when he spoke, was so cold he hardly recognized himself.

"You think I forewarned her."

"More than that," said the king. "I think you assisted her."

"What an odious suggestion, Your Majesty. The very idea is absurd."

"It was quite a while before you answered your door tonight," said Zaal. "I wonder: Were you still slithering back into your rooms? In the dead of night, dragged from your bedchamber, you now stand before me fully dressed, wearing your swords and scabbards. Do you expect me to believe you were abed?"

Kamran laughed, then. Like a lunatic, he laughed.

"Do you deny it?" King Zaal demanded.

Kamran leveled a violent glare at his grandfather, hatred flashing through his body. "With my very soul. That you even think me capable of such unworthiness is so insulting as to astonish me to the point of madness."

"You were determined to save her."

"I asked you merely to consider sparing the life of an innocent!" Kamran cried, no longer bothering to contain his temper. "It was a basic plea for humanity, nothing more. You think me so weak as to go against a formal decree issued by the king of my own empire? You think me so frail of mind, so weak of spine?"

For the first time in Kamran's life, he watched his grandfather falter. The older man opened then closed his mouth, struggling for the right words.

"I— I did worry," King Zaal said finally, "that you were overly preoccupied with thoughts of her. I also heard about your foolishness with the defense minister, who, despite your undisguised loathing of the man, is a prominent elder from the House of Ketab, and your speech toward him was nothing short of mutinous—"

"So you sent armed men to my door? You sentenced me to indefinite imprisonment without trial? You would've risked my head over a mere misunderstanding—an *assumption*? Does this seem to you an appropriate reaction to your concerns, Your Majesty?"

King Zaal turned away, pressed two fingers against his closed lips. He appeared lost in thought.

Kamran, on the other hand, was vibrating with fury.

The unfolding of the evening's events struck him suddenly as so unlikely, so impossible, that he wondered distantly whether he'd detached from his own mind.

It was true that he'd privately considered pushing back against his grandfather's command to find a wife. It was true, too, that in a moment of madness he'd thought to warn the girl, had even fantasized about saving her life. But Kamran always knew, deep down, that those silent ravings were bred only of transient emotion; they were shallow feelings that could not compete with the depth of loyalty he felt for his king, for his home, for his ancestors.

His empire.

Kamran would never have staged a counterattack against the king and his plans—not for a girl he did not know, not against the man who had been more of a father to him than his own had ever been able.

This betrayal— It could not be borne.

"Kamran," the king said finally. "You must understand. The girl was prepared. She was armed. The puncture wounds inflicted indicate she had access to highly unusual weapons, which one can only assume were supplied to her by a third party with access to a complex arsenal. She was prophesied to have formidable allies—"

"And you thought one of those allies might be me?"

Zaal's expression darkened. "Your ridiculous, childish actions—your fervent desire to spare her life even with the knowledge that she might be the death of mine—left me with no choice but to wonder, yes, for it remains highly unlikely that she was able to dispose of six armed men without assistance. Five of the six she flatly murdered; she only spared the last to send back a warni—"

"*The girl is a Jinn!*" Kamran shouted, hardly able to breathe for the vise clamping around his chest. "She is heir to a kingdom. Never mind the fact that she has preternatural strength and speed and can call upon invisibility at will—she was no doubt trained in self-defense from a young age, much like I was. Would you not expect me to easily defend myself against six ruffians, Your Highness? And yet? What? You thought a queen might be easy to murder?"

King Zaal looked suddenly livid.

"You are the heir apparent to the greatest empire in the known world," his grandfather cried. "You were raised in a palace with the best tutors and masters in existence. She is an orphaned, uneducated servant girl who has spent the last few years living mostly on the street—"

"You forget, Your Highness," Kamran said sharply. "You said yourself that she was not an ordinary girl. What's more: I forewarned you. I told you the girl spoke Feshtoon. I shared with you from the first my suspicions of her abilities, her intelligence. I'd watched her dispatch that street child as if he were a twig and not a tree. I've heard her speak; she is sharp and articulate, dangerously so for a girl in a snoda—"

"I say, child, you seem to know a great deal about a young woman you so vehemently deny defending."

A gust of fury blew through Kamran at that, tore through him with a virulence that stripped him entirely of heat. In its wake, he felt only cold.

Numb.

The prince stared at the floor, tried to breathe. He couldn't believe the conversation he was having; he doubted he'd be able to endure much more of the suspicion in his grandfather's eyes.

A lifetime of loyalty, so easily forgotten.

"You underestimated her," Kamran said quietly. "You should've sent twenty men. You should've anticipated her resourcefulness. *You* made a mistake, and instead of accepting fault for your own failure, you thought it better to blame your grandson. How easily you condemn me. Am I so superfluous to you, sire?"

King Zaal made a sound at that, a disbelieving huff. "You think I took pleasure in making the decision? I did what I had to do—what I thought was right given the overwhelming circumstantial indications. Had you assisted the girl tonight you would have become a traitor to your crown, to your empire. I did you the mercy of sentencing you to so gentle a fate as imprisonment, for here, at least, you might be safe. Had news of your treasonous actions been discovered by the public, you'd have been disemboweled by a mob in short order.

"Surely you can understand," the king said, "that my duty *must* be to my empire first, no matter how agonizing the consequences. Indeed you should know that better than anyone. You go too far, Kamran." Zaal shook his head. "You cannot believe I enjoyed suspecting your part in this, and I refuse to listen to any more of this dramatic nonsense."

"Dramatic nonsense?" The prince's eyes widened. "You think me dramatic, Your Highness, for taking umbrage at your readiness to sentence me to *this*"—he gestured toward the dank cage behind him—"without a shred of real evidence?"

"You forget that I first allowed you the opportunity to defend yourself."

"Indeed, you allowed me first to defend myself against a vicious attack ordered against me by His Majesty himself—"

"*Enough*," his grandfather said angrily, his voice rising an octave. "You accuse me of things you do not understand, child. The decisions I've had to make during my reign—the things I've had to do to protect the throne—would be enough to fuel your nightmares for an eternity."

"My, what joys lie ahead."

"You dare jest?" the king said darkly. "You astonish me. Never once have I led you to believe that ruling an empire would be easy or, for even a moment, enjoyable. Indeed if it does not kill you first, the crown will do its utmost to claim you, body and soul. This kingdom could never be ruled by the weak of heart. It is up to you alone to find the strength necessary to survive."

"And is that what you think of me, Your Highness? You think me weak of heart?"

"Yes."

"I see." The prince laughed, dragged both hands down his face, through his hair. He was suddenly so tired he wondered whether this was all just a dream, a strange nightmare.

"Kamran."

What was this, this feeling? This static in his chest, this burning in his throat? Was it the scorch of betrayal? Heartbreak? Why did Kamran feel suddenly as if he might cry?

He would not.

"You think compassion costs nothing," his grandfather said sharply. "You think sparing an innocent life is easy; that to do otherwise is an indication only of inhumanity. You do not yet realize that you possess the luxury of compassion because I have carried in your stead the weight of every cruelty, of every mercilessness necessary to ensuring the survival of millions.

"I clear away the darkness," the king said, "so that you might enjoy the light. I destroy your enemies, so that you might reign supreme. And yet you've decided now, in your ignorance, to hate me for it; to purposely misunderstand my motivations when you know in your soul that everything I have ever done was to secure your livelihood, your happiness, your success."

"Do you really mean it, Grandfather?" Kamran said quietly. "Is what you say true?"

"You know it is true."

"How then, pray, do you secure my livelihood and my happiness when you threaten to cut off my head?"

"Kamran—"

"If there is nothing else, Your Majesty." The prince bowed. "I will now retire to my room. It has been a tediously long night."

Kamran was already halfway to the exit when the king said—

"Wait."

The prince hesitated, took an unsteady breath. He didn't look back when he said, "Yes, Your Highness?"

"Spare me a minute more, child. If you truly wish to assure me of your loyalty to the empire—"

Kamran turned sharply, felt his body tense.

"—there is a task of some importance I wish to charge you with now."

TWENTY-FIVE

پیست وپنج

ALIZEH WAS ON BOTH KNEES in a corner of the grand sitting room, hand frozen on her floor brush; her face was so close to the ground she could almost see her reflection in the glossy stone. She dared not breathe as she listened to the familiar sound of tea filling a teacup, the burbling rip of air as known to her as her own name. Excepting the elixir of water, Alizeh had never much cared for food or drink, but she loved tea as much as anyone in Ardunia. Tea drinking was so entrenched in the culture that it was as common as breathing, even for Jinn, and it sent a little flutter through her chest to be so close to the brew now.

Of course, Alizeh was not supposed to be here.

She'd been sent to scrub this particular corner only after a large bird had flown through the window and promptly defecated all over the marble floor.

She'd not known Duchess Jamilah would be present.

Though it was not as if Alizeh would get in trouble for doing her job; no, the girl's concern was that if anyone saw her in the same room as the mistress of the house, she'd be promptly dismissed and sent to work elsewhere. Servants were not allowed to dawdle for long in rooms where occupants of the house were present. She was to do her job and be gone as quickly as possible—but for the last five minutes,

Alizeh had been scrubbing the same clean spot.

She did not want to go.

Alizeh had never seen Duchess Jamilah before, not up close, and though she could not exactly *see* the woman now, Alizeh's curiosity grew only by the second. From beneath the finely carved legs of the stiff couches, Alizeh was able to observe a horizontal stripe of the woman. Every so often the duchess stood without warning, then sat back down. Then stood up again—and changed seats.

Alizeh was fascinated.

She caught another sliver of the woman's hem then, the peek of her slippers as she moved for the fourth time in as many minutes. Even from this skewed vantage Alizeh could tell that the lady wore a crinoline under her skirts, which at this early hour was not only unusual, but a bit gauche. For ten thirty in the morning, Duchess Jamilah was supremely overdressed with nowhere to go. Doubtless, then, she was expecting company.

It was this last thought that inspired a terrifying flip in Alizeh's stomach.

In the two days since the announcement of the prince's arrival in Setar, Mrs. Amina had worked the servants nearly to death, in accordance with orders issued by the lady of the house herself. Alizeh could not help now but wonder whether the highly anticipated moment had finally arrived— and whether Alizeh herself might see the prince again.

Quickly, she returned her eyes to the floor.

Her heart had begun to pound in her chest at the prospect. *Why?*

Alizeh had not allowed herself to think much of the prince in the last couple of days. For some unfathomable reason, the devil had forewarned her of the young man—and every day Alizeh grew only more baffled as to why. Indeed what had, at first, seemed so foreboding had only recently been proven toothless: the prince was neither a monster nor a murderer of children.

Not only had Omid's recent visit dispelled any lingering concerns Alizeh might've had about the young man's motivations toward the boy, but Alizeh herself now carried evidence of the prince's kindness. Apart from sparing her a fight with a shadowy figure, he'd returned her parcels in the midst of a rainstorm—and never mind how he'd known to find her. She'd decided no longer to dwell on that uncertainty, for she didn't see the point.

The devil's warnings had always been convoluted.

Iblees, Alizeh had learned, was consistent only as an omen. His brief, flickering appearances in her life were followed always by misery and upheaval—and this much, at least, had already proven to be true.

The rest, she would not torture herself over.

What's more, Alizeh doubted the prince spared her a single thought; in fact, she would be astonished if he'd not altogether forgotten their fleeting interaction. These days, Alizeh had precious few faces to look upon and recall, but there was no reason the prince of Ardunia should remember that, for a single hour, a poor servant girl had existed in his life.

No, it did not matter who was coming to visit. It shouldn't

matter. What held Alizeh's attention was this: the rustling of Duchess Jamilah's skirts as she positioned herself in the crook of yet another armchair.

The woman crossed, then uncrossed her ankles. She shook out her hem, draping the material to be shown to its best advantage, and then pointed her toes so that the rounded tips of her satin slippers would peek out from under her skirts, calling attention to her narrow, dainty feet.

Alizeh almost smiled.

If Duchess Jamilah was indeed expecting a visit from the prince, the current situation was only more perplexing. The woman was the prince's *aunt*. She was nearly thrice his age. Watching this grand lady reduce herself to these pedestrian displays of nervousness and pretension was both entertaining and surprising; and proved the perfect diversion for Alizeh's boiling, chaotic mind.

She'd had quite enough of her own troubles.

Alizeh placed her floor brush on the polished stone and fought back a sudden wave of emotion. By the time she'd arrived home the evening prior, she'd been left but three hours to sleep before the work bell, and she spent two out of three tossing restlessly on her cot. A low-level anxiety hummed even now within her, not merely a consequence of being almost murdered—nor even the murdering she'd done herself—but of the young man who'd kneeled before her in the night.

Your Majesty.

Her parents had always told her this moment would come, but so many years had passed without word that

Alizeh had long ago ceased waiting. The first year after her mother's death she'd survived the long, bleak days only by holding with both hands to hope; she felt certain she would be shortly found, would be rescued. Surely, if she was so important, someone would be along to protect her?

Day after day, no one had come.

Alizeh was thirteen years old the day her house was reduced to ash; she'd no friends who might offer her shelter. She scavenged the wreckage of her home for its surviving, mutilated bits of gold and silver, and these she sold, at a great loss, for the necessary sewing and weaving supplies she still owned today.

As a precaution against revealing her identity, Alizeh moved from town to town with some frequency; for in that hopeful first year, it would not occur to her to take a position as a snoda. Instead, she pursued work as a seamstress, making her way south—over the course of years—from one hamlet to a village, from a village to a town, from a town to a small city. She took any job, no matter how small, sleeping wherever she found a reliable place to collapse. She comforted herself with the assurance that the unbearable days would soon come to an end, that imminently she would be found.

Five years, and no one had come.

No one had been there to spare her the gallows. No one had arrived to offer her a path to safety upon arrival in each new town; no one had been around to guide her to a gentle river or stream in the unnavigable crush of the city. No one came for her when she'd nearly died of thirst; or later, when she'd taken a desperate drink of sewer water and was poisoned so badly she'd been briefly paralyzed.

For two weeks Alizeh had lain in a frozen gutter, her body wracked by violent seizures. She had only enough energy to make herself invisible—to spare herself the worst harassment. She was certain back then, as she stared up at the silver moon, her lips chapped with frost and dehydration, that she would die there in the street, and die alone.

Long ago she'd ceased living with the hope of being rescued. Even when she was hunted and besieged by the worst of men and women, she no longer cried out for help—not when her many calls had gone unanswered.

Alizeh had learned, instead, to rely on herself.

Hers had been a lonely, agonizing journey of survival. That someone had finally found her seemed impossible, and she was gripped now by both hope and fear, alternating between the two with such frequency she thought she might go mad.

Was it foolish, she wondered, to allow herself to feel happiness for even a moment?

She shifted, then, felt the nosta move against her chest. She'd hidden the orb in the only safe place she could think of: just inside her corset, the polished glass pressed close to her skin. She felt the nosta glow hot and cold as conversations ebbed and flowed around her, every change in temperature a reminder of what had happened the evening prior. The nosta had turned out to be a gift in many ways, for without it she might've begun to wonder whether her memories of the night before were, in fact, a dream.

Hazan, he'd said his name was.

Alizeh took a deep breath. It gave her great comfort to

know that he remembered her parents, that he had ever been to her childhood home. It made her past life—and his place in her present—feel suddenly real, affirmed by more than her own imaginings. Still, she was plagued; not only by optimism and apprehension, but another, more shameful concern: she wasn't sure how she felt about being found.

A long time ago, Alizeh had been ready.

From infancy she'd been prepared for the day she'd be called upon to lead, to be a force for change for her own people. To build for them a home, to shepherd them to safety. To peace.

Now Alizeh did not know who she was.

She lifted her bandaged hands, staring at them as if they did not belong to her; as if she'd never seen them before.

What had she become?

She startled, suddenly, at the distant, muffled sounds of voices. Alizeh had been so lost in her own thoughts she'd not noticed the new shift in Duchess Jamilah's position, nor the sudden commotion in the front hall.

Alizeh crouched impossibly closer to the ground and peered through gaps in the furniture. Duchess Jamilah was the picture of affected indifference: the casual way she held her teacup, the sigh she gave as she faux-perused a column in Setar's local newspaper, the *Daftar*. The publication was famous for being printed on dusty green pages and had long been a point of interest for Alizeh, who could rarely spare the coin to purchase a copy. She squinted at it now, trying to read the day's headline upside down. She'd only ever been able to peek at the articles on occasion, but—

Alizeh started violently.

She heard the prince's voice, far away at first, and then all at once sharp and clear, the heels of his boots connecting with marble. She covered her mouth with one hand, doubling over so as not to be seen. With her free hand she clutched the floor brush, wondering now at her own foolishness.

How on earth would she escape unnoticed?

The room was without warning swarmed by servants carrying tea trays and cakes; one was collecting the prince's heavy, moss-colored coat—no cloak today—and a golden mace Alizeh had never before seen him carry. Among the bustling staff was Mrs. Amina, who had no doubt invented an excuse to be present upon the prince's arrival. If Mrs. Amina caught Alizeh here now—in the presence of the prince—she'd likely beat the girl just to teach her a lesson.

Alizeh swallowed.

There was no chance she'd go unseen. By the time the visit was over, she was certain every servant in the house would've fabricated a reason to pass through this room for a glimpse of their royal visitor.

Unfortunately for Alizeh, she could only see his boots.

"Yes, thank you," he said in response to a query about tea.

Alizeh froze.

The prince's response came during a chance moment of quiet, his words ringing out so clearly Alizeh thought she might reach out and touch them. His voice was just as rich and complex as she remembered, but he sounded different today. Not unkind, exactly, but neither did he sound pleased.

"I'm afraid I slept poorly last night," he was explaining to his aunt. "More tea is always good."

"Oh, my dear," Duchess Jamilah said breathlessly. "Why should you sleep poorly? Are you not comfortable at the palace? Would you not prefer staying awhile here, in your old room? I've got it all prep—"

"My aunt is very kind," he said quietly. "I thank you, but I'm quite comfortable in my own rooms. Forgive me for speaking thoughtlessly; I meant not to cause you worry." A pause. "I'm certain I'll sleep better tonight."

"Well if you're sure—"

"I am."

Another pause.

"You may go," Duchess Jamilah said in a colder tone, ostensibly to the servants present.

Alizeh's pulse quickened—this was her chance. If she could only scramble upright in time, she might disappear with the others, decant herself into another room, busy herself with a task. It would be a mite tricky to manage with a soapy bucket and brush in hand, but she'd no choice. She'd have to make it work if she didn't want to arrive at the ball tonight with a swollen eye and a bruised cheek.

As quietly—and quickly—as she was able, Alizeh jumped to her feet. She all but ran to catch up with the others, but the hot water in her bucket sloshed as she moved, splashing her clothes—and, she feared, the floor.

For a mere half second Alizeh glanced back to scan the marble for a spill, when she suddenly slipped in the very puddle for which she was searching.

She gasped, reflexively throwing her arms out to recapture

her balance, and only made the situation worse. The jerky movement disturbed the bucket entirely, heaving a scalding wave of soapy water all over her skirts—and onto the floor.

Alizeh dropped the bucket in horror.

In her desperation to flee the scene she moved without thinking, the toe of her boot promptly catching on the wet, dragging hem of her skirt. She fell forward with cruel force, catching herself with both hands only after slamming one knee into the marble.

Pain rocketed through her, branching up her leg; Alizeh dared not shout out, muting the cry in her lungs to a single, dull sound of discomfort.

In vain she implored herself to stand, but the pain was so paralyzing she could hardly think straight; indeed, she could hardly breathe. Tears pricked her eyes in shame, in anguish.

Alizeh had feared many times for the end of her tenure at Baz House, but she knew now without question that this was her finish. She'd be cast out on to the street for this, and today, of all days—when she needed a safe place to ready herself for the ball—

"You stupid, thoughtless girl," Mrs. Amina cried, rushing toward her. "What have you done? Get up this instant!"

Mrs. Amina didn't wait for Alizeh to move; she grabbed the girl roughly by the arm and wrenched her upright, and Alizeh came as close to screaming as she dared, her breath releasing in a tortured gasp.

"I— I beg your pardon, ma'am. It was an acci—"

Mrs. Amina shoved her, hard, in the direction of the kitchens, and Alizeh stumbled, agony shooting up her injured leg.

She caught herself against the wall, excuses dying in her throat. "I'm so desperately sorry."

"You're going to clean this up, girl, and then you're going to clear out your things and get out of this house." Mrs. Amina was livid, her chest heaving with an anger even Alizeh had never before witnessed. The housekeeper lifted her hand as if to slap the girl. "Of all the days to be clumsy and brainless. I should have you whipped fo—"

"Put down your hand."

Mrs. Amina froze, blinking at the unexpected sound of his voice. The housekeeper's hand fell with theatrical slow motion as she turned, confusion sharpening in her eyes, in the language of her body.

"I— I beg your pardon, sire—"

"Step away from the girl." The prince's voice was low and murderous, his eyes flashing a shade of black so fathomless it terrified even Alizeh to look at him. "You forget yourself, ma'am. It is illegal under Ardunian law to beat servants."

Mrs. Amina gasped, then fell into a deep curtsy. "But— Sire—"

"I will not repeat myself again. Step away from the girl or I will have you arrested."

Mrs. Amina released a sudden, fearful sob, scrambling inelegantly to put distance between herself and Alizeh, whose heart was beating so fast she felt both dizzy and faint with fear. Pain spasmed relentlessly in her knee, taking her breath away. She did not know what to do with herself. She hardly knew where to look.

There was a sudden rustling of skirts.

"Oh, my dear!" Duchess Jamilah rushed over, grabbing hold of the prince's arm. "I beg you don't trouble yourself. The fault is mine alone for exposing you to such ineptitude. I pray you will forgive me for subjecting you to this incivility, and for inspiring your discomfort—"

"My dear aunt, you misunderstand me. My discomfort, if any, is inspired only by an overt disregard for the laws that govern our empire, and which we have a duty at all times to obey."

Duchess Jamilah gave a nervous, breathy laugh. "Your strict adherence to our governance does you a great service, my dear, but surely you must see that the girl deserves to be punished—that Mrs. Amina was only doing as she saw fit t—"

The prince turned sharply, disengaging himself from his aunt. "You surprise me," he said. "Surely you don't mean you would condone such cruelty against your servants? The girl was carrying a bucket of water and slipped. There was no harm done to anyone but herself. You would toss her into the street over a mere accident?"

Duchess Jamilah directed a strained smile at the prince, then glared at the housekeeper. "Get out of my sight," she said acidly. "And take the girl with you."

Mrs. Amina paled.

She bobbed a curtsy, said, "Yes, Your Grace," and grabbed Alizeh's arm, jerking her forward. Alizeh stumbled on her throbbing leg and nearly bit through her tongue to keep from crying out.

Under the pretense of offering assistance, Mrs. Amina

drew the girl closer. "If I could, I'd snap your neck right now," she hissed. "And don't you dare forget it."

Alizeh squeezed her eyes shut.

The housekeeper shoved Alizeh down the hall, the sound of Duchess Jamilah's voice fading with her every step.

"Your heart is one of legend," the duchess was saying. "Of course, we all heard the story of your saving that filthy southern child, but now you come to the defense of a snoda? Kamran, my dear, you are too good for us. Come, let us take tea in my personal parlor, where we might have more quiet to reflect . . ."

Kamran.

His name was Kamran.

Alizeh did not know why this revelation comforted her as she was dragged away—or even why she cared.

Though maybe, she wondered, this was the reason why the devil had shown her his face. Maybe it was for this moment. Maybe because his was the last face she'd think of before her life was ripped apart.

Yet again.

TWENTY-SIX

بیست و شش

KAMRAN STARED, UNBLINKING, AS THE girl was half dragged, half shoved down the hall. As if the bandages around her hands and neck weren't evidence enough, he'd noted with a modicum of fear that he'd begun to recognize her now merely from her movements, from the lines of her figure, from her glossy black curls.

Kamran murmured a vacant thanks to his aunt, who'd said something he did not hear, and allowed her to lead him to another room, the details of which he did not notice. He could hardly focus on his aunt as she spoke, nodding only when it seemed appropriate, and offering brief, monosyllabic responses when prompted.

Inside, he was in turmoil.

Why do you not fight back? he'd wanted to cry.

In the privacy of his own mind, Kamran would not cease shouting at the girl. She was capable of killing five men in cold blood but allowed this monstrous housekeeper to treat her thus? Why? Was she really left no recourse but to work here as the lowest servant, allowing her lessers to treat her like trash? To abuse her? Why did she not seek employment elsewhere?

Why?

With that, the fight left his body.

This was the true agony: that Kamran understood why she stayed. Not only had it recently occurred to him how difficult it might be for a Jinn to find employment in a noble house, but as the days wore on his imagination expanded even to understand precisely why she sought work in such a grand home. He'd begun to discern as much when she hesitated to remove her mask even in the midst of a rainstorm; he'd understood fully only when he realized how fraught her life was with danger. Kamran had known the girl but a matter of days, but in that short time he'd already been privy to three different attacks on her life.

Three.

It had been made clear to him, then, not only that she wished to live her life unseen—but that she did not feel safe enough in the city to live alone.

These were two desires directly opposed.

Her work as a servant, Kamran had realized, provided her with more than the basic needs of coin and shelter. The snoda itself offered her a measure of anonymity, but there was safety, too, in the walls of a grand estate. Guaranteed protection. Guards stationed at all access points.

A faceless servant in a busy, heavily secured house— It was, for a young woman in her position, a brilliant cover. Doubtless she accepted as incidental the regular abuse she suffered in exchange for security.

It was a situation Kamran despised.

The tea he sipped turned to acid in his gut, the casual position of his limbs hiding an interior tension coiling him taut from the inside out. He felt as if his muscles were atrophying slowly in the suit of his skin, a silent litany of epithets perched in his mouth even when he smiled.

He murmured, "Yes, thank you," and accepted a second puffed pastry from his aunt's proffered dish. He tucked one pastry next to its sibling, then placed the dessert plate on a low table. He'd no appetite.

". . . much excitement about the ball this evening," his aunt was saying. "The daughter of a dear friend of mine shall be attending, and I was hoping to introduce . . ."

Why Kamran felt this overwhelming need always to protect this nameless girl, he could not explain, for she was not at all helpless, and she was not his responsibility.

"Hmm?" his aunt prompted. "What do you say, dear? You would not mind terribly, would you?"

"Not at all," the prince said, staring into his teacup. "I'd be happy to meet anyone you respect so highly."

"Oh," his aunt cried, clapping her hands together. "What a lovely young man you are, how . . ."

Still, Kamran thought it must be exhausting to live such a life as hers; to know in your soul your own strength and intelligence and yet live each day insulted and berated. The girl went every minute overlooked unless she was being hunted. And devils above, he was tired of hunting her.

The prince had been sent to Baz House as a spy.

It was not the first time he'd done covert work for the empire, and he knew it would not be the last. What he detested now was not the work itself, but the nature of the directive he'd been given.

Though Kamran doubted the anger and animosity he now

felt toward his grandfather would abate, he also knew he was doomed to bury the feelings regardless, carrying on forever as if nothing untoward had transpired between them. Kamran could neither condemn the king nor disregard his duties; he'd no choice but to persist even in his current dilemma, loathsome though it was.

". . . thinking of wearing my lavender silk," his aunt was saying, "but there's a darling cream satin I've not yet worn, and I might . . ."

The king was beyond persuasion: the girl had been prophesied to have powerful allies, and as a result Zaal firmly believed she'd received assistance during the previous night's attack. He now wanted a lead on these unknown allies. If she was working with a team of spies or rebels, his grandfather argued, it was essential that they know immediately.

"We'd hoped to dispose of her with absolute discretion," the king had said. "The events of last night have instead set us back quite a bit, for if she is indeed connected to a larger plan—or a private army—her allies are now aware that an organized attempt was made on her life.

"Should we succeed in our mission upon a second attempt, details of her death might then spread across the empire, inspiring vicious rumors that would cause strife between Jinn and Clay. We cannot afford civil war," his grandfather had insisted. "We must wait to proceed, then, until we know exactly who she's working with, and what they're capable of. We cannot, however, wait too long."

The prince did not know how to undo what he himself had first set in motion. This servant girl seemed fated to be the death of him, and much as he longed to blame others for the position he was in, he could not.

He experienced only unceasing torment.

Kamran took an unsteady breath and startled, suddenly, at the unexpected figure of his aunt, who stood before him holding a teapot. Understanding dawned, but too slowly.

She gave him a strange look.

The prince murmured his thanks, held out his empty cup for a pour, and made himself conjure a smile.

"I'm certain you'll look beautiful no matter what you wear," he said to her. "Everything suits you."

His aunt beamed.

King Zaal's men, it turned out, had trailed the girl relentlessly for nearly two days, and in doing so had gleaned a great deal—but had not found evidence of a more nefarious connection.

"We need access to the girl's quarters," the king had explained. "Any sensitive information is doubtless hidden therein. But as she occupies her room at night, the best time to infiltrate is during the day, when she is working."

"I see," Kamran had said quietly. "And you cannot send mercenaries into Baz House in the light of day."

"Then you understand. It is of the utmost importance to keep the crown's interests—and concerns—as quiet as possible. Already we have risked a great deal by having her followed. If it gets out that the empire is worried about demon-like Jinn hiding in plain sight, the people will scare and turn on each other. But your visit to your aunt's house will arouse no suspicion; in fact, she has long been expecting you."

"Yes," the prince had said. "I am in possession of my dear aunt's letters."

"Very good. Your task is simple. Find an excuse to wander the house on your own and search the girl's quarters extensively. Should you discover anything that seems even remotely unusual, I want to know."

It was a strange predicament.

If Kamran could manage to be both smart *and* lucky, he might be able to fulfill this service to the king while sparing the girl a second attack on her life. He only needed proof that she was working with a formidable ally. The problem was, the prince did not agree with his grandfather's conspiracy. Kamran did not think the girl had received help in dispatching the hired thugs, and as a result he did not know if he could help her. His only hope was to find something— no matter how tenuous the evidence—that might give the king pause.

Kamran heard the sharp trill of silver and china, a spoon stirring in a cup. He forced himself, once again, back to the present moment.

Duchess Jamilah was smiling.

She reached out without warning, placing her hand overtop Kamran's. It was no small miracle that he managed not to flinch.

"I see that there is a great deal on your mind," his aunt said kindly. "I can't tell you how grateful I am that you would visit even with so much to preoccupy your thoughts."

"It's always a pleasure to see my dear aunt," Kamran said automatically. "I only hope you will forgive me for not coming by sooner."

"I will forgive you as long as you promise to visit more often from here on out," she said triumphantly, sitting back in her seat. "I have dearly missed having you here."

Kamran smiled at his aunt.

It was a rare, genuine smile, stirred up by ancient affection. His aunt Jamilah was his father's older cousin, and had been more of a mother figure to him than his own ever had. The prince had spent countless days—months, even—at Baz House during his life, and it was not a lie to say that he was happy to see his aunt now.

But then, it was not the same, either.

"As I have missed being here," he said, staring, unseeing, at a glossy bowl of orange persimmons. He looked up. "How have you been? Are your knees still troubling you?"

"You remember your poor aunt's ailments, do you?" She very nearly glowed with happiness. "What a thoughtful prince you are."

Kamran denied himself the laugh building in his chest; he'd be lying if he said he didn't enjoy the effect he had on his aunt—though she required so little encouragement to praise him that it sometimes left him feeling ashamed.

"My knees are old," she said simply. "Things begin to fall apart when they get old enough. Not much to be done about it. In any case, you need not worry about me when I'm so busy worrying about you." A pause. "Are you merely preoccupied with your regular comings and goings? Or is there something troubling you, my dear?"

Kamran did not answer at first, choosing instead to study the filigree of his teacup. "Are you quite certain," he said finally, "that it is age alone that accounts for our steady decline? If so, I am forced to wonder. Perhaps you and I are the same age, aunt, for I fear I may be falling apart, too."

His aunt's expression grew suddenly mournful; she squeezed his hand. "Oh, my dear. I do so wish—"

"Forgive me. Would you be so kind as to indulge me a brief interlude? I'd love to wander the house a short while, and clear away my nostalgia with fresh memories of your beautiful home."

"Of course, dear child!" Duchess Jamilah placed her tea-cup down with a bit too much force. "This is your home as much as it is mine. Though I hope you will forgive me, as I cannot join you on your tour. My knees, as you know, cannot bear all the stairs unless absolutely necessary."

"Not at all." He stood and bowed his head. "Please remain here at your leisure, and I will rejoin you directly."

She beamed somehow brighter. "Very good. I will see to luncheon in your absence. All will be ready for you when you're finished with your wander."

Kamran nodded. "I'll not be long."

TWENTY-SEVEN

بیست و هفت

THE CURIOUS SERVANTS WERE STALKING his every move.

Kamran made noise as he roamed the halls of Baz House, opening doors and wandering corridors gracelessly, leaving evidence of his interests everywhere. He stood dramatically in doorways, dragged his fingers along the intricate wall moldings; he stared moodily out of windows and picked books off their shelves, holding the leather-bound pages to his chest.

Perhaps Hazan had been right. The prince was quite good at giving performances when he felt them necessary.

He maintained the show for as long as he felt was needed to evince his wistful intentions; only then, when he was certain any suspicions of the staff had been thoroughly defused, did he reduce himself to shadow.

Silent as light, he crept up the stairs.

Kamran's heart had begun to beat a bit too fast, a traitor in his chest. Despite the hateful circumstances, some part of him still sparked at the prospect of discovering more about the girl.

He'd already learned from his grandfather that she was orphaned, that she'd been in Setar but a few months, and that she lived in Baz House as only a trial servant. She did not, as a result, have rooms in the servants' wing, nor was she allowed to interact or communicate with the other servants. Instead, she'd been offered lodgings in an old storage closet at the vertex of the main house.

An old storage closet.

This discovery had shocked him, but his grandfather had quickly assured the prince that the isolated position of her room would only make his task easier.

The king had misunderstood Kamran's astonishment.

Even as he climbed yet another flight of stairs, the prince struggled to imagine what such a closet might look like. He knew servants occupied the most humble housing, but he'd not anticipated the girl might live among rotting vegetables. Did she share a room with sacks of potatoes and pickled garlic, then? Was the poor girl left no recourse but to sleep on dank, moldy floorboards with only rats and cockroaches as her companions? She was worked so hard she nearly wore the skin off her own hands—and yet she was not recompensed with the most basic offering of a clean bed?

Kamran's gut twisted at the thought.

He did not like to think how poorly these revelations reflected on his aunt, but worse: he did not know whether he would've done any better. The prince knew not how every snoda in the palace was treated—and it had never once occurred to him to ask. Though he considered it was perhaps not too late to find out.

Kamran had by now lost count of the flights of stairs he'd climbed. Six? Seven? It was uncanny to experience the arduous commute she made day and night—and it was yet another astonishment to discover how far removed she lived from the breathing bodies of others.

For a moment it made him wonder whether the girl preferred being so far from everything. Certainly no one would make such a journey up into the attic without cause. It was perhaps a comfort to feel so sheltered.

Though it was perhaps desperately lonely, too.

When Kamran finally stood in front of the girl's door, he hesitated; felt a disconcerting flutter in his chest.

The prince did not know what he might discover herein, but he tried to prepare himself, at least, for a vision of abject poverty. He did not look forward to rummaging through the girl's private life, and he closed his eyes as he pulled open the closet door, whispering a quiet apology to her ghost.

Kamran promptly froze at the threshold.

He was met with a soft glow of light, and overwhelmed at once by the intoxicating scent of Gol Mohammadi roses, the source of which he pinpointed to a small, crocheted basket in a corner of the room. The makeshift bowl was stacked high with corollas of slowly desiccating pink petals, a kind of homemade potpourri.

Kamran was stunned.

The small quarters—so small that he might've lain down and spanned the length of it—were warm and cozy, flooded with perfume, rich with color. No cockroach in sight.

Like a madman, he wanted to laugh.

How? How did she always manage to reduce him to this,

to this shameful state? Once more he'd been convinced he understood her—had pitied her, even—and instead he was humbled by his own arrogance.

A vision of abject poverty, indeed.

The room was spotless.

Its walls and floors and ceiling had been scrubbed so clean the boards did not match the black, molding exterior door—which she'd left untouched. There was a small, beautifully patterned rug arranged on the ground next to a modest cot, which was neatly dressed in a silky quilt and pillow. Her few articles of clothing hung from colorful hooks—no, they were nails, he realized, nails that had been wrapped in thread—and a collection of miscellaneous items were placed with care in a clean apple crate. They appeared to be sewing supplies, mostly. But there was a single book, too, the title of which he could not discern, and which he peered at now, taking an unconscious step into the room. The entire space came at once into view—and too late, Kamran saw the candle burning in an unseen corner.

He went suddenly solid.

There was the familiar press of a cold blade at his throat, the feel of her small hand at his back. He heard her soft breathing and could tell merely by the unmuffled sound that she did not wear her snoda.

He must've surprised her.

His flutter of anticipation suddenly magnified. It was a bizarre sensation, for what he felt even as she held a knife to his neck was not fear, but elation. She was not supposed to be here, and he'd not dared to hope he might find himself alone with her again.

A miracle, then: her hand still pressed against his back, her racing pulse nearly audible in the silence.

"Speak," she said. "Tell me what you seek here. Answer honestly, and I give you my word I will leave you unharmed."

Was it terrible that his heart pounded in his chest at the soft sound of her voice? Was it worrisome that he felt nothing but pleasure to be held at her mercy?

What a fascinating creature she was, to be so bold as to offer him his life in exchange for information. What worlds he might be inspired to give up, he wondered, in the pursuit of knowing more of her mind.

She pressed the knife harder. "Speak the truth now," she said. "Or I will slit your throat."

Not for a moment did he doubt her.

"I have been sent here as a spy," he said. "I come here now to rummage through your room in the hopes of gathering intelligence."

The blade fell away.

Kamran heard the familiar slicing sound of metal coming together and realized that what he thought was a blade was, in fact, a pair of scissors. He almost laughed.

But then the girl stepped in front of him, and all thought of laughter died in his throat.

She was not dressed.

Her hair was loose; long, obsidian curls fell into her silver eyes, and she batted them away impatiently. Kamran watched, transfixed, as the silky locks grazed her naked shoulders, the delicate column of her neck, the smooth expanse of her chest. The dangerously low cut of her che- mise was held up only by a corset, and Kamran discovered, to his dismay, that he could not breathe.

The girl was not dressed.

She was not undressed, not at all, but she wore only her underskirts and corset, and was covering herself poorly with one hand, clutching her sopping dress against her exposed bodice, her right fist still clenched around a pair of scissors.

He'd forgotten how beautiful she was.

This revelation was astonishing to him, for he'd spent more time than he cared to admit thinking about the girl, conjuring her face when he closed his eyes at night. He did not think himself capable of forgetting anything about her, and yet he must have, for he was struck stupid anew, drawing near her now like a hungry flame to tinder.

Kamran did not enjoy the feeling that overcame him then. He took little pleasure in this kind of desperation, in a desire so potent it inhaled him. He'd never felt this, not like this, for this was a uniquely powerful force, one that left him dis- oriented in its wake.

Weak.

"Turn around," she said. "I must finish dressing."

It took him a moment to process the request. Not only had his mind been upended, but Kamran had never been ordered around by anyone but the king. He felt as if someone had shoved him bodily into a tragic inverse of his real life— and what surprised him most was that he did not dislike it.

He obeyed her order without a word, silently castigating himself for his own incomprehensible reaction to the girl. Women wore all manner of scandalous garments in his presence; some wore gowns so dramatically low-cut that corsets were done away with altogether. What's more: the prince was not a green child. He was not unaccustomed to the presence of beautiful women. How, then, to explain what overcame him now?

"So," the girl said quietly. "You have come to spy on me."

Kamran heard the distinct rustling of fabric, and he closed his eyes. He was a gentleman of honor. He would not imagine her undressing.

He would not.

"Yes," he said.

More fabric swishing; something hitting the ground with a dull thud. "If that is indeed true," she said, "I wonder why you would dare admit it."

"And I wonder why you would doubt me," he said with impressive calm. "You told me you would slit my throat if I failed to give you an honest answer."

"Then you, of all people, should understand my suspicion. Certainly it will not surprise you to hear that none before you have ever accepted my terms."

"None before me?" He smiled to himself. "Do you often find yourself in a position of negotiation with spies and cut-throats?"

"A great deal too often, in fact. Why—did you think yourself the first to find me a subject of interest?" A pause. "You may turn around now."

He did.

She'd pinned her hair back, buttoned a clean dress up to her throat. It had not helped. The modest frock had done nothing to diminish her beauty. He felt bewitched as he drank her in, lingering too long on her arresting eyes, the delicate curve of her lips.

"No," he said softly. "I daresay I'm not the first."

She stared at him then, surprise rendering her, for a moment, inhumanly still. Kamran watched with some amazement as a faint blush burned across her cheeks. She turned away, clasped her hands together.

Had he made her nervous?

"I gave you my word," she said quietly, "that I would leave you unharmed in exchange for your honesty. I meant what I said, and I will not now go against myself. But you must leave at once."

"Forgive me, but I will not."

She looked up sharply. "I beg your pardon?"

"You asked for a confession in exchange for my life, which I readily offered. But I never once promised to forfeit my task. I will understand, of course, if you'd rather not stay while I rifle through your things—and I suspect you are anxious to return to work. Shall I wait to begin until you are gone?"

The girl's lips parted in shock, her eyes widening with disbelief. "Are you as mad as you sound, sir?"

"That is twice now that you have called me sir," he said, a slight smile on his lips. "I can't say I care for it."

"Pray, what is it you would prefer I call you? Do tell me

now and I'll make a note to forget in future, as there is little chance our paths will cross again."

"I should be very sorry if that were the case."

"You say this even as you kick me out of my own room so that you might surveil it? Do you jest, *sire*?"

Kamran nearly laughed. "I see now that you do know who I am."

"Yes, we are both well informed. I know your legacy as surely as you know mine."

Kamran's smile faded altogether.

"Did you think me a simpleton?" she asked angrily. "Why else would the prince of Ardunia be sent to spy on me? It was you who sent those men to kill me last night, was it not?" She turned away. "More fool me. I should have listened to the devil."

"You are mistaken," Kamran said with some heat.

"On what point? Do you mean to say you are not responsible for the attempt on my life?"

"I am not."

"And yet you were aware of it. Does it matter whose lips issued the order? Did not the directive come from your own crown?"

Kamran took a breath, said nothing. There was little else he could say without making himself a traitor to his empire. His grandfather had more than proven how readily he would decree the prince's head be separated from his body, and despite Kamran's many protests to the contrary, he rather liked being alive.

"Do you deny these allegations, sire?" the girl said,

rounding on him. "How long have your men been watching me? How long have I been a subject of interest to the crown?"

"You know I cannot answer such questions."

"Did you know who I was that night? The night you came to Baz House to return my parcels? Were you watching me even then?"

Kamran looked away. Faltered. "I— It was complicated— I did not know, not at first—"

"Goodness. And I thought you were merely being kind." She laughed a sad laugh. "I suppose I should've known better than to think such a kindness might be granted without a hefty price."

"My actions that night had no ulterior motive," Kamran said sharply. "That much is true."

"Is it really?"

Kamran struggled to maintain his composure. "Yes."

"You do not wish me dead?"

"No."

"The king, then. He wishes to kill me. Does he think me a threat to his throne?"

"You already know I cannot answer these questions."

"You cannot answer the most pertinent questions, the ones most relevant to my life, to my welfare? And yet you smile and tease me, talk with me as if you are a friend and not a ruthless enemy. Where is your sense of honor, sire? I see you have misplaced it."

Kamran swallowed. It was a moment before he spoke.

"I do not blame you for hating me," he said quietly. "And I

will not attempt to convince you otherwise. There are aspects of my role—of my position—that bind me, and which I can only detest in the privacy of my own mind.

"I would ask that you allow me only this in my own defense: Do not misunderstand me," he said, meeting her eyes. "I wish you no harm."

TWENTY-EIGHT

پیست و هشت

ALIZEH STRUGGLED TO BREATHE. THE nosta glowed hot against her skin; the prince had not lied to her once.

It should've been a comfort to know that he meant her no harm, but she was not in full possession of herself. He'd caught her off guard, out of sorts. She seldom, if ever, allowed herself to get so angry, but today was a strange day, made more difficult by the hour.

She'd been dismissed without hesitation.

Alizeh had been sent upstairs to pack her things and exit the premises with all possible haste. She'd managed to avoid the inevitable beating, but only because she'd finally defended herself, terrifying Mrs. Amina in the process. There was no point in taking the hit, Alizeh had rationalized, if she was to be cast out regardless—though she'd not actually *hit* Mrs. Amina. She'd merely lifted a hand to protect herself—and the housekeeper had nearly fainted.

The woman had not expected resistance, and the forceful impact of her hand against Alizeh's forearm was such that it sprained the housekeeper's wrist.

It was a modest victory, and it had cost Alizeh dearly.

At best, Mrs. Amina would deny her a reference—a reference that might've made all the difference in finding another position quickly. At worst, Mrs. Amina might report the sprain to Duchess Jamilah, who might then report Alizeh to the magistrates on charges of assault.

The girl's hands were shaking.

She shook not merely with rage, but with fear for her life, the whole of it. For the first time she had hope of escape, but Hazan himself had said there was a chance their plans could go awry. It was imperative that Alizeh attend the ball tonight, but the deed was to be done with discretion—she would need camouflage in such a situation, which meant she needed a gown. Which meant she needed time and space to work; a safe place to prepare.

How would any of that happen now?

It was all beginning to drown her, the realizations sinking in like sediment. The pain in her knee had begun to ebb, but still it throbbed, and the dull ache reminded her now only of her own inexhaustible torment.

Never was she spared a moment of peace; never would her demons leave her be. She was always fatigued, always tense. She couldn't even change out of her miserable, sopping clothes without being besieged, and now she would be pitched out into the winter streets. Everything she'd tirelessly built—the pocket of light she'd dug free from darkness—had been so easily extinguished.

All the world seemed frightfully bleak.

The magistrates alone would've been terrifying enough, but with the crown in pursuit of her, Alizeh knew her life was forfeit. If she couldn't make things work tonight she'd have no choice but to leave Setar, to begin again elsewhere and hope Hazan could find her again.

She felt suddenly close to tears.

There was a whisper of movement then, a featherlight touch along her arm. She looked up.

The prince was staring at her, his eyes dark as pitch, glittering in the candlelight. Alizeh could not help but be struck by him, even then. His was a face you seldom saw in a crowd; so stunning it stopped you in your tracks.

Her heart had begun to race.

"Forgive me," he said. "It was not my intention to upset you."

Alizeh looked away, blinked back tears. "What a strange person you are," she said. "So polite in your determination to rummage through my things without my permission; to deny me my privacy."

"Would it improve matters if I were rude?"

"Do not attempt to distract me with such tangential conversations." She sniffed, wiped her eyes. "You know very well that you are strange. If you truly did not wish to upset me, you would leave at once."

"I cannot."

"You must."

He bowed his head. "I will not."

"Just moments ago you said you wish me no harm. If that is true, why not leave me be?"

"What if I told you that your safety was dependent on the results of my search?"

"I would not believe you."

"And yet." He almost smiled. "Your safety is dependent on the results of my search."

The nosta glowed so hot Alizeh flinched, then stared, wide-eyed, at the prince. "Do you mean to say you seek to violate my privacy in the interest of my protection?"

He grimaced. "Your summary is distasteful."

"But you scarcely know me. Why would the prince of Ardunia trouble himself to protect a hated stranger?"

He sighed at that, looking frustrated for the first time. "My motivations, I fear I cannot adequately explain."

"Why on earth not?"

"The truth may seem to you farfetched. I wonder whether you will believe a word of it."

Alizeh felt keenly the pressure of the little glass orb then, grateful for its presence more than ever. "I would ask you to try anyway."

At first, he did not speak.

He reached into his pocket instead, retrieving what appeared to be a handkerchief—which he then held out as an offering.

Alizeh gasped, recognizing it at once.

Her body was seized by a static of shock as she took the familiar cloth into her own hands. Oh, she'd thought it lost. She'd thought it lost forever. The relief that overcame her then was such that she thought she might be inspired, suddenly, to cry.

"How? How did you—"

"It is my fault you are now being hunted," the prince said quietly. "When I saw you disarm the Fesht boy that awful, fateful morning, I thought you'd stolen your uniform from an unsuspecting servant, as it seemed more likely to me that you were a Tulanian spy than a snoda. I made inquiries, and in the process, delivered you undue harm."

Alizeh took an unsteady step back.

Even as the nosta glowed warm against her skin, verifying his every word, she struggled to believe him.

"Forgive me," he said, staring now into his hands. "I've been made privy to some details of your life in these last few days, and I—"

Gently, he cleared his throat.

"I think very highly of you," he said. "You may not know much of me, but I've seen enough now to understand that you've been treated abominably by the world and its inhabitants, myself among them. I intend to spare you the worst of what comes next, insomuch as I am able."

Alizeh stilled, blinking against a sudden blow of emotion. She had tried to raise a shield and failed: she was touched.

It had been a long time since anyone had noticed her or found her worthy of basic kindness. What had the prince seen of her life to inspire him so? She dearly wanted to know—wanted to ask—but her pride would not allow it.

She stared at him instead, at his bowed head.

Her eyes traveled over the thick, satin waves of his black hair, the broad shoulders beneath his intricately knit ivory sweater. He was tall and steady, so beautifully in possession of himself. She saw the prince in him then, the elegance of nobility, of honor; he seemed in that moment every grace personified.

"You say," she said quietly, "that you think highly of me."

"I do."

The nosta warmed.

"And you mean to protect me now as a kind of penance?"

At that, the prince looked up. "In a way," he said, and smiled. "Though I experience no suffering in the effort, so I suppose even in this I've managed to be selfish."

Alizeh took a deep breath. She wanted to laugh; she wanted to cry. What a strange day this had turned out to be.

"If all that you say is true, sire, why can you not simply leave here? You need not search my room. You might return to the palace and tell His Majesty whatever you think will best accomplish your goal."

"I never said I was sent by His Majesty."

"Were you not?"

"I cannot answer that."

She sighed, turning away as she said, "I see you are determined to be infuriating."

"My apologies. Perhaps you should return to work."

She spun back, all tender emotion forgotten. "You dare dismiss me from my own room? How do you manage to be so kind in one moment and so vexing in the next?"

He tilted his head at her. "You are the first to think me capable of such dichotomy. I am in fact not known to possess so changeable a character, and I'm forced to wonder whether the source of your frustration is rooted elsewhere."

Alizeh's eyes went wide at the affront. "You think the fault lies with me, then? You think me inconstant?"

"With all due respect, I would point out only that you welcomed my arrival with a promise to slit my throat and have since been moved to tears at least twice in my presence. I would hardly call that sort of behavior constant."

She clenched her fists. "Do you not think I am allowed to experience a full spectrum of emotion when my nerves are so mercilessly attacked—when you lay at my feet all manner of shocking revelations?"

"What I think," he said, fighting back a smile, "is that you will soon be missed by your despicable housekeeper. I ask that you return to your duties only for fear that any further delay will cost you. You need not worry about me." He glanced around the room. "I, too, have a task to accomplish."

Alizeh squeezed her eyes shut.

Oh, she wanted to shake him. There was no use trying to convince him of anything.

She moved away, bending with only a little difficulty to collect her disassembled carpet bag from the floor, and quickly pulled the threads taut, reshaping the small luggage. She was aware of the prince's eyes on her as she worked, but did her best to ignore him.

Quickly, she removed her few items from their hooks— including Miss Huda's unfinished gown—folding them on her bed before tucking them into the bag. She reached for the apple crate next—

"What are you doing?"

She was tipping over the crate, dumping its contents into the bag, when she felt his hand on her arm.

"Why are y—"

"You will not listen to me," she said, pulling away. "I have asked you several times now to leave, and you will neither listen nor sufficiently explain yourself. As such, I have decided to ignore you."

"Ignore me all you like, but why pack up your things? Have I not made it plain that I need to search them?"

"Your arrogance, sire, is astonishing."

"I apologize, once again, for any inconvenience my personality has caused you. Please unpack your belongings."

Alizeh clenched her jaw. She wanted to kick him. "I have been dismissed from Baz House," she said. "I cannot return to work. I have little time left to vacate the premises, after which I must, with all possible haste, run for my life." She yanked the quilt off her bed. "So if you will please excuse me."

He moved in front of her. "That's absurd. I won't allow that to happen."

She stepped aside. "You do not control the universe, Your Highness."

"I control more of it than you might consider."

"Do you even hear yourself when you speak? If so, how can you stand it?"

Improbably, the prince laughed. "I must say, you are a surprise. I'd not imagined you'd be so quick to anger."

"I find it difficult to believe you imagined me at all."

"Why?"

Alizeh hesitated, blinking up at him. "I beg your pardon? What reason would you have to wonder about my temperament?"

"You need only one? I have many."

Alizeh's lips parted in surprise. "Are you making fun of me?"

He smiled at that, smiled so wide she saw the white flash of his teeth. It changed him, somehow. Softened him.

He said nothing.

"You are right, in any case," Alizeh said. "I am not usually so quick to anger." She bit her lip. "I fear there is something about you that makes me angrier than most."

He laughed again. "I suppose I should not mind then, so long as I am memorable."

Alizeh sighed. She shoved her small pillow into her bag, snapped the overstuffed bag closed. "All right, I w—"

There was a sound.

A distant creak of stairs, the sound of wood expanding and contracting. No one ever came up this far, not unless it was absolutely necessary—and if someone was here now, it was without a doubt to make certain she was gone.

Alizeh did not think before she reacted, instinct alone activating her movements. Indeed it all happened so quickly she'd not even realized what she'd done until her mind was returned to her body, sensation returned to her skin.

She felt him everywhere, all at once.

She'd knocked them both back into a far corner of the room, where they now crouched, and where Alizeh had cloaked their bodies and her bag with invisibility.

She also all but sat in his lap.

Ferocious heat spread through her body, something like mortification. She could not move now for fear of exposing them, but neither did she know how she would survive this:

his body pressed against hers, his warm breath at her neck. She inhaled the scent of him without meaning to—orange blossoms and leather—and the heady combination filled her head, startled her nerves.

"Is it possible you're trying to kill me?" he whispered. "Your methods are highly unusual."

She didn't dare answer.

If she and the prince were caught alone in her room together, she could only imagine the fallout for both of them. A plausible explanation seemed impossible.

When the doorknob turned a second later, she felt the prince stiffen with awareness. His hand tightened around her waist, and Alizeh's heart pounded only harder.

She'd forgotten to blow out the candle.

Alizeh tensed as the door creaked open. She had no way of knowing who would be sent to check on her; if it was one of the rarer Jinn servants, her illusion of invisibility would not hold, as it was effective only on Clay. She also knew not whether her attempt to extend this protection to the prince would be successful, as she'd never before attempted such a feat.

A figure entered the room—not Mrs. Amina, Alizeh noted with relief—but a footman. His eyes roved the room, and Alizeh tried to see the space as he did: stripped of all personal effects, save the small basket of dried flowers.

And the candle, the blasted candle.

The footman scooped up the flowers and headed straight for the flame, shaking his head with obvious irritation before blowing it out. Doubtless he wondered whether the girl had planned to set fire to the house upon her exit.

He was gone a moment later, slamming the door shut behind him.

That was it.

The ordeal was done.

Alizeh should have rejoiced in her success, but the small, windowless attic room had gone suddenly, suffocatingly dark, and a familiar panic began to claw its way up her throat, constricting her chest. She felt as if she'd been left at the bottom of the sea, consumed whole by infinite night.

Worse, she found that she could not move.

Alizeh blinked desperately against the jet black, willing her eyes to adjust to the impenetrable darkness, to widen their aperture enough to find a single spark of light, all to no avail. The more desperate she grew, the harder it became to remain calm; she felt her heart beat faster in her chest, her pulse fluttering in her throat.

The prince moved, suddenly, touching her as he shifted, his hands circling her waist. He lifted her, just slightly, to adjust himself, but he made no effort to put space between their bodies.

In fact, he drew her closer.

"I beg your pardon," he whispered in her ear. "But do you intend to sit on me in perpetuity?"

Alizeh felt a bit faint, and she did not know then whether to blame the dark or the nearness of the prince, whose ever-increasing proximity had begun to brew a counterintuitive cure for her panic. His closeness somehow dulled the sharpest edge of her fear, imbuing in her now an unexpected calm.

She unclenched by degrees, sinking slowly against him with unconscious effort; every inch she conceded he easily claimed, drawing her deeper into his warmth, more fully into his embrace. His body heat soon enveloped her so completely that she imagined, for the length of the most sublime moment, that the ice in her veins had begun to thaw, that she might presently puddle at his feet. Without a sound she sighed, sighed as relief coursed through her frozen blood. Even her racing pulse began to steady.

She could not name this remedy.

She only knew he was strong—she could feel it even now—his limbs heavy and solid, his broad chest the ideal place to rest her head. Alizeh had been desperately fatigued for years; she was overwhelmed then by an illogical desire to wrap the comforting weight of his arms around her body and sleep. She wanted to close her eyes, wanted to drift off at long last without fear, without worry.

She'd not felt safe in so long.

The prince sat forward an inch and his jaw skimmed her cheek, hard and soft planes touching, retreating.

She heard him exhale.

"I haven't the slightest idea what we're doing," he said softly. "Though if you mean to take me captive, you need only ask. I would come willingly."

Alizeh almost laughed, grateful for the reprieve. She focused her fractured consciousness on the prince, allowing his voice, his weight, to orient her. He seemed to her so wonderfully concrete, so certain not only of himself, but of the world he occupied. Alizeh, by contrast, often felt like a ship lost at sea, tossed about in every storm, narrowly avoiding disaster at every turn. She was struck, then, by a strange thought: that she might never be shipwrecked if she had such an anchor to steady her.

"If I tell you something," Alizeh whispered, her hand curling unconsciously around his forearm. "Will you promise not to tease me?"

"Absolutely not."

She made a sound in her throat, something mournful.

"Very well." He sighed. "Go on."

"I'm a bit afraid of the dark."

It was a moment before he said, "I beg your pardon?"

"Petrified, actually. I'm petrified of the dark. I feel very nearly paralyzed right now."

"You're not serious."

"I am, quite."

"You killed five men last night—in the dark—and you expect me to believe this blather?"

"It's true," she insisted.

"I see. If you've constructed this falsehood merely to safeguard your modesty, you should know that it only undermines your intelligence, for the lie is too weak to be believed. You would be better off simply admitting that you find me attractive and wish to be near m—"

Alizeh made a sound of protest, so horrified she shot straight up and stumbled, her injured knee having been locked in one position for too long. She caught herself against her old cot and stifled a cry, clinging to the thin mattress with both hands.

Her heart beat harder in her chest.

She shivered violently as her body filled again with frost; her terror, too, had returned, this time with a force that shook her knees. In the absence of the prince—the absence of his heat, his reliable form—Alizeh felt cold and exposed. The darkness had grown somehow more vicious without him near; more likely to devour her whole. She stretched trembling hands out before her, reaching blindly for an exit that refused to illuminate.

She knew, intellectually, that hers was an irrational fear—knew the illusion was only in her head—

Still, it claimed her.

It gripped her mind with two fists and spun her into a vortex of senselessness. It was all she could think, suddenly, that she did not want to die here, compressed by the darkness of the earth. She did not want to be abandoned by the sun, the moon, the stars; did not want to be inhaled whole by the force of the expanding universe.

Suddenly, she could hardly breathe.

She felt his arms come around her then, strong hands steadying her, searching for purchase. He drew a map of her with his fingers until he found her face, which he took into his hands, and upon which he made a discovery that bade him be still. Alizeh felt it when he changed, when his fingers met with the tears falling slowly down her cheeks.

"By the angels," he whispered. "You really are afraid of the dark. You strange girl."

She pulled away and wiped at her face, squeezed her eyes shut. "I only need to orient myself. My—my bed is here, which means the door is just—just across there. I'll be fine, you'll see."

"I don't understand. Of all the things in your life to fear— I've seen you in the dark before, and you never reacted like this."

"It was not"—she swallowed, steadied herself—"it was not entirely dark then. There are gas lamps lining the streets. And the moon—the moon is a great comfort to me."

"The moon is a great comfort to you," he repeated tonelessly. "What an odd thing to say."

"Please don't tease me. You said you wouldn't."

"I'm not teasing you. I'm stating a fact. You are very strange."

"And you, sire, are unkind."

"You're crying in a dark room the size of my thumb; the door is but paces away. Surely you see that you are being nonsensical."

"Oh, now you're just being cruel."

"I'm being honest."

"You are being needlessly mean."

"Mean? You say this to the man who just saved your life?"

"Saved my life?" Alizeh said, angrily wiping away the last of her tears. "How easily you praise yourself. You hardly saved my life."

"Didn't I? Was not your life in danger? Is that not why you were crying?"

"Of course not, that's n—"

"Then you accept my point," he said. "That you were in no real danger. That you were being nonsensical."

"I—" She faltered. Her mouth fell open. "Oh, you are a horrible person. You are a mean, horrible—"

"I am an extremely generous person. Have you already forgotten how long I allowed you to sit on me?"

Alizeh gasped. "How dare y—"

She stopped herself, the words dying in her throat at the muffled sound of his laughter, the palpable tremble of his body as he struggled to contain it.

"Why do you rile so easily?" he said, still fighting a laugh. "Do you not see that your effortless outrage only makes me want to provoke you more?"

Alizeh stiffened at that; felt suddenly stupid. "You mean you *were* teasing me? Even after I asked you not to?"

"Forgive me," he said, the smile lingering in his voice. "I was teasing you, yes, but only because I'd hoped it would distract you from your fear. I see now that you do not laugh easily at yourself. Or others."

"Oh," she said, feeling small. "I see."

He touched her then, a brush of his fingers down her arm, leaving a fiery path in its wake.

Alizeh dared not breathe.

She didn't know when they'd arrived here, or how, but in such a brief time she felt closer to this peculiar prince than she had with most anyone. Even the way he touched her was familiar—his nearness was familiar. She could not explain why, but she felt safe by his side.

No doubt it was the work of the nosta, without which she might've questioned his every word and action. Indeed, knowing unequivocally that all he'd said to her today was true—that he'd sought her out in the interest of her protection, ostensibly against the wishes of the king—had deeply affected her. It was not even that he was handsome or noble, or that he acted the part of a chivalrous prince—

No, her pleasure was far simpler than that.

Alizeh had long ago been forced into a life of obscurity and insignificance. She was accosted and spat upon, beaten and disrespected. She'd been reduced to nothing in the eyes of society, was hardly recognized as a living being, and was promptly forgotten by most everyone she met.

It was a miracle, then, that he'd noticed her at all.

How, she wondered, had this prince been the only one to see something notable in her, something worth remembering? She'd never have said the words aloud, but his discovery—however dangerous—meant more to her than he would ever know.

She heard him draw breath.

"I want very much," he said softly, "to tell you what I am thinking now, but you will no doubt think I exaggerate, even if I swear it to be true."

Alizeh wanted to laugh. "Do you not think it a kind of cheat, sire, to make such a declaration when you know full well I will insist upon your confession? Does it not seem unfair to you to place the burden of interest entirely on my shoulders?"

There was a beat of silence then, during which Alizeh

imagined she could feel his surprise.

"I fear you've mistaken me for a different sort of person," he said quietly. "I displaced no burden. I do not fear the repercussions of honesty."

"No?" Now she was nervous.

"No."

"Oh," she said, the word a breath.

The prince closed the narrow gap between them until they were dangerously close—so close she suspected she'd need only to tilt up her chin and their lips would touch.

She could not calm her heart.

"You have consumed my thoughts since the moment I met you," he said to her. "I feel now, in your presence, entirely strange. I think I might fetch you the moon if only to spare your tears again."

Once more, the nosta flashed warm against Alizeh's skin, proof that only terrified her heart into a gallop, sent a flood of feeling through her body. She felt disoriented, hyper-aware, and still confused; only dimly cognizant of another world waiting for her; of danger and urgency waiting, waiting for her to surface.

"Tell me your name," he whispered.

Slowly, very slowly, Alizeh touched her fingers to his waist, anchored herself to his body. She heard his soft intake of breath.

"Why?" she asked.

He hesitated, briefly, before he said, "I begin to fear you've done me irreparable damage. I should like to know who to blame."

"Irreparable damage? Surely now you are exaggerating."

"I only wish I were."

"If that is true, sire, then it is best we part as anonymous friends, so as to spare each other further harm."

"Friends?" he said, dismayed. "If your intention was to wound me, know you have succeeded."

"You're right." She grinned. "We have no hope even of friendship. Best to simply say our goodbyes. Shall we shake hands?"

"Oh, now you really do wound me."

"Never fear, Your Highness. This brief interlude will be relegated to a graveyard populated by all manner of half-forgotten memories."

He laughed, briefly, at that, but there was little mirth in it. "Do you take pleasure in torturing me with this drivel?"

"A bit, yes."

"Well, I'm pleased to know I've rendered a service, at least."

She was still smiling. "Farewell," she whispered. "Our time together has come to an end. We will never again meet. Our worlds will never again collide."

"Don't say that," he said, suddenly serious. His hand moved to her waist, traveled up the curve of her rib cage. "Say anything but that."

Alizeh was no longer smiling. Her heart was beating so hard she thought it might bruise. "What shall I say, then?"

"Your name. I want to hear it from your lips."

She took a breath. Released it slowly.

"My name," she said, "is Alizeh. I am Alizeh of Saam, the

daughter of Siavosh and Kiana. Though you may know me better as the lost queen of Arya."

He stiffened at that, went silent.

Finally he moved, one hand capturing her face, his thumb grazing her cheek in a fleeting moment, there and gone again. His voice was a whisper when he said, "Do you wish to know my name, too, Your Majesty?"

"Kamran," she said softly. "I already know who you are."

She was unprepared when he kissed her, for the darkness had denied her a warning before their lips met, before he claimed her mouth with a need that stole from her an anguished sound, a faint cry that shocked her.

She felt his desperation as he touched her, as he kissed her in every passing second with a need greater than the one before, inspiring in her a response she could not fathom into words. She only breathed him in, drew the fragrance of his skin into her blood, the darkly floral scent striking her mind like an opiate. He drew his hands down her body with an unconcealed longing she returned in equal measure; one she'd not even known herself to possess. She didn't even think before she reached for him, twining her arms around his neck; she pushed her hands through the silk of his hair and he went briefly solid, then kissed her so deeply she tasted him, heat and sugar, over and over. Every inch of her skin was suddenly so fraught with sensation she could hardly move.

No, she did not want to move.

She dared to touch him, too, to feel the expanse of his chest, the sculpted lines of his body; she felt him change as

she discovered him, breathe harder when she touched her
lips to the sharp line of his jaw, the column of his neck. He
made a sound, a low moan in his throat, igniting a flare of
awareness in her chest that flashed across her skin before his
back was suddenly against the wall, his arms braced around
her waist. Still, she could not seem to get close enough. She
despaired when he broke away, feeling the loss of him even
as he kissed her cheeks, her closed eyes, and suddenly his
hands were in her hair, pulling pins, reaching for the buttons
of her dress—

Oh.

Alizeh tore away, stumbled back on unsteady legs.

Her bones would not cease shaking. They both struggled
to catch their breath, but Alizeh hardly knew herself in that
moment, hardly recognized the violent pounding of her
heart, the unfathomable desire that had risen up inside her.
She now wanted things she could not even name, things she
knew she could never have.

What on earth had she done?

"Alizeh."

A frisson of feeling moved through her at that, at the tortured sound of his voice, her name on his lips. Her chest
was heaving; her corset too tight. She felt suddenly dizzy,
desperate for air.

Heavens, she had lost her mind.

The prince of Ardunia was not to be trifled with. She
knew that. She knew it and yet somehow, for a brief window, it had not seemed to matter; she'd taken leave of her

senses and now she'd suffer for it, for her lapse in judgment. She'd already suffered for it if the ache in her heart was any indication.

Alizeh wanted nothing more than to throw herself back into his arms, even as she knew it to be a flight of madness.

"Forgive me," Kamran whispered, his voice raw, nearly unrecognizable. "I didn't mean— I wasn't thinking—"

"I'm not upset," she said, trying to steady herself. "You need not worry on that account. We were both of us out of our heads."

"You misunderstand me," he said with feeling. "I did nothing I didn't want to do. I want nothing more than to do it again."

Oh, no, she couldn't breathe.

What she realized then, even as her body trembled, was a single, unassailable fact: what had transpired between her and the prince was much more than a kiss. Even inexperienced as she was, Alizeh possessed awareness enough to understand that something extraordinary had sparked between them.

Something uncommon.

It was critical that she first acknowledge this in order to next acknowledge something else: there was no future for them.

Somehow she knew—somehow she saw, with shocking clarity—that a planted kernel between them had bloomed. Quavering green shoots had sprung forth from the ground beneath her feet; shoots that, if nurtured, might one day flourish into something majestic, a towering tree that not only bore fruit and offered shade, but supplied a sturdy trunk against which she might rest her weary body.

This was impossible.

Not only impossible, it was dangerous. Ruinous. Not merely for themselves—but for the realms they occupied. Their lives were pitted against each other. He had a kingdom to one day rule, and she had her own life to pursue. Any other avenue would lead only to chaos.

His grandfather was trying to *kill* her.

No, Alizeh understood then, even as it pierced her heart, that if she did not destroy this fragile bloom between them now, it would one day grow great enough to crush them both.

She had to leave.

She took a step back, felt the doorknob dig into her spine.

"Wait," the prince said. "Please—"

She reached backward, wrapped her hand around the handle, and pushed it open.

A single, faint beam of light penetrated the room. She spotted her carpet bag in a corner, and quickly collected it.

"Alizeh," he said, moving toward her. She saw the anguish in his eyes, a flash of panic. "Please, don't just disappear. Not now, not when I've only just found you."

She stared at him, her heart beating in her throat. "Surely you must see," she said. "There exists no bridge between our lives; no path that connects our worlds."

"How can that matter? Is this not one day to be my empire, to rule as I see fit? I will build a bridge. I can clear a path. Or do you not think me capable?"

"Don't say things now that you cannot mean. We are

neither of us in our right minds—"

"I grow tired," he said, trying to breathe, "of being in my right mind. I much prefer this kind of madness."

Alizeh gripped with both hands the handle of her carpet bag and took a nervous step back. "You should not— You should not say such things to me—"

He drew closer. "Do you know I am meant to choose a bride tonight?"

Alizeh was surprised by her own shock at that, by the vague nausea that struck her. She felt suddenly ill.

Confused.

"I am meant to marry a complete stranger," he was saying. "A candidate chosen by others to be my wife—to one day be my queen—"

"Then—then I offer my congratulations—"

"I beg you do not." He was in front of her now, one hand reaching out, as if he might touch her. She couldn't breathe for not knowing whether he might, then couldn't breathe when he finally did, when the tips of his fingers grazed her hip, then up, up the curve of her bodice, trembling slightly as they drew away.

"Will you not give me hope?" he whispered. "Tell me I will see you again. Ask me to wait for you."

"How can you even say such things when you know the consequences would be dire— Your people will think you've gone mad—your own king will forsake you—"

Incredibly, Kamran laughed, but it sounded angry. "Yes," he said softly. "My own king will forsake me."

"Kamran—"

He stepped forward and she gasped, took another step backward.

"You must—you must know," Alizeh said, her voice unsteady. "I must tell you now how grateful I am for what you did today—for trying to protect me. I am in your debt, sire, and I will not soon forget it."

She saw the change in his expression then, the dawning realization there that she would really leave, that this was how they'd part.

"Alizeh," he said, his eyes bright with pain. "Please—Don't—"

Then, she was gone.

TWENTY-NINE

يست ونه

KAMRAN CHASED AFTER HER, RACING down the stairs like a fool, as if he could ever catch up to a ghost, as if even finding her would be enough. How the prince managed in his mind to reconcile his desire for the girl and his loyalty to his king he did not know, but even as his better sense condemned him for his dissidence, he could not deny the terrifying feelings taking root inside him. His actions were both treacherous and futile, and still he could not stop himself; could not calm the pounding of his heart nor the madness that gripped him.

He had to see her—to speak with her just once more—

"Where on earth have you been, child?"

Kamran came to a sharp, disorienting halt on the landing, his mind returning to his body with the force of a thunderclap.

His aunt was staring up at him from just steps below, one hand clutching her skirts, the other gripping the banister. They were standing but two flights above the main floor, but he saw—in the light sheen at her brow, in the sharp creasing of her forehead—just how much it had cost the older woman to seek him out.

Kamran slowed.

Fatigue hit him as suddenly as if he'd been struck by a

physical blow, and he grabbed the banister, steadying himself against the assault.

He closed his eyes.

"Forgive me," he said, quietly catching his breath. "I lost track of time."

He heard his aunt make a *tsk* of disapproval, and opened his eyes to see that she was looking him over, scrutinizing his hair, his eyes—even the sleeves of his sweater, which he'd at some point pulled up his forearms. Quietly, Kamran put himself to rights, running an absent hand over his hair, pushing the black waves out of his eyes.

It scared him to realize how easily his heart and mind had parted.

Duchess Jamilah pursed her lips and held out her hand, and Kamran quickly closed the distance between them, tucking her delicate fingers into the crook of his elbow. Carefully, he helped the older woman walk back down the stairs.

"So," she said. "You say you lost track of time."

Kamran made a noncommittal sound.

"I see." His aunt sighed. "You seem to have done a thorough job wandering the house, in any case. The servants are all in a dither over your brooding. First the street boy, then the snoda, now you're mooning about the house, staring longingly out of windows. They all think you a tragic, hopeless romantic, and I'll be surprised if all their gossip doesn't earn you a few inches in the paper tomorrow." She hesitated on a step; glanced up at him. "Take care, child. The younger girls might begin to swoon at the mere sight of you."

Kamran forced a smile. "You have a gift, dear aunt. Your

flattery is always the most elaborate fiction."

She gave a rasp of a laugh. "You think I exaggerate?"

"I think you enjoy exaggerating."

She gave him a light smack on the arm. "Impertinent child."

This time, his smile was genuine.

They'd reached the main floor, were now walking through the great room, and still, Kamran's heart refused to slow its erratic beating. He'd been in darkness so long it was a shock to see the sun still shining through the tall windows. He turned away from the glare, burying the sharp pang that moved through him at the sight. Kamran knew a young woman who would dearly enjoy the sun, who would find solace in its light.

The moon is a great comfort to me.

He realized, with some despair, that everything would now remind him of her. The very sun and moon, the shifting of lightness and dark.

Pink roses.

There—they were just there, a vivid spray in a vase, the arrangement centered on a high table in the room they now occupied. Kamran disengaged from his aunt and wandered toward the bouquet without thinking; carefully, he drew a bloom from its vessel, grazing the velvet petals with his fingers before holding the flower to his nose, inhaling the intoxicating scent.

His aunt gave a sharp laugh, and Kamran flinched.

"You must have mercy, my dear," she said. "News of our melancholy prince will spread far beyond Setar if you do not soon exercise some discretion."

With great care, the prince returned the flower to its vase. "Is our world really so ridiculous," he said quietly, "that my every action is newsworthy, ripe for dissection? Am I not allowed a modicum of humanity? Can I not enjoy simple beauty without censure and suspicion?"

"That you even ask such a question tells me you are not yourself." She drew closer. "Kamran, you will one day be king. The people look to your disposition as a bellwether of all to come; the temperature of your heart will define the tenor of your rule, which will in turn affect every aspect of their lives. Surely you do not forget this. You could not resent the people their curiosity—not when you know how dearly your life concerns their own."

"Certainly not," he said with affected calm. "How could I? I should never resent them their fears, nor could I ever forget the shackles that so loudly ornament my every waking moment."

His aunt took a deep, wavering breath, and accepted the prince's proffered arm. They resumed their slow walk.

"You begin to scare me, child," she said softly. "Will you not tell me what has disordered you so?"

Disordered.

Yes.

Kamran had been rearranged. He felt it; felt that his heart had moved, that his ribs had closed like a fist around his lungs. He was different, out of alignment, and he did not know whether this feeling would fade.

Alizeh.

He still heard the whisper of her voice, the way she'd pressed the shape of her own name into the darkness between them; the way she'd gasped when he kissed her. She'd touched him with a tenderness that drove him wild, had looked into his eyes with a sincerity that broke him.

From the first there'd been no falseness in her manner, no pretension, no agonizing self-consciousness. Alizeh had been neither impressed by the prince nor intimidated; Kamran knew without a doubt that she'd judged him entirely on his own merits, his crown be damned. That she'd found him worthy, that she'd given herself to him for even a moment—

Not until that very second did he realize how much he'd longed for her good opinion. Her judgment of his character had somehow become crucial to his judgment of himself.

How?

He did not know, he did not care; he was not one for questioning the movements of his heart. He recognized only that she'd been so much more than he'd known to hope for, and it had altered him: her mind as sharp as her heart; her smile as overwhelming as her tears. She'd suffered so much in her life that Kamran had not known what to expect; he would have understood had she been withdrawn and cynical, but she was instead vibrant with feeling, alive in every emotion, mercifully giving of herself in all ways.

He could still feel her body under his hands, the scent of her skin suffusing his head, his every thought. His own skin grew hot with the memories of her breathless sounds, the way she'd gone soft in his arms. The way she'd tasted.

He wanted to put his fist through a wall.

"My dear?"

Kamran came back to himself with a sharp breath.

"Forgive me," he said, gently clearing his throat. "I am besieged now only by the most unimaginative of human afflictions. I slept poorly last night, and I've not eaten much today. I'm certain my mood will cool after we've enjoyed our meal together. Shall we go through for luncheon?"

"Oh, my dear"—his aunt hesitated, consternation knitting her brow—"I'm afraid we must forgo luncheon today. Your minister has come to fetch you."

Kamran turned sharply to face her. "Hazan is here?"

"I'm afraid so." She looked away. "He's been waiting some time now, and I daresay he's not altogether pleased about it. He says your presence is required back at the palace? Something to do with the ball, I imagine."

"Ah." Kamran gave a nod. "Indeed."

A lie.

If Hazan had come for him personally—had not trusted a messenger to inspire his hasty return—then something was very wrong.

"A shame," his aunt said, forcing cheerfulness, "that your visit was so brief."

"Please accept my sincerest apologies," Kamran said, lowering his eyes. "I feel I have been nothing but distracted and disappointing to you this day." They came to a stop in the front hall. "Would you allow me to make up for this lost visit with another?"

She brightened at that. "That sounds just fine, my dear.

You know you are welcome here anytime. You need only name the day."

Kamran took his aunt's hand and kissed it, bowing at the waist before her. When he met her eyes again, she'd gone pink in the face.

"Until next time, then."

"*Your Highness.*"

Kamran turned at the heated sound of his minister's voice. Hazan could not—and made no effort, in any case—to hide his irritation.

Kamran forced a smile. "Heavens, Hazan, are you having a fit? Can you not allow me even to say goodbye to my aunt?"

The minister did not acknowledge this. "The carriage is waiting outside, sire. Worry not about your horse, as I've arranged for his safe return to the palace."

"I see," said the prince quietly. He knew Hazan well enough; something was definitely wrong.

A servant handed Kamran his coat, another, his staff. In a matter of moments he'd bid goodbye to his aunt, walked the short path to the carriage, and settled into the seat across from his minister.

The carriage door had only just slammed shut when Kamran's expression grew grave.

"Go on, then," he said.

Hazan sighed. "We have received word, sire, from Tulan."

THIRTY

سی

ALIZEH STOOD IN THE MIDDLE of the busy, bustling path, eyes closed, masked eyes turned up toward the sun.

It was a beautifully bright day, the air sharp with cold, not a cloud in the sky. The world around her was loud with the clop of hooves, the rattle of wheels, savory smoke from a nearby kabob shop coiling around her head. Midday in the royal city of Setar meant the gilded streets were alive with color and commotion, food carts busy with customers, shopkeepers shouting loudly about their wares.

Alizeh was equal parts hopeful and devastated as she stood there, both halves of her heart rife with excuses, all of them compelling. Very soon she'd be forced to examine closely her long list of troubles, but right then she wanted only a moment to breathe, to enjoy the scene.

Tiny finches hopped and tittered along the path while large, glittering crows cawed high in the sky, a few swooping low to perch on the heads and hats of passersby, the better to peck at their baubles. Angry shopkeepers chased after the winged beasts with their broomsticks, one unlucky proprietor accidentally knocking in the head a man who promptly fell over into the capable arms of a street child, who then pinched the man's purse and darted into the crowd. The gentleman cried out, giving chase, but his pursuit of the small thief was thwarted by the commotion of a nearby pastry shop, which had flung open its doors without warning, unleashing a stream of servants into the madness.

Single file, no fewer than a dozen snodas cut a serpentine path through the crowd, each carrying a broad, circular tray high above their head, each heavy platter laden with baklava and pistachio brittle, soft nougat, syrupy donuts, and spirals of honey-soaked funnel cakes. The heady aroma of rosewater and sugar filled the air as the procession marched past, all maneuvering carefully so as not to disturb the many parked occupants of the path.

Alizeh turned.

Large, colorfully patterned rugs had been rolled out over the golden cobblestone, upon which women in bright, floral chadors sat cross-legged, laughing and sharing gossip as they sorted through bushels of purple saffron flowers. Their deft hands paused only occasionally, and only to sip tea from gilt-rimmed glasses; otherwise their nimble motions did not cease. Over and over they separated styles and stigmas from their lush flowers, adding the ruby-red saffron threads to the growing piles between them.

Alizeh could not move, she was so mesmerized.

The last time she'd dared stop for so long in the street she'd been assaulted by a child thief, and yet—how could she deny herself such an indulgence now, when she'd not been free to enjoy daylight in so long? This living, breathing world was hers to admire for this single moment in time, and she wanted to breathe it in; to luxuriate in the beating heart of civilization.

After tonight, she would never see it again.

If things went well, she'd be gone from here; if they went poorly, she'd have no choice but to flee.

Tears sprang to Alizeh's eyes even as she smiled.

She managed to forge a path through the saffron spreads, stopping only when startled by a display of blooms arranged in the window of a nearby florist: winter roses, butter-colored camellias, and white snowdrops smiled up at her from their cut-crystal vase, and Alizeh was so enchanted by the sight she nearly collided with a farmer, who'd stopped without warning to feed alfalfa to his shaggy goat.

Unsettled, her nerves would not now quiet.

Hastily Alizeh moved aside, wedging herself against the window of a millinery shop. She tried to shutter her mind but it was no good; her subconscious would no longer submit. She was battered at once by a deluge of remembered sensations: the whisper of a voice against her ear, a smile against her cheek, the weight of arms around her body. She still tasted him on her lips, could still summon the silky texture of his hair, the hard line of his jaw under her hand. The memories alone were devastating.

Over and over Alizeh had tried to understand why the devil had warned her of the prince—and even now she was uncertain. Was this it, then?

Was it because of a kiss?

Alizeh tensed, took a breath. Even as her heart raced, her mind cooled. What had transpired between her and the prince was a moment of foolishness for a myriad of reasons— not the least of which was that he was heir to an empire whose sovereign sought to destroy her. She'd not yet even begun to unpack the ramifications of such a discovery, nor what explanations it might reveal for the beloved friends and family she'd lost to unexplained acts of violence. Did it mean the king had tried to kill her once before? Had it been he who'd issued the orders to murder her parents?

It troubled her that she could not know for certain.

Kamran might've circumvented the orders of his grandfather to help her today, but Alizeh was not a simple girl; she knew that relationships between kin were not so easily severed. The prince might have spared her a moment of kindness, but his allegiance, no doubt, was elsewhere.

Still, Alizeh could not condemn herself too harshly.

Not only had the dalliance been unplanned, it had been an unexpected reprieve—a rare moment of pleasure—from what seemed the interminable darkness of her days. For years she'd wondered whether anyone might ever again touch her with care, or look at her like she mattered.

She did not take lightly such an experience.

Indeed there had been a mercy in it, in its tenderness, which she would now gracefully accept, pocketing the memories before moving forward. Her thoughtless actions would never again be repeated.

Besides, she consoled herself, she and Kamran would never again cross paths, and all the better, though—

A flock of birds at her feet took flight without warning, disquieting Alizeh so thoroughly she gasped and stumbled backward, colliding with a young man who promptly caught sight of her snoda and sneered, elbowing her out of the way.

A sharp knock to her ribs and again Alizeh doddered, though this time she caught herself, and hurried forward through the crowd.

She'd known, of course, even as she bade the prince fare-well, that there was a chance she'd see him again at the ball that evening. She'd not felt it necessary to inform him of her attendance because she thought meeting him again a bad idea; and now that she knew the ball was in fact meant to facilitate his impending marriage—

No, she would not think of it.

It did not matter. *It could not matter.* In any case, their spheres had no hope of intersecting at such an event; she would not have cause to see him.

Alizeh did not know the full scope of Hazan's plan for her escape, but she doubted it'd have much to do with the festivities themselves, and the prince—for whom the ball had been arranged—would no doubt be expected to engage fully in its activities.

No, they would certainly not see each other again.

Alizeh felt a pang at that conclusiveness, a sharp pain she could not decipher; it was either longing or grief, or perhaps the two feelings were identical, split ends of the same sword.

Oh, what did it matter?

She sighed, sidestepping to avoid a trio of girls chasing each other through the crowd, and peered, halfheartedly, through the window against which she was pressed.

A row of children were sitting at a high counter, each devouring sandwiches of pomegranate ice cream, the blush-colored treat pressed between crisp disks of freshly baked waffles. Their grown-ups stood by smiling and scolding, wiping the sticky mouths and tearstained cheeks of the children they could catch, the others tearing wildly about the shop, rummaging through crystal tubs brimming with fruit taffies and colorful marzipan, rock sugar and rose-petal nougat.

Alizeh heard their muted laughter through the glass.

She tightened her grip on her luggage then, tensing as her heart fractured in her chest. Alizeh, too, had once been a child, had once had parents who spoiled her thus. How good it was to be loved, she thought. How very important.

A curious little girl caught her eye then, and waved.

Tentatively, Alizeh waved back.

She was homeless. Jobless. All she owned in the world she carried in a single, worn carpet bag, the sum total of her coin scarcely two coppers altogether. She had nothing and no one to claim but herself, and it would have to be enough.

It would always have to be enough.

Even in her most desperate moments, Alizeh had found the courage to move forward by searching the depths of herself; she'd found hope in the sharpness of her mind, in the capacity of her own capable hands, in the endurance of her unrelenting spirit.

She would be broken by nothing.

She refused.

It was time, then, for her to find escape from the travails of her life. Hazan would help—but she first had to forge a path through her current predicament.

She needed to form a plan.

How might she source the necessary material and notions needed to make herself a gown? She would've had more coin to her name except that Miss Huda had yet to pay her an advance against the five gowns she'd requested; instead, the young woman was waiting first to see how Alizeh might transform the taffeta ahead of the ball tonight, which now lay crumpled inside her bag.

Alizeh sighed.

Two coppers were all she had, then, and they would afford her next to nothing from the cloth merchants.

She grimaced and pushed on, her mind working. An elderly man with a wispy beard and white turban shot past her on a bright-blue bicycle, coming to a terrifying halt not twenty feet away. She watched as he unfolded his narrow body from the seat, unpacked a sign from the basket of his transport, and hooked the wooden board onto the front of a nearby cart.

Teethmaker, it read.

When he saw her staring, he beckoned her close, offering her a discount on a pair of third molars.

Alizeh almost smiled as she shook her head, staring at the scenes around her now with a touch of sadness. For months she'd lived in this royal city, and never before had she been able to see it like this, at its most dynamic, enchanting hour. Troubadours were parked at intervals with santoor and setar, filling the streets with music, flooding her heart with emotion. She smiled in earnest as cheerful pedestrians spared what moments they had to dance, to clap hands as they passed.

Her whole life seemed suddenly surreal to her, surreal because the sounds and scenes that surrounded her were so incongruously life-affirming.

With some effort, Alizeh fought back the maelstrom of emotion threatening to upend her mind and focused her thoughts instead on the many tasks ahead. With purposeful strides she passed the confectionary shop and the noisy coppersmith next door; she shot past a dusty rug emporium, colorful rolls stacked to the ceiling and spilling out of doorways, then a bakery and its open windows, the heavenly aroma of what she knew to be fresh bread filling her nose.

Suddenly, she slowed—her gaze lingering a moment on the large flour sacks by the door.

Alizeh could fashion a garment out of near anything, but even if she were able to source enough of a substandard textile, arriving at the ball in a burlap dress would only make her a small spectacle. If she wanted to disappear, she'd need to look like the others in attendance, which meant wearing nothing at all unusual.

She hesitated, appraising herself a moment.

Alizeh had always taken meticulous care of the little she owned, but even so, her calico work dress was nearly worn through. The gray frock had always been dull, but it appeared even more lifeless at present, faded and limp with relentless wear. She had one other spare gown, and she did not have to see it to know it was in a similar state. Her stockings, however, were still serviceable; her boots, too, were sturdy despite needing a polish—though the tear in one toe had yet to be mended.

Alizeh bit her lip.

She was left with no option. Her vanity could not be spared; she'd simply have to disassemble one of her drab gowns and remake it, and hope she had enough workable material to get it right. She might even be able to repurpose the remainder of her torn apron to fashion a pair of simple gloves . . . if only she could find a safe space to work.

She sighed.

First, she decided, she would visit the local hamam. A scrub and soak she could afford, as the prices for a bath had always been reasonable for the poor, but—

Alizeh came to a sudden halt.

She'd spotted the apothecary; the familiar shape of the familiar shop arresting her in place. The sight of it made her wonder about her bandages.

Gingerly, she touched the linen at her neck.

She'd not felt pain in her hands or throat in at least a few hours; if it was too soon to remove the bandages entirely, it was perhaps not too soon to remove them for the length of an evening, was it? For she would certainly draw unwanted attention if she arrived looking so obviously injured.

Alizeh frowned and glanced again at the shop, wondering whether Deen was inside. She decided to go in, to ask his professional opinion, but then remembered with dawning horror what she'd said to him that awful night—how unfairly she'd criticized the prince, and how the shopkeeper had rebuked her for it.

No, never mind, then.

She hurried down the walk, narrowly avoiding impact

with a woman sweeping rose petals off the street, and came to another sudden halt. Alizeh squeezed her eyes shut and shook her head, hard.

She was being foolish.

It did her no good to avoid the apothecarist, not when she now needed his assistance. She would simply avoid saying anything stupid this time.

Before she could talk herself out of it, she marched back down the street and straight toward the apothecary, where she pushed open the door with a bit too much force.

A bell jangled as she entered.

"Be right with you," Deen muttered, unseeing, from behind the counter. He was assisting an older woman with a large order of dried hibiscus flowers, which he was advising her to brew three times daily.

"Morning, noon, and night," he said. "A cup in the evening will help a great deal with sl—"

Deen caught sight of Alizeh and promptly froze, his dark eyes widening by degrees. Alizeh lifted a limp hand in greeting, but the apothecarist looked away.

"That is—it will help with sleep," he said, accepting his customer's coin and counting it. "If you experience any digestive discomfort, reduce your intake to two cups, morning and night."

The woman offered quiet thanks and took her leave. Alizeh watched her go, the shop bell chiming softly in her wake.

There was a brief moment of quiet.

"So," Deen said, finally looking up. "You've come indeed.

I confess I wasn't entirely sure you would."

Alizeh felt a flutter of nerves at that; no doubt he'd seen her deliberating outside. Privately she'd hoped Deen might've forgotten her altogether; the awkwardness of their last conversation included. No such luck, it seemed.

"Yes, sir," she said. "Though I wasn't entirely sure I'd be coming, either, if I'm being honest."

"Well it's good you're here now." He smiled. "Shall I fetch you your parcel?"

"Oh, I—no—" Alizeh felt herself flush, the insubstantial weight of her two coppers suddenly heavy in her pocket. "I'm afraid I'm not in the market for—

"Actually," she said in a rush, "I wondered whether you might inspect my injuries a bit earlier than we discussed."

The wiry shopkeeper frowned. "That's five days earlier than we discussed. I trust there've been no complications?"

"No, sir." Alizeh stepped forward. "The salves have been a tremendous help. It's only that the bandages are—they're, well, they are a bit conspicuous, I think. They draw quite a lot of attention, and as I'd rather not be so easily remarked upon, I was hoping to remove them altogether."

Deen stared at her a moment, studied what little of her face he could see. "You want to remove your bandages five days early?"

"Yes, sir."

"Is it your housekeeper giving you trouble?"

"No, sir, it's n—"

"You are well within your rights to treat injuries, you know. She is not allowed to prevent your recove—"

"No, sir," Alizeh said again, a bit sharper this time. "It's not that."

When she said nothing else, Deen took a deep breath. He made no effort to hide his disbelief, and Alizeh was quietly surprised by his concern.

"Very well, then," he said, exhaling. "Have a seat. Let's take a look."

Alizeh pulled herself up onto the high chair at the counter, the better to be examined. Very slowly, Deen began unraveling the bandage at her neck.

"You've wrapped this quite nicely," he murmured, to which she only nodded her acknowledgment. There was something soothing about his gentle motions, and for a moment, Alizeh dared to close her eyes.

Never could she articulate precisely how exhausted she was. She couldn't even remember the last time she'd slept more than a couple of hours or felt safe enough to stand still for long. Seldom was she allowed to sit, almost never was she allowed to stop.

Oh, if only she could get herself to the ball tonight, anything might be possible. Relief. Safety. Peace. As for the actual shape of such dreams—

She had little in the way of expectations.

Alizeh was a failed queen without a kingdom, without even a small country to rule. Jinn were fractured across Ardunia, their known numbers too few, and the rest, too hard to find. Long ago there had been a plan for her ascent, the details of which Alizeh had not been made privy to at such a young age. Her parents always insisted she focus instead on her studies, on enjoying her youth a while longer.

Alizeh was twelve when her father died, and only afterward did Alizeh's mother begin to worry that her daughter knew too little of her fate. It was then that she told Alizeh of the Arya mountains, of the magic therein that was essential to unlocking the powers she was rumored to one day possess. When Alizeh had asked why she could not simply go and collect such a magic, her mother had laughed, and sadly.

"It is not so simple a task," she'd explained. "The magic must be gathered by a quorum of loyal subjects, all of whom must be willing to die for you in the process. The earth has chosen you to rule, my dear, but you must first be found worthy of the role by your own people. Five must be willing to sacrifice their lives to give rise to your reign; only then will the mountains part with their power."

It had always seemed to Alizeh an unnecessary, brutal requirement; she did not think herself capable of asking half a dozen people to die for her, not even in the interest of the common good. But as she could not now think of even a single person willing to forfeit their life in the pursuit of her interests—she felt it premature to rely upon even Hazan—it seemed a futile point to consider.

What's more, Alizeh knew that even if, through some miracle, she managed to claim her rightful throne and earn the allegiance of tens of thousands, she'd have already failed them as their queen, for she'd be sentencing her own people to death.

It required little creativity to imagine that the king of Ardunia would crush a rival on his own lands; his recent pursuit of her was proof enough of his concerns. He would never willingly lose his seat nor his people, and Jinn were among his numbers now.

Alizeh opened her eyes just as Deen unfurled the last of the linen at her neck.

"If you would please hold out your hands, miss, I'll unwrap the linen there, too," he was saying. "Though the cut at your throat appears to be healing very well . . ."

Alizeh held out her hands but turned her head toward the window, distracted as she was just then by the sight of a small, ancient woman pushing past a heaving wheelbarrow. The woman had aged much like a tree might, her face so gracefully inscribed by the passage of time that Alizeh thought she might count each line to know her age. Her shock of white hair was made a brilliant orange by henna and tied back with a floral scarf that matched her vivid, floral skirt. Alizeh glimpsed the woman's harvest: green almonds piled high in the cart, their soft fuzzy shells still intact, shimmering with frost.

The old woman nodded at her, and Alizeh smiled.

She had been surprised, upon arrival in Setar, to discover how much she loved the commotion of the royal city; the noise and madness were a comfort to her; a reminder that she was not alone in the world. To witness every day the collective effort of so many people striving and making and working and breathing—

It brought her unexpected calm.

Still, Alizeh was not like the others who lived here. Her differences were many, but perhaps her most problematic

was that she did not accept, without question, the greatness of the Ardunian empire. She did not accept that the
Fire Accords had been an unmitigated act of mercy. In some
ways, yes, they had been a kindness, but only because most
everyone had longed for an end to the millenia-long strife
between the races.

It was precisely why her people had conceded.

Jinn had grown tired of living in fear, of having their
homes set aflame, of watching their friends and families
hunted and massacred. Mothers on both sides had grown
tired of receiving the mutilated bodies of their children
from the battlefield. The pain of the endless bloodshed had
reached its pinnacle, and though both sides desired peace,
their mutual hatred could not be unlearned overnight.

The Accords had been enacted under the banner of
unity—a plea for cohesion, for harmony and understanding—
but Alizeh knew them to be motivated entirely by military
strategy. Enough Jinn had been slaughtered now that their
remaining numbers were no longer considered a threat; by
granting the survivors the veneer of safety and belonging,
the king of Ardunia had effectively subdued, then absorbed
into his empire, tens of thousands of the strongest and most
powerful beings on earth, for whom a little known provi-
sion had been made: Ardunian Jinn were allowed to exercise
their natural abilities only during wartime, and only on the
battlefield. *Four years* all capable citizens were required to
serve in the empire's army, and newly absorbed Jinn were
not exempt.

All of Ardunia thought King Zaal a generous, just ruler,

but Alizeh could not put her faith in such a man. He had, with a single, cunning decree, not only absolved Clay of all atrocities against Jinn, but rendered himself magnanimous, added to his armies a flood of supernatural recruits, and stripped ice-blooded Jinn any right to their constituents.

"All right, then," Deen said brightly. "All done, miss."

His lively tone was so unexpected Alizeh turned at once to look at him, surprise coloring her voice. "Is it good news?" she asked.

"Yes, miss, your skin has restored itself exceptionally well. I must say—those salves were of my own making, so while I know their many strengths, I'm also aware of their limits, and I've never known them to be responsible for such rapid healing."

Alizeh felt a bolt of fear move through her at that declaration, and she quickly withdrew her hands, studying them now in the sun-soaked room. She'd only changed her bandages once since she was last here, and only in the dead of night, overcome by exhaustion, her effort lit by the dim glow of a single candle. Now Alizeh studied her hands in amazement. They were soft and unblemished, no damage, not a scar to be found.

She dropped her hands in her lap, clenched them tight.

Alizeh had often wondered how she'd survived so many illnesses on the street, how she'd recovered over and over even when pushed to the brink of death. Fire, she knew she could withstand—it was the deep frost in her body that repelled it—but she'd never before had such irrefutable evidence of her body's strength.

She looked up at the apothecarist then, her eyes wide with something like panic.

Deen's smile had begun to fade. "Forgive me my ignorance, miss, but as I do not treat many Jinn, I've little basis for comparison. Is this—is this kind of healing uncommon among your kind?"

Alizeh wanted to lie, but worried the misinformation would adversely affect his treatment of what few Jinn did seek his aid. Softly, she said, "It is rare."

"And I take it you were, until now, unaware you were capable of such swift healing?"

"I was."

"I see," he said. "Well, I suppose we should accept it, then, as an unexpected stroke of good luck, which is no doubt long overdue." He attempted a smile. "I think you are more than ready to remove the bandages, miss. You need not worry on that account."

"Yes, sir. I thank you," Alizeh said, moving to stand. "How much do I owe you for the visit?"

Deen laughed. "I did nothing but remove your bandages and announce aloud what your own eyes might've easily witnessed. You owe me nothing."

"Oh, no, you're too generous—I've taken up your time, certainly I sho—"

"Not at all." He waved her away. "It was but five minutes at most. Besides, I've been awaiting your arrival all this day, and have already been paid handsomely for the trouble."

Alizeh froze. "I beg your pardon?"

"Your friend asked me to wait for you," the shopkeeper

said, frowning slightly. "Was he not the essential reason you came in today?"

"My friend?" Alizeh's heart had begun to pound.

"Yes, miss." Deen was looking at her strangely now. "He came in this morning—rather a tall fellow, wasn't he? He wore an interesting hat and had quite the most vivid blue eyes. He was insistent that you would come, and asked me not to close my shop, not even to take lunch, as I often do. He asked that I please deliver you this"—Deen held up a finger, then disappeared below the counter to retrieve a large, unwieldy package—"when you finally arrived."

Carefully, the shopkeeper settled the heavy, pale yellow box onto the worn surface of the workbench, which he then slid across to her. "I thought for certain he'd informed you of his visit here," Deen was saying, "for he seemed terribly confident you would come today." A pause. "I do hope I've not startled you."

Alizeh stared at the box, fear moving through her at an alarming speed. She was afraid even to touch the parcel.

Gently, she swallowed. "Did my—my friend—did he give his name?"

"No, miss," said Deen, who appeared now to be realizing that something was wrong. "Was not my description of the young man enough to engage your memory? He said the whole thing was meant to be a pleasant surprise for you. I confess I thought it seemed . . . great fun."

"Yes. Of course." Alizeh forced a laugh. "Yes, thank you. I was only—I'm only shocked, you see. I'm quite unaccustomed to receiving such extravagant gifts, and I fear I know not how to accept them graciously."

Deen recovered at that, his eyes shining brighter this time. "Yes, of course, miss. I understand completely."

There was a beat of silence, during which Alizeh pinned a smile onto her face. "When did you say my friend came to deliver the package?"

"Oh, I don't know exactly," Deen said, his brow furrowing. "It was sometime in the late morning, I think."

Late morning.

As if Deen's description of the stranger weren't proof enough, Alizeh was now certain the delivery was not made by the prince, who had been at Baz House at exactly that hour. There was only one other person who might've done such a thing for her, but for a single complication—

Hazan did not have blue eyes.

It was possible, of course, that the shopkeeper had made a mistake. Perhaps Deen had misspoke, or even seen Hazan in the wrong light. Hazan was tall, after all, that much was accurate; though Alizeh realized she didn't know enough about him to judge, with any real conviction, whether he was one to wear interesting hats.

Still, it was the answer that made the most sense.

Hazan said he would be looking out for her, did he not? Who else would be paying such close attention to her movements—who else would spare her such generosity?

Alizeh stared again at the beautiful package; at its immaculate presentation. Gingerly, she drew a finger along the scalloped edges of the outer box, the silky yellow ribbon cinching the case around the middle.

Alizeh knew exactly what this was; it was her job to know what it was. Still, it seemed impossible.

"Don't you want to open it, miss?" Deen was still staring at her. "I admit I'm terribly curious myself."

"Oh," she said softly. "Yes. Of course."

A braided thrill of anticipation moved through her—fear and a flutter of excitement—disturbing any semblance of peace her body had recently collected.

With painstaking care, she tugged loose the ribbon, then lifted the heavy lid, releasing a hush of delicate, translucent paper in the process. Deen took the lid from her trembling hands, and Alizeh peered into the box with the wide eyes of a child, discovering, in its depths, an elegant wonder of a gown.

She heard Deen gasp.

At first, all she saw were layers of diaphanous silk chiffon in a shade of pale lavender. She pushed away the wrappings, carefully lifting the gauzy, gossamer article up against the light. The gown was gathered softly down the bodice and cinched at the waist; a long, sheer cape was affixed at the shoulders in place of sleeves. The whisper of a skirt felt like wind in her hands, slipping through her fingers like a soft breeze. It was elegant without ostentation, the perfect balance of all that she required for the evening.

Alizeh thought she might cry.

She would freeze half to death in this gown and she'd not breathe a word of complaint.

"There is a card, miss," Deen said quietly.

Alizeh looked up at him then, accepting the card from

his outstretched hand, which she promptly tucked into her pocket. She'd decided to say her goodbyes to the shopkeeper, to read the note away from his curious eyes, but was stopped by the strange look on his face.

Deen seemed . . . pleased.

She saw there, in the softness of his expression, that he thought her the recipient of a romantic gesture. He had not seen her face in full, she realized, and as a result the apothecarist could only guess at her age. No doubt he assumed Alizeh was a bit older than was accurate, that she was perhaps the mistress of a married nobleman. It was under any other circumstance a deeply unflattering assumption, one that would've rendered her, in the eyes of society, a common harlot.

Somehow, Deen did not seem to mind.

"I am not so miserly as to begrudge you your happiness," he said, reading the confusion in her eyes. "I can only imagine how difficult it must be to live your life."

Alizeh drew back, she was so surprised.

He could not have been further from the truth and still his sincerity touched her, meant more to her than she could say. In fact, she felt suddenly at a loss for the right words.

"Thank you," was all she managed.

"I realize we are strangers," Deen said, gently clearing his throat, "and as a result you might think me odd for saying so—but I've felt, from the beginning, a quiet kinship with you, miss."

"Kinship?" she said, stunned. "With me?"

"Indeed." He laughed, briefly, but his eyes were dark

with some abstruse emotion. "I, too, feel forced to hide who I am from the world. It is a difficult thing, is it not? To worry always how you will be perceived for who you are; to wonder always whether you will be accepted if you are truly yourself?"

Alizeh felt a sudden heat behind her eyes, an unexpected prick of emotion. "Yes," she said softly.

Deen smiled but still his effort was strained. "Perhaps here, between we two strangers, there might exist no such apprehension."

"You may depend upon it," Alizeh said without hesitation. "Let us hope for the day when we might all remove our masks, sir, and live in the light without fear."

Deen reached out and clasped her hands at that, held her palms between his own in a gesture of friendship that flooded her heart with feeling. They remained like that for a long moment before slowly parting.

In silence Deen helped her gather her things, and with only a brief nod, they said their goodbyes.

The shop bell rang softly as she left.

It was not until she was halfway down the street, her heart and mind thoroughly preoccupied with thoughts of the unexpected apothecarist, the weight of her overstuffed carpet bag, and the large, unwieldy box that housed her gossamer gown, that she remembered the card.

With a violent start, Alizeh dropped her carpet bag to the ground. She tugged free the small envelope from her pocket and, heart now racing in her chest, she tore open the thick paper.

She could hardly breathe as she scanned the brief note, the sharp, confident strokes of the script.

Wear this tonight, and you will be
seen only by those who wish you well.

THIRTY-ONE

سی ویک

THE ROYAL PALACE HAD BEEN built into the base of Narenj Canyon, the imposing entrance positioned between treacherously steep cliffs the color of coral, against which the glittering white marble domes and minarets of the palace stood in stark contrast. The magnificent structure that was the prince's home was cradled in a colossal fissure between land formations, at the base of which thrived lush vegetation even in winter. Acres of wild grass and burgeoning juniper touched the perpendicular rise of orange rock, the trees' blue-green foliage twisted upon irregular branches, reaching sideways into the sky toward a vast, rushing river that ran parallel to the palace entrance. Over this tremulous, snaking body of water was built an enormous drawbridge, a fearsome masterwork that connected, eventually, to the main road— and into the heart of Setar.

Kamran was stood on that drawbridge now, staring at the river that had once seemed to him so formidable.

The rains had come only briefly this season, and as a result, the water underfoot was still fairly shallow, unmoving in the windless hour. Everyday Kamran waited, with coiled tension, for the rains to return; for a sweep of thunderstorms to spare their empire. If they did not—

"You are thinking of the cisterns," his grandfather said

quietly. "Are you not?"

Kamran looked at the king. "Yes," he said.

"Good."

The two of them stood side by side on the bridge, a common stopping place for cleared visitors to the palace. All were expected to halt their horses while the guards pulled open the towering, foreboding doors that led to the royal courtyard. The prince had been surprised to discover, upon his return from Baz House, that his grandfather had been waiting at the bridge to intercept him.

The carriage that delivered Kamran back to the palace was now long gone—and Hazan with it—but still, his grandfather had said little. He'd neither asked about the results of Kamran's search, nor said a word about the Tulanian missive—the summary of which Hazan had provided on their ride home.

The news had been disconcerting, indeed.

Even so, the king and his heir did not discuss it. Instead, they watched in silence as a servant girl paddled a canoe on the still waters below, the lithe boat heaving with a vivid starburst of fresh flowers.

Seldom did Kamran spend time here, at the outer edge of the palace grounds, though his hesitation arose not from a fear of feeling exposed. The palace was all but impenetrable to attack, guarded as it was on all sides by natural defenses. The vast grounds, too, were secured by an outer wall, the top of which grazed the clouds, and that was manned at all times by no fewer than a thousand soldiers, all of whom stood by, arrows notched in waiting.

No, it was not that the prince felt unprotected.

Despite the breathtaking views from this vantage point, Kamran avoided lingering too long on this bridge because it reminded him of his childhood, of one day in particular. He found it hard to believe that so much time had passed since that fateful day, for it still felt to him, in certain moments, as if the event had occurred but minutes ago.

In fact, it had been seven years.

Kamran's father had been away from Ardunia then, gone from home for months to lead a senseless war in Tulan. A young Kamran had been stuck at home with tutors, a distant mother, and a preoccupied king; the long stretches of worry and boredom had been interrupted only by visits to his aunt's house.

The day his father was due to arrive back at the palace Kamran had been watching from the high windows. He searched restlessly for the sight of his father's familiar carriage, and when it finally arrived he'd run desperately out the doors, breathless with anticipation, coming to a stop at this very bridge, overtop this very river. He waited outside the parked carriage, lungs burning with exertion, for his father to greet him.

The rainy season had been ferocious that year, rendering the river turbulent, heaving with a terrifying force. Kamran remembered this because he stood there, listening to the heft of it as he waited; waited for his father to open the door, to show himself.

When, after a long moment, the doors had not opened, Kamran had wrenched them open himself.

He later found out that they'd sent word—of course, they'd sent word—but none had thought to include the eleven-year-old child in the dissemination of the news, to tell him that his father was no longer coming home.

That his father was, in fact, dead.

There, on a lush seat in a carriage as familiar to him as his own name, Kamran saw not his father, but his father's bloody head, sitting on a silver plate.

It was not an exaggeration to say that the scene had inspired in the young prince so violent and paralyzing a reaction that he'd desired, suddenly, the arrival of his own swift death. Kamran could not imagine living in a world without his father; he could not imagine living in a world that would do such a thing to his father. He had walked calmly to the edge of the bridge, climbed its high wall, and pitched himself into the icy, churning river below.

It was his grandfather who'd found him, who dove into the frozen depths to save him, who'd pulled Kamran's limp blue body from the loving arms of Death. Even with the Diviners working to restart his heart, it was days before Kamran opened his eyes, and when he did, he saw only his grandfather's familiar brown gaze; his grandfather's familiar white hair. His familiar, gentle smile.

Not yet, the king had said, stroking the young boy's cheek.

Not just yet.

"You think I don't understand."

The sound of his grandfather's voice startled Kamran back

to the present, prompting him to take a sharp breath. He glanced at the king.

"Your Majesty?"

"You think I do not understand," said his grandfather again, turning a degree to face him. "You think I don't know why you did it, and I wonder how you can think me so indifferent."

Kamran said nothing.

"I know why the actions of the street child shocked you so," the king said quietly. "I know why you made a spectacle of the moment, why you felt compelled to save him. It has required of us a great deal to manage the situation, but I was not angered by your actions, for I knew you meant no harm. Indeed, I know you'd not been thinking at all."

Kamran looked into the distance. Again, he said nothing.

King Zaal sighed. "I have seen the shape of your heart since the moment you first opened your eyes. All your life, I've been able to understand your actions—I've been able to find meaning even in your mistakes." He paused. "But never before have I struggled as I do now. I cannot begin to fathom your abiding interest in this girl, and your actions have begun to frighten me more than I care to admit."

"*This girl?*" Kamran turned back; his chest felt suddenly tight. "There is nothing to discuss as pertains to her. I thought we'd finished with that conversation. This very morning, in fact."

"I thought so, too," the king said, sounding suddenly tired. "And yet, already I have received reports of your unusual behavior at Baz House. Already there is discussion of your—your *melancholy*—as I have heard it put."

Kamran's jaw clenched.

"You defended a young woman in a snoda, did you not? Defended her loudly, disrespecting your aunt and terrifying the housekeeper in the process."

Quietly, the prince muttered an oath.

"Tell me," said the king, "was this not the very same girl we meant to extinguish? The very same snoda tethered to my demise? The one who nearly led to the ghastly transplantation of your life to our dungeons?"

Kamran's eyes flashed in anger. He could no longer dull the anger he still felt at his grandfather's recent betrayal, nor could he bear any longer these condescending displays of superiority. He was tired of them; tired of these pointless conversations.

What had he done wrong, truly?

Just today he'd gone to Baz House only to fulfill the duty charged him by his king; he'd not planned for the rest of it. It was not as if he meant to run away with the girl, or worse, marry her; make her queen of Ardunia. Kamran was not yet ready to admit to himself the entire truth: that in a fit of folly he might certainly have tried to make her his queen, if only she had let him.

He did not see the point in dwelling upon it.

Kamran would never see Alizeh again—of this he was certain—and he did not think he deserved to be treated thus by his grandfather. He would attend the ball tonight; he would, in the end, marry the young woman deemed best for him, and he would, with great bitterness, stand aside while his grandfather continued to make plans to kill the girl. His mistakes were none of them irreversible; none of them so foul they deserved such unrelenting condemnation.

"She had dropped a bucket of water on the ground," the prince said irritably. "The housekeeper was going to oust her for it. I interceded only to keep the girl in her position long enough for her to remain belowstairs. Searching her room, as you recall, was my sole mission, and her dismissal would've thwarted our plans. Still, my efforts came to nothing. She was promptly pitched out onto the street; her room was empty when I found it."

The king clasped his hands behind his back, pivoting fully to face his grandson. He stared at Kamran a long time.

"And did not the perfect convenience of her dismissal strike you as unusual? Has it not occurred to you, then, that she likely orchestrated the scene herself? That she'd seen your face, suspected your aim, and designed the hour of her own exit, escaping all scrutiny in the process?"

Kamran hesitated.

A shot of uncertainty disordered him a moment; he needed the single second necessary to review his memories, to consider and dismiss absolutely the premise of Alizeh's duplicity, which, had Kamran been granted but an instant more, he would have gathered enough evidence to deny. Instead, his pause for reflection cost him his credibility.

"You disappoint me," said the king. "How malleable of mind you have been made by such an obvious enemy. I can no longer pretend I'm not wholly disturbed. Tell me, is she very beautiful? And you—are you so easily brought to your knees?"

The prince's hand tightened around the throat of his mace. "How quickly you slander my character, Your Highness. Did you imagine I'd quietly accept such defamation of my person—that I would not challenge accusations so steeped in the ridiculous, so deviated from truth that they could not possibly signify—"

"No, Kamran, no, I expected from the first that you would affect outrage, as you do now."

"I cannot st—"

"Enough, child. Enough." The king closed his eyes, gripped the brass railing of the drawbridge. "This world seeks in every moment to relinquish me, and I find I lack the time and resources necessary to punish you for your foolishness. It is good, at least, that you have such ready excuses. Your explanations are sturdy, the details are well considered."

King Zaal opened his eyes, studied his grandson.

"I take comfort," said the king quietly, "in knowing that you make the effort now to conceal your unworthy actions, for your lies indicate, at the very least, that you possess a necessary awareness of your failings. I can only pray that your better judgment rules victorious, in the end."

"Your Majesty—"

"The Tulanian king will be attending the ball tonight, as you no doubt have heard."

With great effort, Kamran swallowed back the epithets in his throat, bade himself be calm. "Yes," he bit out.

King Zaal nodded. "Their young king, Cyrus, is not to be trifled with. He murdered his own father, as you well know, for his seat at the throne, and his attendance at the ball tonight, while not an outright portent of war, is no doubt an unfriendliness we should approach with caution."

"I fully agree."

"Good. Very g—" His grandfather took a sharp breath, losing his balance for an alarming moment. Kamran caught King Zaal's arms, steadying him even as the prince's own heart raced now with fear. It did not matter how much he raged against his grandfather or how much he pretended to detest the older man; the truth was always here, in the terror that quietly gripped him at the prospect of his loss.

"Are you quite all right, Your Majesty?"

"My dear child," said the king, his eyes briefly closing. He reached out, clasped the prince's shoulder. "You must prepare yourself. I will soon be unable to spare you the sight of a blood-soaked countryside, though Lord knows I've tried, these last seven years."

Kamran stilled at that; his mind grasping at a frightening supposition.

All his life he'd wondered why, after the brutal murder of his father, the king had not avenged the death of his son, had not unleashed the fury of seven hells upon the southern empire. It had never made sense to the young prince, and yet, he'd never questioned it, for Kamran had feared, for so long after his father's death, that revenge would mean he'd lose his grandfather, too.

"I don't understand," Kamran said, his voice charged now

with emotion. "Do you mean to say that you made peace with Tulan—for my sake?"

The king smiled a mournful smile. His weathered hand fell away from the prince's shoulder.

"Does it shock you," he said, "to discover that I, too, possess a fragile heart? A weak mind? That I, too, have been unwise? Indeed, I've been selfish. I've made decisions—decisions that would affect the lives of millions—that were motivated not by the wisdom of my mind, but by the desires of my heart. Yes, child," he said softly. "I did it for you. I could not bear to see you suffer, even as I knew that suffering was inevitable.

"I tried, in the early hours of the morning," the king went on, "to take control of my own failings, to punish you the way a king should punish any man who proves disloyal. It was an overcorrection, you see. Compensation for a lifetime of restraint."

"Your Majesty." Kamran's heart was pounding. "I still don't understand."

Now King Zaal smiled wider, his eyes shining with feeling. "My greatest weakness, Kamran, has always been you. I wanted always to shelter you. To protect you. After your father"—he hesitated, took an unsteady breath—"afterward, I could not bear to part from you. For seven years I managed to delay the inevitable, to convince our leaders to set down their swords and make peace. Instead, as I stand now at the finish of my life, I see I've only added to your burden. I ignored my own instincts in exchange for an illusion of relief.

"War is coming," he whispered. "It has been a long time coming. I only hope I've not left you unprepared to face it."

THIRTY-TWO

سی و دو

ALIZEH DROPPED HER CARPET BAG to the ground out-side the servants' entrance to Follad Place, all too eager to relinquish the luggage for a moment. The large box that held her gown, however, she only readjusted in her tired arms, unwilling to set it down unless absolutely necessary.

The long day was far from over, but even in the face of its many difficulties, Alizeh was hopeful. After a thorough scrub at the hamam she felt quite new, and was buoyed by the realization that her body would not be battered again so quickly by interminable hours of hard labor. Still, it was hard to be truly enthusiastic about the reprieve, for Alizeh knew that if things went poorly this evening, she'd be hard-pressed to find such a position again.

She shifted her weight; tried to calm her nerves.

Just last evening Follad Place had seemed to her terribly imposing, but in the dying light of day it was even more striking. Alizeh hadn't noticed before just how robust the surrounding gardens were, nor how beautifully tended, and she wished she hadn't cause at all to notice such details now.

Alizeh did not want to be here.

She'd been avoiding as long as possible this last, inevitable task for the day, having arrived at Follad Place only to return Miss Huda's unfinished gown, and to accept with grace the lambasting and condemnation she'd no doubt receive in exchange. It was perhaps a minimization of the truth to say that she was not looking forward to the experience.

Already Alizeh had knocked at the door, after which she'd been greeted by Mrs. Sana, who, miraculously, had not dismissed outright the brazen snoda requesting an audience with a young lady of the house. She had, however, demanded to know the nature of the visit, to which Alizeh demurred, saying only that she needed to speak with Miss Huda directly. The housekeeper stared a beat too long at the beautiful garment box in Alizeh's arms and doubtless drew her own more satisfactory explanation for the girl's visit, one that Alizeh made no effort to deny.

Now Alizeh waited anxiously for Miss Huda, who was due to receive her at any possible moment. Despite the blistering cold, Alizeh had been prepared to wait for some time in the case that the young miss had been out for the day, but here, too, Alizeh had encountered a stroke of unexpected luck. In fact, despite the recent challenges she'd lately faced—nearly being murdered, losing her position, and becoming suddenly homeless among them—she felt herself to be the unlikely recipient of a great deal of good fortune, too. Alizeh had uncovered in the process a fairly solid case for optimism, her two most compelling reasons thus:

First, her neck and hands were healed, which was in and of itself a cause for celebration, for not only was it a relief to be rid of the collar around her throat and to have full use of her fingers once more, but the linen bandages had grown itchy and were made easily dirty, which had bothered her more than was reasonable. Second, Hazan had left her a breathtaking gown to wear to the ball tonight, which would not only spare her the time and possible cost of fashioning such a complicated article in a short time, but it spared her the need to find a safe space to work. This was not even mentioning the fact that the gown was somehow imbued with magic—magic that claimed it would conceal her identity from any who wished her ill.

This was perhaps the greatest good fortune of all.

Alizeh, who knew she could not wear her snoda to the royal ball, had decided simply to keep her eyes lowered for the length of the evening, looking up only when essential. This alternate solution was eminently preferable.

Still, she was wary, for Alizeh knew the gown to be of a shockingly rare stock. Even the royals of Ardunia did not wear magical garments, not unless they were on the battlefield—and even then there were limits to the protections such clothing might provide, for there existed no magic strong enough to repel Death. What's more, only an exceedingly complicated technique could provide such personalized protection to a wearer of a garment, and this complexity could be conducted only by an experienced Diviner—of which there were few.

Magic, Alizeh had long known, was mined much like any mineral: directly from the earth. She was not entirely certain wherefrom the empire excavated their precious commodities, for not only was it done in relative secrecy, but theirs was different from the magic Alizeh required from the Arya mountains. That which belonged to her ancestors was of a rarer strain, and though many Clay efforts had been made over millennia, the arcane material had proven impossible to quarry.

Still, all genus of Ardunian magic existed only in small, exhaustible quantities, and were not meant to be manipulated by the uninitiated, for they killed easily any who mishandled the volatile substances. The Diviner population was as a result quite small; Ardunian children were taught little about magic unless they showed a sincere interest in divining, and only a select few were chosen each year to study the subject.

Alizeh could not, as a result, imagine how Hazan was able to procure such rare items on her behalf. First the nosta, and now the dress?

She took another deep breath, exhaling into the cold. The sun was shattering across the horizon, fragmenting color across the hills, taking with it what little warmth was left in the sky.

Alizeh had been waiting at least thirty minutes now, standing outside in a thin jacket and damp hair. With no hat or scarf to cover her frozen curls, she stamped her feet, frowning at the fracturing sun, worrying over the minutes that remained of daylight.

The ground underfoot was thick with decaying purple leaves, all of which had fallen—recently, it seemed—from the small forest of trees surrounding the magnificent home. The newly bare, ghostly branches arced tremulously toward one another, curling inward not unlike the crooked legs of a many-legged spider, intent on devouring its prey.

It was just then, as Alizeh had conjured this disturbing image in her mind, that the heavy wooden door was wrenched open with a groan, revealing the harried face and hassled form of Miss Huda herself.

Alizeh bobbed a curtsy. "Good aftern—"

"*Not a sound*," the young woman said harshly, grabbing Alizeh by the arm and yanking her inside.

Alizeh had only just managed to swipe her carpet bag up and into her arms before they were off, barreling wildly through the kitchen and down the halls, Alizeh's cumbersome baggage knocking against the walls and floors as she struggled to keep up with Miss Huda's sudden, jerky movements.

When they finally stopped moving, Alizeh stumbled forward from the force of residual motion, staggering a bit as she heard the sound of a door slam shut.

Her box and bag hit the floor with consecutive thuds, after which Alizeh steadied herself, turning in time to see Miss Huda struggling to catch her breath, eyes closed as she slumped back against the closed door.

"Never," Miss Huda said, still trying to breathe. "Never, ever show up unannounced. *Never.* Do you understand?"

"I'm terribly sorry, miss. I didn't realize—"

"I was only able to arrange our last meeting because I pretended to have a megrim on an evening I *knew* the family had been invited to dinner, but *everyone* is home now, preparing for the ball, which is why my maid was supposed to come to *you* to collect the gown and *oh*, if Mother discovers I've hired you to make me a dress I'll be reduced to little more than a writhing, bloody sack on the street, for she will *literally* tear all my limbs from my body."

Alizeh blinked. The nosta glowed neither hot nor cold against her skin in response, and Alizeh didn't understand its lack of reaction. "Surely you do not— You could not mean she would *literally*—"

"I meant exactly what I said," Miss Huda snapped. "Mother is the devil incarnate."

Alizeh, who knew the devil personally, frowned at that. "Forgive me, miss, but that's not—"

"Lord, but how am I going to get you back out of the house?" Miss Huda dragged her hands down her face. "Father has guests due any minute now, and if a single one of them sees you—if even a servant sees you— Oh, heavens, Mother will surely murder me in my sleep."

Again, the nosta did not react, and for a single, terrifying moment Alizeh thought the object might be broken.

"Oh, this is bad," said Miss Huda. "This is very, very bad . . ."

The nosta glowed suddenly warm.

Not broken, then.

Alizeh experienced a wave of relief supplanted quickly by consternation. If the little glass orb was not broken, then it was perhaps Miss Huda who was uncertain of the veracity of her statements. Maybe, Alizeh considered with some alarm, the young woman wasn't entirely sure whether her mother might one day murder her.

Alizeh studied the panicked, overwrought figure of the girl before her and wondered whether Miss Huda wasn't in more trouble at home than she let on. She knew the girl's mother had proven overtly cruel, but Miss Huda had never before characterized the woman as a physical threat.

Quietly, Alizeh said, "Is your mother truly so violent?"

"What?" Miss Huda looked up.

"Are you— Are you genuinely worried your mother might kill you? Because if you believe her a serious threat to your li—"

"I beg your pardon?" Miss Huda boggled. "Have you no sense at all of hyperbole? Of course I'm not *genuinely* worried my mother might kill me. I am in a panic. Am I not allowed to embroider the truth a bit when I am in a panic?"

"I— Yes," Alizeh said, quietly clearing her throat. "I only meant— That is, I wanted only to ascertain whether you truly feared for your safety. I am relieved to discover you did not."

At that, Miss Huda went unexpectedly silent.

She stared for what felt like a long time at Alizeh, stared at her as if she were not a person, but an enigma. It was an ungenerous stare, one that made Alizeh decidedly uncomfortable.

"And what, pray," Miss Huda said finally, "did you mean to do about it?"

"I beg your pardon?"

"If I had told you," Miss Huda said with a sigh, "that my mother did indeed intend to murder me, what would you have done about it? I ask because you appeared, for a moment, quite determined. As if you had a plan."

Alizeh felt herself flush. "No, miss," she said quietly. "Not at all."

"You did too have a plan," Miss Huda insisted, her earlier panic dissipating now. "There's no point in denying it, so go on. Let's hear it. Let's hear your plan to save me."

"It was not a plan, miss. I merely— I only had a thought."

"So you admit it, then? You had a thought about saving me from the clutches of my murderous mother?"

Alizeh lowered her eyes at that, saying nothing. She thought Miss Huda was being intolerably cruel.

"Oh, very well," the young woman said, collapsing into a chair with a touch of theater. "You need not speak it aloud if you find the confession so torturous. I was merely curious. After all, you hardly know me; I was only wondering why you cared."

The nosta glowed warm.

Stunned, Alizeh said, "You wondered why I would care if your mother might actually murder you?"

"Is that not what I just said?"

"Are you— Are you quite serious, miss?" Alizeh knew Miss Huda was serious, but somehow she couldn't help asking the question.

"Of course I am." Miss Huda sat up straighter. "Have I ever seemed to you interested in subtlety? I'm in fact quite known for my candor, and I daresay Mother hates my lack of refinement even more than she hates my figure. She says my mouth and hips are a product of that *woman*, that *other woman*—which is how she refers, of course, to my biological mother."

When Alizeh said nothing in response to Miss Huda's obvious effort to shock her, the young woman raised her eyebrows. "Is it possible you didn't know? That would make you the only person in Setar ignorant of my origins, for mine is an infamous tale, as my father refused to hide his sins from society. Still, I am quite illegitimate, the bastard child of a nobleman and a courtesan. It's no secret that neither of my mothers have ever wanted me."

Alizeh continued to say nothing. She didn't dare.

Miss Huda's performance of indifference was so obvious as to be painful to witness; Alizeh didn't know whether to shake the girl or hug her.

"Yes," Alizeh said finally. "I knew."

She saw a flicker of emotion in Miss Huda's eyes then, something like relief, there and gone again. And just like that, Alizeh's heart softened toward the girl.

Miss Huda had been worried.

She'd been worried that Alizeh, a lowly servant, had not known of her parentage; she worried a lowly servant would find out and judge her harshly. Miss Huda's attempt to scandalize had in fact been an effort to out herself preemptively, to spare herself a painful retraction of kindness, or friendship, upon discovery.

This was a fear Alizeh understood well.

But that Miss Huda would lower herself to be bothered by the worthless opinion of a snoda taught Alizeh a great deal about the depth of the young woman's insecurities; it was information she would file away in her mind, and not soon forget.

Quietly, Alizeh said, "I would've found a way to protect you."

"Pardon?"

"If you'd told me," Alizeh clarified, "that your mother had been trying in earnest to murder you. I would've found a way to protect you."

"You?" Miss Huda laughed. "*You* would've protected me?"

Alizeh bowed her head, fought back a renewed wave of irritation. "You asked for my confession—for the thought that crossed my mind. That was it."

There was a brief silence.

"You really mean that," the young woman said finally.

Alizeh looked up at the gentle sound of the girl's voice. She was surprised to discover the sneer gone from Miss Huda's face; her brown eyes wide with unvarnished feeling. She looked, suddenly, quite young.

"Yes, miss," Alizeh said. "I really mean it."

"Goodness. You are a very strange girl."

Alizeh drew a deep breath. That was the second time today someone had accused her of being strange, and she wasn't quite sure how she felt about it.

She decided to change the subject.

"More to the point," she said, "I've come to you today to talk about your gown."

"Oh, *yes*," Miss Huda said, eagerly getting to her feet and moving toward the large case. "Is this it, then? Can I open—"

Alizeh darted for the box and claimed it, bracing it against her chest. She stepped several steps back as her heart beat hard against her sternum. "No," she said quickly. "No, this—this is something else. For someone else. I actually came here to tell you that I haven't finished making your gown. That, in fact, I won't be able to finish making it."

Miss Huda's eyes widened in outrage. "You— But how *could* you—"

"I was dismissed from my position at Baz House," Alizeh said quickly, grabbing blindly for her carpet bag, which she hauled into her arms. "I desperately wanted to finish the commission, miss, but I've no place to live, and no place to work, and the streets are so cold I can hardly hold a needle without my fingers going numb—"

"You *promised* me— You said—you said it would be done in time for the ball—"

"I'm so sorry," Alizeh said, now inching slowly toward the door. "Truly, I am, and I can well imagine your disappointment. I see now that I should go, for I fear I've disturbed your day quite enough—though of course I'll just leave the gown"—she released the latch on her bag, reached inside for the garment—"and leave you to your evening—"

"*Don't you dare.*"

Alizeh froze.

"You said you needed a place to work? Well, here." Miss Huda gestured to the room at large. "You might as well stay and finish the work. You can manage a discreet exit once everyone leaves for the ball."

The carpet bag slipped from Alizeh's frozen fingers, fell with a dull thump to the ground.

The suggestion was outrageous.

"You want me to finish it now?" Alizeh said. "Here? In your room? But what if a maid comes in? What if your mother needs you? What if—"

"Oh, I don't know," Miss Huda said irritably. "But I see no possibility of your leaving now anyway because Father's guests have certainly"—she glanced at the wall clock, its golden pendulum swinging—"yes, they've certainly arrived by now, which means the house is sure to be flush with all the ambassadors ahead of the ball, as their lot is terribly prompt—"

"But—perhaps I could climb out the window?"

Miss Huda glared. "You will do no such thing. Not only is the idea preposterous, but I want my gown. I have nothing else to wear, and you, by your own admission, have nothing else to do. Is that not what you said? That you were discharged from your position?"

Alizeh squeezed her eyes shut. "Yes."

"So you've no one waiting for you, and no warm place to go on this winter evening?"

Alizeh opened her eyes. "No."

"Then I do not understand your reticence. Now remove that godforsaken monstrosity from your face at once," Miss Huda said, lifting her chin an inch. "You're not a snoda anymore; you're a seamstress."

Alizeh looked up at that, felt the pilot light in her heart flicker. She appreciated the young woman's attempt to raise her spirits, but Miss Huda did not understand. If Alizeh had to wait until the whole of Follad Place departed for the ball, she herself would be terribly late. She'd no choice but to arrive to the event on foot, and had planned, as a result, to leave a good deal early. Even with preternatural speed she couldn't move quite as fast as a carriage, and would certainly not dare move too quickly in such a delicate gown.

Omid would wonder whether she'd abandoned him. Hazan would wonder whether she'd been able to secure safe passage to the ball.

She couldn't be late. She simply couldn't. There was too much at stake.

"Please, miss. I really must go. I am— I am in fact a Jinn," Alizeh said nervously, employing now the only tactic she had left. "You need not worry that I will be seen, as I can make myself invisible upon my exi—"

Miss Huda eyes widened in astonishment. "Your audacity shocks me. Do you even know to whom you are speaking? Yes, I am a bastard child, but I am the bastard child of an Ardunian ambassador," she said, growing visibly angry. "Or did you forget that you stand now in the home of an official hand selected by the crown? How you gather the nerve to even dare suggest—in my presence—doing something so patently illegal, I cannot fathom—"

"Forgive me," Alizeh said, panicked. Only now that she was being condemned for it did she realize the weight of her error; a different person might've already called for the magistrates. "I merely— I wasn't thinking clearly— I only hoped to provide a solution to the obvious problem and I—"

"The most obvious problem, I think, is that you made me a promise you've now unceremoniously broken." Miss Huda narrowed her eyes. "You've no good excuse for not finishing the work, and I demand you do it now."

Alizeh tried to breathe. Her heart was racing at a dangerous speed in her chest.

"Well? Go on, then," said Miss Huda, her anger slowly abating. She gestured limply at the girl's mask. "Consider this the dawn of a new age. A new beginning."

Alizeh closed her eyes.

She wondered whether the snoda even mattered now. One way or another, she'd be gone from Setar at the end of the night. She'd never see Miss Huda again, and Alizeh doubted the girl would go gossiping about the strange color of her eyes—something she more than likely would not understand, as most Clay were uneducated in Jinn history and would not know the weight of what they saw.

It had never been for fear of the masses that Alizeh hid her face; it was for fear of a single, careful eye. Exposure to the wrong stranger and she knew her life was forfeit; indeed, her precarious position in that very moment was proof. Somehow, impossibly, Kamran had seen through her guile, had seen through even her snoda.

In all these years, he'd been the only one.

She took a deep breath and cleared her head of him, spared her heart of him. She thought instead, without warning, of her parents, who'd always worried about her eyes, always worried for her life. They'd never given up hope of her taking back the land—and the crown—they believed to be rightfully hers.

Alizeh had been raised from infancy to reclaim it.

What would they think if they saw her now? Jobless, homeless, at the mercy of some miss. Alizeh felt quietly ashamed of herself, of her impotence in that moment.

Without a word, she untied the snoda from around her

eyes, and, reluctantly, let the scrap of silk slip through her fingers. When Alizeh finally looked up to meet the young woman's gaze, Miss Huda went rigid with fear.

"Heavens," she gasped. "It's you."

THIRTY-THREE

سی و سہ

KAMRAN FLINCHED.

The seamstress stuck him with yet another pin, humming quietly to herself as she worked, pulling here, tucking there. The woman was either oblivious or heartless, he'd not yet decided. She never seemed to care that she was maiming him, not even when he'd asked her, several times, to desist from these nonessential acts of cruelty.

He looked at the seamstress, the ancient woman in a velvet bowler so diminutive in stature she hardly reached his waist, and who tottered over him now on a small wooden stool. She smelled like caramelized eggplant.

"Madame," he said tersely. "Are we not yet finished?"

She started at the sound of his voice and stabbed him yet again, causing Kamran to draw a sharp breath. The older woman blinked big, owlish eyes at him; eyes he'd always found disconcerting.

"Nearly there, sire," she said in a weathered voice. "Nearly there now. Just a few minutes more."

Soundlessly, Kamran sighed.

Kamran loathed these fittings, and could not understand why he'd needed one, not when he owned an entire wardrobe full of clothes still unworn, any number of which would've been sufficient for the night's festivities.

It was, in any case, his mother's doing.

The princess had intercepted him the very moment he'd stepped foot inside the palace, refusing to listen to a word of reason. She'd insisted, despite Kamran's protests to the contrary, that whatever the king and his officials needed to discuss could wait, and that being properly dressed for his guests was far more important. Besides, she'd sworn, the fitting would take only a moment. *A moment.*

It had been nigh on an hour.

Still, it was quite possible, Kamran considered, that the seamstress was stabbing him now in protest. The prince had neither heeded his mother upon arrival, nor had he flatly refused to accompany her. Instead, he'd parted with a vague promise to return. An enemy on the battlefield he might've cut down with a sword, but his mother in possession of a seamstress on the night of a ball—

He'd not been properly armed against such an adversary, and had settled for ignoring her.

Three hours he'd spent discussing the Tulanian king's possible motivations with Hazan, his grandfather, and a select group of officials, and when, finally, he'd returned to his dressing room, his mother had thrown a lamp at him.

Miraculously, Kamran had dodged the projectile, which crashed to the floor, causing a small fire upon impact. This, the princess had ignored outright, instead approaching her son with a violent gleam in her eyes.

"Careful, darling," she'd said softly. "You overlook your mother at great cost to yourself."

Kamran was busy stamping out the flames. "I'm afraid

I don't follow your logic," he'd said, scowling, "for I cannot imagine it costs me anything to avoid a parent who so often takes pleasure in trying to kill me."

The princess had smiled at that, even as her eyes flashed with anger. "Two days ago I told you I needed to speak with you. Two days I have waited to have a simple conversation with my own son. Two days I have been ignored repeatedly, even as you made time to spend an entire morning with your dear aunt."

Kamran frowned. "I don't—"

"No doubt you forgot," she said, cutting him off. "No doubt my request fell right out of your pretty head the moment it was spoken. So swiftly am I forgotten."

To this, Kamran said nothing, for if she'd indeed asked for a moment of his time, he could not now recall such a summons.

His mother stepped closer.

"Soon," she said, "I will be all you have left in this palace. You will walk the halls, friendless and alone, and you will search for me then. You will want your mother only when all else is lost, and I do not promise to be easily found."

Kamran had felt an unnerving sensation move through his body at that; a foreboding he could not name. "Why do you say such things? Of what do you speak?"

The princess was already walking away, gone without another word. Kamran made to follow her and was halted by the arrival of the seamstress, Madame Nezrin, who'd entered the dressing room promptly upon his mother's exit.

Again, Kamran flinched.

Even if he deserved it, he did not think Madame Nezrin should be allowed to stab him with impunity. Surely
she knew better. The woman was the crown's most trusted
seamstress; she'd been working with the royal family since
the beginning of his grandfather's reign. In fact, Kamran
often marveled that she hadn't gone blind by now.

Then again, perhaps she had.

There seemed little other explanation for the ridiculous
costumes he regularly discovered in his wardrobe. Her ideas
were meticulously executed, but ancient; she dressed him
always on the edge of a different century. And Kamran, who
knew little of fashion and fabrics, understood only that he
did not like his clothes; he possessed no alternative suggestions, and as a result felt powerless in the face of such an
essential problem, which drove him near to madness. Surely
the mere act of getting dressed should not inspire in a person
such torment?

Even now she dressed him in layers of silk brocade, cinching the long emerald robes at his waist with more silk, this
time a beaded belt so heavy with jewels it had to be pinned
in place. At his throat was yet more of the awful material: a
translucent, pale green scarf artfully knotted, the coarse silk
netting like sandpaper against his skin.

His shirt, at least, was a familiar linen.

On a single, regrettable occasion he'd once said to his
mother—distractedly—that silk sounded *just fine*, and now
everything he owned was an abomination.

Silk, it had turned out, was not the soft, comfortable textile he'd expected; no, it was a noisy, detestable fabric that

irritated his skin. The crisp, stiff collar of his robes dug into his throat now not unlike the edge of a dull knife, and he turned his head sharply away, unable to keep still any longer, paying for his impatience with yet another needle in the rib.

Kamran grimaced. The pain had at least done a great deal to distract him from his mother's ominous parting words.

The sun had begun its descent in the sky, fracturing pink and orange light through the lattice screen windows of the dressing room, the geometric perforations generating a kaleidoscope of oblong shapes along the walls and floors, giving him somewhere to focus his eyes, and then, his thoughts. Too soon, guests would begin arriving at the palace, and too soon, he would be expected to greet them. One, in particular.

As if he'd not been delivered enough suffering this day.

The news from Tulan had been less distressing than Kamran had expected and yet, somehow, so much worse.

"Remind me again, Minister, why on earth the man was even invited?"

Hazan, who'd been standing quietly in the corner, now cleared his throat. He looked from Kamran to the seamstress, his eyes widening in warning.

Kamran glowered.

None of this was Hazan's fault—logically, the prince understood that—but logic did not seem to matter to his abraded nerves. Kamran had been in a hateful mood all day. Everything bothered him. Everything was insufferable. He shot an aggravated look at Hazan, who'd flatly refused to leave the prince's side in the wake of the recent news.

His minister only glared back.

"There's little point in your sitting here," the prince said irritably. "You should return to your own rooms. No doubt you have preparations to make before the evening begins."

"I thank you for your consideration, sire," Hazan said coldly. "But I will remain here, by your side."

"You overreact," said the prince. "Besides, if you should be concerned for anyone, it should not be me, but th—"

"Madame," Hazan said sharply. "I must now escort His Highness to an important meeting; if you would be so kind as to finish the work in his absence? No doubt you have enough of our prince's measurements."

Madame Nezrin blinked at Hazan; she seemed uncertain, for a moment, which of the two young men had spoken to her. "Very good," she said. "That should be just fine."

Kamran resisted the infantile impulse to kick something.

With great care, the seamstress slid loose the robes from his body, collecting every meticulously pinned article into her small arms, and nearly toppling over in the process.

Briefly, Kamran's upper half was left bare.

Kamran, who spent little time staring at his own reflection, and who'd not been facing the mirror when he'd first undressed, was disquieted to see himself so exposed now. The triple-paneled looking glass loomed before him, revealing angles of his body he seldom studied.

Someone handed him his sweater, which Kamran accepted without a word. He took a tentative step closer to the mirrors, drew a hand down the length of his bare torso.

He frowned.

"What is it?" Hazan asked, the anger in his voice tinged now with concern. "Is something the matter?"

"It's different," Kamran said quietly. "Is it not different?"

Hazan drew slowly closer.

It was the tradition of Ardunian kings to hand over their heirs, on the very day of the child's birth, to the Diviners—to have them marked by an irreversible magic that would claim them, always, as the rightful successor. It was a practice they'd stolen from Jinn, whose royals were born with such markings, sparing their kingdoms any false claims to the throne. Clay royalty had found a way to incorporate such protections into their own bloodlines, though what had once been considered a serious precaution had, over centuries, become more of a tradition—one they soon forgot had been borrowed from another people.

On the day of their birth every Ardunian royal was marked by magic, and it touched them all differently.

King Zaal had found a constellation of dark blue, eight-pointed stars at the base of his throat. The prince's own father had discovered black, branching lines along his back, ominous strokes that wrapped partially around his torso.

Kamran, too, had been marked.

Every year of his boyhood the prince had watched, with a kind of horrified fascination, as the skin of his chest and torso gave the illusion of splitting open down the center, revealing at its fissure a glimmer of gold leaf. The burnished gold mark appeared, as if painted, straight down his middle, from the shallow valley of his throat to the base of his abdomen.

The Diviners had promised that the magic would display

its final form by the end of his twelfth birthday, and so it had. The glittering lash had long ago lost his interest, for it had become as familiar to him as his eyes, the color of his hair. It had become so much a part of him that he seldom noticed it . these days. But now—suddenly—

It looked different.

The fissure seemed a fraction wider, the once dull gold shining now a bit brighter.

"I do not see a difference, sire," Hazan asked, peering into the mirror. "Does it feel unusual in some way?"

"No, it feels no different," Kamran said absently, now running his fingers along the gold part. It was always a bit hotter there, at his center, but the mark had never hurt, had never felt strange. "It only looks . . . Well, I suppose it's hard to say. I've not noticed it in so long."

"Perhaps it only seems different," said Hazan quietly, "because you've lately been rendered an idiot, and stupidity has clouded your better judgment."

Kamran shot his minister a dark look and promptly pulled his sweater over his head, tugging its hem down over his torso. He looked around for the seamstress.

"You need not worry," Hazan said. "She's gone."

"Gone?" The prince frowned. "But— Were not *we* the ones who were meant to leave the dressing room? Was she not meant to stay here to finish the work she'd started?"

"Indeed. The woman is a bit batty."

Kamran shook his head, collapsed into a nearby chair. "How much time do we have?"

"Before the ball? Two hours."

Kamran shot him a look. "You know very well to what I am referring."

"To whom you are referring, you mean?" Hazan almost smiled. "The Tulanian king is with the ambassador now. He should be arriving at the palace within the hour."

"Lord, but I hate him," Kamran said, pushing a hand through his hair. "He has the kind of face that should be kicked in, repeatedly."

"That seems a bit unfair. It's not the fault of the Tulanian ambassador that he's charged with an empire so widely detested. The gentleman himself is nice enough."

Kamran turned sharply to face his minister. "Obviously I'm speaking of the king."

Hazan frowned. "The king? Cyrus, you mean? I'd not realized you'd met him before."

"No. I've not yet had the pleasure. I'm merely assuming he has the kind of face that should be kicked in, repeatedly."

Hazan's frown cleared at that; he fought back another smile. "You do not underestimate him, I hope?"

"Underestimate him? The child killed his own father. He stole a bloody crown from the rightful king for all the world to bear witness, and now he shows his shameless face here? No, I do not underestimate him. I think him mad. Though I must say I fear our own officials misprize him, and to their detriment. They underestimate him for the same inane reasons they underestimate me."

"Your lack of experience, you mean?"

Kamran turned away. "My age, you miserable rotter."

"So easily provoked." Hazan stifled a laugh. "You are in

quite a state, today, Your Highness."

"You might do us all a favor, Hazan, and begin to manage your expectations of my *state*. This is where I live, minister. Here, between angry and irritable, lies my charming personality. It does not change. You may be grateful that I am consistent, at least, in being boorish."

Hazan's smile grew only wider. "I say, these are strange declarations from Setar's melancholy prince."

Kamran stiffened. Very slowly, he turned to face Hazan. "I beg your pardon?"

His minister retrieved from the inside of his jacket a folded copy of Setar's most popular evening journal, the *Quill & Crown*. The nightly post was widely known to be trash, a sloppy rehashing of the morning's news, cut with unsolicited opinions from its self-important editor. Indeed, there was little newsworthy about it; it was a spectacle in printed form, useless drivel. It contained rambling letters from breathless readers, and was stuffed with articles like—

Suggestions for the King, Ten Items Long

—and devoted an entire page to baseless gossip of goings-on in the royal city.

"It says right here," Hazan said, scanning the paper, "that you are a sentimental idiot, that your bleeding heart has been laid bare twice now, once for a street child and now for a snoda—"

"Give that to me," Kamran said, jumping to his feet to snatch the paper out of Hazan's hands, which he promptly tossed in the fire.

"I've got another copy, Your Highness."

"You disloyal wretch. How can you even read such gar-
bage?"

"I may have exaggerated a bit," Hazan admitted. "The
article was actually quite complimentary. Your random acts
of kindness toward the lower classes seem to have won the
hearts of common folk, who seem only too eager to praise
your actions."

Kamran was only slightly mollified. "Even so."

"Even so." Hazan cleared his throat. "You were kind to a
snoda, then?"

"It's not worth discussing."

"Is it not? When you spent a great part of the morning
in the company of your aunt at Baz House, where we both
know resides a young woman of interest? A young woman in
a snoda?"

"Oh, shove off, Hazan." Kamran collapsed once again in
his chair. "The king is well aware of both my actions and my
reasons, which should be more than enough for you. Why
are you trailing me, anyway? It's not as if the Tulanian king
will murder me in my own home."

"He might."

"What good would it do him? If you're so concerned,
you should be protecting the king. I'm perfectly capable of
defending myself."

"Your Highness," Hazan said, looking suddenly concerned.
"If you harbor any uncertainty about the life hurtling toward
you, allow me to assure you now: the inevitable is coming.
You must prepare yourself."

Kamran turned away, exhaling toward the ceiling. "You

mean my grandfather will die."

"I mean you will soon be crowned king of the largest empire in the known world."

"Yes," said the prince. "I'm quite aware."

A tense silence stretched between them.

When Hazan finally spoke, the heat was gone from his voice. "It was a formality," he said.

Kamran looked up.

"Your question," said the minister. "You asked why the Tulanian king was invited. It is a long-standing tradition, during peacetime, to invite neighboring royalty to the most elite affairs. It's meant as a gesture of goodwill. Many similar invitations have been made these last seven years, but never before has the Tulanian king accepted."

"Excellent," Kamran said drily. "He's come now to enjoy a bit of cake, no doubt."

"It's certainly good to be cautious, fo—"

Just then there was a sharp knock, immediately after which the door to the dressing room opened. The elderly palace butler entered, then bowed.

"What now, Jamsheed?" The prince turned in his seat to face the man. "Tell my mother I've no idea where the seamstress went, nor what she did with my robes. Better yet, tell my mother to come find me herself if she wishes to speak with me, and to stop pitching you about the palace as if you haven't far better things to do on such an evening."

"No, sire." Jamsheed, to his credit, did not smile. "It's not your mother. I've come because you have a young visitor."

Kamran frowned. "A young visitor?"

"Yes, sire. He professes the king himself granted him permission to visit you, and I come to you now to ask—only out of the greatest respect for His Majesty—whether there exists even a grain of truth to the child's claim."

Hazan stood straighter at that, looking suddenly perturbed. "Surely you cannot mean the street child?"

"He does not look like a street child," said the butler. "But neither does he appear to be trustworthy."

"Yet he's arrived here, at this hour, demanding an audience with the prince? This is outrageous—"

"Don't tell me he has a shock of red hair?" Kamran ran a hand over his eyes. "Too tall for his age?"

The butler started. "Yes, sire."

"His name is Omid?"

"Why— Yes, sire," Jamsheed said, no longer able to hide his astonishment. "He says his name is Omid Shekarzadeh."

"Where is he?"

"He awaits you now in the main hall."

"Did he say why he's come?" Hazan demanded. "Did he give a reason for his impertinence?"

"No, Minister, though his manner is a bit febrile. He seems deeply agitated."

With great reluctance, Kamran got to his feet; this day felt suddenly interminable. "Tell the boy I'll be down in a moment."

The butler stared, stupefied, at the prince. "Then— Then what the child says is true, sire? That he has permission from the king to speak with you?"

Kamran hadn't even the chance to respond before Hazan

moved in front of him, blocking his path.

"Your Highness, this is absurd," the minister said in a forceful whisper. "Why would the boy request an audience at this hour? I don't trust it."

The prince studied Hazan a moment: the flash of panic in his eyes, the tense form of his body, the hand he held aloft to stop him. Kamran had known Hazan too many years to misunderstand him now, and a sharp, disorienting unease moved suddenly through the prince's body.

Something was wrong.

"I don't know," Kamran said. "Though I intend to find out."

"Then you intend to make a mistake. This could be a trap—"

To the butler, the prince said, "I'll meet the boy in the receiving room."

"Yes, sire." Jamsheed glanced from the prince to his minister. "As you wish."

"Your Highness—"

"That is all," the prince said sharply.

The butler bowed at once, then disappeared, the door closing behind him.

When they were alone, Hazan turned to face the prince. "Are you mad? I don't understand why you'd consent t—"

In a single, swift movement Kamran grabbed Hazan by the collar and slammed his back against the wall.

Hazan gasped.

"You are hiding something," Kamran said darkly. "What is your game?"

Hazan went rigid with surprise, his eyes widening with a touch of fear. "No, sire. Forgive me, I meant not to overstep—"

Kamran tightened his grip. "You are lying to me, Hazan. What is your preoccupation with the b—"

The prince cut himself off, suddenly, for he was startled by a soft, buzzing sound in his left ear.

Kamran turned, blinking in surprise. A slight, glowing insect hovered inches from his face, bumping incessantly against his cheek.

Thop.

Thop.

"What on earth—" The prince grimaced and stepped back, relinquishing the minister to swat the fly from his face; Hazan slumped against the wall, breathing hard.

Go, Kamran thought he heard him whisper.

Or was it merely an exhale?

Kamran watched, stunned, as the fly darted straight toward the door and through the keyhole, disappearing into the world beyond.

Had the insect obeyed a command? Or had Kamran lost his mind? He spared his minister a single, strange glance before he quit the room, pulling open the door with forced calm and striding down the hall with unusual speed, his skin prickling with unease.

Where had the blasted creature gone?

"Your Highness—" Hazan called, catching up, then keeping pace. "Your Highness, forgive me— I only worried the child might prove a distraction on such an important evening— I spoke thoughtlessly. I meant no disrespect."

Kamran ignored this as he barreled down the marble staircase, his boots connecting over and over with stone, the sharp sounds filling the silence between them.

"Your Highness—"

"Leave me, Hazan." Kamran made it to the main floor and kept moving, marching toward the great room with unconcealed determination. "I find your shadow cumbersome."

"I cannot leave you now, sire, not with such a threat looming—"

Kamran came to an abrupt, disorienting halt.

Omid.

The Fesht boy was not in the receiving room where he was meant to be. Omid was instead pacing the main hall when they approached and did not wait for permission before he rushed toward the prince, darting out of reach of the footmen who sought to restrain him.

"Sire," the boy said breathlessly, before speaking in rapid-fire Feshtoon. "You've got to help, sire— I've been telling everyone but no one believes me— I went to the magistrates and they called me a liar and of course I tried to inform the king, but n—"

Kamran jerked suddenly back.

Omid had made the mistake of touching the prince, reaching out a trembling hand in a thoughtless, desperate motion.

"*Guards,*" Hazan called. "Restrain this child."

"No—" Omid spun around as guards came rushing from all sides, easily pinning the child's arms behind his back. Omid's eyes were wild with panic. "No— Please, sire, you've got to come now, we've got to do someth—"

Omid cried out as they twisted his limbs, resisting even as they dragged him away. "Get off me," he shouted, "I need to speak with the prince— I have to— Please, I beg you, it's important—"

"You dare lay your hands on the crown prince of Ardunia?" Hazan rounded on him. "You will hang for this."

"I didn't mean no harm," the boy cried, thrashing against the guards. "Please, I just—"

"That's quite enough," the prince said quietly.

"But, Your Highness—"

"I said, *enough*."

The room went suddenly, frighteningly still. The guards froze where they were; Omid went limp in their grip. All the palace seemed to stop breathing.

In the silence, Kamran studied the Fesht boy, his tear-streaked face, his shaking limbs.

"Release him," he said.

The guards dropped the child unceremoniously to the floor, where Omid fell hard on his knees and curled inward, his chest heaving as he struggled for breath. When the child finally looked up again, his eyes had filled with tears. "Please, sire," he said. "I didn't mean no harm."

Kamran was eerily calm when he said, "Tell me what has happened."

A single tear tracked down the boy's cheek. "It's the Diviners," he said. "They're all dead."

THIRTY-FOUR

سی وچھار

ALIZEH STARED BLANKLY AT THE young woman.

"I really can't believe it," Miss Huda was saying, her eyes wide with astonishment. "It's you. How on earth?"

"Forgive me, but I don't understa—"

"*This*," Miss Huda said, rushing toward a chest of drawers. She tugged open one of the compartments and rifled through her things, and not a beat later held aloft a cream-colored envelope. "This. *This*."

Alizeh stared. "A letter?"

"I received it earlier today. Go on." She pressed it into Alizeh's hands. "Read it."

Unbidden, Alizeh's heart began its familiar pounding, nerves crawling slowly across her skin. With great trepidation she tugged free the note from its sleeve, unfolded the paper, and went still at the sight of the familiar script. It was written with the same firm hand as the note she'd received earlier today; the one currently tucked into her pocket.

> *You will meet today with a young woman with silver eyes. Kindly deliver the enclosed package into her hands.*

As if she were an hourglass, Alizeh felt herself fill incrementally with grains of awareness; she grew suddenly heavy with unease, with a feeling of fear. Whosoever had delivered her the gown had also written this note—but if that were true, she should have no reason to worry.

Why, then, did she worry?

"This says there's an enclosed package," Alizeh said, looking up. "Is there a package?"

"Yes," said Miss Huda, who made no effort to move. She only stared, as if Alizeh had grown a third leg.

"Will you not bring it to me?"

"Will you not first tell me who you are?"

"Me?" Alizeh recoiled. "I am no one of consequence."

Miss Huda's jaw clenched. "If you are no one of consequence then I am the queen of Ardunia. Whatever you think of me, I daresay I've never given the impression of being an idiot."

"No." Alizeh sighed. "That you have not."

"Until just now, I'd thought the note was some kind of joke," Miss Huda said, crossing her arms. "People have long loved to torture me with their insipid pranks. This one seemed more peculiar than the others, but still I ignored it, much as I do the frog legs I find in my bed on occasion." She paused. "Do you take part now in some elaborate caper intended to make me appear foolish?"

"Of course not," said Alizeh sharply. "I'd never participate in such a hateful act."

Miss Huda frowned.

It was a moment before she said, "Do you know, I've thought from the first that you speak uncommonly well for a snoda. Still, I thought it snobbish to look down on you for your attempt to educate yourself. And yet—all that time you were measuring me with your pins and needles, I never quite had the measure of *you*, did I?"

Alizeh exhaled, the action loosening something in her bones, some essential tension responsible for securing in place her deferential facade. She didn't see the point in being compliant any longer.

Indeed, she was tired of it.

"Don't be too hard on yourself," she said to Miss Huda. "If you were unable to take the measure of me, it was because I'd not wanted you to."

"And why, pray, is that?"

"I cannot say."

"You cannot?" Miss Huda narrowed her eyes. "Or you will not?"

"I cannot."

"Whyever not?" She laughed. "Why would you not want anyone to know who you are? Don't say you're on the run from assassins?"

When Alizeh said nothing, Miss Huda quickly sobered. "You can't be serious," she said. "Are you in fact acquainted with assassins?"

"In my experience, one does not make the acquaintance of assassins."

"But it's true, then? Your life is in danger?"

Alizeh lowered her eyes. "Miss, will you not please bring me the package?"

"Oh," she said, waving a hand. "There's little point in the package. The parcel was empty."

Alizeh's eyes widened. "You opened it?"

"Of course I opened it. You think I believed a girl with silver eyes would come looking for a mysterious package? Naturally I assumed the box would contain bloody goat brains, or even a small family of dead birds. Instead, it was empty."

"But that can't be right." Alizeh frowned. "Will you not bring it to me anyway, so that I might inspect it?"

Miss Huda didn't appear to hear her.

"Tell me," she was saying, "why would you bother taking work as a seamstress if your life is in danger? Would it not be difficult to meet the demands of your customers if you needed, for example, to flee with little notice?"

Suddenly, Miss Huda gasped.

"Is *that* why you weren't able to finish my gown?" she asked. "Are you running for your life this very moment?"

"Yes."

Miss Huda gasped again, this time lifting a hand to her cheek. "Oh, how terribly thrilling."

"It's nothing of the sort."

"Perhaps not for you. I think I wouldn't mind running for my life. Or running away, generally."

Alizeh felt the nosta glow warm against her skin and stilled, surprised to discover the young woman did not exaggerate.

"I do nothing but avoid Mother most days," Miss Huda was saying. "The rest of my time I spend hiding from the governess. Or a series of grotesque suitors interested only in my dowry."

"Surely you have other interests," said Alizeh, who was growing vaguely concerned for the girl. "You must have friends—social obligations—"

Miss Huda dismissed this with a flick of her hand. "I often feel as if I live in a corridor; I'm neither genteel enough for nobility, nor common enough to mix with the baseborn. I'm a well fed, poorly dressed leper. My own sisters resist being seen with me in public."

"That's awful," Alizeh said with feeling. "I'm truly sorry to hear it."

"Are you really?" Miss Huda looked up. She studied Alizeh's face a moment before she smiled. It was a real smile, something earnest. "How strange you are. How very glad I am for your strangeness."

Surprised, Alizeh ventured a tentative smile back.

The girls were briefly silent after that, both assessing the fragile shoots of an unexpected friendship.

"Miss?" Alizeh said finally.

"Yes?"

"The package?"

"Right." Miss Huda nodded and, without another word, retrieved from inside her wardrobe a pale yellow box. Alizeh recognized the details right away; it appeared to be a cousin of the box that housed her gown, a perfect match in color and ornamentation, but a quarter of the size.

"So—you're not really a snoda, then?"

Alizeh looked up to meet the eyes of Miss Huda, who'd yet to relinquish the parcel.

"I beg your pardon?"

"You're not really a servant," she said. "You never were, I think. Your speech is too refined, you're on the run for your life, and now you receive mysterious packages by way of strangers? You're also rather beautiful, but in an old-fashioned way, as if from another time—"

"Old-fashioned?"

"—and your skin is too nice, yes, I see that now, and your hair too glossy. I'm quite certain you've never had scurvy, or even a touch of the plague, and by the looks of the rest of you I suspect you've never spent time in a poorhouse. And your eyes are so unusual—they keep changing color, you know— in fact, they're so unusual it almost makes one think you might've worn the snoda on purpose, to hide your—"

"Oh," Miss Huda cried, her eyes shining now with excitement. "Oh, I've figured it out, I've figured it out. You only wore the snoda to protect your identity, didn't you? Did you pretend to work at Baz House, too? Are you a spy? Are you employed by the crown?"

Alizeh opened her mouth to respond, and Miss Huda cut her off with a wave.

"Now, listen, I know you said you can't say who you are. But if I guess correctly, will you tell me? You need only nod your head yes."

"No."

Miss Huda frowned. "That seems terribly unfair."

Ignoring this, Alizeh snatched the parcel from Miss Huda's hands and set the box on a nearby table. Without further delay, she lifted the lid.

Miss Huda gave a small cry of delight.

The box was neither empty nor teeming with goat brains; instead, nestled between delicate sheets of tissue-thin paper, were a pair of lavender boots the exact shade of the diaphanous gown. Elegantly crafted of silk jacquard, they had softly pointed toes and short, stacked heels, ribbon ties lacing all the way up the high vamp of the shoe. The boots were so beautiful Alizeh was afraid even to touch them.

Tucked beside one silk boot, was a card.

"Magic," Miss Huda whispered. "That was *magic*, wasn't it? Good heavens. Who the devil are you? And *why* did you let me order you around like you were a servant?" The young woman began pacing the room, flapping her hands as if they were on fire. "Oh, I'm experiencing quite the most painful wave of retroactive embarrassment; I hardly know what to do with myself."

Alizeh paid this small drama no attention. Instead, she picked up the enclosed card, unfolding it with care. It was more of the same script.

When the path is unclear, these shoes will lead the way.

Alizeh was only just beginning to process the enormity of her own astonishment—the enormity of what it all might mean—when the words on the note suddenly disappeared.

She drew a sharp breath.

"What is it?" Miss Huda asked eagerly. "What does it say?"

Slowly, fresh words bloomed on the blank note before her: sharp, dark strokes as substantial as if they were written in real time, by an invisible hand.

Don't be alarmed.

As if on cue, alarm shot through Alizeh with the force of an arrow, startling her backward, her mind reeling as she spun around, searching for something—for someone—

No, she went deathly still.

The words had disappeared once more without warning, displaced now by others, but more quickly now, as if the writer were in a rush—

I am not your enemy.

Miss Huda snatched the note from Alizeh's limp hands and scanned it, then made a sound of frustration.

"Why do the words disappear the moment I try to read them? I take great offense to this. *I want it known that I take great offense to this,*" she said to the room at large.

Alizeh, meanwhile, could hardly breathe. "I must get dressed," she said. "I must get ready."

"What? Get dressed?" Miss Huda turned, blinked at her. "Have you gone quite out of your gourd? Of all the things to be thinking at this moment—"

"Forgive me, but I must," Alizeh said, snatching the two yellow boxes up into her arms, then darting behind a dressing screen in a far corner of the room. "I hope you will understand now why I cannot stay to fix your gown."

"Oh, dash the gown!" Miss Huda cried. "Where will you go?"

Alizeh didn't respond right away, occupied as she was
with disrobing at breakneck speed. The dressing screen
being not at all as opaque as Alizeh would prefer, she went
invisible as she changed, feeling quite exposed standing in
her unmentionables so close to a stranger. This was not how
she'd imagined preparing herself for the ball tonight, not in a
mad rush behind a dressing screen; not within reach of Miss
Huda and her unceasing questions.

"Will you not answer me?" It was the young miss yet again,
only louder this time. "Why do you need to get dressed?
Where do you intend to go? Those boots aren't at all practical for running away. Why, if you look away from your feet
for even a moment you're likely to step in a fresh pile of horse
manure—or even an old pile, you know, as they're never able
to clear the roads quickly enough—and the silk will never be
the same, this you may rely upon, for I speak from personal
experie—"

"I thank you for your wisdom," Alizeh said sharply, cutting her off. "Though I don't know where I'm going just yet,
only that I—"

Like a half-mute bird, Miss Huda screamed.

It was a tortured sound, a strangled cry of surprise. Alizeh
would've darted out from behind the screen if not for her
nakedness—a problem she rushed now to address—and
would've called out a question of concern if her voice had
not been unceremoniously drowned out by another.

"Your Majesty," she heard someone say.

Alizeh suddenly froze.

It was the voice of a young man. "Forgive me," he said. "I meant not to frighten you. I take it you received my packages?"

Alizeh's heart raced wildly in her chest. She knew the sound of Hazan's voice—the evening they'd met had been emblazoned in her memory—and this was not he. This was the voice of no one she recognized.

Who, then?

Hazan hadn't mentioned anyone else in his plans, but then, he'd mentioned little in an effort to spare her in case she should be discovered. Still, it was possible Hazan was working with someone else, was it not?

"I— Yes, I received a package," she heard Miss Huda say. "But, who are you? Why are you here?"

Indeed, the more Alizeh thought about it, the more it seemed entirely probable that Hazan was working with someone else. In point of fact, he'd mentioned something about others searching for her, hadn't he? It was more than just he who'd been looking for her all these years.

At that realization, a degree of tension left her body.

Alizeh adjusted the nosta, tucking it more firmly inside her corset before buttoning up her new gown like a madwoman. She was just stepping into her new boots when she heard the stranger's voice once more.

"Forgive me," he said again, though he didn't sound at all sorry. "I see that I've frightened you. We were in fact never meant to meet like this, but I've received a warning, and I'm duty bound now to escort y—"

"Please, you misunderstand—" Miss Huda tried again. "I'm not— I'm not whoever you think I am."

There was a brief, taut silence.

Alizeh could hardly concentrate for the nerves lancing through her. She'd only just managed to tie her boot laces, kicking hastily aside her old, reliable pair. Her torn boots and worn calico work dress lay there on the lush carpet like an old skin, discarded; Alizeh felt a strange pang at the sight.

There was no going back to her old life now.

Then, the sound of the stranger's emotionless voice— "Pray tell me, who do I think you are?"

"I don't—" Miss Huda hesitated. "You know, I don't actually know her name."

Another tense silence.

"I see," he said, sounding suddenly annoyed. "So you must be the other one."

"The other one? Oh for heaven's sake," she muttered. "Come out here right this second, *Your Majesty*, or I will come back there and murder you."

Alizeh drew back her invisibility, took a deep breath, and stepped out from behind the screen with stunning equanimity, even as her heart beat wildly in her chest. She could not forget herself, especially not now, when fear blew through her with the force of a summer gale.

The stranger, she noted, was a surprise.

His age seemed nonspecific; she suspected he was still a young man, but he presented right away as an old soul wrapped in the cloak of youth. His skin was a burnished golden brown, his hair a sharp wave of red copper. He wore simple, unadorned black clothes—coat, jacket—and clutched in one hand both a tall black hat and a golden mace. He had bright, startlingly blue eyes, but there was something tragic about them, too, a heaviness there that made him hard to look at—and all the more so when he stared at her, his eyes widening a barely there micrometer as she moved into view.

"Oh," he said.

Alizeh did not spare time for niceties. "How do you know me?"

"I never said I did."

"You don't even know each other?" Miss Huda said, glancing wildly from one to the other. To Alizeh, she said, "You don't know this person?"

Alizeh shook her head.

"Then get out of my room, you madman." Miss Huda all but pushed the stranger toward the door. "Out with you— Out at once, you horrible cad, sneaking into young ladies' bedrooms without permi—"

The young man stepped easily out of reach.

"I think you misunderstand," he said flatly. "Her Highness and I are not entirely unacquainted. We have a friend in common."

"Do we?"

"Her Highness?" Miss Huda spun around, staring now at Alizeh. "You really— Are you really—?"

The stranger said, "Yes," and Alizeh said, "Not exactly," and everyone, collectively, frowned.

"There is no time for this now," the young man said, turning to face Alizeh. "Your plans for the evening may have been compromised. We must away at once."

The nosta flashed warm against her skin, and Alizeh stiffened, her heart plummeting in her chest.

Then it was true: things had gone awry.

Alizeh's disappointment was breathtaking, but she bade herself be calm. After all, it appeared Hazan had built contingencies into the plan. The nosta alone was a tremendous gift; the certainty it provided was a great balm even now, steadying her in these turbulent seas. What was it he'd said when he'd given it to her?

So that you never need wonder who your enemies might be.

"It was you," Alizeh said, meeting the eyes of the stranger. "It was you who sent me this dress? And the shoes?"

He hesitated a beat before saying, "Yes."

"Why?"

"I was returning a favor."

"A favor?" She frowned. "A favor to me?"

"No."

Alizeh drew back. "To whom, then?"

"To our mutual friend."

This was twice now he'd mentioned their mutual friend. Was he concealing Hazan's identity in front of Miss Huda?

"So you do this for him," Alizeh said softly. "Which means you've no vested interest in assisting me."

"My interest is only in discharging myself of an old debt," said the young man. "Our mutual friend has asked that I repay him thus, with these specific instructions, and so I have done. I was never meant to come here, not unless the circumstances demanded my intercession, as they do now."

"I see," she said. The nosta was burning hot against her sternum. This stranger was neither friend nor foe, she was realizing, which made the situation rather tricky.

"What is your name?" she asked.

"My name is irrelevant."

"Irrelevant?" she said, surprised. "What am I to call you then?"

"Nothing."

Alizeh could not hide the flash of irritation she felt at that. "Very well," she said stiffly. "Where do we go from here?"

The stranger opened his mouth to speak and hesitated at the sight of Miss Huda's eager face. Her curious eyes.

Gently, he cleared his throat.

"I would really rather not discuss any of this in front of"—he glanced again at Miss Huda—"a third party, though I recognize that, in this, the mistake is mine. Somehow I thought— That is, for a moment, there appeared to be only one person in the room. I thought the young lady of the house had joined her party downstairs."

"I'm standing right here," Miss Huda said sharply. "You need not discuss me as if I didn't exist."

"Ah," he said, tilting his head. "But I would really rather you didn't."

Miss Huda's mouth dropped open.

Quickly, Alizeh turned to her. "Can I trust that you will keep the details of this day to yourself?"

"Of course," said Miss Huda, drawing herself up to her full height. "I've never in my life betrayed a secret. You may depend upon me to be the soul of discretion."

The nosta went ice cold at that, sending a shiver through Alizeh's body.

She grimaced.

As if he, too, had felt the lie, the stranger locked eyes with Alizeh.

"We have only two options," he said. "Kill her or take her with us. The error was mine, so I will leave the decision up to you. It is my strong recommendation, however, that we kill her."

"Kill me?" Miss Huda cried. "You cannot be serious—"

"No— No, we are *not* going to kill you," Alizeh said, shooting an unkind look at Nothing. Then, trying for a smile, she turned to Miss Huda. "Though you did say you thought you might like to run away, didn't you?"

Miss Huda looked suddenly as if she might faint.

"Here," Alizeh said, opening Miss Huda's wardrobe doors and drawers, plucking essential items from their depths. "I will help you pack."

Miss Huda gaped at her. "But— I can't—"

Alizeh located a medium-sized bag in the girl's wardrobe and pressed the small luggage into Miss Huda's frozen hands. "Bring only as much as you can carry."

"But I don't want to run away," Miss Huda said in a whisper, her eyes bright with fear. "Where will we go? How would I live? How long will I be gone?"

"These are all excellent questions," Alizeh said, patting

the girl's shoulder. "You pack, and I will ask."

Mournfully, Miss Huda pulled a gown from a hanger, stuffing it halfheartedly into her bag.

To the stranger, Alizeh said, "There is no need now for subterfuge, is there? You may now inform me of your plan. Where do we go from here?"

Nothing stared at the scene unfolding before him, looking vaguely nauseated.

"The details are spare," he said. "I will extend you a level of protection until we reach the ball, and shortly after our arrival I will escort you to a secure method of transport. This transport will deliver you to your destination."

"But where is my destination?" Alizeh asked. "What happens when I arrive?"

"Oh—and will it rain where we are going?" Miss Huda asked. "Will I need an umbrella?"

The stranger closed his eyes. "I cannot now tell you where you are going, but I can assure you that your destination is safe. Already I've guaranteed you an extra measure of protection with the dress and shoes."

Alizeh blinked at that; at the reminder. "Of course," she said, glancing at her gown and boots. "I nearly forgot. How do the items work, exactly?"

"Did you not read the notes?"

"I did, but—"

"If you don't know where to go, your feet will assist, if you fear being seen, the gown will protect your identity from those who wish you harm, et cetera, et cetera. If you do not, however, follow my exact instructions at all times, I cannot ensure your safety. Heed your own whims and I will not be responsible for what happens to you, and I will not care."

Slowly, Alizeh looked up to face the stranger. "Did you really feel it necessary to add that last part?"

"Which part?"

"*And I will not care,*" she said, echoing his emotionless tone. "Do you enjoy being needlessly petty?"

"Yes," he said. "I do."

Alizeh opened her mouth to say something unkind, then bit her lip, drew back.

She didn't know this stranger, and he knew little of her. Even if unwillingly given, his honest commitment to help her was nothing short of miraculous, for, whoever he was, he was doubtless risking a great deal. Perhaps he was unaware how much his help was worth to her, but if things went well tonight, Alizeh's entire life might be spared; the trials of the last several years would come to an end.

Finally, she'd be free.

She decided then that she could not—would not—allow herself to be rude to this young man, not even if he deserved it, not when she might soon owe him her life.

She cleared her throat.

"Do you know," she said, trying to smile, "in all the excitement I've forgotten to say something rather important."

He cut her a dark look.

"Thank you," she said. "I know the burden is cumbersome, but you render me a great kindness tonight, and I won't soon forget it."

The stranger flinched at that, stared at her a beat too long. "I don't do it to be kind."

"I know."

"Then don't," he said, sounding, for the first time, like he owned a real emotion: anger. "Don't thank me."

Alizeh stiffened. "Very well, then. I retract my formal thanks. Still, I am grateful."

"Don't be."

She raised her eyebrows. "Do you intend to command me not to feel my own emotions?"

"Yes."

"That's absurd."

"And yet, if you are truly grateful for my assistance, you might do me a favor and resist speaking to me altogether."

Alizeh went slack. "Why are you trying to be cruel?"

"Oh, please don't fight," Miss Huda said. "This is bound to be awful enough already—"

"I am inclined to agree," the young man said coldly. "Impossible as my dreams might be, I would much prefer that we persevere in silence, and part as strangers."

"Fine," Alizeh said quietly, her jaw clenching.

"Good." He glanced at Miss Huda. "Now we must be off."

"Wait," said Miss Huda desperately. "Will you not reconsider? Please let me stay here. I promise I won't say a word to anyone about what I've seen— I'll be silent as death, you'll see—"

For the second time, the nosta went cold against Alizeh's skin. She flinched.

"I told you we should kill her," said the stranger.

Miss Huda whimpered.

"Ignore him," Alizeh said. "Listen, it's only for a short while. You can come back home as soon as we're able to get somewhere safe—"

"You give the girl false hope," said Nothing, cutting her off. "The only way she could reliably return home is if we manage to distort her memory, which requires walking her backward through time, which is exceedingly complicated, not to mention painful—"

Miss Huda began to cry.

"Will you not hush?" Alizeh snapped at the stranger, forgetting her promise to be nice. "How can you not see that your bullying only makes things worse? We will never manage to be inconspicuous if she won't stop weeping."

The stranger looked at her, then looked at Miss Huda. He touched his fingers together, and Miss Huda went suddenly silent.

The girl was still crying but made no sound.

When the young woman realized what happened she clutched at her throat, eyes widening in fear as she struggled to speak, no doubt to scream—all in vain.

Alizeh rounded on Nothing. "What have you done?" she demanded. "I insist you change her back this instant."

"I will not."

"Are you some kind of Diviner?"

"No."

"A monster, then?"

He almost smiled. "Don't say you've been speaking with my mother?"

"How do you have access to so much magic, then? The dress, the shoes—now this—"

"And this," he said, placing his hat atop his head.

Without warning, Alizeh was pitched forward into end-less night.

THIRTY-FIVE

سی و پنج

MUSIC SWELLED IN KAMRAN'S EARS, the screaming darkness of his mind punctured occasionally by the sound of laughter, the clink of glass and silver. His dark eyes were lined with kohl; his neck bound heavily in ropes of sapphire; a single, hammered gold circlet nestled in the midnight of his hair. He stood tall in weighty layers of dark green silk, an emerald-encrusted harness crisscrossing his chest and cinched at his waist, and from which hung, as always, his swords. He was both immaculate and uncomfortable as he nodded his head, greeting, unseeing, the nobles who bowed before him, the young women who curtsied low at his feet.

Occasionally Kamran glanced at the glittering throne beside him, which was occupied by his grandfather, and the one beyond that, in which sat his mother, drinking deeply from a goblet of wine. Both royals were smiling, but the king's jolly countenance was a necessary facade, doing a great deal to belie what was no doubt an interior tempest straining at the capacity of his self-control.

This would describe how Kamran felt, too.

Just steps away, half obscured by a potted olive tree, was the Tulanian ambassador, who'd been ordered to stand by, ready at any time to identify the Tulanian king should the young man ever arrive. Farther in the shadows stood Hazan, awaiting orders.

Kamran had not yet decided what to feel about his minister, or how best to proceed; for though the prince's instincts insisted something was amiss, Hazan's actions had yet to draw an obvious line to deception. Kamran, however, was watching him closely, waiting for even a hint of unusual behavior.

The Fesht boy, at least, had not lied.

Omid had been living at the Diviners Quarters these last days, and, by his own account, had grown quite close to the priests and priestesses who'd saved his life. He'd gone to bid them goodnight for the evening when he discovered that all twenty-five Diviners had been slaughtered in their beds.

Kamran and the king had gone, of course, to bear witness.

There'd been no blood to mop up, no clear evidence of violence to investigate. Their faces had been peaceful, hands clasped across their chests. Only a thorough search had revealed proof of an attack: a subtle growth of frost between their cold, parted lips.

Dark magic, the king had whispered.

Nothing else could've so easily killed Diviners capable of wielding great power. As to the owner of the crime, there was little doubt there, too. The Tulanian king, who, earlier in the evening had been seen and spoken with at a gathering of Ardunian ambassadors, had deserted his party without notice, disappearing into the ether. Neither had he met with the king ahead of the ball, as was expected.

Kamran knew not whether the young King Cyrus would

show his face at the fete tonight, but his absence would indicate its own answer, for such actions were without question a declaration of war—one of the more barbaric instigations the prince had ever witnessed.

Still, there was no proof.

Worse, it would take weeks to collect and deliver to the Royal Square the rare other Diviners scattered throughout the empire, and until then, all of Ardunia would be left vulnerable, lacking an essential layer of protection long provided by the quorum at the Diviners Quarters.

Even so, there were pretenses to be maintained.

The king did not want the horrible news spread throughout the empire, not just yet. He did not want people to panic before he was ready to formally address their fears, which would not be possible until tomorrow morning, for the brutal events of the evening had rendered the ball only that much more important. More acts of violence could arrive at anytime—could threaten the crown at anytime—

Which meant Ardunia needed to secure the royal line, and quickly, with another heir.

Kamran, whose mind was resigned even as his heart protested, stared indifferently at the faceless horde, at the individuals peeling off to pay respect to the Ardunian royals. The prince was meant to choose a bride from among these strangers, and yet, the ladies all looked the same to him. They were all of them in nearly identical gowns, their hair styled in a similar fashion. He could not tell them apart save the occasional unflattering impressions they left behind: a barking laugh, a set of stained teeth; one girl in particular who could not stop biting her fingernails, not even when she spoke.

The vast majority could scarcely look Kamran in the eye, while a select few had leaned in dramatically, whispering in his ear illicit invitations for that very evening.

It all left him feeling exhausted.

Among the many travesties of the day, Kamran had not been able to relinquish the memories of one young woman in particular. He wondered, as he nodded his head at yet another girl curtsying low before him, whether Alizeh would remain with him always in his mind, in the occasional manifestation of sensation across his skin, in the sharp breath he might take at the reminder of her touch. It was a thought both strange and thrilling, and which imbued in him a striking fear.

Would he forever compare all others to her?

Would anyone else ever make him feel as much? And if not, would he be cursed forever to live only a half-life, a life of quiet acquiescence, of unfulfilled expectations? Was it worse, he wondered, to never know what you might have— or worse to have it snatched away before you might have it?

"You are making no effort," the king whispered sharply, startling the prince out of his reverie.

Kamran dared not turn his head to look at the king. He'd not even realized the curtsying young woman had gone.

"You might ask the girls a single question," King Zaal was muttering, "instead of standing there like a statue."

"Does it truly matter, Your Highness, when I already know you will choose for me whomever you think is best?"

King Zaal went quiet at that, and Kamran's heart wrenched at the confirmation of his fears.

"Even so," the king said finally. "You might at least act as if you are at a ball and not a funeral, dire though the circumstances may be. I want your engagement announced before the week is out. I want you married before the month is done. I want an heir before the year is finished. This night is not to be disturbed before its purpose is fulfilled. Are we clear?"

The prince tensed his jaw and studied the crowd, wondering how their numbers seemed to bloat before his eyes. "Yes, Your Majesty," he said quietly.

Kamran's gaze landed unexpectedly on the Fesht boy, who stood idly by, wringing his hands. The child stared often at the entrance, and with obvious anticipation. His eyes were red from sobbing, but as he'd been expressly forbidden from crying at the ball—under threat of expulsion—he only bit his lip and flinched every time a name was announced.

Kamran frowned.

He could not understand what the child was searching for. Certainly Omid knew no one else here; he had no family to name. No friends.

Why then, did he seem so eager?

A finely dressed older woman came suddenly forward, and the prince, distracted, did not at first discern the familiar face of his aunt—and then, disarmed, could not hide his relief. Kamran was so pleased to see Duchess Jamilah that he took her outstretched hand and bowed before it, paying the woman an undue level of respect that attracted a number of unwelcome stares.

A beat too late, he realized his aunt was not alone.

"Your Highness," said Duchess Jamilah, flushing slightly under his attentions. "It is my great thrill this evening to introduce to you the daughter of a dear friend of mine."

Kamran felt—and heard—the king straighten in his seat. The prince steeled himself as he turned, studying now the young woman standing beside his aunt.

"Please allow me the pleasure of formally presenting Lady Golnaz, daughter of Marquess Saatchi."

Kamran nodded, and the girl fell into a graceful curtsy, rising before him to reveal clear brown eyes and an uncomplicated smile. She possessed ordinary, familiar features neither remarkable nor plain. Her brown waves were pulled back from her face in a loose chignon; she wore a nondescript gown with little to recommend its color or shape. Intellectually, Kamran understood that the girl was an approximation of pretty, but he felt nothing when he looked at her, and would never have noticed her in a crowd.

Still, she seemed self-possessed in a way he appreciated. Of all things, Kamran thought he could never be married to someone he didn't consider his emotional equal, and he struggled always to respect young ladies who only simpered, never holding up their heads with conviction. Dignity was, in his opinion, an essential quality in a queen, and he was at least relieved to discover that Lady Golnaz appeared the owner of a spine.

"The pleasure is mine," he forced himself to say to the

young woman. "I trust you are enjoying yourself this evening, Lady Golnaz."

"I am, thank you," she said in a bright voice, a smile touching her eyes. "Though I think the same cannot be said for
you, Your Highness."

The prince stilled at that, studying the young woman now
with a renewed appreciation. "My pride would insist that I
disagree, though I—" Kamran paused, blinking up at a blur
of a girl in the distance, there and gone again.

"I . . ." he said, returning his eyes to Lady Golnaz, struggling now to remember the original purpose of his statement.
"I cannot . . ."

Another flash of color and Kamran looked up again, wondering, even then, why he should be so distracted by a single
movement when the entire room around him was a madness
of motion and—

Alizeh.

The prince was transfixed. Blood rushed from his head
without warning, leaving him light-headed.

She was here.

She was here—*just there*—incandescent in shimmering waves of lavender, obsidian curls pinned away from her
unmasked face, a few loose tendrils glancing off her cheeks,
which had gone pink with exertion. If he'd thought her
breathtaking in the drab garb of a servant's dress, he could
not think how to describe her now. He only knew that she
seemed apart from this mundane world; above it.

The mere sight of her had paralyzed him.

There was no linen at her throat, no bandages wrapped

around her hands. She seemed to glow as she moved, float as she searched the room. Kamran lost his breath as he watched her, felt his heart hammer in his chest with a violence that scared him.

How? How was she here? Had she come for him? Had she come to find him, to be with him—?

"Your Highness," someone was saying.

"Sire, are you quite all right?" Another.

The prince watched, as if from outside himself, as a young man grabbed Alizeh's hand. She spun around to face him, her eyes widening in surprise, then recognition.

He said something, and she laughed.

Kamran felt the sound spear him like a blade, his chest seizing with an unfamiliar pain. It was an ache unlike any he'd known; one he wished to tear out of his chest.

"That's him," Hazan whispered suddenly in his ear.

Kamran took a breath and drew back, the scene around him coming sharply into focus. Alizeh had gone; disappeared into the crowd. He saw instead the worried eyes of his aunt, the curious gaze of Lady Golnaz. The frenzy of the bloated crowd before him.

"It's the gentleman with the copper hair, Your Highness. The one carrying the unusual hat. The Tulanian ambassador has confirmed it."

It was a moment before the prince was able to say: "Is he quite certain?"

"Yes, sire."

"Bring him to me," Kamran said softly.

THIRTY-SIX

سی و شش

ALIZEH HAD SPIRALED AS SHE fell, plummeting through layers of night, nearing a death that grazed her skin without claiming her soul. She thought she'd heard herself scream as she tumbled, but she'd wondered, too, in a flickering moment, whether she might actually be dreaming, whether her whole life was not some strange, shimmering tapestry, infinite threads of nonsense.

She'd felt her feet hit the ground first, the impact shuddering up her legs, her hips, rattling her teeth. When she opened her eyes she'd crashed against him, braced herself against his chest. Music roared in her ears as she reared back, her head spinning, the din of chatter and laughter piercing the fog of her mind, the smell of sugar in her nose, the crush of bodies against her skin.

There was heat and sweat, sound and sensation—too much of everything. Still, she realized at once where she was, and worried right away for Miss Huda. She pushed away from the stranger and began to search for her new friend, wondering whether the girl had made it through, wondering whether she'd lost forever the ability to speak.

Alizeh trusted the stranger no longer.

She didn't care if he was an ally of Hazan's. How could she

now believe anything he said? He'd proven both cruel and capricious, and she would never again le—

Someone took her hand and Alizeh spun, startled, to discover the very same blue-eyed, capricious stranger. She stared at their clasped hands, then at his face, wondering whether she imagined the terror that flitted in and out of his eyes.

"Where are you going?" He sounded different; the antithesis of the impassive young man she'd first met. "You don't intend to run away, do you?"

Alizeh was so surprised by the fear in his eyes that she laughed. "No, I'm not running away, you ridiculous creature. I'm searching for Miss Huda. She is doubtless terrified somewhere and unable to call for help—because of what *you* did to her."

Alizeh tugged her hand free from his and pushed on through the crowd, grateful for the protections offered her by the gown—and then frowned, biting her lip as she remembered who'd given her the garment.

He'd not lied to her about this, at least. The dress really was a miracle.

People seemed to pass by her as if she did not exist, their gazes never quite touching her face. It was unsettling to think so many strangers did not wish her well, but it was a comfort, too, not to worry about her eyes or her snoda. There was no one here to spit at her, no one to shove her out of the way, no one to order her to scrub feces out of porous stonework.

Still, Alizeh was made uneasy by the knowledge that she

owed this peculiar stranger any thanks for her safety, for everything about him seemed suddenly traitorous. If he had the ability to render Miss Huda mute, what might he do to Alizeh if she crossed him? In fact, it was possible the dress and shoes were a trap. What if they'd been bewitched to carry her somewhere unsafe? What if she followed her feet to her own demise? Perhaps she should discard the gown— or destroy it. But then what about the shoes? What would she wear instead?

How would she escape?

"I have undone it," the stranger called, trailing close behind.

Alizeh started, turned back. "You've undone what?"

"The other girl. The loud one," he said. "She will be able to speak again." He made no effort to lower his voice even as he closed the gap between them, evincing no apparent worry for being overheard.

It made Alizeh wonder whether he carried magical protections on his own garments, too.

"You've undone it, just like that?" Alizeh said, staring at him as he approached. His was a disconcertingly fickle character.

"Yes," he said. Up close, his eyes were a truly shocking shade of blue, all the more so under the refracted light of so many chandeliers. "In exchange, I ask for your word that you will not run away, no matter what happens."

"My word?" she said, surprised. "But why are you so worried I might try to run away?"

"Because this night will be difficult. I was sent here to collect you, which is my primary goal, but while I'm here I intend to complete certain tasks, in return for which I will be absolved of some rather large debts." A pause. "Do you frighten easily?"

Alizeh bristled at this. "You insult me even by asking the question."

"Good. Then I ask for your word."

"You will not have it."

His eyes narrowed. "I beg your pardon?"

"I will only grant such a request if you first swear you won't harm her."

"Who? The loud girl?"

"Swear you won't hurt her, or use magic on her—"

"Oh, come now, you ask for too much."

"You want my word I will not run away?" Alizeh said. "Well, I need to be able to trust you. Give *me* your word that you will not harm her. That is my condition."

"Very well," he said bitterly. "But I must warn you—if you go back on your promise, there will be repercussions."

"What kinds of repercussions?"

"I will not be nice to you."

Alizeh laughed. "Do you mean to imply that you are being nice to me now?"

"I will come find you at half past the hour," he said, scowling. "I must escort you to our transport before midnight, else our ride will fall asleep, and getting things running again will cost us a great deal of time."

"Our ride will fall asleep? Don't you mean the driver?"

He ignored this. "Do fetch the girl, and quickly, for I fear she will be difficult to corral."

Alizeh frowned. "And what will you be doing?"

"As I mentioned, I've a bit of business to settle. It shouldn't take long."

"A bit of business?" Alizeh felt a flutter of nerves at that. "With Hazan, you mean?"

The stranger blinked. "Hazan?"

"Yes—I have a great many questions for him. Where is he now, do you know? Will he make it to the ball?"

The stranger's eyes widened, then narrowed, not unlike the focus on a telescope. "I don't know."

"Oh." Alizeh bit her lip. "Well, will y—"

"For now, just fix upon finding that girl. If you need help getting anywhere, your shoes will deliver you where you need to go."

"If that's true, why must you be the one to take me to my transport?"

"Because it's *my* transport," he said in a flash of anger, "and you're only meant to borrow it."

She recoiled at that, at the venom in his voice.

"And I'll have you know," he said, "that while you're so busy wondering whether I'm reliable, I'm wondering the same about you. I can assure you, *Your Highness*, that I do not want to be here, either. I am forced into your company only by the order of a merciless master, and I'm not at all pleased about it."

Alizeh opened her mouth to protest but the stranger turned abruptly away—and left.

She watched him push through the crowd, disappearing into a sea of bodies with ease. How he moved so quickly among so many was both surprising and confusing, though not nearly as much as his last words.

He was forced into her company by a *merciless master*? That didn't sound like Hazan, but then, what did she really know of him? Of anyone?

Alizeh stared at the broad back of the stranger as he retreated, at the simple lines of his black ensemble, the peculiar hat he carried in one hand.

She could not take the measure of him, and it worried her. How could she reliably place her life in the hands of someone she could not trust?

With a sigh, Alizeh turned to go, stopping only when she saw her blue-eyed companion intercepted by Hazan himself, the back of his dusty-blond head a stark contrast to the rich amber of the stranger's copper.

Alizeh nearly cried for relief.

So they *did* know each other; they had indeed planned her escape together. A crashing wave of calm overcame her nerves, soothing her many worries. The stranger's methods were unorthodox, yes, but she'd been wrong; he was not untrustworthy. He had undone his hex on Miss Huda, he'd given his word he'd not hurt the young woman, and now she had proof that he'd not lied to her. All this time Alizeh had trusted the nosta to guide her, but there was great comfort to be derived from the kind of proof only her own eyes might provide.

Finally, Alizeh felt as if she could breathe.

He and Hazan were speaking quickly now, and Alizeh was torn between searching for Miss Huda and joining their small party. She had so many questions for Hazan she was eager to ask, and perhaps—

Perhaps if she did not search for Miss Huda, she might not find the girl, and could then safely allow the young woman to return to her life. After all, what difference would it really make if Miss Huda told people what she'd seen? Alizeh would be long gone by then.

Though it was possible the gossip would not hurt *her*, but her blue-eyed companion. Knowing now that he was not a wretch made it harder for her to be careless with his life, especially as she considered all he'd done to spare hers.

Alizeh bit her lip, her eyes darting back and forth between the room at large, and the tall forms of the two young men.

Oh, dash it all.

She would let Miss Huda go. She needed to speak with Hazan; there was too much uncertainty.

Alizeh began forcing her way back through the crush, weaving between bodies to catch up with the gentlemen, who'd begun moving quickly in the opposite direction.

"Wait," she called out. "Where are y—"

The copper-headed stranger turned around at that, catching her eyes with a narrowing of his own. He gave her a single, firm headshake.

Danger, he seemed to say. *Do not follow.*

Alizeh felt the nosta warm, and she gasped in surprise. How had the nosta understood an unspoken warning?

She stood in place, struck still by the many curiosities of the evening, when she felt the dregs of a familiar, silky whisper flood her head, fill her with dread.

A crawling fear overtook her heart, shattered across her skin, filled her mouth with heat.

Blindly, she ran.

It was panic that propelled her jerky movements, panic that sought irrational escape, as if she could ever outrun the devil. She knew the futility of retreat even as she pushed desperately through the densely packed room, even as she knew her efforts were in vain.

Like vapor, his whisper filled her head.

Beware the gold, the crown, the eye

"*No*," she cried as she ran. "No, n—"

Beware the gold, the crown, the eye
One is a king who is loath to die

"Stop," Alizeh shouted, clapping her hands around her ears. She didn't know where she was going, only that she needed air, needed to flee the crush of the crowd. "Get out, get out of my head—"

Beware the gold, the crown, the eye
One is a king who is loath to die

Ford the darkness, scale the wall
Two have a friend who is foe to all

"Leave me alone! Please, just leave me alone—"

The serpent, the saber, the fiery light
Three will storm and rage and fight

Alizeh caught a marble column around the middle and sagged against it, pressing her uncommonly overheated cheek to its cool skin. "Please," she gasped. "I beg you— Leave me be—"

Always the jester will interfere
For there cannot be three sovereigns here

Something broke, smoke unclenching from around her throat, and just like that, he was gone.

Alizeh felt dizzy in the aftermath, breathless with fear. She pressed herself against the glossy marble, felt the cold penetrate her skin through her gauzy gown. She'd been so certain she'd freeze in this dress, but she'd not anticipated the crush of bodies, their collective heat, the unusual warmth she'd feel this night.

Alizeh closed her eyes, tried to calm her breathing.

She didn't know where she was and she didn't care; she could hardly hear her own thoughts over the sound of her heart, beating wildly in her chest.

She'd not even been able to decode the first riddle she'd

received from the devil—how was she supposed to understand this second one?

Worse, so much worse: his visits had proven over and over to be an omen. It was just days ago that he'd filled her head with whispers of misery, and oh, how she'd suffered the consequences. How dramatically had her life changed and collapsed since she last heard his voice in her head? What did that mean for her now? Would she lose every crumb of hope she'd recently collected?

There was no precedent for this precipitous visit from Iblees. Alizeh usually experienced months, not days, of a reprieve before his torturous voice infected her mind again, bringing with it all manner of calamity and unrest.

How, now, would she be tortured?

"Alizeh."

She stiffened, turning to face an altogether different torment even as she grasped for purchase at the cool column. Alizeh's heart pounded now in an entirely new fashion, her pulse fluttering dangerously at her throat.

Kamran stood before her, magnificently turned out in a heavy green coat, the open, buttonless front cinched closed with a complex emerald harness, his neck wrapped up to his chin in more gleaming jewels. His eyes were made impossibly darker with kohl, more devastating as they searched her now. But it was the glint of the circlet in his hair that sent a terrifying bolt through her heart.

He was a prince. She'd nearly forgotten.

"Alizeh," he said again, though he whispered it now, staring at her with a longing he did nothing to conceal. The infinite darkness that was his eyes took in every detail of her face, her hair, even her gown. Alizeh felt weak standing this close to him, disjointed in her mind. Nothing was going according to plan.

How had he even spotted her in the melee?

She'd glimpsed him, briefly, from afar, watched him coolly receive a long line of guests she'd been certain would distract him through the night. Surely he had responsibilities he could not abandon—surely someone would soon be along to collect him—

The prince made a sound of distress that startled her, sharpening her instincts; Alizeh drew closer without thinking, stopping just short of touching him. She watched as Kamran winced a second time, gently tugging the collar away from his neck, doing his best to find relief without disturbing the artfully constructed ensemble.

"What is it?" Alizeh asked softly. "Are you in pain?"

He shook his head, attempting a brief laugh that did little to deny his obvious discomfort. "No, it's nothing. It's only that I find these costumes suffocating. This coat is supposed to be made of silk, but it's frightfully stiff and coarse. It was uncomfortable before, but now I swear it feels as if it's full of needles." He grimaced again, pulling at the lapel of his coat.

"Needles?" Alizeh frowned. Tentatively, she touched him, felt him stiffen as she drew her hand along the emerald brocade, its raised embroidery. "Do you— Do you have a sensitivity to gold?"

His brows furrowed. "To gold?"

"This is silk, yes," she explained, "but it's silk woven with a gold-spun weft. The threads are, in some places, wrapped with gold fibers. And here"—she grazed the raised embroidery at the collar, at the lapels—"here it's overlaid with yet more goldwork. These are real gold threads, did you not know?"

"No," he said, but he was staring at her strangely; for a moment his gaze dropped to her mouth. "I didn't know one might weave gold into fabric."

Alizeh took a breath, stole back her hand.

"Yes," she said. "The garment should feel heavy, and perhaps a bit rough against the skin, but it shouldn't hurt you. It certainly shouldn't feel like needles."

"How do you know this?"

"Never mind that," she said, avoiding his eyes. "What's more important is that you are in pain."

"Yes." He took a step closer. "A great deal of it."

"I'm—I'm sorry to hear it," she said, nervous now. She began to ramble. "It's quite rare, but I think you might have an aversion to gold. You should perhaps avoid wearing such textiles in future, and if you want a softer fabric, you might be more specific and ask your seamstress for silk charmeuse, or satin, and avoid georgette and certain types of, of taffeta or—or even—"

She stopped breathing when he touched her, when his hands landed at her waist, then moved down her hips, his fingers grazing her skin through the layers of sheer fabric. She gasped, felt her back sink against the marble column.

He was so close.

He smelled like orange blossoms and something else, heat

and musk, leather—

"Why did you come tonight?" he asked. "How? And your injuries— This dress—"

"Kamran—"

"Say you came back for me," he whispered. There was a thread of desire in his voice that threatened the good sense in her head, her very composure. "Tell me you came to find me. That you changed your mind."

"How—how can you even say such things," she said, her hands beginning to tremble, "on an evening you are meant to choose another as your bride?"

"I choose you," he said simply. "I want you."

"We— Kamran, you cannot— You know it would be madness."

"I see." He bowed his head and drew away, leaving her cold. "So you've come for another reason entirely. Will you not share that reason with me now?"

Alizeh said nothing. She could think of nothing.

She heard him sigh.

It was a moment before he said, "Then may I ask you a different question?"

"Yes," she said, desperate to say something. "Yes, of course."

He looked up, met her eyes. "How, precisely, do you know the Tulanian king?"

THIRTY-SEVEN

سی و هفت

KAMRAN SCHOOLED HIS EXPRESSION AS he waited, masking the pain that seized him now. Twin agonies assaulted his heart, his skin. The clothes he wore this evening had grown only more painful by the minute, and now this—*this spasm*—that threatened to fissure his chest. He could hardly look at Alizeh as he waited for her to speak. Had he misjudged her altogether? Had he become every inch the fool his grandfather and minister had accused him of becoming? At every turn she was a surprise, her intentions impossible to grasp, her actions confounding.

Why would she be so friendly with the sovereign of an enemy empire? How—when—did their friendship begin?

Kamran had hoped Alizeh might absolve herself of any objectionable suspicions by admitting she'd come tonight for him, to be with him; that she'd so easily dismissed this possibility had been both a blow and a confirmation—an endorsement of his silent fears.

For why, then, had she come at all?

Why would she sneak into a royal ball held inside his home, her injuries miraculously healed, her servants' clothing miraculously gone? Why, after so many desperate efforts to cling to her snoda—to hide her identity—would she discard the mask now, revealing herself in the middle of a ball where any stranger might see her for who she was?

Kamran could practically hear the king accuse her of duplicity, of manipulating his mind and emotions like some impossible siren. The prince heard every word of the imagined argument, saw every piece of plausible evidence that might condemn her, and still, he could not denounce the girl—for reasons so flimsy as to be laughable:

He had a feeling she was in danger.

It was his instincts that insisted, despite all damning evidence, that she was not herself a threat. On the contrary, he worried whether she might not be in trouble.

Even to himself he sounded a fool.

He recognized the glaring errors in his own judgment, the many missing explanations. He could not comprehend, for example, how she might've afforded such a stunning gown when just days ago she'd barely enough coppers to purchase medicine for her wounds. Or how, when just this morning she'd been scrubbing the floor of Baz House, she looked now every inch a breathtaking queen, laughing easily with the king of another empire.

King Zaal, the prince knew, would say she'd come to lead a coup, to claim her throne. The ball was, after all, the perfect venue to declare aloud—where all the nobility of Ardunia might hear—that she had a right to rule.

Perhaps Kamran had gone mad.

It seemed the only feasible explanation for his inaction, for the fear that gripped him even now. Why else did he worry for her, when he should turn her over to the king? She would be arrested, no doubt sentenced to death. It was the correct course of action, and yet—he made no move.

His paralysis was an enigma even to himself.

The prince had ordered Hazan to deliver him King Cyrus, but Kamran had changed his mind when he saw the young man's exchange with Alizeh. Cyrus had said something to her and left; not long after which Alizeh ran madly through the crowd, looking nothing short of terrified.

Kamran had followed her without thinking, hardly recognizing himself when he moved. He only knew he had to find her, to make certain she was okay, but now—

Now, Kamran could not fathom her reaction.

Alizeh seemed perplexed by his question.

Her lips parted, her head canted to one side. "Of all the things you might wonder," she said. "What a strange question you would choose to ask. Of course I do not know the Tulanian ki—"

"Your Highness," came the sound of his minister's breathless voice. "I've been searching for you everywhere . . ."

Hazan trailed off, coming to an abrupt halt at the prince's side. The minister's body was rigid with shock as he stared, not at the prince, but at Alizeh, whose silver eyes were no doubt all he needed to verify her identity.

Kamran sighed. "What is it, Minister?"

"*Minister?*"

The prince turned at the surprised sound of Alizeh's voice. She stared at Hazan curiously, as if he were a puzzle to be solved, instead of an official to be greeted.

Not for the first time, Kamran thought he might be

willing to part with his soul simply to know the contents of her mind.

"Your Highness," said Hazan, bowing his head, his eyes cast down. "You must go. It's not safe for you here."

"What on earth are you talking about?" Kamran frowned. "This is my home, of course it's safe for me here."

"There are complications, Your Highness. You must go. Surely you received my message."

Now Kamran grew irritated. "Hazan, have you lost your mind?"

"Please trust me, Your Highness. Please return to your quarters and await further direction. I worry greatly for your safety so long as you remain here. Things are not going according to plan—did you not receive my message?"

"That is quite enough, Minister. Not only do you exaggerate, but you bore the young lady with talk of politics. If that is all—"

"No— No, sire," he said, lifting his head sharply. "The king has requested your presence at once. I'm to deliver you back to the throne with all possible haste."

Kamran's jaw tensed. "I see."

He watched as Hazan glanced from Alizeh to the prince, looking suddenly frantic—and Kamran couldn't be entirely certain, but for a moment he thought he saw Hazan shake his head at her.

Or did he nod?

Alizeh surprised them both by dropping into an elegant curtsy. "Good evening, sir," she said.

"Yes—yes, good evening." Awkwardly, Hazan bowed. To the prince, he said quietly, "Sire, the king awaits."

"You may tell the king that I'll b—"

"*Alizeh!*"

Kamran went immobile at the sound of the unexpected voice.

Of all people, Omid Shekarzadeh moved fast toward them now, ignoring both the prince and his minister in his pursuit of Alizeh, who beamed at the boy.

"Omid," she called back, rushing forward to meet him.

And then, to Kamran's utter astonishment, she drew the child into her arms. She *hugged* the street urchin who'd nearly murdered her.

Kamran and Hazan exchanged glances.

When the unlikely pair drew apart, Omid's face had gone bright red. In Feshtoon, the boy said nervously, "I wasn't even sure it was you at first, miss, because I've never seen you without your mask, but I've been searching for you all night, and I asked near everyone I could find if they seen a girl in a snoda—in case you were still wearing yours—but they only kept pointing at the servants, and I said no, no, she's a guest at the *ball*, and everyone laughed at me like I was crazy except one lady, of course, one lady, I forget her name, Miss something, she told me she knew just who I was talking about, and that you were here wearing a purple dress, and that you weren't a snoda, but a queen, and I laughed so hard, miss, I said—"

"I beg your pardon?" Hazan interjected. "Who is this

person? Why would she say such things to you? How does she know anyth—"

"While we're asking questions, how on earth do you know this young woman's name?" Kamran interjected. "How are the two of you even on speaking terms?"

"Begging your pardon, Your Highness," Omid said, "but I could ask you the same question."

"You little blighter—"

"Actually, Omid is the reason I'm here tonight," Alizeh interjected quietly, and Kamran went taut with surprise.

Always, she astonished him.

He watched as she smiled fondly at the child. "He invited me to the ball as an apology for trying to kill me."

Impossibly, Omid went even redder. "Oh, but I was never gonna kill you, miss."

"You used your credit with the crown to invite a girl to a ball?" Kamran stared at the boy, agog. "You conniving rascal. Do you imagine yourself to be some kind of young libertine?"

Omid scowled. "I was only trying to make amends, sire. I didn't mean nothing inappropriate by it."

"But who was the woman?" Hazan demanded. "The one who told you that"—nervously, he glanced at Alizeh—"that this young lady was a queen?"

Kamran shot his minster a warning look. "Surely it was a lark, Minister. A silly jest to startle the child."

"Oh, no, sire." Omid shook his head emphatically. "She weren't joking. She seemed pretty serious, and scared, actually. She said she was hiding from someone, from a man who'd done some awful magic on her, and that if I found Alizeh I should tell her to run away." He frowned. "The lady was mighty strange."

A shock of fear moved through the prince then, apprehension he could no longer push aside. A man who'd done magic? Surely there could be little doubt as to the identity of the culprit?

All of Setar's Diviners were dead.

None but King Cyrus was suspected of using magic this night. What other havoc might the monstrous king have wrought?

The prince locked eyes with Hazan, who looked similarly panicked.

"Omid," Alizeh said quietly. "Will you show me where this lady was hiding?"

"Your Highness," Hazan said abruptly, turning his eyes to the floor once more. "You must go. Go now. With all possible haste you must lea—"

"Yes, very well," Kamran said coldly. "You need not have a fit, Minister. If you would please excuse me—"

He was interrupted by a sharp, bloodcurdling scream.

THIRTY-EIGHT

سی و هشت

ALIZEH RUSHED HEADLONG INTO THE chaos, her heart beating hard in her chest, Omid trailing close behind. Her mind was already spinning with the weight of so many revelations—and now this? What was happening?

She'd hardly a moment to wrap her head around the realization that Hazan was minister to the prince, and even less to analyze a disconcerting suspicion that Hazan had not been speaking to Kamran, but to *her* when he'd issued those warnings to leave the ball, that things were not safe.

Indeed, Hazan had seemed so worried it scared her.

Perhaps he feared she was running out of time; the stranger had said Alizeh needed to leave the palace before midnight, but he'd abandoned her with so little apprehension that she hadn't thought he meant it literally. And yet, if what he'd said was true—she glanced up at the towering clock in the hall—there were thirty-five minutes left in the hour. That felt like plenty of time.

Did Hazan mean for her to get to the transport alone, without assistance of the stranger? He said he'd sent messages, but to what message did he refer? Surely he meant the notes that came with the gown and shoes? Or was it the appearance of the copper-headed young man?

No, Alizeh considered, Hazan must've been referring to the shoes; for what other message had she received today that might aid in her escape?

Oh, if only she could get Hazan alone—if she could secure even a minute of his time—

Alizeh looked around as she moved, searching for a glimpse of Hazan's face, but Kamran and his minister had been enveloped by the surging mass more easily than she, as the horde knew to make way for the prince even in the midst of chaos.

Though even the chaos was strange.

The screaming had stopped, but so, too, had the music. Most people were flocking toward the source of the commotion, while others were rendered immobile by confusion; everyone seemed to be waiting to know whether the terrifying scream could be ascribed to an overstimulated attendee—maybe a young woman had fainted, maybe someone had been overly startled. All seemed to wonder whether they might continue enjoying their evening without worry, as no one had yet confirmed a cause for panic.

Alizeh pushed against the swell of the crowd, worried for the fate of Miss Huda, wondering where she'd gone, when the silence was split open by yet another shriek of terror. Alizeh froze in place, struck by the sound of the young woman's familiar voice.

"No," Miss Huda was shouting. "No, I will not—You cannot—"

Dread pooled like tar in Alizeh's gut. The stranger was

no doubt accosting Miss Huda now—of this Alizeh felt certain—though she struggled to understand his motivations. Why had he so easily broken his promise? What reason did he have to torture Miss Huda?

Alizeh's hands clenched, her body seizing with a desperate need to do something, when someone tugged at her arm. *Omid.*

"Miss," he said urgently. "That's the voice of the lady who was hiding earlier. I think she needs help."

Alizeh glanced up at the tall twelve-year-old. "Yes," she said. "Can you take me to her? And quickly?"

"Right away, miss," he said, already moving. "Just follow me."

Alizeh trailed the boy without a word, the two of them weaving between bodies, wending around chairs, occasionally crawling under tables. Omid, she realized, was quite good at uncovering the narrow, unexpected path through madness, for no matter his reformed ways, he had been a street child, and knew well how to find his way through a crowd.

He led Alizeh through the throng with astonishing swiftness, delivering them both to a dark cove in a far reach of the ballroom, where Miss Huda was backing away from what appeared to be a tall shadow of a person, her arms held up defensively in front of her body.

Alizeh felt she recognized that shadow.

"Wait," she said sharply, holding out an arm to halt Omid's forward march.

She pulled them both behind a perforated wooden screen,

where they ducked low, peering at the scene through a series of star-shaped cutouts. Alizeh had a vague idea of what she was expecting to see, but her imaginings were so far from truth that her mouth dropped open in surprise.

Miss Huda did not hold aloft her arms, but a candelabra, and she was approaching the tall shadow as if she might strike him. "Not so powerful now, are you?" she was saying. "Not so scary anymore, no, not when you're at my mercy."

"Listen, loud one," came the acerbic, familiar voice of the stranger. "I've tried to be patient with you for her sake, but if you won't cooperate, I've no choice but t—"

"No," Miss Huda shouted. "You will never again use magic on me, sir, never again, or, or I'll—I'll do something terrible— I'll have you trampled by a team of horses—"

"I never said I would use more magic on you," he said sharply. "Lest you forget, I was minding my own business when *you* hit *me* on the head—in a most unladylike fashion, I might add—exhibiting such violence, and when I've been nothing but accommodating—"

"*Accommodating?*" she cried. "You stole my voice! And then you dumped me unceremoniously into the heart of a royal ball in my muslin day dress! I'm not with my family, I was never formally announced, no one even knows I'm here, and now I'll never meet the prince." Her chest heaved as she struggled for breath. "Do you even realize the cruelty of your actions?" she said, swiping at him with the candelabra. He dodged her attacks. "I can't let anyone see me like this. As if my social standing wasn't already in tatters, now I'm at the palace—for possibly the biggest event of the season—and I've not done my hair, I've got food in my teeth, I've not changed my slippers, I've no idea how I'll get home from here—"

"Do you know, I've changed my mind," said the young man. "Perhaps I will kill you. Though, alternatively, if you're so apprehensive about the opinions of others I could always knock back your brain an inch—"

For the third time, Miss Huda screamed.

"Oh no," Omid whispered. "This isn't good."

People came running now, a crowd beginning to gather, among them Hazan and the prince. Alizeh and Omid watched from the shadows as the blue-eyed stranger sighed, muttered an ungentlemanly word, and stepped out of the darkness—revealing himself to all and sundry with a broad smile.

Alizeh felt suddenly sick with trepidation.

"Welcome, one and all," the stranger said. "I see you've come for a show. I'm eager to oblige, though I confess none of this is happening as I'd envisioned it! Then again, I've always appreciated a bit of spontaneity."

Without warning, a ring of fire several feet in diameter erupted around himself and Miss Huda, flames three feet high, the heat so oppressive Alizeh could feel it even from where she stood.

Miss Huda began to sob, this time sounding close to hysteria. Alizeh's heart was pounding furiously in her chest; she heard Omid's sharp intake of breath.

This entire night was nothing short of a disaster.

Kamran stepped forward then, and the crowd surged back with a collective gasp, leaving him exposed. The prince drew

as close to the flames as he dared, and Alizeh's lungs constricted. She was terrified and somehow livid—*furious* as he
studied the madman now holding her friend hostage.

Fool, she wanted to scream at the unhinged stranger. *You
stupid, stupid fool.*

The prince, meanwhile, approached the aforementioned
fool with sangfroid so assured one might think there was no
danger at all.

"Your Excellency," Kamran said. "This is no way to treat
our guests. I will ask you once to douse your fire and release
the lady."

Alizeh froze, then frowned. *Your Excellency?*

Was Kamran making fun of him? She could think of no
other reason why the crown prince of Ardunia would say
such a thing, though even in jest it was—

Alizeh closed her eyes; felt the room spin. The memory of
Kamran's voice filled her head.

How, precisely, do you know the Tulanian king?

If the prince had been able to spot her in the crowd, he
must've also seen her speaking with the blue-eyed stranger—
and, devils above, what he must've thought of her. She'd
been consorting with the Tulanian king just hours after kiss-
ing an Ardunian prince.

It struck a traitorous image, even she could see that.

Shame suffused Alizeh's skin with a sudden heat; shame
she need not own or claim, but felt regardless. Her confusion
and apprehension tripled; for her mind would not now cease
conjuring new questions.

Had Hazan struck a deal with the Tulanian king? If so,

how? Why? What grand favor would a minister have been
able to provide a king, so much so that he'd risk his reputation as sovereign of a formidable empire to assist her? What
on earth had Hazan done?

Alizeh looked up again when she heard the stranger's
voice.

"And you must be the prince," he was saying. "The beloved
Prince Kamran, the melancholy royal of Setar, friend to street
child and servant alike. Your reputation precedes you, sire."

"How dare you speak to the prince in such a manner, you
miserable swine," Miss Huda cried, angrily swiping at her
tears before lifting the candelabra above her head. "Guards!
Guards!"

"Oh, yes, by all means," said the young king. "Please do
summon the guards. Bring them forth, have them confess
aloud their sins. All under the order of King Zaal are com-
plicit in his crimes."

Kamran drew his sword and approached the flames at a
proximity that made Alizeh gasp.

"You would speak ill of the king in his own home—on his
own land?" said the prince with thunderous calm. "Release
the girl now, or I will have your head."

"Pray tell me, sire, how will you reach my head? With what
magic will you walk through fire to claim it? With what power
will you extinguish mine when your Diviners are all dead?"

At that, the room erupted in gasps and shouts, cries of
astonishment and fear. Alizeh spun around, taking it all in.
Her heart wouldn't stop racing in her chest.

"Is it true?"

"He's a madman—"

"Where is the king?"

"—but it cannot be—"

"Don't believe a word of it—"

"The king! Where is the king?"

King Zaal appeared then, came forth through the crowd with a silent dignity, his head held high even under the weight of a hulking crown.

The young king extinguished his fire at once, releasing Miss Huda in the process. Several people rushed to her side, helping her to safety, while the blue-eyed fool charged forward to meet King Zaal, erecting another fiery circle that trapped the two sovereigns inside.

Alizeh realized then that she would rather rot in the gutter than go anywhere with this copper-headed scoundrel. So these were the few tasks he'd meant to accomplish? This was the business he'd claimed wouldn't take long?

Oh, she wanted to slap him.

"Your fight is with me, is it not?" King Zaal said quietly.

"Not at all," said the fool brightly. "There will be no fight, Your Majesty. When I am done with you, you will be begging me to end your life."

King Zaal barked a laugh.

Someone in the crowd screamed, "Call for the soldiers! The magistrates!"

"The magistrates?" The southern king laughed aloud. "You mean your weak, corrupt officials? Tell me, fine nobles of Ardunia, did you know that your magistrates are paid extra by the crown to collect street children?"

Alizeh felt Omid tense beside her.

"Ah, I can see by the looks in your eyes that you did not. And why would you, really? Who would even miss a surplus of orphaned children?"

"What do you want here?" King Zaal said sharply. He looked different then—angry, yes—but Alizeh thought he looked, for a moment—

Scared.

"Me?" The madman pointed to himself. "What do I want? I want a great deal too much, Your Highness. I've been bled dry for too long in repayment for my father's sins and I'm tired of it; tired of being in debt to so cruel a master. But then, you know what that's like, don't you?"

King Zaal drew his sword.

Again, the southern king laughed. "Are you really going to challenge me?"

"Your Majesty, please—" Kamran moved forward as if to enter the fiery ring, and King Zaal held up a hand to stop him.

"No matter what happens tonight," King Zaal said to him, "you must remember your duty to this empire."

"Yes, but—"

"That is all, child," he said thunderously. "Now you must leave me to fight my own battles."

"As I've already told you, Your Highness." The madman again. "There will be no battle."

The Tulanian king raised his arm with a flourish and King

Zaal's robes tore open at the shoulders, revealing large swaths of skin that were both scaly and discolored.

The king's face went slack, stunned as he studied himself, then his southern enemy. "No," he whispered. "You cannot."

"Will you not speculate?" the madman shouted into the crowd. "Will you not hazard a guess as to what the magistrates do with the street children they find?"

Alizeh felt suddenly as if she couldn't breathe.

The sounds of the room seemed to quiet, the lights seemed to dim; she heard only the sound of her own harsh breaths, saw only the horror unfolding before her.

She closed her eyes.

There once was a man
who bore a snake on each shoulder.
If the snakes were well fed
their master ceased growing older.

What they ate no one knew,
even as the children were found
with brains shucked from their skulls,
bodies splayed on the ground.

"It's true," Omid whispered, his voice trembling. "I—I've seen it, miss. I seen it happen. But no one believes the street kids, miss, everyone thinks we're lying—and they started threatening us if we said anything, said they'd come for us next—"

Alizeh gasped, clapped a hand over her mouth. "Oh,

Omid," she cried. "Oh, I'm so sorry—"

Two leathery white snakes reared up from the shoulders of the Ardunian king, snapping and hissing hungrily.

King Zaal's sword fell, with a clatter, to the ground.

THIRTY-NINE

سی ونه

KAMRAN FELT HIS HEART SHATTER in his chest even as he refused to believe what his eyes swore to be true.

This was a horror too great.

The prince knew—had heard, of course—that all around the world there had been kings who made deals with the devil; they sold a bit of their souls in exchange for power, or love, or land. The stories said that Iblees presented himself to every sovereign on earth on the day of their coronation.

Never did these stories end well.

For the entirety of Kamran's life King Zaal had warned him of Iblees, warned him never to accept an offer from the devil. How, then—

"No," Kamran whispered. "No, it's not possible—"

"Your dear king should have died years ago," Cyrus was saying. "But your melancholy prince was too young to lead, was he not? He was still too sad, too scared, too heartbroken over the death of his dear father. So the great, righteous King Zaal made a bargain with the devil to extend his life." A pause. "Didn't you, Your Majesty?"

"Enough," King Zaal said, lowering his eyes. "You need not say more. It would be better for everyone if you simply killed me now."

Cyrus ignored this. "What he didn't realize, of course, was

that a bargain with the devil was a bloody one. The snakes lengthen his life, yes, but even a serpent needs to eat, does it not?"

Kamran could hardly breathe.

He knew not what to do, knew not what to say. He felt paralyzed by the revelations, confused by the chaos of his own emotions. How could he defend a man so debased? How could he not defend the grandfather he loved? The king had bartered with his soul to spare the young prince, to give Kamran time to live a bit longer as a child—

"Yes, that's right," said Cyrus. "They eat the fresh brains of young children." From nothing he conjured a soggy mass of flesh, which he tossed at the snakes. "Street children, to be more specific. For the wretched and the poor are the most easily expendable, are they not?"

The snakes hissed and snapped at each other, swinging their necks around to catch the morsel, which one triumphant serpent caught in his open, distended maw.

Shrieks of horror pierced the silence; one woman fainted into the arms of another.

The prince saw a flash of steel.

A sword materialized in Cyrus's hand and Kamran reacted without thinking, launching himself forward—but too late. The Tulanian king had already impaled his willing grandfather straight through the chest.

Kamran nearly fell to his knees.

He caught his breath and charged, brandishing his sword as he leaped through the searing flames to reach Cyrus, not feeling his flesh as it burned, not hearing the screams of the crowd. Cyrus feinted, then lunged, swinging his sword in a diagonal arc; Kamran met his opponent's blade with an impact so violent it shuddered through him. With a cry he pushed forward, launching Cyrus back several feet.

Quickly, the Tulanian king steadied, then attacked, his blade glinting under the glittering lights. Kamran dodged the blow and spun, slashing his sword through the air and meeting steel; their blades crashing, slicing the air as they slid away.

"My fight is not with you, melancholy prince," Cyrus said, breathing heavily as he took a step back. "You need not die tonight. You need not leave your empire without a sovereign."

Kamran stilled at that, at the realization that his grandfather was truly dead. That Ardunia was his now.

To rule as king.

He cried out as he advanced, lunging at Cyrus who parried, then brought his blade down with crushing force. Kamran dropped to one knee to meet this blow, but his sword arm, which had been badly burned by the flames, could not withstand the force for long.

His sword clattered to the floor.

Cyrus withdrew, his chest heaving, and lifted his blade above his head to deliver what was no doubt the finishing blow.

Kamran closed his eyes. He made peace with his fate in that moment, accepting that he would die, and that he would die defending his king. His grandfather.

"*No!*" he heard someone scream.

Kamran heard the mad dash of boots pounding the marble floors and looked up, startled, hardly daring to believe his eyes. Alizeh was rushing wildly toward him, shoving people aside.

"Don't!" Kamran shouted. "The fire—"

FORTY

چھل

ALIZEH RAN STRAIGHT THROUGH THE inferno without care, her diaphanous gown going up in flames, and which she beat down quickly with her bare hands. She looked at Kamran, her heart seizing in her chest, sparing what moments she had to see that he was alive, to make certain he wasn't too badly injured.

He was only staring at her in wonder.

A broad strip of his right arm was bleeding profusely—had been burned straight through his clothes. The rest of the outfit was damaged beyond repair, singed more in some places than others, but he appeared otherwise okay, save a few nasty scrapes he'd collected in the match. Still, he seemed oblivious to his injuries, even to the gash across his forehead, the blood dripping slowly down his temple.

The crowd, which had previously gone silent with shock, suddenly began whispering, gasping aloud their heartache and disbelief.

Alizeh turned on the Tulanian king.

She charged up to him in a singed gown and sooty skin and yanked the sword from his frozen hand, tossing it to the floor, where it landed with a clatter. The young king was staring at her now like she was some unfathomable sea monster, come to swallow him whole.

"How dare you," she cried. "You horrible cretin. You useless monster. How *could* you—"

"How—how did you—" He was still staring at her, gaping. "How did you walk through the fire like that? Why are you not—burning?"

"You despicable, wretched man," she said angrily. "You know *who* I am, but you don't know *what* I am?"

"No."

She slapped him, hard, across the face, the potent force of her strength sending him reeling. The southern king reared back, colliding with a column against which he both knocked his head and braced himself. It was a moment before he looked up again, and when he did, Alizeh saw that his mouth was full of blood, which he spit out onto the floor.

Then he laughed.

"Damn the devil to hell," he said softly. "He didn't tell me you were a Jinn."

Alizeh startled. "Who?"

"Our mutual friend."

"Hazan?"

"Hazan?" The copper-headed king laughed at that, wiped a bit of blood from his mouth. "*Hazan?* Of course not *Hazan.*" To Kamran, he said, "Pay attention, King, for it seems even your friends have betrayed you."

Alizeh swung around to meet Kamran's eyes just in time to see the way he looked at her—the flash of shock, the pain of betrayal—before he shuttered closed, withdrew inward.

His eyes went almost inhumanly dark.

She wanted to go to him, to explain—

Kamran exchanged a look with a guard, scores of which now swarmed the ballroom, and Hazan, soon revealed to be the sole person trying to flee the crush, was seized not moments later, his arms bound painfully behind his back. The silence of the room was momentarily deafening; Hazan's protests piercing the quiet as he was dragged away.

Alizeh was gripped then by a violent terror.

With agonizing slowness, she felt a tapestry of truth form around her; disparate threads of understanding braiding together to illustrate an answer to a question she'd long misunderstood.

Of course not Hazan.

Hazan had never planned this fate for her. Hazan had been kind and trustworthy; he'd truly cared for her wellbeing. But this—this was all a cruel trick, was it not?

She'd been deceived by the devil himself.

Why?

"Iblees," she said, her voice fraught with disbelief. "All this time, you have been speaking of the devil. Why? Why did he send you to fetch me? What interest does he have in my life?"

The Tulanian king frowned. "Is it not obvious? He wants you to rule."

Alizeh heard Kamran's sharp intake of breath, heard the rumblings of the crowd around them. This conversation was madness. She'd nearly forgotten they had an audience—that all of Ardunia would hear—

Again, the southern king laughed, but louder this time, looking suddenly disturbed. "*A Jinn queen* to rule the world. Oh, it's so horribly seditious. The perfect revenge."

Alizeh felt herself pale then, watched her hands begin to tremble. A fragile hypothesis began to take shape in her mind; something that shook her to her core:

Iblees wanted to use her.

He wanted to bring her to power and control her; no doubt to ensure the mass chaos and destruction of the Clay who wronged him; the beings he blamed for his downfall.

Alizeh began slowly backing away from the blue-eyed king. A strange madness had overtaken her, a fear beyond which she could not see. Without thinking, she glanced up at the clock.

Five minutes to midnight.

Alizeh bolted for the exit, fleeing the fiery circle for the second time unscathed; the remains of her gown going up in flames once more. She beat the fire from her dress even as she ran, even as she knew not where she was headed.

The Tulanian king called after her.

"Wait— Where are you going? We had a deal— Under no circumstances were you allowed to run away—"

"I must," she said desperately. She knew it sounded crazed even as she said it, for there had never been escape from the devil, never a reprieve from his whispers. Still, she could not help the anguish that overcame her then. It made her irrational.

"I'm sorry," she cried. "I'm sorry, but I have to leave— I need to find somewhere to hide, somewhere he won't—"

Alizeh felt something catch her in the gut then. Something like a gust of wind; a wing. Her feet began kicking without warning, launching her body upward, into the air.

She screamed.

"Alizeh!" Kamran bellowed, rushing up to the edges of his fiery cage. "Alizeh—"

Panic filled her lungs as her body soared. "Make it stop," she cried, her arms pinwheeling. "Put me down!"

She felt at once paralyzed and weightless; the movements of her body utterly beyond her control.

Would this dark magic float her up to the moon? Would it drown her in a lake? Impale her on a sword?

All she could do was scream.

She was nearing the rafters now, rising up to the ceiling. The people below were hard to distinguish, their voices inaudible—

And then, a crash.

A massive beast broke through the palace wall, its leathery body bright with iridescent scales, its wingspan as wide as the room. The crowd shrieked and hollered, dove for cover. Alizeh, meanwhile, could not look away.

She'd never seen a dragon before.

It swooped low and roared; its long, studded tail whipping along the wall, leaving gashes in the marble.

And then, like a shot, Alizeh was released.

She plummeted to the ground with terrifying speed, the sounds of her own screams filling her ears, drowning out all else. She hardly had time to process that she was about to die, that she would snap in half when she hit the floor—

The dragon dove and caught her, hard, on its back.

She fell forward with superlative force, nearly losing her seat before she caught the studded nape of the beast that took flight without delay. Alizeh was knocked back as it launched upward, her head spinning, heart hammering in her chest. It was all she could do to hold on and keep her wits about her. The dragon gave another roar before flapping its massive wings, propelling them out the destroyed palace wall and into the night sky.

For a long time, Alizeh did not move.

She felt paralyzed by fear and disbelief; her mind assaulted by a tumult of uncertainty. Slowly, sensation returned to her limbs, to the tips of her fingers. She soon felt the wind against her face, saw the night sky drape itself around her, a midnight sheet studded with stars.

By degrees, she began to relax.

The beast was heavy and solid, and seemed to know where it was going. She took deep lungfuls of air, trying to clear the dregs of her panic, to convince herself that she would be safe for at least as long as she clung to this wild creature. She shifted, suddenly, at the feel of soft fibers grazing her skin through what was left of her thin gown, and looked down to examine it. She hadn't realized she was in fact sitting on a small carpet, which—

Alizeh nearly screamed again.

The dragon had disappeared. It was still *there*—she felt the beast beneath her, could feel the leathery texture of its skin—but the creature had gone invisible in the sky, leaving her floating on a patterned rug.

It was deeply disorienting.

Still, she understood then why the creature had disappeared; without its bulk to blind her, she could see the world below, could see the world beyond.

Alizeh didn't know where she was going, but for the moment, she forced herself not to panic. There was, after all, a strange peace in this, in the quiet that surrounded her.

As her nerves relaxed, her mind sharpened. Quickly, she yanked off her boots and chucked them into the night. It gave her great satisfaction to watch them disappear into the dark.

Relief.

A sudden thud shifted the weight of the rug, startling her upright. Alizeh spun around, her heart racing once again in her chest; and when she saw the face of her unwelcome companion, she thought she might fling herself into the sky with the boots.

"No," she whispered.

"This is *my* dragon," said the Tulanian king. "You are not allowed to steal my dragon."

"I didn't steal it, the creature took— Wait, how did you get here? Can you fly?"

He laughed at that. "Is the mighty empire of Ardunia really so poor in magic that these small tricks impress you?"

"Yes," she said, blinking. Then, "What is your name?"

"Of all the non sequiturs. Why do you need to know my name?"

"So that I may hate you more informally."

"Ah. Well, in that case, you may call me Cyrus."

"Cyrus," she said. "You insufferable monster. Where on earth are we going?"

Her insults seemed to have no effect on him, for he was

still smiling when he said, "Have you really not figured it out?"

"I'm entirely too agitated for these games. Please just tell me what horrible fate awaits me now."

"Oh, the very worst of fates, I'm sorry to say. We are currently enroute to Tulan."

The nosta burned hot against her skin, and Alizeh felt herself go rigid with fear. She was stunned, yes, and horrified, too, but to hear the king of an empire denigrate his own land thus—

"Is Tulan really so terrible a place?"

"Tulan?" His eyes widened in surprise. "Not at all. A single square inch of Tulan is more breathtaking than all of Ardunia, and I say that as a discernable fact, not as a subjective opinion."

"But then"—she frowned—"why did you say that it would be the very worst of fates?"

"Ah. That." Cyrus looked away then, searched the night sky. "Well. You remember how I said I owed our mutual friend a very large debt?"

"Yes."

"And that helping you was the only repayment he would accept?"

She swallowed. "Yes."

"And do you remember how I told you that he wanted you to rule? To be a Jinn queen?"

Alizeh nodded.

"Well. You have no kingdom," he said. "No land to lord over. No empire to lead."

"No," she said softly. "I don't."

"Well, then. You are coming to Tulan," Cyrus said, taking a quick breath. "To marry me."

Alizeh gave a sharp cry, and fell off the dragon.

Keep reading for a sneak peek at *These Infinite Threads*,
the searing sequel to *This Woven Kingdom*!

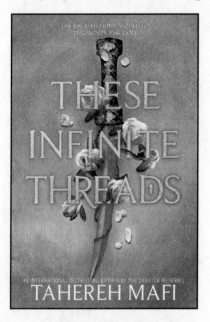

ONE

یک

"DON'T!" KAMRAN SHOUTED. "THE FIRE—"

The words died in his throat.

He watched Alizeh charge toward the thigh-high blaze with an astonishment so complete he sank to the ground, the cold of the stone floor seeping through the tattered silk of his trousers. Kamran had the benefit of heavy layers and jewel harnesses at least; the fire had been unable to devour him with any speed. But Alizeh—Alizeh wore little more than a whisper, so fine was the fabric of her gown.

The fire will melt the flesh from her bones.

He thought it even as she crossed the blaze without care, her gossamer dress inhaled in an instant by the fiery ring, an abomination magicked to life by the young Tulanian king. Cyrus, the monarch in question, stood just opposite Kamran, sword still held aloft in anticipation of a fatal blow, his hand stayed only by the sight of Alizeh, who headed toward him now. As if from outside himself Kamran watched as she batted away flames from her dress with bare hands, snuffing the fire as one might a light. He stared down at the remains of his own disintegrated garments, then at the blood dripping between his knuckles. Slowly, he looked back up at Alizeh, possessing clarity of mind enough to register that she'd emerged from the inferno unscathed, even as her gown suffered. He blinked at the impossibility of it; he was either dreaming or deluded. He could not make sense of her.

No, he could not make sense of anything.

Alizeh, who'd nearly tripped over the king's fallen crown in her haste, had sent the weighty heirloom spinning toward Kamran as she ran. He stared at that crown now, stared at it as a sudden tremor seized him, shock and cold combining, reminding him—

His grandfather was dead.

King Zaal was supine before the world, blood pooling beneath his lifeless body in the imperfect oval of an open-mouthed scream. His grandfather had bargained with the devil to extend his life—and in the end Death had devoured the king swiftly and without dignity, the sovereign and his sins withering in unison. The limp, corded muscle of twin white snakes still soldered to the pale shoulders of a beloved king painted a scene so grotesque it inspired in Kamran a sudden impulse to heave; he braced his unsteady hands on the icy floor and wondered, with increasing horror, how many street children had been sacrificed for his grandfather's serpents.

It was an imagining too monstrous.

Kamran was ill with disillusion, with denial. He willed himself to remain calm, to marshal his thoughts, but an unidentified agony clawed at his consciousness, the pain seeming to emanate from his left arm. He wished to be someone else. He wished to turn back time. Above all he wished, without a mote of hyperbole, that Cyrus had been allowed to kill him.

The whispers of their heretofore silent audience had been growing steadily in the interlude and now built to an alarming crescendo, the din awaking in Kamran years of training and awareness. His mind sharpened against the gossip, duty piercing the fog of grief and replacing it with anger, focus—

A sudden clatter.

Kamran looked up in time to see Alizeh toss Cyrus's sword to the floor, the young man flinching as glinting steel struck marble. The foreign king stared at Alizeh with an astonishment to rival Kamran's, fear torpefying his features as she rounded on him.

"How dare you," she said. "You horrible cretin. You useless monster. How *could* you—"

"How—how did you—" Cyrus fumbled back an inch. "How did you walk through the fire like that? Why are you not—burning?"

"You despicable, wretched man," she cried. "You know *who* I am, but you don't know *what* I am?"

"No."

Alizeh struck Cyrus across the face with the force of a bludgeon, the impact so violent the young king staggered, audibly striking his head against a column.

Kamran felt the shock of it in his bones.

He knew he should rejoice in this moment—knew he should celebrate Alizeh's actions against the depraved royal—but his mind would not submit to relief, for the scene unraveling before him did not align with reason.

Cyrus appeared entirely too unnerved.

The trepidation in his eyes, his astonishment at her

approach, the blind steps he took backward as she advanced—
it made no sense. Alizeh had insisted to Kamran but
moments ago that she did not know the southern king; yet
Cyrus, who'd more than proven his ruthlessness, displayed
every sign of alarm in her presence. If they were truly strangers, why would he cower now at the unarmed advance of a
girl he did not know? She'd tossed his sword to the floor,
insulted him repeatedly, and slapped him in the face—and
the young king who'd minutes ago buried a blade in Zaal's
heart hadn't so much as lifted a hand in his own defense.
He'd only stood there and stared at her and all but *allowed*
her to strike him.

Almost as if he feared her.

Kamran dared not breathe as a terrifying suspicion
dawned in his mind, the thought provoking in him a spasm
so acute he thought his chest might crater.

From the first, Kamran had been mystified by Alizeh's
transformation at the ball. In a matter of hours her injuries had miraculously healed, she'd discarded the iconic
snoda of her servant's uniform, and her drab work dress had
been replaced by an extravagant gown no maid could ever
afford—and still he'd denied the truth, so desperate was he
to absolve her of artifice. Finally, he understood.

He had been deceived.

His eyes flickered again to the fallen figure of his grandfather.

King Zaal had tried to warn him; he'd begged Kamran to
see how Alizeh was tethered to the prophecy, to the end of
Zaal's life—and only now that his grandfather was dead did

Kamran understand the magnitude of his own folly. Every foolish word he'd spoken in her defense—every stupid, childish action he'd taken to protect her—

Without warning, Cyrus laughed.

Kamran looked up; the southern king appeared pale and disordered. From where he knelt, Kamran could not see Alizeh's face; he saw only the horror in Cyrus's eyes as he looked her over. The young man had killed his own father for the throne of Tulan; he'd newly murdered King Zaal, the ruler of the greatest empire on earth; he would've killed Kamran, too, had he been granted but a moment more to accomplish the task. Now the copper-headed tyrant steadied himself slowly, blood seeping from his lips, smeared across his chin. Of all the adversaries they might've encountered, it seemed they'd both been cowed by the poor, gentle servant of Baz House.

"Damn the devil to hell," the Tulanian king said quietly. "He didn't tell me you were a Jinn."

"Who?" Alizeh demanded.

"Our mutual friend."

"Hazan?"

Kamran recoiled. He'd not been prepared for the blow of yet another betrayal, and the impact of that single word lanced through his body with a ruthlessness against which he had no defense. That she was somehow allied with Cyrus was torture enough—but that she'd gone behind his back with *Hazan*?

This was more than he could bear.

She'd playacted at fear and innocence, had outmaneuvered

him at every turn, and worst of all—*worst of all*—he had fallen, madly, for her manipulations. In all the time he'd known her, Alizeh had clung to her snoda, fighting to hide her identity even in the midst of a rainstorm; now she stood unmasked before a sea of nobles, glowering at the formidable sovereign of a neighboring nation, declaring herself to the world.

All this time, Alizeh had been making plans.

Already Kamran had been attacked by grief and anger; he struggled even then to digest the magnitude of the last moments, could hardly piece together his discordant thoughts about his grandfather—but now— Now he was expected to make sense of this? He, who prided himself on the strength of his instincts—he, who believed himself to be a capable, intuitive soldier—

"Hazan?" Cyrus laughed again, his hand trembling almost imperceptibly as he wiped blood from his mouth. "*Hazan? Of course not Hazan.*" Cyrus locked eyes with Kamran and said, "Pay attention, King, for it seems even your friends have betrayed you."

Alizeh turned suddenly to face him—eyes wide with panic—and her obvious flush of guilt was all the evidence Kamran required. Just hours ago he would've sworn an oath that her desire for him was as palpable as the press of satin against his skin; he'd tasted the salt of her, had felt the exquisite shape of her body tremble under his hands. Now he knew it had all been a lie.

Hell.

This was hell.

But to say that this revelation had broken his heart would

be to misrepresent the truth utterly; Kamran was not heart-broken, then, no—he was incandescent with rage.

He would kill her.

Any naive, lingering softness in Kamran's heart evaporated. He'd been seduced by a siren while being deceived by his own friend—and had all but spat in the face of the only person who truly cared for his well-being. King Zaal had sold himself to evil in the pursuit of Kamran's happiness—and the man was repaid with only disloyalty and treason. This dark night had been wrought by Kamran's actions alone; he understood that now. The entire Ardunian empire had been left vulnerable because he'd been frail of mind and body.

Never again.

He would never again allow a woman to own his emotions; he would never again be made weak by such base temptations. He swore it then: this monster from the prophecy would die by his hand—he would drive a blade through her heart or die trying.

But first, Hazan.

Kamran caught the eye of a guard hovering—awaiting orders—and with a single glance he issued his first decree as king of Ardunia: Hazan would hang.

Kamran experienced no victory as he watched his former minister seized, then dragged away; he felt no triumph at the sound of Hazan's feeble protests ringing out through the astonished silence of the room. No, Kamran suffered only the ascent of a terrifying madness as he forced himself upright, daring to bear weight on his injured arm in the process, and realizing only in the excruciating effort that his legs, too, had been badly burned. His skin and clothes were sticky with blood; his head felt leaden. It was a truth he was loath to admit: that he did not know how much longer he could stand here without the aid of a surgeon. Or a Diviner.

No. The royal Diviners were dead. Slaughtered by Cyrus.

Kamran's eyes squeezed shut at the reminder.

"Iblees."

His eyes flew open at the sound of her soft, traitorous voice. Kamran's heart began pounding anew, startling him with its intensity. He couldn't decide then what disturbed him more: to realize that she and Cyrus shared *a mutual friend* in the devil, or to discover that his body still wanted her, still heated at the mere sound of her voice—

She had disappeared.

Panicked, Kamran searched for her and was unsuccessful; instead he saw Cyrus, still staring intently at what could only be Alizeh, who'd a moment ago been speaking—

Without warning, she materialized.

Alizeh stood in precisely the same spot, except now she appeared hazy, oscillating in and out of focus with a dizzying consistency.

Was she doing this to him? Had she access to dark magic? He couldn't think how else to explain his broken vision, her injuries, her superhuman immunity to fire, or the way heart seemed to bleed in his chest at the sight of her. How ght he defend his own stupidity in the face of such reachery?

nce was Alizeh stood now a milky blur of move-ce warped and waterlogged, reverberating as if she were speaking from inside a glass jar.

"Ssssttt you you sspeakthe the the vvvvil . . ."

Kamran dragged bloody hands down his face. As if each revelation weren't already more annihilating than the last— he was now blind and deaf, too?

"Sssssendyyou you iiiinterest heeeee my my llllife?"

His injured legs failed as his mind fractured; he trembled, hands grasping at air as he sought purchase, and fell hard onto one badly burned leg. He nearly cried out in agony.

But then, a mercy—

The Tulanian king spoke, his words lucid: "Is it not obvious? He wants you to rule."

A terrible thunder filled Kamran's head. There was no time to rejoice in the restoration of his hearing. The demon-like monster with ice in its veins had been foretold to have formidable allies, and here was further evidence of the Diviners' wisdom, of his grandfather's warnings—

The devil himself was assisting her.

The crowd was growing louder now, and he could hear *them*, too, whispers having evolved into shouts and hysterics. Kamran was reminded once more that all the nobles of Ardunia were collected in this room; the highest ranking officials from across the empire had been brought together for an evening of decadence and celebration; instead, they would bear witness to the fall of the greatest empire in the world.

Kamran did not know how he would survive it.

He heard Cyrus laugh again, heard him say clearly: "*A Jinn queen* to rule the world. Oh, it's so horribly seditious. Th perfect revenge."

Again, Kamran attempted to draw himself up. His head pounded with a vengeance, his eyesight still an uncertain thing. The room, the floor—Cyrus himself—were all perfectly clear, but Alizeh remained more nimbus than person, a series of halos stacked in the general shape of a body. Then again, just knowing where to aim might be enough.

This evening's admissions had more than proven his grandfather's every warning about the girl—and Kamran would die before he failed the man twice. His sword lay a few feet away, and though the distance seemed insurmountable, Kamran would force himself to clear it. He might be able to bury the blade in her heart now, kill her now, end this tragedy tonight.

He'd just managed to take an agonizing step toward his sword when the haze of her shifted away from Cyrus; then, in a flash of kismet, Kamran could see Alizeh's face.

She looked terrified.

The sight speared him through the chest at the precise moment the cataracts in his eyes seemed to clear; her figure came suddenly into sharp, disorienting focus and, oh, this was a cruel fate, indeed. Alizeh was an enemy possessed of power he never could've imagined. Even now her shining ˙ glittered with an emotion that destroyed him. Her guile ˙ graceful, so natural; she searched the room as if she ly frantic.

cursed the wretched organ in his chest, then ˙nched fist against his sternum as if to kill it. ˙rrible anguish ripped through his body, so n it took his breath away; it was as if a tree had planted in a single shot at his feet, the trunk suturing to his spine, tremendous branches pushing violently through his veins.

He doubled over, gasping, almost missing the moment when Alizeh glanced up in his direction and then bolted without warning, exiting the inferno once again unscathed.

Had she seen him reaching for his sword? Had she gleaned his intentions?

Alizeh was a maddening sight even as she fled, the gauzy layers of her gown having now been incinerated twice. She flew past in little more than scraps of transparent silk; he could see every lush curve of her body, the lithe shape of her legs, the swell of her breasts, and he hated himself for wanting her, even now. Hated himself for the hunger he felt as he watched her go, hated the instincts that screamed at him, despite all logical evidence to the contrary, that she was in danger—that he should go to her, protect her—

"Wait— Where are you going?" Cyrus shouted. "We had a deal— Under no circumstances were you allowed to run away—"

We had a deal.

The words rang in his head, over and over, each syllable striking his mind like a scythe, drawing blood. By the angels, how many more blows need his body survive tonight?

"I must," she cried, the agitated crowd leaping apart to let her pass. "I'm sorry, I'm sorry, but I have to leave— I need to find somewhere to hide, somewhere he won't—"

At once Alizeh doubled over, as if struck by an invisible force, and was promptly jerked upward, into the air.

She screamed.

Kamran reacted without thinking, a rush of adrenaline propelling him upright, dregs of stupidity compelling him to cry out her name. He pushed as close to the edge of the flaming bastille as he dared, the anguish in his voice no doubt betraying him to the world, if not to himself—but he could not think on it then. Alizeh was being launched higher and higher in the air, twisting and screaming, and Kamran condemned himself for his tortured response to her suffering; even then he couldn't fathom the battle being waged inside his body.

"Make it stop," she screamed. "Put me down!"

Sudden understanding forced Kamran to look Cyrus in the eye. "*You*," he said, hardly recognizing the rasp of his own voice. "You're doing this to her."

Cyrus's expression darkened. "She's done it to herself."

Kamran was prevented from responding by the sound of yet another tortured cry. He spun around in time to see Alizeh spiraling toward the rafters—she was without a doubt in the grip of a very dark magic—and promptly lost his battle with sense. He could not fathom this chaos into order, could not answer the multitude of questions that hounded him.

Kamran felt unmoored as he watched her.

Alizeh was a force so powerful she claimed the devil as 'iend, knew the sovereign of an enemy nation as an ally. ' used dark magic to create illusions so compelling he'd lieved she'd suffered physical blows to her hands, her face. She'd tricked even King Zaal into believing 'oless, ignorant servant girl. And yet, she sobbed 'teria so believable that even he—

"You can see her."

The statement startled him. Kamran turned back to Cyrus, assessing in an instant his enemy's copper hair, his cold blue eyes. Of all the things Cyrus might've said, *this* was particularly strange, and Kamran was too discerning to dismiss it as meaningless. That Cyrus appeared surprised Kamran could see her seemed to point to a simple inverse—

Perhaps others could not.

It was a theory that explained nothing yet seemed somehow vitally important. Kamran wondered then about the source of his temporary blindness, and renewed fear branched up his back.

"What," Kamran said carefully, "did you do to her?"

Cyrus did not answer.

Lazily, the southern king pushed himself off the column before bending to pick up his sword. He walked toward Kamran with affected unconcern, dragging the blade behind him like a dog on a leash, the eerie exhalation of steel against stone briefly overpowering the sounds of Alizeh's screams.

"I thought she broke through the fire to punish *me*," Cyrus was saying. "I see only now that she did so to protect *you*."

There was a flicker in those blue irises, and for a single second Cyrus betrayed himself. Beneath his placid surface was something desperate and unrestrained, if not broken. Kamran cataloged the moment as a kind of mercy, for he realized then that the young man was a king weaker than he appeared.

"You know her name," Cyrus said softly.

Kamran felt a pulse of trepidation but said nothing.

"How," Cyrus demanded, "did you come to know her name?"

When Kamran finally spoke, his voice was heavy, cold. "I might ask you the same question."

"Indeed you might," said Cyrus, who was lifting his sword by inches. "But then, it's my prerogative to know the name of my bride."

A sharp pain exploded in Kamran's chest just as an ear-splitting crash broke open the room. He fought back a cry, clasping his ribs as he fell once more to his knees, heaving through the brutality of the blow. Kamran had no idea what was happening to him, and there was no time to hazard a guess. He could only force his eyelids open in time to witness not merely the destruction of his home but the arrival of an enormous, iridescent dragon, the sight of which seemed to drain the blood from his body.

The Diviners would never have allowed a foreign beast to enter Ardunian skies.

But the Diviners were dead.

Kamran watched the dragon catch Alizeh just as she began a sudden, dizzying descent, the monstrous creature seating the young woman firmly on its back before launching upward once more. The animal gave a stalwart roar, flapped its leathery wings, and, in a blink, both beast and rider were gone, vanishing into the night through the cavernous hole newly blown through the palace wall.

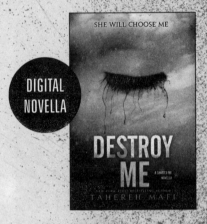
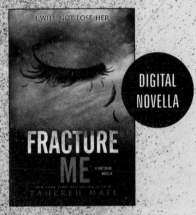

Don't miss these stunning novels from the *New York Times* bestselling author of the **SHATTER ME** series.

"The very best books move you to reconsider the world around you, and this is one of those."

—Nicola Yoon, #1 *New York Times* bestselling author

HARPER
An Imprint of HarperCollinsPublishers

epicreads.com